MAIA

AND THE

SECRETS OF ZAGRAN

S. G. BASU

H. G. R

YOU MAKE THE CHICANES OUT-OF-THIS-WORLD FUN

MAIA

AND THE

SECRETS OF ZAGRAN

GALACTIC MAP

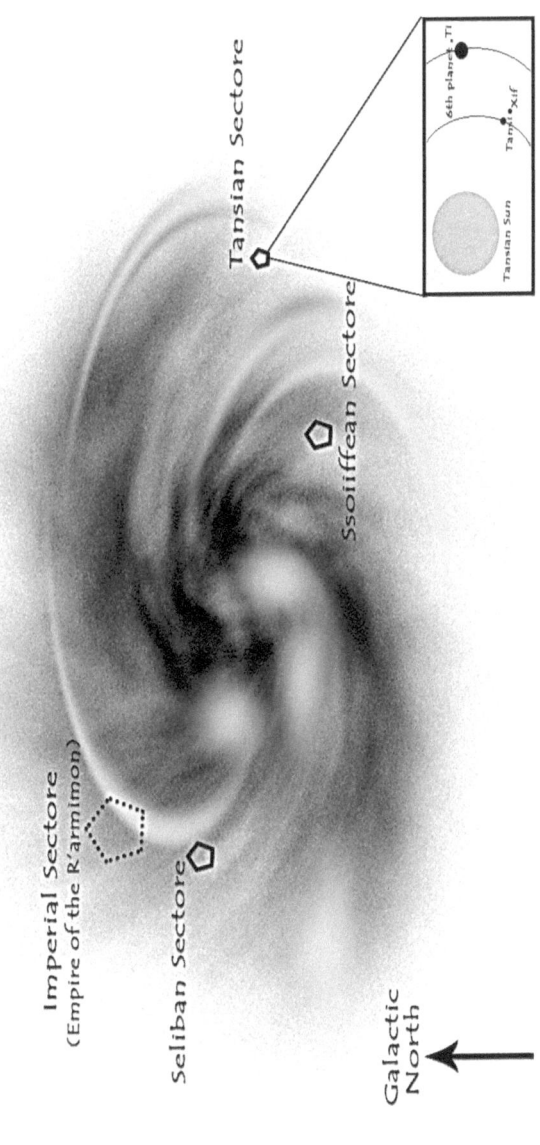

Imperial Sectore
(Empire of the R'armimon)

Seliban Sectore

Tansian Sectore

Ssoiiffean Sectore

Galactic
North

Tansian Sun

Tansi Xif

6th planet, Ti

The Map of Tarsi

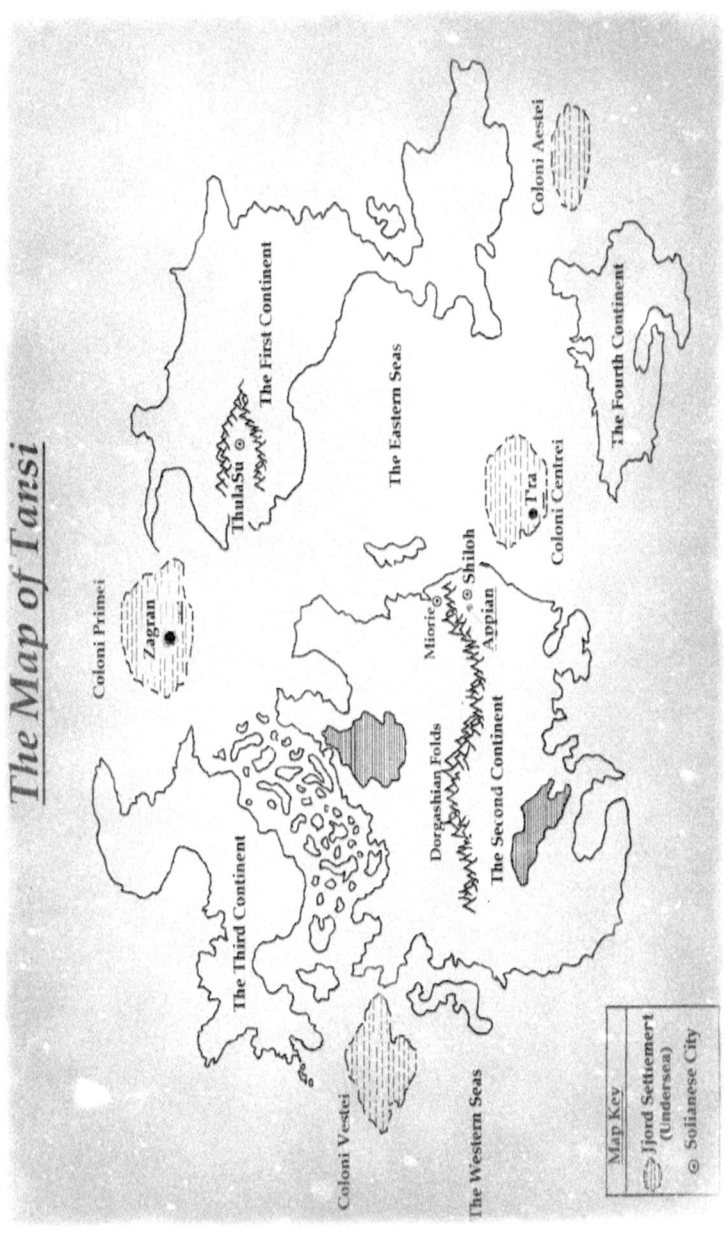

CHAPTER ONE

THE CHANCELLOR'S WOES

The Xifarian chancellor was an illustrious man. His friends admired him, his critics respected him, and the public treated him with utmost veneration. He had a reputation for being honorable and straightforward, and his life was a study of honesty and determination. Not many things frightened him; not many things worried him either. Born the sixth son of a poor miner, he had worked his way up to the highest seat of the Xifarian power structure by hard work and diligence. As chancellor, he had ruled with quiet dignity for fourteen long and peaceful years. There was scarcely a voice of discontent among the population. In short, he had done well.

"This is going to be a problem," the chancellor snarled, barely managing to keep his voice low. He shot a quick glance around to see if anyone had heard him. He knew he had to keep his composure; he could not show his agitation or *they* would think he was losing control.

He hurried along the thickly carpeted hallways of the Chancery, down the staircase that led away from the official section, and into the living quarters. Passing the double-arched doorway that led to the private suites, the chancellor turned and dashed into the first room on the left.

Someone was already inside—a tall man who stood with his back to the door, looking out the ornate windows at the dark grounds outside. He did not turn around to greet the chancellor; he did not even move. But he spoke almost immediately.

"You are late." His voice was sharp and unforgiving. "We cannot afford to lose time. Not anymore."

"My apologies." The chancellor bowed hastily.

"You do know why I am here," the man spoke again. His voice had softened a little.

"I presume it is time for the announcement to be made, sire," the chancellor replied, running a nervous hand to wipe the copious perspiration that shone on his shaved head. "And that old man has to be—"

"I am not worried about those."

"What else, sire?" the chancellor muttered.

The man whirled around. "The girl, Chancellor . . . the girl."

"Oh yes, yes, of course." the chancellor nodded vigorously, his gaze skimming the floor.

The man hissed as he strode toward the door. "Find out about her, as quickly as you can."

He reached the threshold and stopped abruptly.

"And if I were you, I would keep a close eye on that son of yours." His words cut through the air like a knife. "Miir got away this time, but one more mistake and there will be no saving him or . . . you."

As the man twisted the handle and yanked the door open, the impressive array of jeweled rings on his fingers blazed like fire.

CHAPTER TWO

A MIDSUMMER'S DAY

Through the darkness and the fog, Maia fell. Faster and faster, lower and lower, she plummeted into the bottomless pit until her heart went numb until she had stopped feeling the rush. It was a murky blur of senses when she hit the surface. The water, surprisingly warm and soft as it engulfed her, spilled over the top of her head, swirling around her face and her neck, suffocating her.

Maia screamed.

She bolted upright in her bed like an uncoiled spring. The heaviness dropped away from her head forming a dappled white, black, and amber shape of Dusty the cat. Struggling with the lingering feeling of weight that crept along the fringes of her heart, Maia realized it had been a nightmare. There had been too many of them lately.

Over a week had passed since thirteen-year-old Maia had returned home to Appian after a successful run at the Alliance Initiative on Xif. Her team, Core 21, had topped the first phase. They were one of the twenty teams selected for the second phase in the undersea city of Zagran, the Jjordic capital. Maia had intended to enjoy every moment of this brief break between the phases, and she mostly did. Except for the nights. Every night was a battle against the inevitable, and every day started in a haze of outlandish dreams from the night before. There were scores of them, but one kept coming back—the one with the fires. Time after time, Maia woke up screaming inside as the raging inferno engulfed her.

These nightmares were triggered by the simplest of things. One night it was the curtains that billowed as an early morning storm swept through. In her dreams, Maia found herself pursued by a man in a flowing white cloak across the desolate streets of some dead, abandoned city. This morning it was Dusty, the spirit of the untamed wild packaged into the petite frame of a calico cat. He was barely a month old when Dada had brought him home for Maia. While Maia had taken to the little creature instantly, Dusty never seemed happy to be confined within the walls of the house. Soon, Maia realized that Dusty was not the kind of pet every other child possessed. He came and went at will, never staying for more than a few weeks at a time. There was no wavering in his affection toward Maia during his whirlwind tours of the house though.

Dusty had now settled peacefully on Maia's lap, his loud and content purrs making her smile. It was good to be home, Maia thought, as she eased back against the pillows and gazed out the window. She reached for the ends of her pigtails and twirled them around her fingers, as she often did when immersed in thought. Her hazel-green eyes, partially covered by wayward locks of dark-brown hair, scanned the cheery clouds swimming across a bright, sunny sky. But before she could savor the beauty of the day, the memories barged in.

Sophie! The message!

Emptiness swirled inside, and a chill coursed through. Shuddering, Maia slid under the covers, seeking some warmth in its confines. There was no comfort to be found. Grudgingly, she let her thoughts roam.

Up until six months ago, Maia thought her mother, Sophie, had betrayed the cause of the Tansian people during the Exchange. Maia had taught herself to shun Sophie's memory. Then, everything Maia had thought about her mother turned out to be false when Dada gave her a message Sophie had left for her. While it was true that Sophie had taken the Xifarians' side during the Exchange, that was just a ploy to gain the Xifarians' confidence so she could thwart their scheme of destroying Tansi's sun. And Sophie had succeeded. She had ruined the Xifarians' plans. Sophie was no traitor but an unsung hero.

Maia's fingers reached for the broken pendant her mother had left for her, that now hung over her heart. She traced its contours, feeling the smoothness of the filigreed metal. In her message, Sophie had worried about the Xifarians' wrath on her child. A familiar iciness stirred at the base of Maia's spine at the thought.

Stop it! Maia chided herself. She sat up, fingers still clutching at her mother's pendant. The facts were painfully clear; it did not matter how hard she tried to hide, the Xifarians would find her if they wanted. She had nowhere to run. There was only one option—she had to forget about Sophie and her message. Thinking about it did not help. At all. It only made Maia nervous and weak.

I can't live in fear all the time. I won't!

Maia let go of the pendant and breathed in with all her might. A part of her wanted to take the ornament off and put it away in the farthest corner of a bureau drawer. That would surely let her forget more easily. But, even though she had mulled it over a zillion times now, she could not . . . it was one of the very few things her mother had left behind, and Maia could not let go.

I have to keep training my mind instead. I can. I have to.

Excited voices drifting in through the windows drew her attention away from the dismal thoughts.

"You'll have to leave quietly, Herecule," a woman said in a matter-of-fact tone. "If you don't like it, then you're to put off your trip. Maia needs to catch up on her sleep."

So typical of the hyper-anxious Emmy, Maia mused. She concentrated on catching more of the conversation, wondering what trip the housekeeper was trying to hide from her.

"But, Emmaline," Herc pleaded, almost piteously. "She wouldn't wanna miss a trip to Shiloh. Yeh know she loves going there—it's her fav'rite place in the world."

Shiloh! Of course!

Maia whispered a quick thanks to Herecule, the groundskeeper, for disputing Emmy's stand. Shiloh, the biggest town in the vicinity, was her favorite haunt, and the monthly trips to Shiloh had always been her only chance at freedom from Emmy's constant vigilance.

"If it were up to her, she would go to Shiloh every day, and you would happily permit it." Emmy, the housekeeper, was not one to give in so easily. "I forbid you to mention anything about this while she's around, do you understand? It's not safe for her to ramble around Shiloh."

Maia chuckled a little, thinking how her last trip to Shiloh had changed it all. She had always wanted to go to ThulaSu, the last standing Solianese university from before the Collapse. She would have been there now if her life had not turned upside down six months ago. Right before her induction into ThulaSu, Maia had been spotted by Xifarian scouts while flying a glider above Shiloh. She had been forced into accepting the Xifarians' invitation to join the Alliance Initiative, a peace summit between the three nations—the Solianese, the Jjord, and the Xif. For the first of the three planned phases of the Initiative, Maia had journeyed to the Xifarian cities inside the planet-spaceship of Xif. And she had had quite an adventure. Only Emmy did not seem to appreciate them, at all. Ever since the housekeeper had heard of Maia's stories, she had gone into a frenzy of finding ways to keep "the child" safe.

"Thank goodness I had enough sense to simplify matters for Emmy and Herc," Maia said, sighing. Dusty purred wisely in response, his green eyes peering through slits.

Maia had told her grandfather of all her adventures on Xif, but she had requested him to not tell Emmy or Herc everything. Dada had kindly obliged, they carefully made it sound as if none of the dangers Maia faced on Xif were directed specifically at her. Only Maia and her Dada knew the real truth—how Yoome, a fellow contestant at the Initiative who turned out to be a R'armimon assassin tried to use a soul extractor on Maia, and if had not been for Miir, their Xifarian mentor, she would be dead.

Matters had become complicated afterward, however. And now, the Xifarian chancellor suspected Maia to have aided the R'armimon in a plan to attack him. He threatened retaliation against Maia and the Resistance, and in no unclear terms.

It's such a big mess now.

With a shake of her head, Maia shooed the worrisome memories away. She was intent on enjoying her vacation from the rigorous training schedules at the Initiative.

And that's why Emmy can't know.

Emmy was prone to fussing, so much so that Maia often wondered if Emmy actually considered it a hobby. The woman fretted and frowned, continuously expecting villainous hordes to arrive and whisk Maia away.

Herc, on the other hand, did not think Maia was in any danger at all. Maybe he was a bit too naive or maybe he wanted to take the worry off Maia's mind. Herc had always been that way—the farmhand and Maia's martial arts teacher was more of a friend and confidante than anything else.

"Now I know what you feel like being stuck inside the house, Dusty," Maia whispered as she lifted the cat off her lap and set him on the floor. She dressed quickly and grabbed her sword Bellator before running out of her room and down the stairs to meet Herc.

Hurtling down the staircase, Maia came to a screeching halt after barely managing to dodge Dada who was walking up the stairs.

"Where are you off to?" Dada asked in a teasing voice.

"I have to catch Herc before he leaves for Shiloh," Maia replied, casting a frantic look at the porch door. "Can I go, Dada? Please?"

Dada hesitated. His eyes darkened, and his face became rigid.

I can't let his fear get to me. Focus!

"Please? It's been so long since I was there.

"Where's Emmaline?" Dada asked, still not consenting.

"Emmy is outside with Herc, doing everything she can to keep me home."

"Maia, she worries about you," Dada said, his tone carrying a mild sting of reproach. "She can only protect you while you're here. Soon you'll be off to some strange place again."

Maia studied his face, trying to decide whether this was a ploy to hold her up. Dada could not stop being anxious about her safety, Maia understood that, but she needed her escape.

"She raised you, Maia. And your mother before you," Dada said, sighing. "We lost her so soon. Too soon. That's why—"

Sophie, Dada's only daughter, had passed away when Maia was an infant. Thirteen years had gone by, yet the household mourned her every day.

"I'll be fine, Dada," she tried to reassure him. "Herc will be with me in Shiloh. And when I'm away for the Initiative, I'll have a lot of friends with me. There's hardly anything to worry about as long as I'm with them. Besides, I enjoy seeing new places and learning new things. I really do."

Maia truly liked the incredible cities inside Xif, the sunken Seliban temple on its surface, and all the fantastic subjects she had studied during her stay there. Now, she was looking forward to visiting the undersea colonies of the Jjord. When she left for Xif six months ago, she had been upset and scared, but things had changed a lot since then. She had changed.

"I'm glad to hear that." Dada chuckled. "Now you better run and catch Herc before he leaves. And please . . . please be careful in

Shiloh."

A quick hug later Maia was out on the porch just in time to stop Herc and the carriage. Emmy, who was not pleased with the new development, finally settled for a packed breakfast for Maia and the promise that they would return before sunset. With her food satchel in hand and the promise in mind, Maia set out with Herc for Shiloh.

CHAPTER THREE

THE MAN IN WHITE

The ride to Shiloh was peaceful until a sorry-faced dog decided to cross their path right after they had entered the city. Herc swerved in an attempt to avoid crashing into the mutt, and they found themselves sitting squarely in a pothole. The carriage had splintered a right wheel, and Herc announced that it needed immediate attention. For some time, Maia simply sat gawking at the broken wheel, fighting off tears of disappointment. Her plans for the day were dashed, there would be no time left for frolicking around Shiloh after the repairs were completed. When Herc towed the carriage to the nearest repair shop, Maia shuffled along glumly behind him. The mechanic was short on help so Herc had to give him a hand with the repairs. Maia found a bench in one corner and opened Emmy's food pack. Herc rushed over when she was halfway through.

"Miss," he said, panting, "what to do 'bout Dada's medicines? 'em repairs gonna take a while."

It took a moment for Maia to realize the problem. Doctor Hsu's dispensary was on the other side of Shiloh, and if they waited until the wheel was fixed, they would not make it in time for today's orders. There was one easy way to solve this: Maia could walk over alone. But she knew Herc would not agree to that; no one would after hearing all the dire scenarios Emmy had prophesied over the past week.

"I can walk over and place the order, Herc," she offered anyway.

"But . . ." Herc scratched his head and looked away. Maia had guessed right; her plan was not going to fly. "Maybe we can find someone to walk with yeh," Herc suggested brightly.

"Yes, whatever." Maia shrugged and refocused on her breakfast. The babysitting was getting really annoying.

Herc returned shortly, behind him was a small dopey-eyed boy with straggly brown hair.

"This is Merrick, miss," he announced. "Merrick, greet Miss Maia."

Maia sized the boy up; he could not be older than ten. Maia had serious doubts about the help the scrawny kid could provide in case of danger, but she decided to keep her thoughts to herself. The prospect of walking around with a tag-along was somewhat better than spending the day sitting in the mechanic's shop.

She started in a dejected mood, dragging her feet along the shiny cobbled roadways, with Merrick in tow. But she could not stay miserable for long. The day was glorious, and the town of Shiloh was spilling at its seams with the infectious joy and vigor of life. It slowly seeped into Maia. Townspeople of all shapes and sizes thronged the roads; shops filled with colorful merchandise beckoned the passersby inside. Doctor Hsu's shop, where Herc would later pick her up, sat at the opposite end of Shiloh, so Maia decided to take a shortcut through the middle of the town. She strode forward, knowing fully well that Merrick was having a hard time catching up. It was not the boy's fault that Herc had sent him, but she still felt irritated by his presence.

Maia walked along the road that circled the high rim of the beautiful and sprawling Lake Lupitiali. The sunken lake at the heart of Shiloh was teeming with migrating birds at this time of year. Their incessant cackle filled the air as they huddled in mottled masses of black, gray, and white on the placid surface of the waters. Lupitiali looked serene, and it was hard to believe that people could keep away from its waters. However, they did. Ever since the Collapse, the lake frothed up from time to time and the townsfolk came to believe its waters were contaminated. Now, a high metal fence around its periphery kept adventurous kids away. Only the migratory birds and a stray animal or two would venture into the lake anymore.

At the center of the enormous lake, rising from the depths, the top of a grayed spire peeked out. Legends spoke of an ancient city of Lupitiali that lay deep below the surface of the lake. One fateful summer day, the entire city sank during a string of massive earthquakes. The rains that followed filled the crater and Lake Lupitiali was born. The story never ceased to fascinate Maia, and even though Dada called it a sham, each time she passed the lake she felt drawn to the mysteries that rested deep beneath its surface.

On this day, Maia did not linger by the paved walkways along the side of the lake but quickly walked toward the beautiful houses that stood along the eastern shores. This was where Shiloh's richest lived, their regal abodes placed in perfect symmetry along the tree-lined streets. Beautiful as it was, the gleaming and flawless neighborhood was quiet, snobbish, and perfectly boring. Past them, a few more steps toward the east, the wide street narrowed into a decimated alleyway leading up to the series of flat, windowless yellow buildings that sat in a long, depressing line, looking forlorn even in the bright sunlight. Some ingenuous townspeople had named this alleyway the "Narrows." Cold and gloomy, constricted by the buildings on both sides, at places so tight that only one person could pass through at a time, the Narrows always felt like a trap to Maia. However, a trek through the Narrows was unavoidable today, especially because she had to reach the dispensary before it closed for orders.

On her first walk through the Narrows, Maia had counted the number of steps she needed to take to make it through its suffocating confines. It was a monumental 1,003 then, but it had dropped to a manageable seven hundred in recent times. Maia wondered if she would make it through even faster today.

"Miss Maia?" A sharp, squeaky voice interrupted her thoughts. Merrick bounded up to her, breathing rapidly. "Can you wait a bit, miss? I spotted something my mama wanted me to get. I can buy it and be back in a moment."

She was not going to wait for anyone, certainly not for Merrick, even if that meant facing the Narrows on her own.

"That's all right, Merrick," Maia replied, smiling as sweetly as she could. "Why don't you catch up after you're done? I'll head through the Narrows."

"All right." Merrick nodded eagerly before scurrying away toward a pottery shop.

That was easy. Smiling, Maia turned her attention back to the Narrows. Taking a bracing breath, she set foot on the road that snaked through the dingy buildings. She walked briskly, trying hard to ignore the damp yellow walls that almost touched her shoulders or the mossy cobblestones that seemed to suck the warmth away from her boot-clad feet. Maia was up to two hundred eighty-five steps when she felt a presence behind her. She turned around and cast a quick look backward, finding nothing but the dim, dark road. She dismissed it as a figment of her imagination, but the feeling persisted. At the pit of her stomach, nervousness formed an uneasy knot. Maia quickened her pace, her clammy fingers firmly encircling Bellator's hilt. The end of the Narrows was near, and she broke into a run.

Within moments, she found herself inundated by the clamor and aromas of the bustling Spice Market. Rows of shops lined the road on both sides, their walls painted in bright hues, their shelves stacked with colorful bottles of spices. Men and women busily went about their daily chores; shopkeepers traded their wares, while shoppers meandered from one store to another.

Maia felt the alarm rise through her once again as she headed toward Physicians' Lane, making her way slowly through the crowd. It was as if someone was watching her. Maia's heart picked up the pace. She kept glancing backward, trying to find anything out of the ordinary, but no one seemed to glance in her direction. The feeling continued to grow—cold fingers were prying and leafing through her mind, an icy gaze sweeping over her every memory. She nervously looked around again and almost fell over a peddler's cart, inviting a glare from the merchant who narrowly survived her assault. Maia walked faster, struggling to drive the thoughts out of her head as she took one last look behind. Suddenly, she crashed into someone, lost her footing, and fell face-first on the hard cobbled surface of the road.

As Maia scrambled to her feet, a stinging pain throbbed in her knees. Then she realized with a start, the strange feeling was gone.

"Are you all right?"

Maia held her breath in surprise when she looked up at the man with whom she had collided. A long white cape was draped across his shoulders. He was not handsome, but his appearance was far from unpleasant. He was not overly large, but his slender frame made him seem taller than he really was. His face was pallid, his ashen hair hung long and straight, and she could have sworn that the color of his eyes had changed from a frosted white to a dark gray as they looked into hers. His gaze, comforting and brimming with kindness, mesmerized Maia.

"Are you all right?" the man asked again as she stood transfixed before him.

"Y-yes," she stammered, still gawking at the man.

"Your palms are bleeding. We should get them treated." His voice was warm and serene, almost hypnotic.

Maia nervously glanced around. "I'm fine. Sorry for bumping into you, sir."

"You seem to be looking for something? Or someone?"

Maia hardly ever spoke to strangers and never trusted anyone she had not known for a while, but it felt like she had known this man for years. Something in his smile almost coaxed her into trusting him; an unknown rush of emotions swept through her mind and labeled him a "friend." She yearned to talk to him, to tell him everything that was bothering her.

"It was as if someone was watching me or . . . following me," she blurted.

The man's eyes narrowed and he looked around at the milling crowd before turning back to Maia.

"Maybe you're tired and need some rest. Sometimes exhaustion can play tricks on the mind," he said helpfully.

"Yes, maybe," Maia replied absent-mindedly and turned in the direction of Dr. Hsu's shop. Suddenly, she wished Merrick were around. "I'd better go now."

"May I know the name of the young lady I have had the pleasure of talking to?" the man said cheerfully as she prepared to step away.

Maia stopped, feeling a little embarrassed.

"Maia. I'm sorry . . . it's . . . I'm feeling a bit stupid for being jumpy about nothing," she tried to explain. "I should've been brave. Should've turned around and faced whatever I thought was following me."

The man smiled. "You're quite brave already. Sometimes when you don't know what you're up against, there's no cowardice in turning around and running away. Trying to fight something you don't know well enough can be foolishness."

"Guess you're right."

"And I see that I haven't introduced myself yet. I'm Ruche U'Kien and pleased to make your acquaintance, Miss Maia."

"Your name sounds very *foreign*," Maia blurted.

"Indeed, I am. Foreign that is." Ruche chuckled and pointed in the northern direction. "I come from the mountains up there."

"Those mountains? You mean the Dorgashians?" Maia asked incredulously. "But no one lives up there; it's only the ruins and the wild beasts. I've heard tales of creatures so huge that could squash a man like an ant."

"Well, I've been there for a while, and all I can say is that some tales are just . . . tales," Ruche said with a teasing smile. They had come to a stop at a crossroads. "Here we part ways, my friend, until we meet again. And be careful on your journey back home."

"I will." Maia smiled. "You be careful on the mountains."

Ruche waved before walking away toward a group of antique peddlers. Maia was about to leave when she saw something fall from his hand. It sparkled and clinked away, rolling past her feet and toward the edge of the road. By the time she picked it up and turned around to look for Ruche, he had vanished into the crowd.

"Ruche," she shouted, hoping he was still within earshot. But apart from attracting curious stares from passersby, her cries did not do much. She tried peeping into a few stores, but could not see the fair-haired man. As Maia walked back in the direction of the doctor's shop, she opened her palm to look at the object in her hand. It was a crudely carved ring of dull gray metal, with twelve white stones surrounding a round black one at the center. The gems caught the light and glittered brightly.

"Maybe I'll see him again before I leave for Zagran," Maia said to herself as she slipped the ring into her coat pocket.

CHAPTER FOUR

AN UNEXPECTED VISIT

On the ride back home, Maia sat atop the coach next to Herc, enjoying every bit of the warm sunshine that bathed her from head to foot. The sun had begun to set when they started their slow trot up the hill toward the house. The world was luminous—orange-red rays made the browned grass on the hillsides glow, and it looked as if the entire valley had been set ablaze.

Maia spotted the glint of pale gold hair on the porch steps as soon as the carriage crossed the oak and faced the open white gates of the farmhouse. A girl sat on the steps, her hands cupping her face. Her eyes scanned the approaching carriage intently before it came to rest on Maia.

"Dani?" Maia shouted, promptly scrambling down the coach that was still in motion.

Maia found it hard to believe that she had only known Dani for six months. A Jjord from Coloni Centrei, Dani had befriended Maia on the journey to Xif, and they had become teammates and good friends.

"What brings you here?" Maia asked after she had released Dani from a bear-hug. "I didn't think I would see you before getting to Zagran."

"I was worried about you, Maia." Dani smiled, but her bright blue eyes were dim. "I kept remembering how close Yoome was to killing you and all those terrible things the chancellor said to you."

Maia remembered their adventures on Xif. Some of the situations were scary, as was the encounter with Yoome, the R'armimon assassin. But with so little time to spend in Appian before the Initiative resumed, Maia had forced herself to forget those unpleasant memories. The one thing she just could not stop thinking about was Sophie's message, of course. She wondered what Dani would say if she knew, but it was not time to tell her yet.

Maia quickly stifled a sigh. Her situation was agonizing at best—how she yearned to recall every nuance of her mother's voice, yet she could not bear to face the terrifying implications of the communication. Sophie had found out about the Sedara—the artificial star that hung inside the hollowed-out planet of Xif. At the heart of the Sedara lay the Verto-balancer Capsule—a contraption that enabled Xif to fly across galaxies. This Capsule generated the power to propel Xif by sucking the energy out of the nearest star. That meant one thing—if Xif were to leave the Tansian system, it would destroy the Tansian sun. Left behind with a dead sun, life on Tansi would perish. Sophie knew she was the only hope for Tansi because she was born a Shimugien, one who had power over light—the only one who could break the Capsule. And she had broken it just in time to stop Xif from leaving, robbing the planet-spaceship of its ability to fly and stranding it forever in the Tansian system.

Breaking the heart of the Sedara had a terrible effect on Sophie, and she died within a year, right after Maia was born. In her message, Sophie had asked Maia to stay away from the Xifarians and keep her relationship with Sophie a secret.

Ever since learning this, Maia often stayed awake at night thinking about her mother, trying to understand the true meaning of her message, and the depth of the revelation. The more Maia thought about it, the more fearful she became. She half-expected Xifarian troops to barge in and arrest her any moment. So much so that even the sound of a rustling leaf made Maia break into a sweat. After two days of putting up with the panic, Maia realized something—she was turning into an "Emmy."

Maia was sure that was *not* a path she wanted to follow. The only way to stop, she figured, was to refuse to believe in Sophie's message. It was hard and painful to sow distrust in her mother's words, but the ploy worked like a miracle. Slowly, Maia let in the doubts. They crept in one at a time, and each day saw more of it occupying her mind, to the point that now, a week later, Maia found it somewhat easy to wonder if what Sophie said were just the imaginings of a gravely ailing woman and nothing more. She questioned the improbability of it all every waking moment, wondering how the Xifarians had not realized what had been taken from them. It seemed impossible. It *had* to be untrue. Maybe there had never been a Verto-balancer Capsule within the Sedara at all; Sophie could have simply heard stories and thought them to be true.

"I finally broke down yesterday and told Hans all about Yoome. I couldn't keep it a secret anymore." Dani's voice pulled Maia out of her thoughts. "He suggested that I come and see you immediately. And here I am."

Maia felt warmth creep over her face at the mention of Dani's nineteen-year-old brother Hans. It was obvious, of course, that Dani would not travel all the way to Appian alone without her brother's permission, but somehow the idea that Hans knew about the attack of the R'armimon and the chancellor's threats made Maia ill at ease. It was one thing that her friends knew about it, but quite another if the whole world found out.

"Where's Hans?" she asked slowly, taking care to conceal her embarrassment.

"He's inside speaking to your grandfather."

It was a stupid question, Maia realized. Of course, he would be inside talking to Dada about all that had happened and the implications of it.

"What have you told Dada?" Maia whispered urgently, grabbing Dani's wrist as nervousness swept over her. Dada already knew everything, but it would be terrible if Emmy overheard.

"Um, not a lot," Dani replied. "Hans didn't want to scare him too much."

Maia heaved a sigh of relief. "Well, he knows. But, I didn't want to scare Emmy, so—"

"I understand. Hans and I were a bit worried though." Dani smiled, slipping an arm around Maia's. "You know, you live out here in the country with not much to protect you. The rest of us are much more secure."

"Dani—"

"I know. You don't want to make your family panic. We don't want that either. That's why Hans plans to casually suggest a basic security system along the fence."

Maia flinched. "Security system? Emmy barely needs a reason to—"

"It won't have anything to do with you. Trust me. Hans will find a way to make it sound spontaneous."

"Trust me, Dani. Emmy will find a way to make a point about how defenseless I am. She always does."

Dani chuckled and tugged Maia's arm. "It'll be all right. Come on, let's go in."

It was close to nightfall, and Maia walked into the sitting area expecting a dimly lit room, a low fire in the grates, and maybe more than just one candle burning on the table in honor of the visitors. As they stepped through the door, the bright white light made her stop and stare in amazement. It bathed every corner of the small room, spilled through the open entrance, and washed away the everyday shadows. The source of the beautiful light was a small box that Hans was in the process of setting up on the table. It looked like a small silver lantern with glass windows surrounding it on all sides. At the center of it sat a glowing white globe. Dada and Emmy stood next to

Hans, watching in hushed reverence, their eyes wide with wonder.

"That's a LumTorch. Once charged in the Challowist farms, that little globe can emit light for ten days," Dani whispered, her voice bubbling with excitement. Seeing Maia's perplexed face, she went on to explain. "The Challowist farms are energy farms. Well, I don't want to drive you crazy with too much detail right now; you'll see the farms when you visit us."

Waiting until later was definitely a good idea, Maia thought. Her head was swimming. Since the days of the final challenge in the Xifarian phase, things had been happening around her. And while she expected a gazillion wonders in the Jjordic settlements, she was not ready just yet.

"Maia, there you are." Hans walked over to the two girls with a smile that was far more luminous than the LumTorch. The dimples on his cheeks were still as charming, and his hair was longer now, falling in dark gold waves to his shoulders. His eyes, a shade deeper than Dani's, shone with kindness. "You look all grown up. Whatever happened to the little girl I met a few months ago?"

Maia felt warm, and she knew a blush had flooded her cheeks. She looked for a place where she could safely fix her gaze.

"I haven't grown any taller," she squeaked when she managed to find her voice. She had been a little upset with that particular fact for a while now, especially since all of her friends had easily managed to add some length to their frames over the last few months. Maia was sure that she would be the shortest of them all.

"I didn't mean it that way." Hans found a perch on the arm of a chair and smiled reassuringly. "It's your eyes, Maia . . . those are the eyes of a brave and capable young woman."

"Things . . . have happened," Maia said slowly, thinking of all the situations she had been through since meeting Hans a few months ago—the attack of the R'armimon, the Xifarian chancellor's threats, the message from Sophie. Maia knew her experiences had made a difference in her, and she wondered if it was indeed a change so easy to spot.

"All of you have been through a lot on Xif," Hans said in a warm, earnest tone. "I'm glad to see you're holding up well, and you look strong and confident."

"My little girl is brave, Hans." Dada had stepped closer to the group as they talked. He beamed at Maia. "And I know I have no reason to worry with friends like you around."

"Of course, she's very capable, sir. They all are," Hans replied. Maia held her breath, hoping that Hans would not linger on this topic. Hans changed the subject quickly enough. "They had so much fun together on Xif that Dani already missed her friends. She kept begging me to let her visit Maia. I hope you won't mind her staying here for a few days?"

"Dani can stay here with us for as long as she wants. I'm sure there's nothing Maia would love more than to have her friend here," Dada said with a broad smile. "You will stay too, I hope?"

"I really wish I could, but . . ."

"Hans has to get back to work," Dani explained. "I'm so glad we made this trip though, we had a blast traveling to Appian. Didn't we, Hans?"

They settled down around the fireplace as Dani chattered with excitement, narrating her first ever over-land travel. The conversation drifted to a variety of topics, Hans and his work, Appian and its people, and, of course, the Alliance Initiative. Soon, it was time for dinner. Everyone did justice to the sumptuous meal—roasted potatoes, skewered seafowl, and Emmy's special spiced bread.

Hans had plans to leave for Zagran early the next morning, so he soon retired. Maia helped Dani unpack, and with the incessant chat, everything took longer than expected.

"Oh, Maia," Dani squealed midway into her unpacking. "I forgot to show you this."

She pulled out a piece of paper from her travel-box and waved it eagerly in Maia's direction.

"What is it?" Maia leaned forward to look.

The paper was honey-colored and the words stylishly scripted.

THE ALLIANCE INITIATIVE—A GRAND SUCCESS

The first phase of the Initiative was concluded with great fanfare with the winners being presented with medals of honor by the chancellor of Xif. Twenty teams have been chosen to advance to the Jjordic phase. Stay tuned for more news as these fearless youngsters continue their journey.

"The time we spent on Xif will be the most memorable of our lives, our team unanimously agrees. None of us expected to learn so much, yet have so much fun and find new friends among people we would have never met if not for the Initiative." – Core 21, Winners, Xifarian phase.

"This is about us," Maia said breathlessly. "Where did you get this?"

"They were mailed to every house in the Colonies," Dani replied, rolling her eyes and shaking her head. "And not once, but three times already in the past week. People are totally tired of this publicity overload."

Maia found it odd that there was no such buildup around Appian. Xifarian propaganda never reached her village. There was something strange about her village and it probably had to do with the Resistance, the Solianese rebels who opposed the Xifarian domination of Tansi.

"And did you recognize that quote?" Dani asked. "That's from our final paper, remember?"

Maia nodded, recalling the last task they had been assigned during the Xifarian phase – to write about their time on Xif. The two girls sat up for the longest time reminiscing the good times and speculating about the upcoming months. It was not until Emmy came by and made them turn out the lights that they finally went to sleep.

CHAPTER FIVE

THE CANDY SHOP

Hans was already up and about when Maia and Dani came down to the kitchen the next morning. He had been working since daybreak, Emmy informed the two girls, putting up a "perimeter shield" around the house. Apparently, Hans had found it bizarre that houses on Appian had so little security. Luckily enough, he also just *happened* to have enough hardware and tools with him to install a basic system along the farmhouse fence. Dada had no reason to disagree with his proposal of setting up a shield, Emmy was ecstatic, and Herc was not given a chance to speak. So, Hans had set off on his mission.

"Finally, I find someone who is bothered by the lack of security around here," Emmy declared a little too loudly, raising a triumphant eyebrow at the figure seated at the table. Herc was bent over a plate of food, his face scrunched up in annoyance. He made a dismissive grunt at the comment, and Emmy smiled smugly at her slouching opponent. Dani broke into a giggle as Maia sighed; fervently hoping that Dani would not motivate Emmy any further.

Maia slipped out of the kitchen, dragging a still-giggling Dani behind her. As they walked out to the porch, Maia decided to settle the matter.

"Dani, please don't aid Emmy in this. If she could, she would keep me locked up in a room. I'll die if you guys expect me to stay indoors for the next few days," Maia said in one feverish breath.

"Oh, come on, Maia. You are overreacting." Dani tried her best to reassure her friend in-between giggles. "Don't you worry; I plan to have plenty of fun with you in Appian. Too bad I missed the trip to Shiloh. Now, let's find out what Hans has been up to." Dani strode down the porch steps in search of her brother, followed by a half-calmed and half-anxious Maia.

They did not find him in front of the house, so Maia led Dani toward the stable at the back. Halfway to their destination, something large and silvery sitting near the side of the house made Maia stop and squint.

It looked like a large upside-down saucer, not quite round but more of an oval with a pinched middle. The frame of the body sat on tiny wheels that ringed the entire rim. The top of the saucer was transparent, while the rest of the body was silvery white, and a pair of blue stripes spanned it from head to tail.

"That, my friend, is the one my brother has given his heart to, the one who has his eternal allegiance. Don't you dare touch her or give her the evil eye, for if you do, you risk my brother's everlasting wrath." Dani gestured at the vehicle with a flamboyance that reminded Maia of Geir-Sei, the melodramatic vice principal of the Xifarian Defense Academy or the XDA. "Maia, I present to you the 'Hansmobile.'"

Now it was Maia's turn to burst into a fit of giggles as Dani tiptoed to the vehicle and imitated Hans professing his eternal love to the Hansmobile.

"Please don't believe everything my sister tells you, Maia." They had not noticed Hans emerge through the kitchen doors. "I just happen to like this Aqumob a little, that's all."

"Words cannot capture the depth of his feelings, Maia, believe me," Dani said in a mock whisper. "You know who this reminds me of? Our distinguished and cranky mentor on Xif and his Raptor."

It was good that Dani had brought it up; Maia did not want to be the only one to remember how proud Miir had been of *Shadow*, his Onclioraptor.

During the Xifarian phase, Core 21 had been placed under the guidance of a senior from the Xifarian Defense Academy that hosted the Alliance Initiative. This senior, Miir, was also one of the scouts who had recruited Maia. Although Maia and her teammates shared at best a tumultuous relationship with their sixteen-year-old mentor, there was no denying that he was a prodigy of a pilot and one of the best students at the XDA. He was also related to the high and mighty of Xifarian society, being the son of the Xifarian chancellor, the supreme ruler of Xif.

"I still don't understand why you should talk of Miir that way, Dani," Hans protested. "I found him most amiable, and he was the one who helped Maia and Ren, if you care to remember."

"I do, dear brother." Dani continued to argue; she was not about to give up so easily. Dani's spirited exchanges with her brother made Maia smile. The usually quiet girl was always remarkably lively with Hans. "But I also remember that Miir didn't even think of saying goodbye to us. I find that quite rude and very unpleasant."

"I would rather not fight about this at all," Maia commented solemnly. "We're never going to see him again, so who cares whether he is nice or not?"

"I wouldn't be so sure, Maia," Dani said. "Of course, we'll get a new mentor for the Jjordic phase, but with Miir's talents, I'm quite sure he'll rise through the ranks of Xifarian leadership. And if that happens, given the ideas the chancellor had about us, we'll surely cross paths soon."

The trio fell silent for a while before Dani spoke again.

"Hans, you should definitely take Maia out for a ride when we're in Zagran. She needs to see how wonderful the Hansmobile is, won't you, please?"

Hans chuckled. "All right, I will. I have to get ready now. And please don't bother her while she is foraging."

Dani laughed as Hans disappeared into the house.

"The Aqumob's power supply comes from the sunlight it stores in its solar packs. That's what he means by foraging, in case you are wondering. Let's give her some privacy while she has her breakfast, shall we?"

Maia and Dani spent some time walking around the house as Hans left to prepare for his trip back to Zagran. After all goodbyes had been said, and all directions about the perimeter shield conveyed to Dani, Hans got into his gleaming Aqumob. The engine started with a soft purr as the glass top closed noiselessly. A set of tiny jets erupted from the edge of the wheels that lined the rim of the vehicle. As the jets grew louder, the cushions of air around the Aqumob raised the vehicle a little so that it hovered above the ground. Hans waved, and a loud growl of the engine later, he vanished in a flash of silver and blue.

"He's off to Zagran, is he?" Herc asked Dani later as the girls sat watching him feed the horses.

"Yes, he'll enter the porthole for T'ra—that's where our home is," Dani explained. "From there he'll take the Transoceanic Highway 25 that goes straight up to Zagran."

"Transoceanic Highway? And this highway is underwater, right?" Maia asked.

"Yes, it is. There's a sizeable mesh of roads and highways under the seas. They're all enclosed in super resilient materials and laid out to form a grid of paths connecting all our settlements," Dani explained.

"Mus' be beautiful down there," Herc said. He had been listening with rapt attention.

"It *is* quite beautiful," Dani said softly and fell silent for a moment. "Maybe when the Initiative is over, all of you can come to visit us. I'll show you around T'ra. You'll love it."

"Why, thank you, Miss Dani. I woulda love it." Herc grinned. "But now we need to show you 'round our Appian, don' we, Miss Maia?"

Maia nodded vigorously. Appian was small, rather dull compared to the spectacular underwater settlements, but she wanted to show Dani the places she loved and treasured.

After a hearty breakfast of stringed potatoes, poached eggs, and cured seafowl meat, Maia decided to take Dani out on a tour of the village. Herc was confident that the two girls would be fine by themselves, but Emmy's insistent pleas won Dada over. So, after the girls were wrapped in hooded coats to safeguard against the light chill, the trio headed toward Appian's famous candy shop.

The trio walked along Market Street, a narrow paved road lined on both sides with rows of quaint and pretty shops, their walls painted in bright colors. Appian was a rather sleepy place; men and women went about their daily chores at a relaxed pace. Herc had to stop for some supplies at the food store, so the two friends continued their journey to the candy shop without him. They walked to the end of the street where the road made a twisty turn toward the East-West high roads. Studded across this turn were a few shops; the smallest had a lopsided sign that read, "Mama Bililo's Candy." Maia strode toward its worn door that stood open on its well-oiled hinges.

They had almost reached the door when a flash of orange and yellow emerged from inside, streaked past the girls' feet, and disappeared among the shops on the other side of the road. A flying broomstick came next, tracing an ambitious path through the air, and landed noisily on the pavement. The flash of orange was Chico, the resident tabby cat of the candy shop. A robust voice that exuded effortlessly from inside of the shop promised things of great misfortune for the escaped feline.

"Watch out," Maia cautioned her friend, stepping closer to the doorway gingerly, ready to dodge any other projectile that might come their way. "Anything can happen at the Bililo's."

The duo walked in guardedly. The legendary Mama Bililo sat

crouched on her bench behind a wall of huge glass tubs full of colorful candy, her hands clamped over her ears. Time and again, she looked with annoyance at the back door of the shop, which opened into the house and the candy factory beyond. It was from the other side of this door that the stout voice continued its long tirade against the plots of the evil cat and the people who had brought that source of mischief home. On seeing Maia and Dani at the doorway, Mama Bililo flashed a wide, toothy grin. She was well built on a smallish frame and looked young for her fifty years.

"Maia, come in," she welcomed, smiling sheepishly, "don't mind my sister. She is mad at that thief of a cat. I don't understand why Chico does it, he is so well-fed. Sometimes I suspect that he steals for the thrill of it all. Poch never should've brought that tabby home."

It was about four years ago on a rainy afternoon that Mama Bililo's youngest son, Poch, rescued a bunch of stray kittens from the Woods of Penning. No one knew where they came from, but the whole village impinged on the little candy store to help raise the tiny ones. Two of the infant sisters never made it through that night. Little Chico survived and so did his brother, the equally troublesome Dusty whom Maia adopted. The third kitten found a home in neighboring Shiloh.

"And who is this, Maia, a friend of yours?" asked Mama Bililo as threatening sounds continued to stream through the open doorway.

"Yes, this is my friend Dani from—"

"The seas, I think," Mama Bililo finished the sentence, and Maia nodded. "Will she be staying for a while in our little village?"

"Yes," Dani replied quickly, "I will be here until—"

"Maia leaves for that contest or peace summit or whatever." Mama Bililo was not shy about finishing Dani's sentence either. She turned toward Maia next. "Now, Maia, what would you like today? I think you'll have your usual, ginger candy. And you'll want a little more today to share with your friend here, am I right?"

"Yes, you are," Maia replied, counting the coins. "I'd like two sacks of candy please."

"That's so sweet of you, darling." Mama Bililo handed each of them a bag full of ginger candy. "Here you go. See if you like our grubby sweets, little girl from the seas."

"And oh, Maia," Mama Bililo exclaimed as the two girls were about to leave. "If you see Herecule, tell him to go to the mouth of the power grid, please. Poch and his boys are trying to fix some stuff up there, and they said they could use some help."

CHAPTER SIX

THE MOUTH OF THE POWER GRID

Herc was still at the food store chatting busily with the keeper when Maia and Dani came looking for him. As soon as he heard of Mama Bililo's message from Poch, Herc set out to meet him. Dani was eager to see more of the village, so the girls decided to follow Herc to the mouth of the power grid. Maia was excited, hoping that the repairs meant she would get a closer look at the grid itself.

There was a time on Tansi when the power grids formed an immense underground network that bore through the surface of the planet like a colony of termites. The ground below the cities was hollowed out, and a mesh of cables and pipes spread out like a net. They carried the source of life—light and heat from the generator farms—to the towns and cities all over Tansi. One of the bigger grids south of the Dorgashians was underneath Shiloh; from there it branched out south and west. The western branch flowed through Appian all the way to the Western Seas.

Since the colonization of the planet of Tansi, the mighty Solianese

Empire had ruled with an iron fist. Civilization on Tansi flourished under their reign, but with unbridled power came excesses and decadence, many of which proved harmful to Tansian ecology and endangered the planet's future.

A group of Solianese protested against the empire and seceded from it. Driven away from the land settlements, this group took refuge in the nascent underwater colonies and named themselves the Jjord. Since then, Tansians were divided into two nations, the surface-dwelling Solianese and the Jjord of the undersea colonies. The Jjord persistently warned the Solianese of the consequences of unchecked industrial growth and reckless practices of stripping the planet of its resources. They predicted a doomed future, an apocalyptic demise of Tansi.

About a hundred years ago, the prophecy of the Jjord came true. The Solianese Empire started to crumble, and the era of the Collapse began. First came the virus—it infected livestock, and then a mutated variant of it crossed over to infect people. It was a catastrophic calamity as the virus spread through the population, wiping out villages, towns, and cities within days. The Solianese government attempted to decontaminate the affected areas, and in the process unleashed a horror far more menacing and uncontrollable than the virus.

The government released bio-cleansers—nanobots that could seek out contaminants and eliminate them. But the bio-cleansers were barely half-developed. Hordes of out-of-control nanobots scorched the ground at the slightest suspicion of toxins, obliterating the vegetation on Tansi and most sources of food, and leaving the surviving people homeless, hungry, and barely alive. That was the beginning of the Scarcity, which continued for decades.

During the days of the Scarcity, the power grids were the first to fall. The generator farms on Tansi were located strategically in remote pockets, and when the nanobots wiped out the food sources, the supply lines to these faraway power stations were disrupted almost immediately. The starving custodians of these bases either fled or died, and left unattended, the generator farms collapsed. As darkness descended over the cities, marauding hordes swarmed the grids. Unable to change the fate they were destined to face, the mob did the only thing that made them feel powerful and in control. They wrecked the empty grids, brick by brick, stone by stone, fiber by fiber, until they tired. Then they set the fire. It was a spontaneous show of anger against the empire that had led the planet to this end, but the mutiny was too late to save anything; it only hastened the ruin.

The rebellion spread quickly. It spilled from the cities to the towns and tainted the villages, as did the madness of self-destruction. When the Jjord finally came to aid the last surviving Solianese refugees, the planet was a burned-out shell. The Jjord helped set up food supplies, but only after the weakened Solianese had agreed to pay a price for their greed. The Solianese agreed to a life of abstinence from technology. The Jjord disallowed the use of machines by the Solianese, only permitting the surface dwellers to rebuild remnants of their broken civilization with tools from before industrialization. They repaired the power grids to a point where the cities could receive a paltry donation of energy from their undersea power stations. The surviving Solianese lived, but they had been herded into a bygone era of hardship and misery.

Of the bigger towns south of the Dorgashians, only Shiloh was left standing, mostly because of its proximity to the Troughs and its miraculous water table. It was also because, as fate would have it, Shiloh's local power grid and standby generators were not damaged as extensively after the Collapse. So was the case with Appian. Everything else to the south and west of Appian was annihilated. The power grid that emerged from Shiloh was used up to Appian, but because of the terrible condition of the channel, barely a trickle of energy reached the village. Dredging the power channels was a daunting task, something beyond the technological capabilities of the Solianese. Time and again the villagers of Appian asked for help, but they were refused tenfold.

Tired of the rejections, the villagers of Appian started collecting funds for building a wind turbine to supplement the meager supply of energy through the grid. It was a fortunate gamble—soon a lucky grant from the Continental Parliament and the blessing of the Jjord followed. The first wind turbine was built on the Windehill, the highest hillock to the east of Appian that stood directly across from Hen's Beak. Slowly but diligently, the villagers of Appian added to their pride. The lone structure was joined by three more—the Windehill along with two other neighboring hills sported the four wind turbines of Appian.

It was toward the top of the Windehill that Maia, Dani, and Herc were headed in hopes of finding Poch and the others. Herc lumbered ahead of the girls. Dani chattered excitedly as Maia pointed out their farm on Hen's Beak and other landmarks in the valley.

Some villagers were gathered around the control base of Appian's power grid, a rounded well-type structure that stood at the summit of Windehill. The fringe of the control base was made of small orange-red bricks dating as far back as the colonization of the planet. The mortar on them had fallen off in many places, revealing an intricate patchwork of seams and joints that frantically tried to hold the structure together. It always reminded Maia of Tansi itself—the thinnest threads of protocols and policies tried hard to keep the disintegrating people in place, but it was only a matter of time before it all fell apart. Poch Bililo stood in front of the group that sat around the base of the well, describing something animatedly. At the sound of their footfalls, he turned to welcome the trio.

"Herecule," he exclaimed and flashed a quick smile. "Just the man I was looking for."

Poch was a swarthy man, solidly built on a stocky frame. His wide face was always cheerful, forever ready to break into a smile. Dark stringy hair sat like a bird's nest on his head, and his eyes were endlessly darting from one thing to another.

"The second turbine is broken," he announced. "Like one was not enough bad luck for us."

"What d'ya mean broken? How?" Herc demanded.

"I don't know, Herc. All I know is there's not a single trickle of power coming from this one." Poch pointed at the wind turbine to the right of the control station. "The flow from Shiloh is almost down to nothing now. And with two of these gone, what are we gonna do?"

"No need to panic jus' yet, Poch." Herc patted the man lightly on the back in an attempt to calm him. "We'll have these fixed up by the time the days grow colder."

"And who'll do that?" Poch seemed truly upset. "The only one who knows anything about anything is that crazy old Moritz who blew up the first one. Too bad those fat cats living under the seas don't think we're fit to do the simplest of work. You remember what that tall, snobby one said when he came to approve the last mill?"

Poch stopped briefly, took a deep breath, and rambled on.

"That Jjord said, 'Too much learning is dangerous, and your people have proved that once already. We cannot risk losing the planet we share because of your greed.'" Poch scrunched his face in disgust. "But how long is this going to go on? Forever? Because someone did something bad more than a hundred years ago? Isn't a hundred years long enough for punishment?"

Maia flinched. She did not like the way Poch's rant was shaping up, especially with Dani there. She knew the history of animosity between the Jjord and the Solianese well; she had heard it a zillion times already. Tansi's history was dismal and sad, but Maia knew they had to move on and think more about the future and less about the past. Dani was a good friend, regardless of whether she was Jjord or not, and Maia was not about to let that friendship down. She decided to chime in and divert Poch's attention.

"There's no point thinking about the past, is there, Poch?" she said. "Why don't we try to find Moritz instead?"

"Yes, that crazy man is our only hope." Poch's face was dark with despair. "There's no help coming from them water people anyway. I wish that one day they'd understand what it feels like to beg for the smallest things you need to survive. And when that day comes, I'll sure kick them in the face."

Maia turned around in alarm to look at her friend. Dani stood quietly, looking sad rather than angry or annoyed.

"Maybe *I* can fix it for you." Dani's voice was as soft and soothing as the first summer showers.

Poch's eyes grew wide and his mouth fell open. "How would you do that, little girl?" he said, recovering quickly. "How would you know what to do?"

"She's a friend of Miss Maia's from the seas, she knows." Herc sounded upset.

Poch's eyes grew wide once more, and this time it took him longer to speak again. "She's one of them," he whispered. "Why would she offer to help? Is this some kind of trap?"

"Poch, please," Maia said sharply. She was beyond annoyed at his constant harping on the same matter. "She's my friend, all right? She wants to help just because she's nice. If you want her to take a look at the circuits, then show us around."

"Neva' mind, Poch. I'll show Miss Dani around," Herc said gruffly.

They walked past the still-gawking Poch and the other startled villagers to the malfunctioning wind turbine.

CHAPTER SEVEN

THE WIND TURBINES

H erc pushed the buttressed door open and led them inside the base of the giant tower. A complicated set of machines, connected by serious-looking shafts and rods, were neatly placed around the room. Everything was dull gray, and the room smelled faintly of grease and grime. Maia did not recognize any of the parts, but Dani had already started inspecting a series of cables that looked particularly distressed.

"Seems like something has burned out in here," Dani informed Herc and Maia, who stood watching from a distance. "We need to open some connector units, Herc. Could you get me some tools please?"

"Tools?" Poch, who had walked in behind them, repeated incredulously. "We don't have tools, not allowed any."

"You must be joking," Dani said. "You must have something. You do fix your household stuff, don't you?"

"Oh, come on, Poch, get 'em boxes up here." Herc almost growled. Poch blinked rapidly at him and quickly slipped outside without a word.

"They don't trust me." Dani sighed. "And why should they? I'm one of *them*."

"No, Dani." Maia kneeled next to her. "You can't be sad because of what Poch said. Half of the people here have never met a Jjord before, let alone one who is kind and helpful. I never thought I could have a friend from the seas before I met you."

"I know that my people can be quite snooty and obstinate about things," Dani said earnestly, "but we need to trust each other a little more than we do. Hans always says that we need to give people second chances."

"And that's why you came over to Kusha and me in the Holding Pod, right?" Maia remembered how Dani was the only Jjord to speak to them during their flight to Xif.

"I simply wanted to meet someone who was not like everyone else I knew." Dani smiled. "And look what great friends I found."

Maia nodded. She too was thankful for every one of her teammates. Besides Dani, there were the two Solianese members Kusha and Nafi, as well as Ren, a Xifarian boy. Maia smiled to herself as she thought of them. She had not been lucky in life in most ways, having lost her mother in infancy, and having never known her father, but she was blessed in her friendships. Maia's thoughts were interrupted as the door flew wide open and Poch came stumbling in. Piled up on his thick arms were a few large, rickety boxes. He shuffled closer to where the two girls sat and slowly placed the load on the floor.

"This is all we have." He breathed heavily as he quickly opened up the boxes and showed the contents to Dani. "Here are the tools, and here are the parts that we bought from Moritz."

After he had shown all of the bigger boxes, Poch picked up the last one. It was smaller than the rest, and it was strangely out of place with its neatness.

"And this has some snacks Mama made for you. Just in case," he added shyly and placed it in front of Dani.

Dani laughed. The carefree laughter told Maia that all misgivings had been forgotten; all was well between Poch and her friend.

"Thank you. But I won't need that in a hurry. Emmy has fed me all too well," Dani said. "I might need help from you if we have to replace the circuitry."

Poch nodded eagerly. The happy man that Maia knew had surfaced again.

"I'll be right here . . . anything you need . . . right here."

As Dani began working on the blackened cables, Maia inched closer to observe. When Herc left to finish his errands, Dani and her two eager apprentices were crouching and crawling all over the floor. All the connector units lay open, and soon Dani found the problem and was working to fix it. The real hard work started after that, and when they had closed the last unit after replacing wires, fuses, rotors, teeth, and a dozen other broken or almost broken parts, it was midafternoon.

The one thing that remained to be done was to go to the measurement station at the control base and check whether the repairs had fixed the turbine. So Poch led them back to the well and down the half-broken staircase. An enormous door of thick ancient wood stood at the bottom of the steps. It was bolstered with iron belts that ran up and down and across its body. An equally impressive black lock hung at the center of it.

"This is the entrance to the power grid. The measurement station is inside," Poch explained as he opened the lock with a stout key that hung on a chain around his waist. "It's dark in there, but we don't need to go too far in."

Maia held her breath as Poch pushed the door open. She was about to see what was once the lifeline of the Solianese civilization—the power grid of Tansi. Although Maia had ventured quite a few times to the Windehill and strolled around the well, this was the first time she walked past the closed doors of the control base. Herc believed it held memories of evil and was no place for Maia.

The smell of standing water hit Maia as soon as she stepped in. A dark wave of hopelessness swirled in her mind, bringing an ominous feeling of broken promises and death. A small flight of stairs led to a worn-out, raised platform overlooking the long tunnel that stretched endlessly on both sides. The arched roof of the tunnel and its shabby walls still bore the markings of old fires. Cables of enormous girth that looked like a mass of giant sleeping snakes occupied almost the entire floor of the tunnel. The measurement station, where Dani and Poch headed was on the left of the platform. Away from the station, nestled between the charred walls and the sea of cables was a pair of rail tracks. Running parallel to the walls, they stretched along the length of the tunnel and disappeared into the darkened ends.

"It works!" Dani's gleeful shout made Maia take her eyes off the misty blackness in the distance that threatened to hypnotize her. "We have a steady flow of power."

Poch stood behind a smiling Dani, his face frozen into the widest grin Maia had ever seen.

"I think I'm ready for some food now," Dani declared happily, as she sprinted out of the doors and up the stairs. "Let's go, Maia, we have to look at the other one."

After a sumptuous snack, Dani dove under the mesh of shafts in the other broken turbine. The work was finished hours later, almost close to sundown. By that time, Herc had reappeared carrying a box of food from Emmy, who was reportedly furious that a visitor should have been made to do such messy and frightful work.

They went back down the stairs to the mouth of the grid once more. As much as Maia feared that the discomfort would strike her again, she felt absolutely nothing this time around. She watched the cables as Dani and Poch went to look at the power measurements. The ancient tunnel mesmerized her; even the darkness that Maia feared so much felt inviting down here.

"They say it stretches all 'round the planet." Herc's voice startled Maia. He stood behind her staring at the dark eastern end. "See 'em rails, Miss Maia? The legends speak of cars that ran on them with the work crew that supervised the grid. They could drive 'em cars from one town to 'nother, 'cross continents and oceans. 'Twas all connected, you see."

"And now?" Maia asked.

"Parts hav' caved. And then there's jus' a handful of our cities left anyway, so the Jjord patched up bits of it. Only now, 'tis not them who feed the power, but the Xifarians."

Maia sighed, recalling the tale she had heard a million times over, the story of Xif—the planet that had suddenly turned up next to Tansi. Xif was not just a planet but also a spaceship and the Xifarians were no different in appearance from the people on Tansi, except for their eerie, incandescent eyes. They seemed kind and friendly at first contact. The Jjord maintained a wary aloofness from the new arrivals, but for the land-dwelling Solianese, reeling from the crippling devastation of the Scarcity and the strict sanctions laid by the Jjord, Xif was the first glimmer of hope in years. The impoverished land dwellers lined up in droves for the mining camps on Ti, the frozen moon of the sixth planet. But that interest soon waned. Horrifying tales about Ti started to circulate, and none of the recruits returned from Ti to tell otherwise. Anger stirred up unrest; frustration swelled into revolts. The leaders of the Solianese, the Jjord, and Xif agreed to meet at the Continental Parliament in the Solianese capital of Miorie in an attempt to soothe the rising tensions between the three nations. On the third day of the summit, the Resistance, a ragtag band of Solianese rebels, went up in arms against Xif.

The Xifarians swiftly retaliated. They crushed the fledgling rebellion, held the leaders of both the Solianese and the Jjord captive, and destroyed the energy sources of the planet. The people of Tansi teetered on the brink of extinction over the two-day standoff until their leaders were forced into the terms of what became known as the Exchange. The Solianese promised the Xifarians workers for the mining operations on Ti, and the Jjord agreed to an annual bartering of scientific and industrial knowledge—all in return for a stringently calculated supply of energy from Xif.

And since then, our lives . . . lives of all Tansians, the land-dwelling

Solianese and the Jjord of the undersea alike, have been dictated by the Xifarians.

Maia suppressed a sigh and turned her attention back to the tunnel.

"Have you ever walked into the tunnel, Herc?" she inquired.

Herc shook his head. "No, Miss Maia. 'Tis not safe," he said. "But way back then, yeh could prob'ly reach Shiloh if yeh walked eastward along it."

Sounds of laughter told Maia that the second turbine was now alive as well. Dani and Poch soon emerged from the measurement station.

"We did it," Dani announced, rushing to hug Maia.

A giddying wave of pride and happiness flooded Maia's heart. She had known that her friend was smart, but she did not know how much until this day.

A warm sunset was coming to an end when the group walked back home, happy and content. Poch led the way alongside Herc, Maia and Dani followed closely, and a band of chatty villagers brought up the rear. Poch promised them a tour of the woods the following day, as well as one of his candy factories.

Emmy was waiting for them at the gates when the party walked in. She wasted no time in ushering the girls inside, even before Poch and the villagers had the chance to bid them a proper goodbye. This night there was no talking after dinner, as Maia and Dani were exhausted, and within moments, they drifted into a sound, peaceful sleep.

CHAPTER EIGHT

TOGETHER AGAIN

The next few days flew by in the blink of an eye. Dani had grown so popular overnight that people who had never set foot in Dada's farm stopped by to meet the "kind girl from the seas." They brought gifts, trinkets, sweets, cakes, pastries, and anything else they could find. Overwhelmed by the outpouring of gratitude, Dani started brooding over the sad state of affairs between the two nations that had formerly been one. By the fourth and final day of the stay, Maia could not bear to see her downcast eyes and lightless face.

Dani kept busy tinkering with the perimeter shield that Hans had started. Maia accompanied her every day, and together they installed some monitoring devices along the fence lines. The more Maia worked with Dani on the security system, the more fearful she grew. She had been happier not thinking about the hazards she had faced, but now a gloom weighed on her mind. The Xifarian chancellor's threats kept ringing in her ears.

The Xifarians are capable of anything. What if they hurt my family?

The next moment she restrained herself.

I have to stop thinking this way, or I'll end up worrying like Emmy all my life. The chancellor's words were just a random outburst of anger. He meant nothing to me in particular, he couldn't have. I'm just an ordinary girl to him, by now he must've even forgotten all about me.

Debating her fears brought relief, but only briefly. Doubts, obstinate as they always were, persisted anyway. Maia was almost glad when it was time to leave Appian, this time there was little regret in her mind.

No one will bother my family if I'm away, and they'll be safe.

Maia could not wait to leave.

The village was still struggling to catch a few winks of fitful sleep on the very warm and humid night when Herc readied the carriage for their trip to the drop-off point. They arrived at the Troughs a little before daybreak, the soft light making the vast expanse of pockmarked fields look ethereal. Maia was a little surprised to find Dani as affected by the landscape as she had been on seeing it the first time. Dani trod the soft ground with the utmost care as if making sure she did not hurt the carpet of green underneath her feet. The Holding Pod that would take the contestants to the venue in the Jjordic colonies sat sure and steady in a trough as it had six months ago, a similar white tent standing next to it. A Tokii clerk scooted out of the parted curtains and peeked at the trio. There was no need for passkeys this time since both Maia and Dani wore their assigned identification numbers. The Tokii simply brought his prong closer to scan the numbers and nodded.

"What is that?" he asked sharply, glancing at the case Dani was carrying.

"My belongings," Dani explained. "I was visiting my friend here, so—"

"All right," the Tokii interjected. "It is up to your security protocols to allow luggage in. Please board."

After waving goodbye to Herc, Maia and Dani walked into the Holding Pod. It looked smaller than Maia remembered and there were certainly fewer people in it. A dark-haired girl Maia recognized was sitting on the floor, and just like the last time, she did not glance at the new arrivals. A boy with bright red hair stood with his back to the door, staring out of the clear glass walls. He turned around and flashed a half-hearted smile. Maia remembered her last ride on the craft and suddenly missed Kusha—it had been comforting to have him by her side. Now that the circus his parents owned was camped in the Third Continent, Kusha would take a different pod, likely along with Nafi, to Zagran.

They did not speak much. Dani was still in a contemplative mood. The pod took off, landed at a few more places, and gradually familiar faces trickled in. Jiri, the lanky boy who looked even ganglier now, scuttled toward the pair.

"We're back together again," he exclaimed.

"Yes, we are." Maia twittered happily. "Had a fun break, Jiri?"

"Sure did, but it was a little too short. How was yours?"

"Great, couldn't have been better," Maia replied.

They went on to speculate what this phase of the contest would be like and mused over the various adventures they had had while on Xif. Before long, the craft was skimming past the bright blue waters over Coloni Primei. They went down the funnel and bobbed up in the brightly lit cove of the Jjordic settlement.

Dani broke her silence. "Let's go. We have to disembark here."

She led the way down the stairs and onto the sparkling white ledge. Maia felt a distinct sharpness in the air as she followed Dani out of the pod. A woman and a man stood on two sides of the stairs, intently scanning the visitors. Their faces were like masks, their eyes unsmiling and cold. They nodded curtly at Dani as she walked past and continued staring icily at the others who followed. A young man in a white uniform beckoned them to the other end of the ledge; behind him was a large door marked, "To Checkpoint." After everyone had gathered in this area, he turned around and threw the door open.

A crowd of familiar faces thronged the room on the other side.

"Maia," a familiar voice rang out. A girl with bouncy auburn curls rushed to Maia's side. "How have you been?" Nafi's bright green eyes sparkled.

"Great," Maia laughed, throwing her arms around her friend. "Been here long, Nafi?"

"Very long," Nafi said, rolling her eyes. "Our pod was the first to arrive and I've grown tired of waiting."

"Hello, Nafi," Dani chimed in softly.

"Dani?" Nafi's eyes widened. "What are *you* doing here?"

"I just got off the pod with Maia," Dani replied. "Happy to see me?"

"Of course, of course," Nafi chirped, struggling to catch up. "I just wasn't expecting you *here*. Wait, does that mean you were visiting Maia?"

"Yes, she was." Maia eagerly summarized the long story of the surprise visit from Dani and her brother.

"Why don't I get to visit anyone?" Nafi grumbled. "All I get is to travel back with Mister Grumpy."

"Mister Grumpy?" Maia raised a curious eyebrow.

"Kusha," Nafi explained. "He's been silent all through the trip, I don't know why. I'm so bored."

"Where's he now?" Dani asked as she looked around the room.

"I don't know. He took off right after we came in here." Nafi shrugged listlessly, and then a mischievous look came over her face. "Maybe, he has a girlfriend," she whispered, her eyes shining with the thrill of making the greatest discovery. "That would explain why he was grumpy all along—he must be missing his dearest."

"You're crazy," Dani declared. "I'm going to ask Kusha and see what he has to say about it."

"Why?" Nafi crossed her arms and tapped her right foot as she squinted at Dani. "You think he can't have a girlfriend? Do you know something that we don't?"

"I didn't say that, I just—"

Dani did not get a chance to finish, as the door behind them opened once more and another bunch of youngsters filed in. A gregarious boy with mottled eyes and spiky black-and-white hair came swaggering into the room. He wore a bright red shirt with a gold hawk emblem. His face broke into a big grin when he saw the three girls.

"A receiving party for me?" Ren, their friend and teammate from Xif, said loudly, tipping an imaginary hat for effect.

Nafi shook her head and exhaled as noisily as she possibly could. "What's this you're wearing?" she demanded as she tugged at the sleeves of his shirt.

"Hey, hey . . ." Ren flinched, pulling his arm back. "Don't touch my team shirt, ignorant girl."

"What?" Nafi barked. The frown on her face was not a happy sight. "What did you call me?"

Maia and Dani exchanged a glance, both deciding this was the right time to intervene before war broke out.

"You're all here . . ." The voice that came from behind them was as welcome as it was effective in distracting everyone. Kusha stood smiling, his dark hair as unkempt as ever, his eyes shining through curly strands that escaped the red headband stretching across his forehead.

"Where were you hiding, Kusha?" Dani asked. "We've been here for ages."

"Just walking about," Kusha replied.

"He speaks," Nafi observed as she peered at the boy.

"Great discovery, Miss Smartness," Ren chortled.

Nafi glared at Ren, Ren made a face at Nafi, and then they both looked away. Both seemed really keen on hiding from each other the smiles that played on their lips.

Maia felt her heart swell, and her face stretch into an uncontrollable grin that kept on going. They were together again. There was little else in the world that could have made her happier.

"Are you well, Maia?" Kusha asked, leaning closer.

As Maia nodded, she could not help but notice the pallor on his face. Fear lurked in his eyes, subduing their sparkle.

"Nafi said you were worried," she said to Kusha. Next to them, Dani fought hopelessly to contain another imminent war of words between Nafi and Ren.

"I was." Kusha sighed and turned to face her. "I was worried about you, Maia . . . almost thought I'd never see you again."

"Oh, Kusha, I was fine." Maia linked an arm through his. "Besides, Dani stopped by and spent almost a week with me."

"Really?" A wave of emotions coursed through his face. He glanced at Dani, who had finally managed to bring peace between Nafi and Ren. "That was nice of her. I would've shown up at your house too if I could've found a fast-enough transport. I was worried sick—I was sure the R'armimon would attack you again."

Maia's heart skipped a beat. Seeing her friends so concerned made the realization sink in some more—her face-off on Xif with Yoome, the assassin of the R'armimon, had been dangerous indeed. A shudder went down Maia's spine as she recalled how powerful Yoome had been. She had overpowered Maia and Ren so easily and put up a stiff fight with Miir. Maia had been lucky to have escaped her clutches.

"Visitors traveling to Zagran will please follow the signs to the Aquiccela terminal," an icy voice announced over the loudspeaker, the voice's lifelessness lingered and spread uncomfortably across the room. The crowd silently gathered around the door that said, "To Terminal."

CHAPTER NINE

BROKEN APART

There was no one to show them the way, no smiles or welcomes. The door opened silently, revealing a brightly lit corridor ahead. On the ceiling, a brilliant green arrow flashed intermittently. The floor was white, shiny, and slick; the tap of each footstep on its hard surface reverberated through the emptiness. A hushed silence had fallen, and the group of youngsters walked quickly in the direction of the arrow. They came to a vaulted doorway leading to another corridor framed by lighted arches as far as Maia could see. Ahead of the entrance, the entire path seemed to ripple forward.

"Follow me," Dani said as she made her way through the crowd.

Maia marched onward. Kusha, Nafi, and Ren tagged close behind. When Dani stepped beyond the doorway, Maia gingerly hopped on the moving walkway, a little fearful of the floor that crawled below her feet. The other teams soon followed. A curious few even started walking and skipping ahead of the rest.

"Where are we going?" Maia asked Dani.

"To the Aquiccela terminal," Dani explained. "There we board our transport to Zagran, a train that runs between the settlement and the fringe port."

"Fringe port?" Nafi asked.

"That's what we call the cove where the pod landed. These fringe ports are the points of entry from the external world to our settlements, sort of like what Arpasgula is to Xif."

"That reminds me, it's weird that no one came to greet us," Maia commented. During the Xifarian phase, Vice Principal Geir-Sei of the Xifarian Defense Academy or the XDA had received them at the spaceport of Arpasgula where the Holding Pod had taken them. Maia had expected someone from their current host institution, the Jjordic University of Advanced Arts and Sciences or the UAAS, to meet them the same way.

"Yes, that surprised me too," Dani admitted.

"No one cares," Ren said casually. He diligently brushed off some invisible dust from his bright red shirt.

Above and around them, the rows of lighted arches glowed in a soft, soothing blue. It did little to calm Maia—she stared eagerly ahead, wondering what to expect next. The wait soon came to an end, and after a few sharp turns, the walkway reached a wide room similar to the one they had started from. The far side of this room was lined with a row of booths where ten women sat. They all had short hair, wore white uniforms, and sported equally somber expressions. The women stared at the visitors with cold, disapproving eyes.

"They will check our credentials," Dani said loudly enough for the entire company to hear. A voice crackled overhead not long after.

"Visitors traveling to Zagran, proceed to the agents for verification and authorization."

Soon, Maia made it to one of the counters. The agent asked her name, scanned the number the Tokii had assigned to her during the last phase of the contest, and then directed her to another side of the room where more agents waited next to a closed door. Nafi and Ren were already waiting there, looking away from each other pointedly, perhaps because of yet another disagreement.

"So, Ren" — Maia nudged his elbow — "what exactly is this 'team shirt' thing?" She could feel Nafi steal a furtive glance.

"It's my racing team jersey," Ren replied, his eyes sparkling with excitement. "We won the Sword of Ataii this year, so this is very special."

"Racing team? What race?" Maia asked. Next to her, Nafi shuffled closer.

"The annual Cylopede race," Ren replied, and then added, flushing a little, "I'm part of the juniors' team though. The real race is open only to people eighteen years and older."

"What's the Sword of Ataii?" Kusha joined the conversation.

"It's the winner's trophy, named after the legendary Seigvard," Ren said dreamily.

"Seigvard is a wonderful name. Ataii was your last queen, wasn't she?" Dani, who had joined the group moments before, must have recalled what Ren had mentioned during their stay on Xif. "There must be incredible tales about this sword."

"Not really." Ren shook his head. "The Royal family and its history is a well-guarded secret. I've always heard those names, but not much more."

A small murmur rose from where the two agents stood guarding the door, making all of them forget the matter of the Xifarian queen for a while. The door had opened and the two guards directed people through it. One of them thumbed through the pages of a shimmery notebook, while the other pointed people in different directions on the other side of the door.

"They're showing us to the Aquiccela. Come on." Dani directed the group to the agent with the notebook.

The man looked through the book, then back at the group, and back and forth a few times. Maia assumed he was crosschecking their identification numbers with their biometrics before letting them inside.

"You have been checked in," he informed Nafi, who stood at the head of the line. "You will pass through the doors and await the boarding call."

As Nafi stepped aside, Dani walked up to the man.

"You will please take a seat." The man smiled at her, pointing at a bench along the wall behind him. "You will be boarding the fore after everyone else has been boarded. An escort will be here shortly to walk you over to your seat."

Dani looked uncertainly at the bench. "Why do I have to sit there?" she asked. "I would rather be here with my friends."

The expression on the man's face changed from confusion to sudden comprehension, and then to cold outrage.

"I am sorry. You will *not* be boarding the same section as your *friends*." He articulated the last part of the sentence with a chilly vehemence. "Your place has been chosen, and you will be taken there at the appropriate time."

"Why?" Dani spat angrily.

"That is the rule. There are assigned sections for everyone, and yours is different from theirs. You cannot travel with them, not here in the settlements."

Maia's heart stilled. *We're being separated based on our heritage.* For a brief moment, she simply wanted to run away from the humiliation. To think that the Jjord would treat them this way; they were one people not so long ago. But of course, they would, she reasoned. They had kept the Solianese away for a century, and they intended to keep that segregation alive. Just because the Solianese children were competing alongside the Jjord in the Initiative did not mean their nations had turned into compatriots.

"You can't tell me whom I should travel with. That's my choice," Dani almost shouted. Her face was a vivid shade of red, and her lips trembled as she argued with the man. "Where I want to sit is my choice too."

Proud as she was of Dani's resolve to be with them, Maia also felt a sharp pang of embarrassment. Next to her, Kusha fidgeted while Nafi stood quietly. Ren watched with an expressionless face, his eyes flitting from the man to Dani and back. People were starting to stare. Around them, eager and inquisitive faces gathered, some concerned, some worried, and some simply enjoying the spectacle.

Dani's refusal to follow orders did not seem to sit well with any of the personnel. The man had nodded in the direction of the booths, and two women walked over to them promptly, their heels clicking on the hard floor with the sound of finality. Their eyes scanned the group and came to focus on Dani's flushed face.

"You will please observe the rules. If you don't, we will have to take steps to enforce them," one of the women said. "And we do not want to do that to one of our own."

"But . . ." Dani protested. She did not seem to care for the consequences. The woman's face hardened and her eyes narrowed to slits.

"Dani, please," Kusha interrupted before she could say any more. "I . . . we know you don't like this, but you're making this awkward for us, so just go with them. Please."

Dani stared at Kusha, her eyes blazing. Then a pall of gloom fell across her face. Maia expected her to say something, but Dani did not utter a sound. She strode past the two women and the man and sat down on the bench without another glance backward. The agents seemed a little taken aback by her sudden compliance; it was not until a few moments later that they turned around to face the remainder of the group. Kusha was next, and he was directed toward the door where he joined Nafi. Ren took his turn after Kusha.

"What plans do you have for me?" Ren stood with his arms crossed, his head cocked at the three agents.

"You will please join your friend over there," the man said, pointing toward the bench where Dani sat alone.

"Interesting," Ren declared. He turned to Maia and whispered loudly enough for everyone to hear, "Not sure if I should be happy or sad."

After Maia was sent in the same direction as Kusha and Nafi, the trio walked together silently to the open door. The man at the door ushered them toward an empty seat on a sparkling platform that stretched endlessly in both directions.

CHAPTER TEN

TO ZAGRAN

The terminal felt cold as Maia sat with Kusha and Nafi, waiting for their transport. No one spoke, and Maia hoped the train would arrive soon. She always found Nafi's silence hard to endure. Every time the vivacious girl refused to speak, it was as if the heart of the group had stilled. Maia shifted uncomfortably, trying to think of things to talk about, yet failing to break the silence. The quiet had grown unbearable when Kusha sat up and started the much-needed conversation.

"There it is, the Aquiccela," he said, smiling at the sleek tubular vehicle that pulled into the terminal. "Looks quite snazzy."

Nafi gave the Aquiccela a detached look-over. "Hmmm," she said finally, her voice low and gloomy.

"Wonder how long the trip to Zagran will be," Maia chimed in. Keeping the conversation going could not have been more difficult. Nafi did not even look in her direction. "Hope it's not as boring as traveling through the tunnel into Xif."

"I don't think so," Kusha replied eagerly. "I've heard that the transoceanic lines are laid right across the seas, no tunnels down here."

"Guess it's time to find out," Maia said, looking at the men in uniform who had emerged from the transporter and were now asking the scattered groups of children to board.

Maia, her two teammates, and the rest of the Solianese contestants were shown into the third compartment from the fore. As the groups filed in slowly, the air filled up with light chatter. The compartment was long, and its body lined with clear windows. Inside, rows of seats ran perpendicular to the length of the train. Two consecutive rows faced each other forming groups of four on both sides of an aisle that ran along the center of the coach.

Maia observed the flurry of activity on the platform. After all the contestants had boarded and the doors of the compartment were closed, more doors on the platform opened. People streamed out and slowly entered the coaches in the rear.

"They had this compartment reserved for the participants of the Initiative," Kusha observed. "Now they are boarding the public sections behind us."

"There they are," Nafi said, looking toward the front of the train. "The whole gang from Xif and Dani are getting into the second car."

"Hey, did you notice that Karhann's team is missing?" Maia exclaimed, suddenly realizing the team rumored to have been disqualified during the last phase had not shown up. Karhann and his teammates—Loriine, Baecca, Yoome, and a boy whose name Maia could not recall—made up Core 7. They had been fierce competitors during the Xifarian phase. However, because they violated the Code of Honor during their combat with Maia during the final challenge, the team's actions had been under scrutiny. And then Yoome had turned out to be an assassin of the R'armimon. By the time the groups had left Xif, no decision about Core 7's further participation had been released.

"Serves them right," Nafi said gruffly. She had not been able to forgive the group for their sneaky attack on Maia.

"I keep wondering about the challenges for this phase." Kusha stretched himself across two seats. "And what we get to learn from these people."

"I don't have high hopes," Nafi commented wryly. "They don't seem even half as nice as the Xifarians, and we all know how charming those people were."

Maia had to chuckle. Nafi was always to the point, not always pleasing, but hardly ever off the mark.

A tiny noiseless vibration started below their feet and slowly grew stronger. Then, with a small shake and a wobble, the transporter pulled away from the platform. Maia remembered their passage into Xif through the darkened lock gates and hoped the journey this time around would be more pleasant.

CHAPTER ELEVEN

INTO THE BLUE

The Aquiccela entered a passageway that was nothing like the dark tunnel leading into Xif. This one had shiny walls, silvery ribs spiraling around its entire length, and bright lights glittering like gems at closely spaced intervals. Not too long after it had left the terminal, the transporter turned sharply to the right and plunged downward along a steep incline. Midway through the fall, a wave of water rushed up the sides of the tunnel and splattered across its shiny length, making Maia shrink back from the windows. They had entered the seas. All around them swirled the clearest water Maia had ever seen. As the train sunk lower, it turned darker.

"I thought we were quite deep under the seas already." Nafi seemed a bit agitated. "Why are we going down again?"

"Wish Dani were here to explain," Maia said with a sigh.

Outside the passageway, the water grew murkier. Maia had started to wonder what Dani and Ren were up to in the next compartment when she heard a voice.

"This is my home, and all I wanted was to tell you more about it on our way to Zagran," Dani's voice rang crisp and clear in Maia's ears.

"Dani?" she exclaimed, turning to look at Kusha and Nafi.

"I hear her too," Kusha whispered as Nafi nodded. "But how?"

"Maia . . . you can hear me?" Dani asked. "But how is that possible? I was simply talking to Ren."

Maia looked around at the other groups. Everyone was busy staring out of the windows; no one spared a glance in their direction. It seemed as if they were the only ones who could hear Dani.

"I know!" Ren's excited shout almost threw Maia backward with its sudden intensity. "It has to be the wristbands."

Three pairs of eyes turned immediately to the dark and sparkly band that stretched around their wrists, the prize from Mahswa Tabrin for their bravery during the Seliban challenge. Mahswa was a Tierremorphe; she could terraform or shape land freely with her mind. Maia remembered her words clearly: "The firestones have special powers that not many know about." Maia remembered the words of another man, the Emeritus Professor Phocluus who had known Sophie: "These stones helped you protect the Tyrillic Converter."

"But how did you make it work?" Kusha whispered. "It was as good as dead all along."

"Don't know," Dani replied.

"We can figure that out later," Nafi whispered. "Now, Dani, tell us why we're heading toward the bottom of the ocean."

"We're not going to the bottom of the ocean." Dani's laughter filled Maia's ears. "We're simply getting out of the fringe port through the North Central Spout. The transport lines almost always merge below the city levels, so these openings, or spouts, have to face downward in the direction of these interchanges. We're now heading toward the Northern Interchange and we shall take the TTL to Zagran from there."

"What's a TTL?" Ren asked.

"Transoceanic Transport Lines," Dani explained. "These are

connectors between settlements, highways for the transporters like the one we are on. Then there are the Transoceanic Carriage Lines for private carriages driven by citizens themselves."

"Like the Hansmobile?" Maia asked.

"Well, not exactly." Dani laughed. "The Hansmobile can also use uncharted routes outside the tunnels — a vehicle like that is called an 'off-liner.' The Hansmobile doesn't like to limit itself to the confines of defined transport systems; rather, it makes its own road, so to speak."

Kusha stared at Maia, and Nafi's eyebrows shot up a tad higher at this exchange, but before anyone could ask questions the rapidly changing scenery outside drew their attention.

The transporter slowed for a moment and immediately picked up speed as it entered the "mesh" — a web made of innumerable tunnels just like the one their own transporter was speeding through. They came from all possible directions at various levels above and below, a gigantic ball of shimmery yarn that spun around in the depths of the blue. Some of them merged, some intersected, and some diverged. Within them, vehicles moved swiftly in a frenzied blur.

"This is the Northern Interchange," Dani informed.

Their Aquiccela sped through the complicated net, twisting and turning for a very long time before it was swallowed up by a tunnel nearly double the width of the first one it was in. Once inside, the transporter steadily climbed up and away from clustered transport lines of the interchange. Maia assumed this to be the TTL to Zagran; the long stretch under the Eastern Seas that it was designed to cover explained its wider girth. As the transporter climbed higher, the waters around it grew refreshingly lighter.

"We should be able to see the fringe port behind us," Ren inferred. Maia, Kusha, and Nafi craned their necks to catch a glimpse.

"Not for this one, we can't," Dani was quick to correct him. "This fringe port is built behind an underwater ridge. We are outside that embankment now, so — "

Nafi groaned, obviously let down by the information.

"Don't be upset, Nafi," Dani chuckled. "Wait until we get to

Zagran. You'll forget all about the fringe port once you see the city."

Suddenly, something stirred in the waters, and ripples spread across in a swift, circular motion. Rising through the curtain of blue were milk squids, creatures Maia had read about in books. She had never imagined they could be so large or so imposing. Their large, bulbous heads were as big as a pachyderm's, and twenty long tentacles emerged from the base of the heads and dangled like hooks. It was not just one milk squid but a huge colony that rose and lingered around the speeding transporter, their mass casting a dark shadow on the area. Maia felt a bit unnerved by their presence, but thankfully the group sunk back into the depths as noiselessly as they had arrived.

The transporter moved on through reefs and canyons, some a mosaic of colors and some dull and lifeless. But there was never a lack of things to talk about—a zillion enticing and amazing creatures went about their ways. Shoals of colorful fish swarmed past; some stopped for a while and peeked at the Aquiccela with curiosity while others passed without care. Some were small and some large, some in groups and some alone, and they were of the strangest shapes and sizes. Between Maia and her friends, it was an endless conversation about every new thing they saw, and Maia hardly noticed how time flew by.

"We're almost there," Dani said as the transporter glided past a bluish-yellow embankment. "As soon as we turn around that ridge, you'll see—"

The transporter made its way past the ragged edge of the underwater hillock. A stunned silence descended on all conversation, and Maia forgot to breathe.

Chapter Twelve

The City of Dreams

Sprawled all along the left of the transport line was a structure that could have popped out of a dream. It was a breathtaking arrangement of shimmering shapes, a composition of gigantic bubbles stacked and connected through a complex series of tunnels, passages, and corridors. Its transparent surface gleamed in the soft blue light filtering through the waters; the curves and the bulges that housed the city reflected the myriad of colorful sea creatures that swam all around it.

"This is it." Dani's reverential voice came over the wristband. "This is Zagran."

As the transporter drew closer to the colossal mountain of bubbles, the lights of the glistening city inside it slowly became visible. The Aquiccela suddenly seemed minuscule—the length of the whole structure could easily rival the Dorgashians, Maia guessed.

Dani's voice sounded again. "Zagran is built around Mount Setna, an underwater mountain. You can think of the Setna as Zagran's backbone, it forms the axis to which the frame of the city is anchored. The city now looks like a cluster of berries, but it wasn't always like this. The first few levels of it were partially carved into the mount, and partly erected upon an impervious rocky ledge. Slowly the structure grew. When our technology was advanced enough, the buildings grew taller. The bubble meshes were built over them as a protective cover."

On nearing the city, the TTL subdivided into narrower transport lines. The Aquiccela picked one of these smaller lines that circled halfway around the underwater city and plunged into the side of a shabby-looking dome protruding rather sorely from the middle of the superstructure. Within moments, the transporter came to stop at a platform.

The doors opened one by one, and people streamed out of the Aquiccela. By the time Maia, Kusha, and Nafi made their way out of the transporter, Dani and Ren were already waiting on the platform.

"So, what do you think?" Dani asked the instant they were together. Her eyes shone with pride.

"It's ridiculously big," Nafi exclaimed. "I have to say, I didn't expect anything as huge as this."

The crowd around them hummed excitedly among themselves, everyone seemed moved and upbeat after the ride. No one knew what they were supposed to do, so they simply waited on one side of the half-empty platform for further directions.

"And we wait once more," Kusha observed with a grimace. "You would think the organizers would arrange for someone to meet us."

"Yes, I never thought I'd say this, but right now I miss Geir-Sei." Maia chuckled as she remembered the flamboyant vice principal of the XDA who had received them at the spaceport of Arpasgula.

A door next to the huddled group opened noisily no sooner than Maia had spoken. A woman wearing a crisp white uniform walked in, her head held high, her posture stiff, and the heels of her shoes clip-clopping on the hard floor. She was tall and skinny. It was as if the thinnest fabric of pallid skin had been draped upon her bones. Her eyes were sunken and sharp, her lips a thin and disapproving presence below a harsh and unforgiving nose. Gray hair was swept away from her brows that knit in a tight frown on her cold, humorless face and tied up into a sleek ponytail that stood on her head like a flagpole. She crossed her long bony arms, her eyes sweeping over the faces around her as she faced the group.

"Welcome to Zagran," she said icily.

No one made a sound or moved.

"I am Aerika from the University of Advanced Arts and Sciences. I will be your training supervisor during your stay here in Zagran. As you already know from the first stage of this contest, you will be expected to learn some of our skills and master them to be able to successfully compete in the two challenges. This will, of course, require your attention, application, and commitment, which I hope you have plenty to have survived the Xifarian phase. Each team will be paired with a mentor who will help you adapt to your new home. Your mentor will show you around, introduce you to our rules and regulations, and advise you when needed."

The supervisor paused, and Maia let out the breath she had been holding. She found it very odd that they were being introduced to the contest at a place as public as the transporter terminal. People walked past, staring, and some even stopped to listen. Maia wondered if this was a deliberate attempt by the Jjord to show their displeasure at this whole exercise.

"Your mentors are here," Aerika said.

A group of girls and boys, who looked about sixteen or older, gathered behind the ponytailed woman. They were a mixed bunch, their expressions ranging from happy and eager to simply bored. They were dressed in white and a dark blue that reminded Maia of the midnight sky; the boys wore blue trousers, white shirts with blue-bordered oversized collars, and red ties; the girls wore blue skirts, similar white shirts ,and ties. All of them had an abalone talisman indicating their Jjordic heritage pinned to their shirt.

"Your mentors will now escort you to your dormitories," Aerika continued. "Some of your teammates will join you there directly."

She was referring to the participants from the Jjordic colonies, Maia surmised. With the obvious exception of Dani, Maia had not seen a single Jjord contestant.

Aerika clapped her hands. "That's all then. I will see you at the university tomorrow."

With that, she turned and left. As the door closed behind her, the group of mentors came to life. One girl waved at Dani and walked purposefully in their direction. Her hair was the color of honey, a thousand curls ringing her head like a summer cloud.

"If I'm not mistaken, you're Dani," the girl said, her pretty, brown eyes dancing as Dani nodded.

"I think I know exactly who everybody is," the girl said, squinting at the team. She pointed out each person with practiced perfection. "You must be Kusha, Nafi, Maia, and Ren. Am I right?"

Maia grinned, as did everyone else.

"I'm Joolsae," the girl said, smiling. It was the most beautiful smile Maia had seen in a while. "I welcome you to the city of Zagran, the university, and the second phase of this awesome contest that you guys are lucky enough to participate in. I wanted to try out for it but could not take a year off from my classes, so . . ."

Joolsae looked a little sad and lost in thought for a moment, but then she chuckled and continued.

"So, I'm thrilled to have been chosen as a mentor. And I think I'm extra lucky to be assigned to the winners of the Xifarian phase. We've been hearing all about you from the promotionals," she beamed. Maia guessed Joolsae was referring to the pamphlets the Xifarians had been distributing about the Alliance Initiative, like the one Dani had shown her in Appian.

Joolsae gushed again, "Now if you'll follow me, I shall show you around my fabulous city."

CHAPTER THIRTEEN

JOOLSAE AND THE 500TH

Maia glanced at her friends as they followed Joolsae out of the terminal; everyone looked happy and relaxed. Nafi caught her gaze and shuffled closer.

"This girl is too good to be true, don't you think?" Nafi whispered. "Do you remember our terrible first meeting with Miir?"

Maia tittered. Of course, she remembered that and every other encounter with their foul-tempered mentor on Xif. It was not something she could forget in a hurry. It was indeed a welcome change to have someone as nice as Joolsae as a mentor, and Maia was nothing but thankful for her presence.

Joolsae stopped when they reached a giant hall with a domed ceiling. The expansive area was decorated with innumerable trees, shrubs, and flowering plants. It seemed like a meeting place—tables and chairs were scattered around in neat groups, some of which were occupied. About ten glass-enclosed elevators scuttled up and down a central wall, rising from the floor and disappearing into the ceiling high above. To the right, an enormous curved window faced the waters outside. Beyond it was the glittering scenery they had seen from the transporter on their way in.

"Which floor is this?" Ren asked.

"This is the 300th," Dani replied. "All transporter terminals in Zagran are on the 300th. And every transporter terminal is placed right next to an atrium, which provides easy access to the entire length of the city."

"That's right," Joolsae chimed in. "We're now standing in the North Central Atrium. There are fifty atriums in the entire city of Zagran. They serve as connectors across the many levels of our city."

Joolsae pointed at the elevators that ran back and forth forever. "Those elevators can take you from the topmost floor of the city to the lowest end. We will take one of those and rise to the 400th floor — that's where the UAAS starts."

"What do you mean 'starts?'" Kusha asked, frowning.

"The UAAS takes up the entire North Central section from the 400th. We, the students of the UAAS, have access from the 400th to the 499th floors, and so will you. Floors above the 500th are used by the government and closed to public access."

"A *hundred* floors for the university?" Kusha sounded incredulous.

"Well, only the North Central section. I know it seems like a little too much, but this is a big place with a lot of students and a lot of activity," Joolsae said as she held open the door of a waiting elevator that would carry the group to the UAAS. "The first few days might be a little crazy, but very soon you'll get used to the size."

"I was totally lost when I first visited Zagran," Dani added as the group filed into the elevator. "T'ra, my home city, is tiny compared to this, and it took me months to finally find my way around here. I don't know how Hans manages to remember every nook and cranny of this place like the back of his hand."

"Because Hans is ah-mazing," Joolsae said. There was something about the way her voice flitted that made everyone turn around and look at her. A small flush crept into her cheeks, and as if to divert attention, she quickly added, "We're going up to the 500th now."

Nafi squinted hard at Joolsae. "But I thought students don't have access to the 500th."

"You're such a smart li'l thing." Joolsae chuckled loudly and ruffled Nafi's hair, making her squirm. "Yes, the 500th is not for general access, but this exercise is sort of a government program. So, a small section of the 500th has been modified to house your teams. You'll have limited access to the rest of that floor or the floors above. You'll mostly be restricted to the dorm and the atrium on the 500th. But that section of the North Central atrium has the most fantastic views. You guys are really lucky."

The elevator had started to rise and it swiftly climbed along the atrium. The stunning surroundings kept everyone quiet for the most part, and by the time the elevator came to a stop on the 500th floor, Maia felt slightly dazed.

"Here we are." Joolsae smiled brightly as she stepped out. "Welcome to your new home on the 500th. I hope you have all the fun in the world."

The walls of this section were a beautiful aquamarine, and the décor was similarly hued. A large meeting area with tables and chairs far larger and more opulent than the ones on the 300th made up the center of the atrium. On one side were shops that displayed a variety of foods, gifts, and a host of other items.

Maia had to agree that the view from here was indeed more spectacular than on the other floors. Right outside the window was the most vibrant reef she had seen so far. A part of it jutted close to the left side of the window; it felt almost near enough to touch.

"It's beautiful," Nafi said, gazing at the reef and the thousand different water creatures swimming all around it. The group plopped down on the narrow bench that formed a circle in front of the glass wall.

They had spent a long time watching in silence when Joolsae rose to her feet. "Sorry, guys, I know it's quite fascinating. I could spend hours simply sitting here and looking outside, but . . . I have to show you to your dorms," she said.

Maia followed her quite reluctantly. Joolsae led them toward the side of the atrium behind the elevator walls. This area was quiet and somewhat isolated. A flight of stairs was built into the side of the walls, rising about two stories above the floor. As they took the stairs, Maia noticed several doors on the floor level that were closed. At the top of the steps, the corridor split in two, and there were small signs at the junction that said "Girls" on one side and "Boys" on the other.

"Here are the dorms. Your team has been allotted units D1 on both sides," Joolsae announced. "Each dorm houses six people. So you will be sharing the room with members from other teams."

Nafi's face immediately twisted into a grimace, and Kusha raised an eyebrow.

"So the team doesn't get to stay together?" Kusha asked.

Joolsae shook her head vehemently. "Oh no, the boys' and girls' sections are separate," she informed. "You'll find your uniforms inside, as well as your other necessities. If you need anything in particular, you have to let me know and I'll arrange to get it for you. Have a good night's rest, and I'll see you in the morning."

She patted Nafi lightly on the cheek. Nafi cringed and as her face reddened Joolsae chuckled and patted her again. Then she left.

"She thinks I'm her pet monkey or something," Nafi grunted loudly when Joolsae was out of earshot. "She's strange, that girl."

"I like her," Maia said. "I didn't expect our mentor to be so nice."

"I totally agree," Kusha declared as Nafi shrugged at Maia's comment. "Would you rather have someone as grumpy as Miir?"

"I'm more worried about who we'll be sharing our dorm with," Ren said. "And are we expected to starve tonight? She forgot to show us the dining area."

"You won't die if you don't get to eat one night," Nafi said with more than her usual air of wisdom.

Ren would not have taken her comment so lightly had it not been for a shrill beep that made them jump. It came from Dani; the small, flat, translucent square that hung from her waistband persistently screamed for attention until Dani unhooked it from her belt and pressed some buttons to silence it.

"That's my Urso, it's a messenger device. Hans has sent a note welcoming you all to Zagran," she declared, flushing bright on noting the slightly alarmed faces around her. "I'll set the volume to the lowest, so I don't startle anyone."

"Yes, please do," Nafi snapped.

"And don't forget to thank Hans," Maia added quickly, frowning at Nafi for her curtness.

Dani's fingers danced over the Urso. "All right, done," she said. "Let's check out our living quarters. Maybe we can come back out after we've freshened up."

That suggestion seemed to go down well with everyone. Kusha and Ren stepped away toward the boys' section while Maia and the two girls went to find the girls' room. D1, the first door on the left, was ajar when the trio walked up to it. Maia gingerly pushed it open.

CHAPTER FOURTEEN

THE GIRL IN THE ROOM

The room was rectangular — three beds, complete with canopies and curtains, stood along each of the longer sides. At the foot of every bed stood a box with the name of the person it was assigned to, except for the first two on the left. Maia immediately spotted their names on the right side. On the bed farthest from the door, a dark-haired girl sat staring fixedly at Maia and her friends. Maia recognized her as the girl she had seen in the Holding Pod; they had traveled together from Shiloh a few times, but the girl had neither talked nor smiled.

"You seem like you've seen a ghost or something," the girl said in a flat, drab voice.

Maia stepped forward, smiling sheepishly. "I'm Maia," she said. "We've been on the Holding Pod together."

The dark-haired girl did not reply, but tilted her head and watched the trio march in.

"Anja from Shiloh," she said simply when they had gathered around her.

It was funny, Maia mused, although they were practically neighbors on Tansi they had never spoken to each other before.

Anja pointed at the two unassigned spaces. "Don't know who those are for, no names, nothing."

"Maybe it's just the four of us then." Maia plopped happily onto her bed before starting to fiddle with the box with her name on it. A pile of uniforms lay neatly stacked inside, along with a lot of stationery.

"No way I'm going to wear this." Nafi held up a uniform that looked exactly like the one Joolsae was wearing, only the skirt was cerulean, not dark blue.

"Why not?" Dani asked, raising a curious eyebrow at a distraught Nafi. "It looks perfectly fine to me."

"It's . . . blue." Nafi seemed to have the utmost difficulty speaking. "It's *not* my color."

"Not your color?" It was Maia's turn to be surprised.

"Blue represses my spirit," Nafi declared, sounding almost irritated by the ignorance of her audience.

"Too bad. You're under a whole ocean of blue. I doubt if there's any hope for you in here." Anja's flat voice was surprisingly bold and precise.

Nafi glared at the girl, making Maia wonder how interesting the next six months were going to be. She had just started to worry about the prospect of Nafi and Anja sharing a room when the door flew open. Two girls stepped inside—the one with a dark, luminous complexion stood in front, and behind her lurked the other's wearied, pale face.

"You," Nafi said incredulously, as Loriine's beautiful face broke into a twisted smile. "Why are *you* here?"

"Same reason you are, little cousin." Loriine's drawl was as infuriating as Maia remembered. Loriine walked in, sat on one of the unassigned beds, crossed her legs, and leaned back. Her companion, the perpetually bored Baecca, busily inspected her surroundings as everyone else stared in shocked surprise. Maia found it hard to fathom the situation—Loriine and Baecca belonged to Core 7 along with Karhann, and they had been fierce competitors during the Xifarian phase. However, because of their dishonorable attack on Maia at the Seliban Temple, there had been discussions about banning the team from the Initiative.

"But . . . you were disqualified," Dani said, frowning.

"Of course not. What happened at the Seliban Temple was simply the result of a miscommunication. It was not a serious-enough offense for the team to be disqualified," Loriine crooned as she lazily swung her legs. "So, be ready for some tough competition, girls, because this time there will be no mercy."

Nafi opened her mouth to reply, but Maia grabbed her arm and pulled her away. The girls occupied themselves with inspecting their boxes. Loriine seemed annoyed that she had failed to engage Nafi in a fight but soon busied herself with something else. After everything had been looked at, the trio walked out of the room in search of the boys.

***

Kusha and Ren were sitting at the atrium watching the waters around the reef.

"Guess who showed up?" Ren said.

"Must be that stupid Karhann and his posse," Nafi said grumpily, depositing herself next to Kusha. "His sweethearts barged into our dorm not too long ago, as if we didn't have enough trouble with that loud-mouth Anja."

"Besides Karhann and his mate, who are the others in your room?" Dani asked the boys.

"Jiri and his buddy Nair," Kusha replied. "I'm surprised that Karhann's team was allowed back into the competition."

"They have connections," Ren commented.

"As in they have ties to the Xifarian chancellor," Maia said, remembering that Karhann was Miir's cousin.

Ren shook his head. "They wouldn't need to go that far," he said slowly. "Karhann comes from a powerful family of politicians, and Loriine's father is quite influential as well. They would have enough backing to get past their disqualification."

Maia sat wordlessly, bristling inside at the unfairness of it all. Judging by the quiet that fell around them, Maia knew her teammates felt equally disappointed.

"Hello," a nervous voice broke their companionship of silence. Jiri stood behind them, a friendly smile adorning his earnest face. "We've been asked to retire to our rooms, and food has already been served."

"Don't tell me we have to eat in our rooms with that nasty lot," Nafi blurted, forgetting that Anja was Jiri's teammate and possibly his good friend.

"We were told this is just for tonight." Jiri graciously ignored Nafi's remark.

The group rose to their feet half-heartedly, hardly interested in getting back to their rooms. Nafi walked ahead, Kusha and Dani followed. Maia took time to tear her eyes off the school of striped fish whose scales sparkled in a rainbow of colors in the reflected light of the atrium. Ren sat next to her, he had not moved either.

"Maia," he said in a hesitant whisper. "Can you wait a while?"

His dejected tone startled Maia a little. Ren continued to stare fixedly at the dark waters beyond the glass, and he did not speak until the rest of the group had started up the stairs.

"What is it, Ren?" Maia asked.

"I . . ."

"Yes?"

His eyes brimmed with sadness when he finally turned to look at her. "I'm sorry," he said. "I let you down . . . couldn't protect you when . . . Yoome attacked. I was so weak and . . . stupid —"

"Ren," Maia cut him off forcefully. "Please don't say that. Don't say that ever again." She paused to collect her thoughts as she watched the gloom on Ren's face. "You were not weak, you were really brave." She placed a hand on his. "But you were stupid . . . and crazy enough to fight Yoome, who was no match for any one of us. She could've killed you, Ren, and you knew that, yet you tried to help me."

"I failed." Ren looked away.

"You tried." Maia pulled his shoulder to make him face her again. "And that's all that matters to me." Ren did not reply, but the air of sadness seemed to fade a little. Maia got to her feet and tugged at his arm. "Come on, you don't want Nafi to come back and yell at us, do you?" Maia teased, hoping that she had managed to clear his mind.

A small smile played uncertainly on Ren's face before he flashed a grudging grin. Together, they headed up the stairs.

Maia found the girls gathered around a small table that had been set at the center of their room. It was stacked with food—a basket of bread, colorful plates heaped with vegetables and fish, and a bowl filled with fruits, jams, and tarts. A pang of hunger twisted in Maia's stomach as soon as she laid her eyes on the fare. She took quick steps forward, almost running up to join the others. They ate in silence, and soon afterward, an attendant came by to clear the table. After the attendant had left, the group prepared to retire for the night. Except for a few whispered "good nights" exchanged strictly among friends, not much was said.

Maia lay staring into the darkness for the longest time. She was tired, but her mind was racing. She had been through a lot since the morning, and not everything had been pleasant. Yet, Maia felt hopeful. She recalled her first night on Xif—she had been distraught then, but even with the setbacks, the visit to Zagran seemed uplifting and not as ominous.

CHAPTER FIFTEEN

THE INITIATION SPEECH

Maia woke up to utter chaos the next morning. A battle was raging in the room, and surprisingly enough, Nafi was not involved. Loriine and Baecca were trading their candid opinions of Anja at the top of their voices, and Anja replied in no gentle terms her own views of the two girls. What had caused the current grief, Maia had no idea, but she noticed that Dani and Nafi had wasted no time in getting out of the warzone. Maia decided to follow their example and quickly began to get ready for the day.

By the time they managed to slip out of the room, Anja had casually thrown a pillow at Loriine and shut herself in the dressing room. Baecca soon called it quits while Loriine still fumed indignantly at the nerve of the "stupidest girl in the whole universe."

"I hope they don't kill each other." Maia was genuinely worried about the situation they left behind in the room.

"I hope they do," Nafi said with a harrumph and strode faster than ever in the direction of the stairs. They met Joolsae halfway down the staircase. The sweetest smile flooded Joolsae's face as soon as she saw the girls, and she rushed forward to slip an arm over Nafi's shoulders.

"Hope you slept well," she said. As they waited at the base of the stairs for the boys to arrive, Joolsae decided to acquaint herself with the group's quests on Xif.

"You guys are really brave," she said when she had heard of some of their adventures. "Wish I was there."

"Wish you were too," Maia replied. "Our stay would have been a lot happier if we had a mentor like you."

Joolsae laughed. "I'm sure we'll have our share of fun together. It all begins today. I'll show you the refreshment center and then take you to the Initiation Arena where the trainers will introduce themselves and present the agenda for the next six months. After that, we can take a tour of the university floors. That's all we've got planned for today. Starting tomorrow though, you have to be prepared for a real lot."

After the boys joined them, Joolsae led the group triumphantly to the elevators.

"The refreshment center, the RC, is on the 450th floor," she stated as the elevator zoomed past floors.

When it came to a stop, Maia and her friends followed Joolsae through some corridors up to a gigantic silver door. Its surface was etched with precision, and the lights shone and rippled in an eye-catching pattern. At the center of the door was a picture of a mermaid leaning on a rock that jutted out of the water. Her gaze was soft and felt almost real, her hair a cascade of curls, and her tail gracefully bowed in the water. Arched over her elegant figure, "University of Advanced Arts and Sciences" was written in big, bold letters.

"That's our emblem," Joolsae said, nodding at the ethereal being as the group stood transfixed, admiring its beauty. She held up her abalone talisman. At the center of the swirls of white and blue was the shimmery image of the same mermaid. "See, it's also here."

Joolsae then pushed the door open to reveal a large hall with at least a hundred tables and about a thousand people gathered around them. All along the walls were food kiosks where cooks busily prepared food, and throngs of students queued up in front of them. A wonderful and appetizing aroma whirled throughout the room making Maia's stomach growl in an instant. Maia recognized some of their fellow contestants in the crowd as Joolsae led them forward. Soon they had picked seats for themselves, lined up for food, and returned to the table with their food trays.

"Now *this* is what I call food." Nafi's eyes sparkled as she affectionately eyed the steaming pile of bread, eggs, vegetables, and fruits. "Not stuff wrapped up and shoved into boxes."

Maia chuckled. Evidently, Nafi had not been able to forget or forgive the boxed food they were served at the XDA.

"And *this* is what I call the lack of privacy," Ren countered, grimacing at the open surroundings.

Nafi did not reply; she either agreed with Ren's comment wholeheartedly or was too distracted by the food on her plate. They finished breakfast quickly and left the table earlier than most. Joolsae led them back to the elevators and up a few floors to the 455th, and down a maze of busy passageways to a room that was filled with rows of chairs and desks.

"Aerika will be here shortly for the initiation speech," Joolsae informed. She picked a chair in the first row after seating Maia and her friends in the row behind her. And then they waited. Soon the room filled up, but there was no sign of Aerika or any other trainer. The wait grew long; the contestants huddled in groups, chatting. Joolsae was never short of questions and answering them kept Core 21 busy, but the incessant chatter made Maia feel exhausted.

Maia was wishing for a little quiet when the harsh clip-clopping of Aerika's shoes drifted in through the open doors. The sound reverberated across the room and a hush descended immediately. The training supervisor walked in with two men in tow. Once again, there were no smiles and no greetings from Aerika. The two men looked equally impassive; their shiny heads were devoid of hair, they wore tightly fitted white suits, and they looked like identical twins. Even as they stood, their postures and the expressions on their faces were mirror images of each other. The trio placed themselves at the central podium, the men flanking Aerika on both sides. The crowd quickly settled back into their seats, and Aerika started to speak.

"Mentors, please pick up the booklets and distribute them to your respective teams," she said, pointing at the corner of the room where satchels were stacked high. Joolsae and the other mentors immediately headed to the corner.

Aerika cleared her throat and addressed the gathering.

"While those are being distributed, let me introduce you to your instructors, Trainer Palak and Trainer Dill. Trainer Palak will be assisting you with the backgrounders." The man to the right of Aerika nodded curtly.

"Trainer Dill will help you with the hands-on work." The man to the left nodded exactly in the same way as the other man had.

"The rules booklet can be found in the book bag, and I advise you to pay attention to it. Please note the floors to which you are allowed access. I will not have you loitering around on the secure levels. I will also not have you talking politics around here. Any debate or discussion of anything other than what is in your curriculum is strictly forbidden." Aerika paused.

Meanwhile, Joolsae had dumped a bag that weighed like a ton of bricks on Maia's lap. The dark blue satchel had the emblem of the UAAS at the center and "Core 21" emblazoned below it. Maia could feel the hard outlines of thick-bound books inside.

"And they call these booklets?" Ren whispered.

"Any violation of the Code of Conduct will be met with the severest penalties. Each time you fail to adhere to instructions, it will be counted as a strike against your group. And the moment you manage to accumulate five strikes, you will be asked to leave this contest. There will be no considerations, no exceptions, and no second chances.

"Mentors will also collect your personal weapons now. We, the Jjord, do not believe in the need for arms. So, we will not allow you access to any. These will be handed back to you during the challenges, although their use during the time will be strictly monitored. Any unjustifiable use will result in your scores being diminished, so I suggest that you get used to a life without these tools of bloodshed," Aerika stated.

Maia started unhooking Bellator from her belt. The announcement did not surprise her. After all, she had heard of the Jjord's passion for non-violence, so it made sense that they would take away the weapons. Even the Xifarians did not allow weapons at the XDA, and Bellator had been stowed away in the counsel room for most of the first phase of the Initiative. A dull racket erupted as the weaponry was collected and placed in a large storage locker. Aerika waited until the din reduced to a few murmurs and then resumed her speech.

"Now for a quick overview of the stages. In about three months we will have the first challenge; only fifteen teams will advance. The second challenge will be in six months from now and of the remaining teams, we will pick the top ten to participate in the Solianese phase."

Aerika paused as if to ponder. Maia sensed a faint hesitation in her voice when she started again.

"The UAAS believes education should be tailored to fit individual sensibilities. In our opinion and experience, this sort of universal training is impractical and ineffective. So we do not expect grand performances from all of you. We do demand, however, that each of you apply yourselves and learn to be respectful of our heritage, our beliefs, and our way of life."

The room was quiet. Aerika's speech was strange, Maia thought grimly to herself. *It's going to be a very long six months.*

"You are free to leave now. Take the rest of the day to familiarize yourself with the area. The mentors will show you the training floors where you will congregate starting tomorrow morning," Aerika said and gestured dismissively at the audience.

"Excuse me?" A lone hand rose tentatively in the air. It was the always-curious Jiri. "What about team leaders? Should we pick new team leaders for this phase?"

"We, the Jjord, believe in the power of the collective. We believe that *many* are more important than *one*. So we will not place one person above the rest. In this phase, all team members shall remain equal."

A wave of murmurs rose, and heads turned to exchange glances. Maia felt an unexpected emptiness inside her. She could not quite pin down the feeling.

I am . . . sad. But why? I never wanted to be a leader anyway. I hated it when I was forced to be one in the last phase. I should be relieved.

Maia suppressed a wry chuckle – there was no denying it, this *was* a disappointment. How hard she had tried to give up her position as a team leader during the Xifarian phase, but now –

Aerika cleared her throat loudly. "We are done here. Please disperse."

As the crowd rose to leave, Aerika walked over to Maia and her teammates and tapped their desk.

"This team will stay behind."

Maia could feel the stares and the frowns as she waited breathlessly for the trainer to say something. Aerika spoke after the last person had shuffled out of the room.

"You will need to take that off," she said, pointing at Kusha's signature red headband.

Kusha froze, and so did everyone else around him.

Chapter Sixteen

The Ultimatum

Kusha's hand trembled slightly as it touched the dark red band circling his forehead. The rest of the team simply gaped in disbelief. Maia knew how Kusha felt about that headband. She remembered how heartbroken he had been when he had misplaced it in the design studios on Xif, only to find it later in a parts bin. The fabric was faded and worn out in places, and a symbol that looked like a child's drawing of the sun was sewn on it in gold thread. It was an inheritance, Kusha had said, and irreplaceable.

"Why?" That was all Kusha could ask when he finally found his voice.

"I am not required to justify our rules, but I will answer your question," Aerika said curtly. "Because it does not fit in with the regulation uniforms."

"It's an heirloom," Kusha said with increasing vigor. "I can't take it off."

Aerika's eyes narrowed. She shifted slightly backward and crossed her arms. "It is up to you," she said rather casually. "If you should choose to wear it, it will be considered a strike against your team. So you decide."

Kusha threw a frantic look around; for the brief moment that Maia looked into his eyes, she found the helplessness in them unbearable. She did not care if they had five strikes against them—she wanted Kusha's eyes to sparkle and shine again.

"You can't give that up." Maia's confident voice broke the oppressive silence.

"Yup. We'll take the strike or whatever," Ren added brusquely. "Kusha gets to keep his band."

"Yes, you should keep it, Kusha," Nafi asserted.

Dani nodded. "Yes, Kusha."

A wave of cold rage swept through Aerika's ice-blue eyes. Then she smiled. It was more like she bared her teeth than smiled; there was nothing but viciousness on her face.

"All right," Aerika murmured in a low, guttural voice. "So it will be."

She flashed that cold gaze once more over the gathered group, clicked her heels, and turned away toward the door. She had almost walked out when Kusha jumped up and took a few stumbling steps after her.

"No, please . . . wait," he yelled.

Aerika turned to face him, anger and disdain still deeply etched on her face.

"I'll take it off. Please excuse my friends' words," Kusha said, peeling the band off his head.

A ghost of a smile drifted across Aerika's face before her lips hardened again. At that moment, Maia realized that it probably did not matter anymore that Kusha chose to respect her wishes; she would not forget the group's bold stand anyway.

"All right, I accept your decision, a little late as it may be. I have to tell you, this is a wise choice. I like that you made this choice for your team's sake—that was commendable. And since this is practically your first day here, I shall waive your first strike. But"—

Aerika paused and raised an ominous finger — "try not to defy me again." With that, she abruptly left the room.

The gang, along with Joolsae, did not waste a moment in gathering around Kusha, who still stood quietly with the band in his hand, staring at the doorway.

"You did the right thing," Joolsae said emphatically. "Aerika wouldn't tolerate disobedience, especially not from your kind."

"Our kind?" Nafi burst out.

"I mean visitors, of course," Joolsae mumbled.

"You mean visitors?" Nafi asked, frowning. "Really?"

Joolsae fidgeted.

"What about my kind?" Ren smiled impishly. "Does she tolerate people from Xif any better?"

"You should never *ever* challenge Aerika, no matter what your heritage," Joolsae said to Ren. "She does not forget things easily, and you don't want to be on the wrong side of her."

"You should've kept it, Kusha." Maia ignored Joolsae's comments. "We still had four more penalties to go and that's plenty."

"Yes," Nafi piped up.

"It's all right, I'm fine with this," Kusha said, although he did not sound fine.

"All right, we've had enough of that discussion," Joolsae interrupted rather rudely. "We have a lot to do today, so let's get going."

They followed her around the seemingly endless floors, corridors, and elevators. Joolsae was quite a nice guide, and she was overly enthusiastic about the tour around the UAAS, but no one seemed to be very much into it anymore. They tagged along listlessly all day and were looking forward to a good night's rest when Joolsae led them out of the RC after dinner.

A familiar figure waiting for them right outside the RC made them forget the unpleasant encounter with Aerika almost immediately. Hans stood at the door flipping through the pages of a magazine.

"Hans," Dani squealed.

The moment he saw the group, he smiled widely and walked over. He was wearing a white-and-blue uniform quite similar to Aerika's garb. Not only did he look strangely formal in the uniform but also remarkably dashing, Maia noted.

"There you are." There was nothing formal about his warm and friendly voice. "I've been trying to find you all day and had almost given up hopes of locating you. You've been busy tourists today, haven't you?"

"I've tried my best," Joolsae chimed in before anyone else could reply. She looked extremely happy and joyful for some reason.

Hans smiled back. "Joolsae, nice to see you. And thanks. If you don't mind, I'll walk them to the dorms."

"Sure, no problem," Joolsae replied with a large grin, but her voice did not sound that cheerful anymore. Then she left, waving a quick goodbye.

"She has quite a crush on you," Nafi announced casually as they boarded the elevator up to the 500th.

Hans stared at the diminutive girl before chuckling loudly. "And you have quite a personality," he said. "Be careful with Aerika though, she is not very fond of spirited children. She usually likes them timid and docile."

Everyone nodded in agreement. No one seemed eager to relate the incidents of the day to Hans, as the memories were still too fresh and painful. Hans led them out to the sitting area next to the glass wall when they came out on the 500th.

"I wanted to meet you not just to say hello," Hans said as he sat down on a bench. "I have some news to share with you."

The group quickly deposited themselves around Hans, curious to hear what he had to say. Hans glanced over the small assembly and took a deep breath before he started.

"I'm not telling you this because I have to, but because I want to. This news is not supposed to be shared outside the government offices, but I'll tell you because I know that all of you risked your lives trying to protect our settlements."

Maia felt pride swell inside when Hans referred to the incident with the Chrysocolla key during the Xifarian phase. Maia and her friends had stumbled upon a plot—it involved sabotaging the energy supply to the Jjordic settlements, thus endangering the lives of thousands. Unable to warn the settlements of the impending peril, the teammates had taken it upon themselves to pursue clues, and after a daring face-off with two masked saboteurs in the Grotto, they had foiled the conspiracy.

"What I'm about to say isn't about a specific person or a particular people, but about a situation we face together."

Hans paused briefly as if to collect his thoughts.

"Two days ago, an envoy from the Xifarian Senate requested an audience with our governments. Some leaders of the Solianese Houses and our premier's office met with them right away. It wasn't a very long meeting or one with a pleasing outcome." Hans stopped once more.

The silence that swooped in now felt unbearable. No one batted an eyelid; no one even breathed. For a moment, darkness descended around Maia, making everything distant and unreal.

"What did they say?" Dani asked.

"That . . . is the most intriguing part," Hans said, his eyebrows furrowed deep. "I've never heard of anything so strange in my life, it almost seems impossible to believe.

"The envoy said that we, the people of Tansi, are responsible for the loss of a valuable artifact, something that has impaired their planet beyond imagination. And unless we restore the item to them along with the unconditional surrender of the Resistance, whom they believe to be the mastermind behind the theft, there would be no helping us. We have three hundred days to comply and after that, there will be a siege."

"A siege?" Nafi asked.

Maia felt a wave of dread sweep through her, the rush threatening to stop her heart. She feared what Hans was going to say next. Somehow, she knew it had something to do with her mother. She did not want to hear it. Yet she had to ask, she had to know.

"What is this artifact?" Maia asked hesitantly.

"Something that resides in the heart of the Sedara, that's all I know. We were not told exactly what it was and how or when it was taken. All we were told is that Xif lies broken because of this, and we, the people of Tansi, are collectively responsible for it."

Maia sat frozen, the terrifying burden clamping tightly over her throbbing heart. She alone knew the hopeless truth—there was no returning that artifact because Sophie had destroyed it. A cold nervousness coiled at the pit of her stomach as she saw the gloom in everyone's eyes.

Next to her, Ren shook his head vigorously. "That's impossible," he exclaimed. "The only thing that resides within the Sedara is the Verto-balancer Capsule and it makes no sense . . ."

Hans leaned forward as Ren's words trailed off. "What's the Verto-balancer Capsule?" Hans asked.

"And why doesn't it make any sense?" Kusha probed.

Ren sat up straight, took a bracing breath, and faced his audience.

"The Verto-balancer Capsule is comprised of a chalice that envelops a core of light. No one knows much about how it works, but it's part of the mechanism that channels the energy of the neighboring star into the Sedara, making it mimic the day and night patterns of the system we are visiting. Not only is it next to impossible to access the Capsule, but the Capsule is not something one could simply pick up and walk away with. And as I understand, the Resistance is nothing more than a ragtag band of rebels who could have no possible way to get into Xif, let alone breach the Sedara."

Eyes grew wider and brows shot up. Ren spoke again, sensing the lingering questions around him.

"You see, only a handful of Xifarians know anything more about the Capsule than the fact that it exists. You can imagine how few actually know how to reach it. It's not a place that anyone, let alone someone other than an extremely highly ranked Xifarian, could even think of accessing.

"And then, this is not just *any* object—it's a living entity like the L'miere crystals. You can't simply take it away—it would kill you if you were even in its presence, such is its power. That's why I don't see how anyone could steal it, and that's why it doesn't make sense."

"Do you mean that this claim might be untrue?" Hans asked.

Ren turned away abruptly and stared into the darkness outside the glass atrium.

"Sorry, Ren," Hans said immediately. "Didn't mean to offend you."

"No, it's not that." Ren flashed a quick half-smile. "I was just thinking about what you asked, and it reminded me of something I've always wondered. It's unusual that we've stayed so long in the Tansian system. Xif has been flying through galaxies for centuries, and the longest we've been in one system until now is about fifteen years. Our time in the Tansian system is close to thirty years. I'd figured it was because we still had unfinished business here on Tansi, but now I wonder if it's because something stopped us from leaving."

"Like the loss of the Capsule?" Kusha asked. "You mean, the Capsule gives Xif the power to fly?"

Ren shrugged. "I don't know. Maybe? I mean, I don't see anything else broken on Xif. But anyway, the point is no one from Tansi could've ever done it."

"But, wait a moment." Nafi interrupted, waving her arms wildly. "What about this siege, Hans? Do you mean the Xifarians will attack us or something if we don't return this artifact?"

"Yes, in a way, they will," Hans replied in a calm, deliberate tone. "We were told, in no uncertain terms, that the energy curfews we had been hearing about were not true. It would be far more than that—it would be a total and complete withdrawal of support. The Xifarians will stop giving us the energy we need to survive."

Chapter Seventeen

Burdened

Maia had never been a devious child. She had been taught to value honesty over everything else, but that was until she found out about her mother Sophie. She had spent every moment since trying to avoid facing her past, and the effort was exhausting. For a long time, Maia thought her mother was a traitor and she was ashamed. That changed when she received Sophie's message a few weeks ago. But while her opinion of her mother had transformed, Maia realized nothing had changed about her need for secrecy. The burden of knowing that her mother had been the one to destroy the heart of the Sedara, an act that stranded the Xifarians' traveling planet, was no lighter.

As the wave of murmurs rose around Maia, as theories and counter-theories flew among the friends keen to understand the unfortunate situation, she sat dumbfounded and sad. She wanted to tell them about Sophie—her heart ached to say everything about herself and her mother, but she could not bring herself to speak the words. And with every moment that passed, the opportunity slipped slowly through her fingers.

"Maia." Someone nudged her rather forcefully. "You all right?"

Dani was staring at her, a worried look clouding her face. Maia nodded fast, desperate to hide once more. The murmur around her had now grown into a loud chatter.

"Well, there's not much we can do right now." Hans tried to calm the excited group. "We'll learn more about this in time, and I'll let you know as I hear more. However, be careful discussing the matter. Not only is this a confidential issue, but Aerika does not condone talk of politics among her students."

"Bones doesn't condone anything," Nafi said, scowling. "She would rather have some mindless zombies as her students."

Hans chuckled, and the rest of the group nodded vigorously in agreement. Soon after, he herded the team toward the dormitories and went his way.

The girls' room was quiet; the other three seemed fast asleep after the long day. Maia slipped into her bed as noiselessly as she could. But while Dani and Nafi seemed to drift off to sleep quickly, Maia lay awake staring into the darkness. The newest nightmare came not too long afterward.

The dark expanse of the room lay in front of her. There was no movement or sound except for her breathing. Her footsteps were hesitant, feeble, and awkward. She was looking for something, but she did not know what. She saw nothing but the unseeing darkness. Then there was the flicker.

A small flame came to life at the farthest corner of the room. She gasped and tried to push herself backward. In front of her, one spark of light grew into thousands, and they crackled and danced in a timeless rhythm all across the back of the room. She had to call for help, but not a sound escaped her mouth. The light was intense as the flames raced across the floor toward her. But even as they engulfed her, she could not run. The heat overpowered her senses, and she simply stood there, sweat and tears trickling down her face, her heart beating fast and furious. She closed her eyes tightly as the wall of fire swept over her.

Maia woke with a violent jolt as the weight of her nightmare threatened to bury her. She sat up in her bed shaking, her body drenched in sweat. She breathed heavily, inhaling the cold air in quick, short gasps. Nothing stirred around her; the sound of soft, peaceful breathing was all Maia could hear. The memory of the fire refused to budge.

Unable to clear her mind, Maia shuffled out of bed. Grabbing her coat from the top of her trunk, she tiptoed out of the room and into the dimly lit corridor. All was quiet. Maia wrapped the coat around her, slipping her hands into the well-worn pockets. She had taken a few steps toward the atrium when her right hand touched something small, hard, and cold. Stopping abruptly, she dug out the object—a small ring with a central black stone surrounded by small white ones. *Ruche's ring!* She slowly slipped the ring on her right index finger and it fit perfectly as if it were made for her. She took a moment to admire the subdued glitter of the stones before heading down the stairs.

The atrium looked gloomy in the faint light. Maia walked toward the benches, hoping that watching the waters would calm her mind a little. The dark waters swirled outside. In them, a thousand murky shapes swam relentlessly. Maia was staring vacantly at the indistinct forms when the right side of the window darkened. A shape, dark and enormous, loomed in the shadows. Maia could tell a streak of white among the black and a pair of large, gleaming eyes that seemed to watch Maia as she peered. Something beckoned her to take a closer look. She walked to the curved pane, kneeled in front of it, and squinted hard.

The bulky size can only mean a whale. But that's . . . impossible.

The whales in the Tansian oceans had long been extinct, first hunted for sport until their numbers dwindled to just a handful. Later, when the Northern Waters warmed up, the remaining few perished. Maia had barely touched the glass with her hands when the noise of footsteps marching across the floor made her turn around.

CHAPTER EIGHTEEN

OLD ACQUAINTANCES

Two young men and an attractive girl with curly red hair, wearing the black uniforms of the Xifarian Defense Services, had stepped out of the elevator. They stopped abruptly on seeing Maia, and then the girl strode swiftly in her direction.

"You're Maia," the girl said on nearing the benches where Maia was crouched. "Am I right?"

Maia nodded as her eyes flitted from one face to another. The red-haired girl, Amanii, had been the mentor of Core 7 in the Xifarian phase. The heftier of the two boys sported a wide smile—Maia recognized him as the one who had broken up the brawl Maia and her teammates had had with Lex's group on Xif. The third person, who seemed to drag himself reluctantly forward, was none other than Maia's own mentor from the Xifarian phase, Miir. He looked distracted, his pale face looked paler, and his dark eyes scanned the atrium with the intensity of a warrior in battle. Maia's eyes lingered a moment too long on his neurogenic interface, the triangular patch of gray metal that stretched from his left brow to cheek, which gave him access to memories from his ancestors.

"This is just too awesome," Amanii exclaimed. "I can't wait to see my gang. They've arrived here, right?"

Maia nodded again. She wondered what the Xifarian trio was doing in Zagran and how the Xifarian Defense Services could be allowed to walk the restricted floors of the UAAS.

"We should let these two catch up," Amanii suggested brightly to the other boy. Maia could not think of a single thing she wanted to discuss with Miir. She hardly wanted Amanii and the other boy to leave.

"You should tell Maia about your token of D'tsani," Amanii declared, laughing as Miir frowned at her words. Maia recalled what Ren had told them about the token of D'tsani—it was an honor given by the XDA to the year's top graduate. Sophie, her mother, had also received it during her stint at the XDA.

Amanii rolled her eyes at Miir. "He's student of the year, but it kills him to tell anyone about it."

Maia watched Miir's compatriots leave, turning toward him only after they were gone. She found him observing her, his sharp gaze scrutinizing her face. For a moment they stared at each other, and then Maia looked away hastily. She struggled to find a topic for conversation. Her mind drew a blank.

Silent moments passed awkwardly.

This is ridiculous. There has to be something we can talk about.

The last time Maia had seen Miir was right after Yoome, the R'armimon assassin, had attacked Maia and Ren at the Sanctuary of the Stars on Xif in a supposed assassination attempt on Miir's father, the Xifarian chancellor. Miir had fought long and hard to save them that day.

Maybe I can thank him for—

"What are you doing here?" Miir broke the silence in the gruffest possible way.

"I should ask you that," Maia retorted as she got to her feet. "I'm here for the Jjordic phase, but why are you here?"

She expected him to at least scowl, but he did nothing of the sort.

"I am an apprentice of the Scientific Defense Services. A part of its commitment is to oversee the Initiative and make sure it proceeds safely. But when I asked you about being here, I meant about being out here in the atrium, alone and at this late hour," he said in a manner that did not befit the Miir she knew. "It is not safe for . . . you to be here on your own."

"Why?" Maia did not understand why she should be afraid while she was here in Zagran, of all places. Appian was a different matter altogether; there was little to stop someone from harming anyone if they chose to. But the Jjordic colonies, with their elaborate security systems, were supposed to be safe. "What should I be afraid of here?"

Miir frowned. It was not the angry, impatient frown that Maia was used to seeing, but a worried, thoughtful one. He seemed to try hard to choose the right words.

"You have not forgotten about Yoome, have you?" His voice was a hush. "Those people are not to be trifled with. You should be very watchful."

He means the R'armimon.

"What's that got to do with anything now?" Maia asked.

Miir stared for a while. Maia felt a hesitation in his eyes as if he was trying to decide whether to be annoyed at her answer or laugh at her ignorance. He ended up doing neither.

"You do understand that she was there for you, right?" he asked solemnly.

Maia's heart skipped a beat. She had thought about that possibility before; it was a particularly nagging doubt after she had received the message from Sophie. But Maia had pushed away the fears—it was all too fantastic to believe that the R'armimon would be looking specifically for her. Now, hearing it from Miir of all people meant something else altogether.

"Why do you say that?" she asked, her voice trembling a little. "I thought we were just in her way, Ren and I. The real target was—"

"My father? No, she was planning to use her weapon, possibly an extractor, on you," he said, almost rushing through the words. "Had she been after my father, she could have just hurt you enough to make you unconscious as she did with Ren. She did not, because she had precise plans for you."

"But she said she was going to deal with both of us." Maia did not want to believe she was the target. "She happened to pick me first."

"I do not think so," Miir replied calmly. "Think about it . . . if you were trying to best a foe, who would you deal with first? I would pick the one who poses the most threat to me. Ren tried to resist, yet Yoome deemed him secondary. Even when he was unconscious and would have made easy prey, she chose to come after you. And there has to be some reason behind it."

Maia did not quite understand. She did not *want* to understand. Her mind raced to remember something else.

"Why did you ask us to lie to your father? You asked us not to tell him that Yoome fought us for such a long time. Why?" she said, crossing her arms and standing as tall as she could to meet his gaze. "You know what your father thought? He thought that I was somehow involved in this plot to assassinate him."

Miir shifted uneasily and his face twisted into a grimace. His eyes flashed briefly with the old, familiar rage.

"What choice did I have?" he hissed. "Do you know what they would have done to you had my father suspected that the R'armimon was in fact after *you*? Do you have *any* idea?"

"They wouldn't come after my people, at least. Innocent people will now be accused of this assassination plot," Maia snapped back. "I could've tried to explain."

Miir's sarcastic laughter tore a jagged path through Maia's heart.

"You think he would listen to you? Had he known Yoome was after you, you would be taken into custody, and neither your claims of innocence nor any explanation could have stopped that," he said. "You would have ended up in the Gnelexian chambers, and after they had finished with their probes, you would be no more than a mindless, soulless shell. But then, I guess you could have handled it all just as easily as you handle everything else. You always know the best, don't you?"

Maia simply stared, half-understanding and half-dazed at his harsh words.

"If you are still keen on becoming the hero for your people, it is not too late," Miir continued, still unforgiving and ruthless. "When you want to face the Gnelexians, let me know. I will surely receive a medal of honor if I hand you over to the authorities."

Maia slumped on the bench. There was so little she understood. She did not know what the R'armimon wanted from her; she did not even know who these dreaded Gnelexians were. She stole a glance at Miir. His face was taut, brows knitted in a deep frown. He would likely snap at her, but Maia needed to ask.

"Miir?" she started hesitantly.

Miir flinched. He shifted, just a little, in Maia's direction.

"The Gnelexians . . . who are they?"

He turned sharply, his eyes smoldering as they scanned her face. Maia could not fathom why he was so cross, nor did she have a clue about how to calm him. She held his gaze, however, and waited patiently for him to answer her question. After what seemed like an eternity, Miir let out a long sigh. Suddenly the darkness passed, and his face softened.

"They are mind readers," he stated simply, before pausing as if to deliberate. "Gnelexians can penetrate a person's mind. The most powerful of them can sift through years' worth of the target's memories within moments. They can do that with or without direct contact—some breach the subject through thought waves, some through eye contact, and some simply by touching the target's head. No one can stop a Gnelexian mind probe, not even by learning blocking techniques and putting up mental barriers to shield the information."

Maia let out a sigh when he stopped. The Gnelexians surely seemed formidable already and Miir had even more to tell.

"No one has survived a full probe of the Gnelexians. Their scans, along with the information they seek, suck out consciousness from the mind. A subject won't necessarily die but will exist like a mindless corpse."

"Have you met a Gnelexian?" Maia asked, curious.

Miir chuckled. "Of course," he said. "You would have as well. They don't have a sign that says 'Gnelexian' plastered across their foreheads, in case you are wondering."

"I might've met one?"

"Sure. Most Gnelexians are non-practicing and they mingle freely among the population. Also, it is illegal to practice mind-reading outside of the Gnelexian sector. If someone were to be caught using any mind-reading techniques outside the sector without the explicit consent of the subject, they can be accused of an intrusion which is a punishable offense."

"What's the Gnelexian sector?"

"It is a penal colony, a massive prison basically," Miir replied. "It is rumored to be an underground structure, twenty floors deep. I have never been near it, only heard horror stories of the torture chambers in there."

Breathlessness. A rush of fear. A dark curtain swayed before Maia's eyes. She inhaled. As hard as she could. The air felt stale and strangely inadequate. She could not believe that the chancellor would have sent her to these terrifying Gnelexians if he had known about Yoome's true intent. Questions spun around in Maia's mind at a dizzying speed.

Clearly, the Xifarians are bothered by the R'armimon's presence. But why? And why do I matter to the R'armimon?

Maia cast a sidelong glance at Miir again.

Does Miir know something that he isn't telling me?

"I don't understand. What could the R'armimon have wanted from me?"

"They must think you have something," he blurted, "something that might help their cause."

Thoughts raced in an indistinct rush. *It has to be about Sophie.* Then again, she had known next to nothing about her mother at the time Yoome had attacked.

Did the R'armimon know about my mother even before I did? But how?

Maia rested her throbbing forehead on her palms and took in a long breath. "I wish I could run away somewhere . . . disappear."

Miir shifted uneasily on his feet. For a moment, it seemed to Maia that he would simply walk away, but then he sat down next to her, his movement slow and posture stiff, his gaze fixed on the window ahead.

"You really need to be careful," he whispered, staring at the dark waters.

"Why is the R'armimon here? Why did your father believe they were out to hurt him?" Questions spilled out of Maia like a gushing spring.

Miir did not reply. He either did not know or did not want to tell her.

"All I can tell you, and all I know, is that we have a shared past," he said finally. "Old scores that are yet to be settled . . . ancient feuds that call for bloodshed."

"So, the R'armimon think I have something that would help them in this feud." Maia tried to piece the puzzle together. "That makes me a threat to—"

"To us," Miir completed the sentence Maia was afraid to finish.

"Then why . . . ?" She could not comprehend why Miir chose to help her that day. "Why did you still help me?"

"Because I was supposed to," he said without a moment's hesitation. "My task was to guide you and protect you. And I thought you were innocent. You did not know anything that could be a threat to anyone."

The explanation was simple, honest, and effortless. And Maia did not have to try hard to believe.

"Thank you," she whispered. There was nothing but stony silence from Miir.

The stillness seemed to stretch forever. Maia fidgeted inside; there were a million questions that she still itched to ask and quite a few things she wanted to tell.

"You should get back to your room now." Miir broke the uneasy peace.

The moment had passed.

He walked with Maia to the base of the stairs. He offered no goodbyes, but simply waited for her to walk up the stairs and into the safety of the corridor.

CHAPTER NINETEEN

PALAK AND DILL

A rush hit early the next morning. Maia woke to a lot of shouting and yelling. As she sat up groggily, she found herself in the middle of a frenzy—clothes being thrown around, beds being made, satchels and books gathered, and to top it all off, words that bordered on civility being exchanged. She slowly crawled out of bed and made her way through the craziness. By the time she was done, only Dani and Nafi remained in the room waiting for her. They were already running late for their first day's training session.

It was not until they reached the RC that they had a little time for some decent conversation. In between the gulps of food, Maia related the incident of the previous night to the wide-eyed group.

"That's ridiculous," Ren declared with a disbelieving shake of his head. "Why would the R'armimon pick you? I mean, what's so special about you?"

Maia sat tongue-tied. Sophie was the reason. If only she could tell. If only she could find the courage. She looked around at the faces surrounding her, searching for that elusive strength. But she only found reasons to prolong her silence. Ren would never forgive Sophie's actions; he was a Xifarian after all. Maia recalled a conversation they had had on Xif—traveling across galaxies on their planet was a way of life for Xifarians, their heritage, and a source of immense pride. Sophie had taken that away.

Ren will hate me by extension. Of course, he will.

Swallowing the lump of hurt in her throat, Maia looked at the others. Dani would understand; she always did. Maybe Kusha would handle it well also. Then there was Nafi. Nafi would probably get too excited.

And then what? What if she tells someone? No, it's too risky. I can't —

"Never mind the reason," Dani said in a worried voice. "If Miir thinks you ought to be careful, then you really should be careful, Maia."

Kusha nodded. "Don't walk about on your own like you did last night, all right?"

"So, Miir is a high-flying apprentice now, huh?" Nafi asked.

"Wonder what really brings the apprentices here," Dani muttered absentmindedly. "We don't see them around much, so what are they overseeing?"

No one had an answer to that question. They concentrated instead on finishing their breakfast so they could reach the training room soon. Dani, an able and efficient guide, led the team to the designated room without too much trouble. Most of the other groups had already assembled when they reached the high-ceilinged and airy classroom. A tall dais was located at the front end, where a cluster of very large screens hung suspended from the ceiling. Trainer Palak stood near the podium, watching. Huge desks were strewn across the entire room in a seemingly random fashion. Each was stacked with stationary, books, and a lot of other strange-looking equipment. A high stool that stood next to every desk had the name of the core printed on them.

Maia and her friends walked along, trying to find their spot. They found the five seats with "Core 21" marked on them clustered toward the right side of the podium at the head of the room. Dani and Ren took the seats in the front, and Kusha sat right behind them followed by the two girls. The cluster behind Maia and Nafi was still empty.

As they waited for the remaining groups to file in, Maia peeked at the mountain of books that towered on the two sides of the table. She read some of the titles: *Water: A Treatise on the Beginnings of Life, Ocean Currents, Power of the Fluid,* and *Harnessing the Blue.* Reaching out for the thinnest of the lot, she flipped the cover open. The pages were light green and the pale-grayish letters were hard to make out in places. The paper had a funny texture—it was coarse and grainy in areas. A conversation with Dani from the night before came to her mind; these were recycled kelp paper, she had said, and the ink was harvested from squid colonies.

"Maia," Nafi whispered. She was poking at the enormous volumes. "You think we'll need to get through all of these?"

Maia sighed. "Looks like that to me. Not to mention the ones we have been lugging around in our satchels."

"Yes, those too." Nafi inhaled noisily. "This is too much work."

Maia had the same feeling. If the Xifarian phase was demanding, then this would be grueling. A small commotion sounded behind them as stools were drawn, satchels thrown, and legs scrambled on the seats. Maia turned around to check out their new neighbors and immediately fought to suppress a scowl.

Loriine was sitting right behind her. The grimace that Maia managed to hold back was splayed all across the girl's face. Beside her was Karhann; he matched the impressive glare that Nafi threw in his direction.

"This is so not going to be good," Maia muttered to herself as she turned away quickly. Next to her, Nafi shook her head and fiercely flipped through the pages of the thickest book she could find on her table.

"If I may have your attention please." Trainer Palak had a rather arresting voice. "I shall begin with a few words for our friends from the land settlements. You will likely find our curriculum rather challenging. You have an intellectual handicap because of your underprivileged background. But that is nothing to be ashamed of. Do not be afraid to ask for help. We expect a need for supplemental lessons for you, and we are prepared to work with you. Just stop by and talk to us."

Intellectual handicap? How can he simply assume that the Solianese are stupid?

Maia felt her cheeks grow warm at the sound of a chuckle behind them. Her brows came together; she could not quite believe his words. A painful silence gripped the assembly until Palak spoke again.

"Now we start with the basics. My sessions will complement the practical lessons you will need to undertake with Trainer Dill.

"It is always critical that we understand the nature of this world that we live in. So, we will study the water — its properties, its powers, and most of all, its needs. Also, you will be expected to learn the geography of the under-ocean territories on your own.

"You will be evaluated on a weekly basis. I will assign you reading tasks, and I will expect you to complete them. If you fail to obtain a passing grade in any of the evaluations we plan to start next week, you will earn a penalty against your team. And as Supervisor Aerika already said, you will be eliminated if you have five such strikes."

At this point, there was no stopping the murmurs and the turning of heads.

"Nice," Nafi said as she exchanged an anxious glance with Maia. "Weekly evaluations — this is just crazy."

"Yes, and they talk about this being fun," Karhann commented from behind them.

Nafi's face scrunched up; it changed from surprise to annoyance to anger. Even before Maia understood the situation, let alone intervene, Nafi whirled around.

"You think I spoke to you?" she hissed. Karhann sat up in surprise at the sudden offense. "I don't want to hear you speak. I would rather not hear you breathe."

"You rude, nasty . . ." Loriine started, and Maia braced for the fireworks.

"If I may have your attention back please," Palak interrupted, and Maia breathed a sigh of relief. He directed everyone to a book containing maps of the oceans, and the large display screens lit up with complicated charts and measures. Books had to be opened and studied, and every head was soon buried deep in thick volumes.

When the session ended well past midday, Maia was beyond exhausted. Palak's opening address still sat heavily on her heart. Dani rounded up the team before they headed out for lunch.

"Sorry," she said in a hushed voice. "Palak probably just meant to help. But it sounded —"

"Offensive," Nafi declared.

"Yes," Dani agreed. "It wasn't proper of him to speak that way."

"Your people think very lowly of us," Kusha scoffed. "Like it or not, that's the truth."

"I wish I could change how my people think," Dani said. "But I'm just one person. And there's so much prejudice around here."

"Forget about it, Dani." Kusha waved a dismissal and marched away in the direction of the RC.

Lunch was had in silence, but the food did a lot to refresh Maia. She trooped in optimistically to what was to be Dill's instruction area and looking at her teammates' lit-up faces, Maia knew they too felt revitalized. Dill stood smiling near the door. He greeted every person by name and ushered them through a turnstile into his training room.

Chapter Twenty

Saskawatching

Maia froze the moment she stepped inside. They had walked into a massive forest—plants and trees of all shapes and sizes grew everywhere, and the musty smell of wet soil overwhelmed Maia's senses. Such lushness was a rare sight on Tansi. The sound of birds twittering and insects chirping created a world of wilderness that Maia had only read of in books. In the middle of the room was a clearing, and a giant pool of water occupied its center. Built into nooks and corners of this gigantic greenery, and surrounding the central clearing, were rustic benches. On each bench sat a large glass bowl; within it was a miniature piece of the underwater world, not unlike the one surrounding Zagran.

"Wow! I didn't expect *this*," Dani said as they walked toward the center. She rushed to the edge of the pool of water and gazed at it. "And a dive bay too."

The water was dark and it seemed deep. "Is this pool . . . dive bay connected to the outside?" Maia asked.

"Yes, it is," Dani replied. She went on to explain, "Dive bays are connected to the seas through chutes equipped with lock gates to equalize water pressure. You can swim all the way from this room to the reef outside if you want."

"All right. It's all great. That's enough about swimming. Now let's grab some seats." Ren quickly moved to a side where a few benches were still empty. He dropped his satchel and peeked at the glass bowl that sat on the bench.

"This is amazing," he declared after a moment. "I mean, look at this thing. It even has tiny fish swimming in there."

"For real?" Kusha asked as he moved closer to investigate.

"It's sort of real," Dani stated, drawing curious stares from her teammates. "This glass bowl is called a Saska. It's a miniature replica of the world that surrounds us. Every Jjord child receives a personal Saska on their fifth birthday. It's a symbol of the ties that bind us to our environment."

"And I will explain more if you will be patient for a little longer." Dill had stepped closer, unnoticed. Dani flushed immediately, and the group hastened to take their seats. The trainer walked over to the area near the pool of water and addressed the assembly.

"Dear friends," he said cheerfully, "welcome to this corner of our city which we will call home for the next few months. Make yourselves comfortable and make yourselves happy, for that will be the key to what we will learn while we are here."

He cast an amused glance at Dani before resuming his speech.

"Now, as some of you have already been told, that glass globe on your table is called a Saska. It is a replica of the world that surrounds us and a measure of how well we are attached to that world. It is not entirely real; it is more of a projection of your mind in the very real water that is contained within it. So, the more you adapt and embrace the life around you, the more your Saska will thrive. If you cannot adapt, I am sorry to say that your Saska is doomed. And from now until the day you leave this city, you will watch and tend to the tiny world you create, and thus learn the art of Saskawatching."

The trainer walked around the rim of the pool and stood in front of Jiri, who was sitting across from Maia and her friends.

"Now, I want you all to touch the Saska with your hands like this," Dill said, placing Jiri's hands on the sides of the bowl of water. "And embrace it with your mind."

Dill looked at the somewhat hesitant faces around him. "Come on now. Give it a try, it won't hurt you."

Maia carefully placed her hands on the sides of her Saska. The surface felt cold to the touch but comforting as well. She held her breath and looked intently at the colorful little creatures swimming around gaily. She closed her eyes. Wishing with all her might that she would have better luck with this bowl than she had with the L'miere crystal on Xif, she let her mind embrace the Saska.

A chill tingled Maia's spine, and her eyes fluttered open with a strange sensation. She let go of the bowl with a loud gasp. Swimming in the clear waters next to the tiny fish was a gigantic black whale, with patches of white on its belly and sides. It stared intently at Maia from within its watery confines.

"I have never seen this happen at first contact. That is most interesting," Dill declared, squinting at Maia's Saska. Everyone around had turned to look as well. Maia glanced at her friends' globes—they all looked perfectly regular. No one had managed to create a life form yet.

Dill continued to stare thoughtfully at Maia's bowl for the longest time. "Where did you hear of a Timiti whale?" he asked finally, tearing his eyes from the creature that gamboled within Maia's Saska. "Have you read about it?"

Maia shook her head. Not only had she never seen what was being called a Timiti whale, she had never even heard of it. She felt embarrassed, especially with the stares and the whispers.

"All right, everyone, let's keep working." The trainer turned away to attend to the rest of the gathering and Maia sighed in relief.

"That is cool," Ren whispered as he peeked at the replica of the whale. His own Saska was now a melee of milk squids, evidently inspired by the bunch they had encountered on their journey to

Zagran. "How did you conjure it?"

"She would tell you if she knew, Ren," Nafi chided. She had managed to create some snub-nosed dolphins that cavorted in the water.

Kusha only had a few new fish in his Saska, but Dani's was teeming with a variety of creatures—hers was a beautiful world, sparkling with color and meticulous detail. As Maia looked at Dani's Saska, she realized something; Dani had not even glanced at Maia's Timiti. It was odd that while everyone else, including the trainer, had stared in surprise, Dani had chosen to ignore the incident.

CHAPTER TWENTY-ONE

THE DAY OF ALL DISPUTES

The next couple of weeks passed in a daze. The first week's evaluations were a living nightmare. It was either a miracle or immense kindness on Palak's part that no one received a failing grade. But there was no dearth of stern warnings; even Aerika graced the congregation with her unsmiling presence. The second week, however, went a little better as the teams grasped the complex charts and the maps of the seas.

The only relief was the sessions in Saskawatching. Everyone seemed to have embraced the ocean world quite well, as was obvious from the flourishing little realms they had all managed to create. Maia was glad that no other strange creatures popped up in her bowl. The Timiti, however, did appear to grow friskier by the day.

Maia was thankful that time passed peacefully, at least until the fifth day of the fourth week. Then it went awry right after breakfast. The meal was sumptuous, and the gang had found a few precious moments to spare before Palak's session. To make good use of the extra time, they stood at the door of the RC, admiring the portrait of the mermaid that shimmered with unusual brilliance that morning.

"It looks like she'll spring to life any moment," Kusha said, admiration evident in his voice.

"Would be nice if she did. We could have a pretty mermaid friend," Ren added with a chuckle.

Nafi turned toward Dani. "Do mermaids really exist? Have your people ever seen one?"

"No," Dani said with a wave and a laugh. "Don't get crazy ideas, Nafi. Mermaids are just fantasy."

"Can you imagine swimming around with a real mermaid?" Nafi had never looked so excited. She practically skipped all the way to the elevator. "I wish I could swim once in my life, with or without a mermaid friend."

"Well, maybe they'll let us out in the waters one day," Dani said as they waited for the elevator to arrive.

Kusha flashed a huge grin. "Now that would be something to look forward to," he said.

The sound of footsteps behind them made Maia turn around. It was Karhann—he trudged in, yawning. Nafi's face grew rigid as soon as she saw him. Karhann, however, smiled warmly, and so did the rest of the team.

"Sleepy, huh?" Kusha asked the boy, who nodded groggily in response.

"These sessions are tough."

"Yup. Make sure you get a good night's rest."

Maia squinted, suddenly curious. That was most unusual, the friendliness with which Kusha spoke to Karhann.

"But I thought you have lakes and rivers on Tansi, Nafi," Ren resumed the halted discussion from earlier. "How could you have not swum before?"

"It's all about the condition of the water," Maia started to explain. "Most of the water on Tansi is toxic from the days before the Collapse."

"Yes. Swimming in Tansi's waters is dangerous business—you

might get mutated or even die," Kusha added. "That's probably a risk not worth taking."

"I still would give it a try," Nafi sighed. "But I live in a desert; we hardly have enough water to drink, let alone think of frolicking in it."

"Not much different from Xif, I guess." Everyone turned to stare when Karhann chimed in. "All our water is tightly regulated—it's easier to break into the Chancery than to steal a glass of water. You wouldn't know about all that as guests though. Their needs are catered to with the greatest care."

Nafi glared at Karhann, shook her head angrily, and took a few deliberate steps toward him. "Who do you think wants to speak to you?" she shouted, her face blushing a vivid crimson. "Haven't I told you to be quiet? Don't you understand?"

Karhann fell back in surprise. It took a moment for the astonishment on his face to turn into anger.

"You're the rudest girl I've ever met," he said, glaring back at Nafi. "Can't you get over the Seliban challenge? Why can't you understand that it was nothing personal?"

"Oh, no, no, no . . . this is more than just the challenge and your disgraceful behavior out there." Nafi shook a threatening finger. "This is totally personal. If you and your nasty girlfriend think that you could mock my sister's name—that makes it *very* personal."

Maia blinked in surprise. *Sister?* She had never heard about Nafi having a sister.

"No one mocked anything." Karhann seemed to have been taken aback at Nafi's accusation. "Loriine simply suggested a few names and I picked one I liked."

A moment of silence fell like a sliver of rain on a raging inferno. But the small flash of quiet was gone before it could begin.

"You . . . have . . . no . . . right . . ." Nafi wheezed. She was trembling from head to foot like a leaf. "What you did was inexcusable, and I'll never ever forgive you for that."

The elevator came to a stop with a small thump. As soon as the door opened, Karhann stepped out. He looked more pained than angry when he turned around to look at Nafi once more.

"I do not need your forgiveness," he said in a cold, steady voice that was surprisingly free of anger. "And you should know this—you do not own that name. I can and I will use it as I choose. Go on and hate me, see if I care."

A pall of gloom fell on Nafi's face as Karhann strode away toward Palak's classroom. No one dared to speak as they shuffled along until Maia finally decided to brave the storm.

"You never told us about your sister," she said softly, taking a step closer to Nafi.

"And I'm not going to start now," Nafi growled before stomping forward.

Maia trudged onward with the rest of her teammates, hoping that by the end of the day all would be forgotten. Little did she know that this was just a preview of things to come.

CHAPTER TWENTY-TWO

THE MESSAGE IN A BOTTLE

A quiet class and a quieter dinner later, the team walked back to the dormitories. While Nafi had started to look a tad cheerful again, no one was willing to venture in her direction just yet. After spending months in each other's company, they had all learned to give each other space when needed. And the current situation demanded all the distance they could possibly afford to put between each other. Things changed in a heartbeat when they saw their mentor, Joolsae, waiting for them at the atrium.

Joolsae smiled happily as Maia and her friends gathered around her. After the usual hellos and the expected pats on Nafi's head, she held out a small bottle for Dani. It was a transparent blue-green bottle, sealed with a silver stopper. A scroll of paper lay inside it.

"Hans asked me to give this to you," Joolsae informed. "He said the message is for you and your friends."

After Joolsae left, the group settled down at their favorite nook next to the glass window.

Nafi was back to her usual self. "A message in a bottle, huh?" Her eye shone as she kneeled next to Dani.

"Of all the ways people can send messages, you have to use something like this?" Ren asked incredulously. "I mean, what about security? Anyone could have read that."

"Yes, what about that thing you use all the time? What's the name . . . the Urso?" Nafi pointed at the small tablet that was always tucked securely in Dani's pocket, beeping softly every other moment. It was a device for exchanging messages with friends, Dani had once explained.

Dani laughed. She reached below her collar and pulled out a delicate silver chain that encircled her neck. A blackish object that looked like a ring hung from the chain.

"*This* is security," Dani declared, holding up the ring and showing it to the group. "This is a PR key, short for Personal Restrictive key. It works with the assistance of biometrics."

She explained more as the team listened intently.

"Primitive as this bottle looks, it's far from that. The stopper can only be opened with a key that is paired with the key that seals it. If anyone tried to break the bottle or the cap by force, the contents inside would be destroyed by a corrosive gas released through the inside of the container. So, this is far safer than any electronic transmission, free from interception of any kind."

"Hmm," Kusha tapped his chin thoughtfully. Strands of hair hung over his forehead, creating an attractive mess. "But what if someone steals that key from you?"

"Like I said, the PR key works with the assistance of biometrics, which means it wouldn't work if I were not using it."

"What if someone forces you to open it for them?" Maia asked.

"Again, the key would not work if it detects changes in my biometrics due to stress," Dani said with a smile.

"All right, I think we all get it. Let's open the bottle now," Nafi chirped restlessly. Dani chuckled as she placed the key on the silver stopper, waited a brief moment, and then pulled the cap out. She rolled out the note and read the message from Hans.

Please take care to keep this information as much of a secret as you can for reasons I have explained to you before. I wanted to meet you in person, but with all the unexpected work we have been getting lately, I could not find the time. But I think you should know this now.

Since receiving the ultimatum from the Xifarians, the Jjordic Council has been working to find the best way to handle the possible fallout. The first step is to find a way to placate the Xifarians by supporting them in their search. In that, we have been mostly unsuccessful, at least so far. We know they want to get their hands on the Resistance, but what they want to do with the rebels is beyond our comprehension. We also do not understand much about this lost artifact. The Xifarians have been unresponsive to all of our questions regarding the nature of this object. They have demanded that we provide them UTAP throughout our settlements, as well as the planet's surface, which we have not consented to and do not plan to consent to in the future.

"Wait," Ren interrupted. "Explain UTAP."

"It stands for Unrestricted Territorial Access Pass," Nafi explained. "It's a protocol granting a foreign national visiting, exploring, recruiting and investigative access. Like what you get for a week during the annual drafting for the mines on Ti."

"We do?"

"Of course," Nafi replied. "Why do you think Tansians are so mad at your people? Your troops can walk into anyone's home and take them away if they meet the recruiting criteria. But, drafting session is limited to only a week. The current demand, I'm guessing, is for either a long-term or perpetual UTAP."

Ren stared for a while at Nafi, the disbelief in his eyes slowly turning into embarrassment, until he could look at her no more.

Kusha spoke, ending the crushing silence. "That's one thing. But why won't they tell us what they are looking for?"

"Maybe because they don't know what they're looking for either," Ren said thoughtfully. "As I said the other night, the heart of the Sedara is not just an object but almost a living entity. I doubt it's even possible to take the heart away. And even if anyone has managed to do that, who knows what it could've morphed into. It could be a rock, a tree, a cat, a fish, or maybe even a human for all we know."

"Are you serious?" Nafi asked, her eyes wide.

"Of course."

"So, they're searching blindly?" Nafi asked.

Ren shrugged. "Maybe they have some clues. I've no idea."

Something stirred vaguely in Maia's mind. In her message, Sophie had said something about scattering the pieces. Did the Xifarians know the heart was shattered?

Dani continued to read.

The second step is to come to an understanding with our compatriots from the surface. While we are aware that the Resistance is denying any responsibility in the loss of the artifact, we were hoping to make them talk to the Xifarians. However, it seems that not all House leaders are willing to even try to make the Resistance recognize this need. So, we are planning a series of meetings to convince the Solianese House leaders.

We also need some time to prepare ourselves in case the Xifarians do withdraw all support. Although it is doubtful whether things will come to that since a siege would hardly help the Xifarians' cause, we have to be prepared. We have to find ways to preserve as much life as we can on this planet in case all negotiations fail. In a few months, we can manage to have more than we need for the underwater cities, but we have come to a crossroads when it comes to sharing the modest surplus. It will certainly not be possible to sustain everyone in the land cities of

Tansi, so we have to plan and choose which areas we want to protect and preserve.

Dani stopped abruptly. Gloom had descended on the group as Dani read the last few sentences. A vision of the picture-perfect Appian flashed before Maia's eyes. She wondered how long it would survive on its own with its rusty old wind turbines. It would definitely not be for very long; a few breakdowns would be the end of the simple folk of Appian. Anger, unrelenting and intense, throbbed in her veins.

"Go on, Dani," Nafi urged softly. "Keep reading."

Given the incidents before the Collapse that had almost led to Tansi's extinction, our leadership was never too eager to cooperate with the Solianese Houses. The current situation with the Resistance, and the disinterest of most of the Houses to persuade them into talking with the Xifarians, is once again making us question the dependability of our allies. Their lack of concern for the well-being of the planet we share seems very much like what we have seen in the past. Our leaders are apprehensive and in my opinion, quite rightly so.

In the next few months, as the discussions progress, we hope to decide on a course of action. Solianese House leaders will be arriving shortly to meet with our premier and the Jjordic Council, but it is questionable that there will be a positive outcome for everyone on Tansi.

This is a difficult situation that none of us deserve to be in, and there is little we can do now to alter our collective history. But we can surely choose our individual destinies. Now that you know what is happening around you, you should make your own choices early and fast.

Hope to see you soon.

Please destroy this letter after reading it.

They sat in silence for a while before Kusha scrambled to his feet.

"Make our choices early? What does he mean by that?" he said sharply. "Does that mean we should choose to ignore the fate of our people and look out for ourselves now?"

Dani blinked. "Kusha . . ." she started. "I'm sure Hans didn't mean anything like that —"

"Then explain to me what he meant," Kusha demanded.

"I . . . I don't know," Dani replied. "I'm as shocked by this news as you are. I can't think of anything at the moment."

"You are simply shocked." Kusha laughed sarcastically. "And I'm practically mourning the end of my world. Do you see the difference here?"

"But what am I supposed to do?" Dani almost wailed.

"Stay safe," Kusha shot back. "And have fun watching while we die."

"Kusha!" Maia and Nafi exclaimed in unison. However distressed Kusha might have been, there was no reason for him to be unkind to Dani. There was hardly anything Dani alone, or even Hans for that matter, could do to change the situation. Kusha did not show any signs of regret at what he had said. He stared a moment at the group, then turned and left.

"See you guys tomorrow," Ren said before he got to his feet and ran after Kusha.

Maia and Nafi sat in the atrium with Dani. After a long while, they plodded back to their dormitory to end what had been a very bad day.

Chapter Twenty-Three

Seigvard

The dispute between Dani and Kusha made the days gloomy, to say the least. For the next few weeks, neither spoke unless absolutely necessary and the air hung heavy around the group. The warring duo threw furtive glances each other's way, but that was all. Maia made a few attempts to get them talking and failed miserably. And, after one futile try a week later that drew a chastising glare from Kusha, Ren also gave up.

There was no end in sight to their miserable existence. Dani had not heard from Hans, so all Maia could assume was that the talks between the Solianese and the Jjord were in progress. Nafi was bored and anxious enough to suggest that they ask Joolsae about the talks. But good sense, inspired by a stern look from Dani, had prevailed over her impulsive urges.

It was a much-welcomed change when they walked into Palak's classroom to find the usually darkened display screens ablaze with pictures and diagrams.

"Now that we have gathered some basic knowledge of the oceans, it is time to start a more intensive research," the trainer declared, immediately drawing a barrage of sighs and groans. Maia and Nafi exchanged a quick, fearful glance.

"Your first challenge is coming up in a few weeks," Palak continued. "You will be required to navigate through a complicated route in the ocean in an extremely specialized vehicle."

Murmurs stopped the moment he mentioned "vehicle," and "navigation." Maia breathed in relief; they would finally be set free from their tiresome, cooped-up lives.

"You will learn more about these vehicles and their operation in Trainer Dill's session, so hang on to that excitement. Right now I will show you some maps."

What came right after was intricate. A myriad of paths, nooks, and hideaways that formed a convoluted maze on the ocean floors flashed on the screens. Then there were the ocean currents that created an invisible network in the waters. The currents were the key, Palak stated over and over again, to figuring out the best pathways through the ocean. There were hundreds of calculations and estimates to be made to devise the easiest and fastest routes, and another hundred to switch from one current to another with precision. At the end of the session, Maia found herself in a daze, as if a storm had caught her out in the open.

"Whew, that was intense," Ren said as they walked toward the RC.

"And that's just the first day," Maia added with a sigh.

"Six more weeks until the challenge," Nafi said as she punched the buttons of the elevator. "By then we'll all have turned half crazy."

They were laughing and poking fun at each other when the elevator came to stop on the 450th floor.

"You guys go ahead," Dani said softly as the others filed out. "I have to pick something up from the dorm. I'll catch up with you later."

"Oh no, you won't." Maia slipped right back into the elevator; she was not going to let the team splinter any further. "We're coming with you."

Everyone else followed, including a sulking Kusha. It was a quick stroll to the dorm where Dani picked up a book for the next session, and the gang headed back to the RC. They were about to turn toward the elevators when a flash of brown at the other end of the atrium caught Maia's eye.

"Mahswa Tabrin," Maia exclaimed before sprinting forward toward the fast-disappearing figure.

By the time the rest of the gang had decided to follow Maia, she had already caught the woman's attention. Mahswa Tabrin, the Xifarian Tierremorphe who had given the team their firestone wristbands during the Seliban challenge, smiled indulgently as she watched them run up to her, panting and heaving.

"Mahswa Tabrin," Maia gushed. "Honored to see you."

"What a wonderful surprise to see you again, Maia," the Mahswa said. "How have you all been?"

"Fine, we're all fine," Maia replied.

"What are you doing here, Mahswa?" Nafi blurted. "Are you here for the Council as well?"

"Nafi . . ." Dani's attempt to stop Nafi came a little too late.

Mahswa Tabrin smiled at a flushing Nafi.

"Come in here and we can talk a little," she said, holding open the door at the end of the corridor, exposing a large, cozily furnished hallway. Mahswa Tabrin led them to a group of sofas that were stacked opulently with piles of pillows.

Maia noticed the dark circles under the Mahswa's eyes as she took her seat. The woman looked worried, almost sad, and far from the calm and serene presence Maia had always found her to be. Something must have been bothering Mahswa Tabrin, and Maia wondered if it had something to do with the lost Xifarian artifact. She also noted the long sword that hung from the Mahswa's waist, its bejeweled pommel peeking out of its sheath. Even the sight of the handle was breathtaking; it held the promise of a sword that would be no less than grand. Maia had not seen the Tierremorphe carry a weapon before and wondered if it was customary to bear arms during travels outside Xif.

"Yes, Nafi, I am here for the talks," the woman said. "And do not worry, Dani, I will not tell anyone what you know. I can keep secrets."

It was astonishing that she remembered their names, Maia thought. She remembered another secret that Mahswa Tabrin held in her heart, of Maia being a Shimugien, a person with power to control light.

"This is a sad situation," Mahswa Tabrin said in a deep, almost broken voice. "It seems like you all know this by now. An artifact of the most precious nature has been lost."

"It's true then? The heart of the Sedara has been taken?" Ren exclaimed. He still sounded disbelieving.

"I cannot confirm that, but I will not deny it either," Mahswa replied, sighing deeply. "I can simply tell you that it might be a possibility."

"But how?" Ren sounded indignant. "I've heard that the light consumes anyone who comes in direct sight of it, let alone touch it."

"You have heard correctly," Mahswa Tabrin replied, her gaze sweeping over the group. Maia felt the woman's glance rest on her a tad longer. "Unless someone with the power of the light tried to touch it."

"A Shimugien," Ren exclaimed.

"A what?" Kusha asked immediately.

"A Shimugien," Ren gushed. "One who is born with power over the L'miere crystals and can absorb their light and their energy. Only such a person could've taken the heart of the Sedara."

"And such a person is easy to find?" Dani asked.

"No, not at all." Mahswa Tabrin chuckled loudly. "A Shimugien is a marvel of nature, just as rare as the L'miere crystals themselves. I have only seen one in my lifetime, and I do not believe I will see another."

"But, hold on, I still don't follow." Ren raised his hand and shook his head vehemently. His face was scrunched up in confusion.

"Yes, Ren?" the Mahswa smiled.

"The heart, or the Verto-balancer Capsule, is made of two parts, right? The lighted core and the chalice that envelops and holds the core, isn't it?"

Mahswa Tabrin nodded.

"And I thought the chalice is impenetrable and immovable. Then how could it have been broken or stolen?"

"The chalice could be dissolved, and then the core extracted."

"But a Shimugien couldn't have gotten past the chalice," Ren said, his voice rising.

"And why not?" Nafi looked baffled. "Seems to me the Shimugien could practically do anything, like magic."

Mahswa Tabrin broke into soft, gentle laughter. It was soothing to hear her laughter spread across the room and twitter and fall.

"No, Nafi, that's not true. There is no magic. Ren is correct," Mahswa Tabrin said.

"So, someone else had to break the chalice first so the Shimugien could take the core out," Ren continued his deduction.

"That is a possibility, yes." Mahswa Tabrin nodded gravely.

"Wait," Nafi interrupted again. "What's so special about this chalice?"

"This chalice is not a clay pot, Nafi," Ren replied with a generous smirk. "It's supposedly made of super-refined Calbion. Only an extremely gifted Tierremorphe could've broken that sheath. Once that sheath was broken, the Shimugien could've taken the lighted core. Right?"

"So, there had to be at least two people working together," Kusha inferred. He continued after a pause, "Why can't they find them and ask? There can't be more than a handful of Tierremorphes and even fewer Shimugien, right?"

Maia found it hard to keep thinking clearly. Even listening quietly to all that was being discussed felt like an impossible task. Thoughts, questions mostly, swirled incessantly in her dazed mind.

Two people? But Sophie had never mentioned anyone else. And why not? To protect the other person who had helped her?

"I told you already. Because they would probably be dead by now," Ren explained. "The light they released on opening the Capsule would have consumed them. Not as fast as it would an ordinary person, but they still wouldn't survive more than a year or two."

A year was too much. Sophie had not lived that long, Maia knew. Her thoughts wandered again.

Sophie must've known the light would consume her. She must've been scared. Yet, she faced it anyway.

Maia relished the surge of pride inside her.

"So, if the people who had taken the heart have perished already, what do you expect to find now, Mahswa Tabrin?" Nafi asked.

"I cannot tell you that," Mahswa Tabrin said. "I would be divulging state secrets if I did."

"I guess we're hoping to find the chalice *and* the core?" Ren wondered aloud. "I assume that once we find them, we shall resurrect the heart of the Sedara."

"Possibly," Mahswa Tabrin replied.

"What does the chalice look like? And the core?" Kusha asked.

"Didn't I tell you? They are formless entities capable of morphing freely. No one could know or predict what they look like," Ren replied, and Mahswa Tabrin nodded in agreement.

"Then how can anyone hope to find them?" Nafi asked again.

"Nothing in this world stays lost forever," Mahswa Tabrin said. "You can trace anything if you try hard enough or long enough."

"I still don't understand something, Mahswa Tabrin," Dani interrupted. "If the lighted core is so deadly and the chalice so tough how did you put this thing together in the first place?"

Mahswa Tabrin chuckled. "Now, this I can answer. It was put together by one person, a princess named Ataii, back in the days when Xif had not yet been a traveling planet. She was one with the power of the light and the land, what you could call a Shimugien and a Tierremorphe rolled into one. Her power over the elements was absolute. The light could not harm her, and she was the one who could truly embrace it."

Mahswa Tabrin paused. Once again Maia felt the woman's gaze linger a moment too long on her face. Maia fought the urge to tell Sophie's story. There was nothing more to know from Sophie's tale than what people already knew, other than the fact that Sophie had claimed to have broken the heart into pieces. Sophie had not said anything about what she had done to the broken fragments, nor if anyone else had assisted her, but no one would believe that.

The Xifarians will come after me and destroy anything that stands in their way.

My friends . . .

There was no reason to endanger her friends more than they needed to. Maia decided to keep her secret just that, a secret.

"Ataii was a princess of the R'armimon, right?" Ren asked.

Mahswa Tabrin sat quietly. She did not say a word, not even offering a reason for her refusal to answer.

"But, wait a moment." Nafi leaned forward, fixing a puzzled gaze on Mahswa. "What if the person who took the heart apart was just like Ataii? What if there was another Shimugien and Tierremorphe rolled into one?"

The Mahswa shook her head, smiling. "A Shimugien is a rarity, and we have not had a perfectly formed Tierremorphe in generations. It would be a miracle to see both traits manifested in one person, given our current environs. And if by chance it had happened, we would have known. It would be rather difficult, almost impossible, for such a powerful being to stay hidden for so long."

A hush fell. Maia let her mind drift away.

Mahswa Tabrin is right; Sophie was not a Tierremorphe. She only ever mentioned being a Shimugien. Someone else must have helped her, someone who . . .

"Mahswa Tabrin," Maia blurted as she remembered something her mother had mentioned in her message. It had confused her then, and if anyone could clear it up, it would be Mahswa. "What is the Afterlight?"

Mahswa hesitated. "That's a name for the lighted core of the Capsule after it's released. The Afterlight is—" She stopped abruptly and sat staring at Maia, as if a thought had frozen her. The silence was prickling.

"That's a beautiful sword." Kusha broke the quiet. He was gazing in admiration at the jeweled pommel.

The Mahswa smiled and rose to her feet to take the stunning object out of its sheath. Maia held her breath as Mahswa put the sword down on the table. It was indeed a thing of astounding beauty. Its broad, silver surface sparkled, and all along the center of the blade was a long line of scriptures that trailed from right below the guard down to the tip. The hilt was the most beautiful of all, with its intricate work of metal encrusted with jewels.

"This is Seigvard," Mahswa Tabrin said in a voice that exuded reverence.

"*The* Seigvard?" Ren almost fell over the sword; he did not blink even once as he muttered, as if in a trance, "The sword of Ataii?"

"Yes, this *is* the sword of Ataii," the Mahswa replied. "Seigvard has seen more than any one of us hopes to see in a lifetime, or will."

Maia had barely opened her mouth to ask more about Seigvard when the door at the opposite end of the hallway opened wide and the familiar clicking of heels sounded. The clip-clopping drew closer, frighteningly fast in its approach.

"Bones . . . we're as good as dead," Nafi whispered as the ominous form of Aerika strode up to the corner, nodded curtly at Mahswa Tabrin, and stared with cold displeasure at the team.

CHAPTER TWENTY-FOUR

SECRETS

As the group scrambled, Maia wished they could make Aerika disappear by some magic. But hard as she wished, nothing of that sort happened.

"Don't you have a training session right about now?" Aerika snarled after she had bestowed her glare on the group long enough. "And this is a restricted area, are you not aware of that?" Aerika frowned, and Maia fidgeted under her stare.

"It is my fault." Mahswa Tabrin came to the rescue. "I brought them here, got rather too excited on seeing old friends. My apologies."

Aerika did not like the intervention one bit. Her face fell for a moment. She squeezed a small smile to her lips and nodded at Mahswa Tabrin. Then she waved dismissively at the five.

"Run along now. We do not have the entire day to chat."

After muttering quick goodbyes to Mahswa Tabrin, Maia and her friends rushed out to the atrium and gathered near the elevator doors.

"I hope they find the heart of the Sedara soon," Kusha said as their elevator sped past the floors. "I hope they find it in one piece. It would solve all of our problems if they do."

"Yes," Ren replied. "I'm sure we'll get it back and then things will go back to normal. No more fights and no more threats. We'll live together in peace."

At that moment, Maia knew she had to tell her friends the truth. She *had* to tell them. There would be no finding the heart in one piece. And then, even if they did find the pieces and put them back together, there would be no living in peace. For the Solianese and the Jjord, there would be no Tansi to call home.

"Wait," she said as the group sprinted toward Dill's classroom. It was hard to find the right words, and Maia knew it would get more difficult with every passing moment.

I have to do this. Now.

"We can't make it to this session."

They stopped and stared. Maia had been the leader of the team during the Xifarian phase, and while she had not been very keen on taking the responsibility to begin with, she had slowly embraced her position. She had defended and fought for her team's success over and over again. Gradually, she had earned the respect of her teammates. And now, even though she was not the designated leader anymore, her words still grabbed everyone's attention.

"You sure, Maia? Aerika will probably come to check on us," Dani said after a moment's pause.

"Yes, Bones will eat us alive if she finds us missing," Nafi added, making some menacing gulping noises to drive her point home.

"There's something I need to tell you." Maia looked at them resolutely. "And no, it can't wait."

Dani sighed and looked around to check if Aerika was walking up behind them. Then she grabbed Maia's arm and walked briskly in the direction opposite Dill's classroom. She led Maia into a room at the corner of the atrium while the rest of the team followed.

The room was small and sparsely furnished. As Nafi, Ren, and Kusha hurriedly pulled up some chairs, Maia stood with her arms wrapped around herself, bracing for the doubts and the questions.

Dani kept fiddling with a portal on the door. She unhooked the PR key from her chain and fitted it into a small slot on the white panel with buttons.

"That'll stop people from barging in, I hope," Dani said after a while. "I have access to these study rooms, and I can bar entry to others while I'm using them. Unless, of course, Aerika finds out and overrides my access privileges."

"Go on, Maia. Tell us," Ren looked expectantly at Maia.

Maia did not know where to start; words seemed to be slipping away from her mind like water spilling from a broken cup.

"I'm a Shimugien," she stated simply.

Gaping mouths and shocked silence greeted her statement. Not seeing a single eye blink, Maia decided to continue. With great care, she related everything that had happened on Xif, up to finding out about her power over light. Maia recounted how she had assimilated a precious light-generating L'miere crystal, and how Principal Pomewege and Mahswa Tabrin had come to her rescue. By the time she ended that story, a little normalcy had returned to the room.

"That's how Mahswa Tabrin knew you," Nafi exclaimed. "I'd always wondered."

"Is that why the principal asked Miir to teach you telekinetics?" Ren asked, and Maia nodded.

"But, Maia," Kusha waved eagerly to draw her attention. "You should've told us, we could've kept that secret."

"I know you could." Maia looked away, not bearing to face them until she had told them everything. "I was asked to not tell anyone."

"Anyway, your being a Shimugien has nothing to do with what's going on now," Dani reasoned. "And you're safe here with us. We should get back to class now."

"No, we can't." Maia was surprised at the conviction in her own voice. "I have to tell you more . . . about Sophie."

"Who's Sophie?" Kusha looked utterly confused.

"My mother. Her name was Sophia Avaroh," Maia replied. It was strange how she felt stronger and taller the moment she had said her mother's name aloud. It was as if she could take on any threat that would dare to confront her or the memory of her mother. She told them everything she knew about her mother. She waited for the questions to come in torrents, but there was absolutely nothing until Ren let out an anguished groan.

"It can't be true," he almost whimpered, holding his head in his palms. He sounded devastated. "How can this be happening?"

"I don't know if any of this makes sense either, Ren," Maia said, toiling to find the strength to keep on talking. "I, too, had hoped it was all a terrible mistake, that my mother wasn't responsible for destroying the heart of the Sedara. I thought I could forget it all. But with everything that's happening around us now, I'm convinced that it's indeed true. And I have to accept that."

"Why did you ask the Mahswa about the Afterlight?" Nafi asked sharply.

"Because my mother had said the Xifarians would be looking for it," Maia explained. "And I had also heard of it before . . . at the meeting of the Order of the Fyrstell."

She slumped into the nearest chair as she recalled the conversation she had overheard at the secret meeting of the Order of the Fyrstell on Xif. The Order had been plotting to use the stolen Chrysocolla Key to disrupt the flow of energy to the Jjordic settlements by decoupling the Jjordic channel from the Stabilator. The chief of the saboteurs had also mentioned the Afterlight, but neither Maia nor any of her teammates had understood the meaning of it then. Now, at least this much was clear to Maia—the Order of the Fyrstell was struggling to restore the same object her mother had destroyed.

"Maybe we should tell someone about this," Dani suggested.

"Tell what?" Nafi shot back. "Who will believe that Maia doesn't know anything other than the heart of the Sedara was broken? They will hound her for things she doesn't know, they will torture her for something her mother did."

"You're right. We can tell no one." Kusha paced the room. "But now we know for sure that the heart was broken and the pieces have been scattered."

"Hey, we could try to find the pieces ourselves," Nafi exclaimed.

"Really?" Ren scoffed. "You think finding them will be that easy? My whole nation is looking for them, and you think we can beat them to it?"

"You never know," Nafi retorted. "We could get lucky."

"What if we do get lucky? What then?" Dani asked. "What do we do when we find a piece?"

"Give it back, of course," Ren said. "So the heart can be restored."

"We can't do that," Nafi argued. "It would mean the end of our world. Didn't you hear what Maia said?"

"Maybe it's not true," Ren muttered wistfully. "Maybe the Sedara doesn't destroy the sun—maybe it's just a myth."

"And maybe we can all live happily ever after," Nafi taunted.

"It's too early to fight over that, guys," Kusha said as Ren turned away crossly.

"Right now we should get back to our session," Dani reminded, forever the voice of reason.

Ren walked over to Maia, held out his hand, and smiled. "Come on, Maia. We're a team, remember? We'll figure this out."

Maia took his hand and got to her feet. Although she knew this problem could not be solved as easily as Ren hoped, the warmth in his voice was reassuring. A smile escaped her lips as she looked at the group. The kinship she felt with her teammates gave her more courage than she could ever have alone. She was never going to hide anything from her friends again, she decided. Together, they marched toward Dill's classroom.

CHAPTER TWENTY-FIVE

FIRST STRIKE

Maia had hoped to escape Aerika's clutches that day, but those hopes died a violent death the instant the team slinked into the classroom. Aerika stood near the pool with her arms crossed, her eyes fixed on the doorway—she was ready to pounce on her hapless prey the moment they set foot inside. At the forefront of the luckless group was Kusha. He slowed to a halt at the sight of Aerika, and behind him, Maia could almost feel his urge to turn around and flee. But Kusha stood his ground and so did his teammates as Aerika strutted up to them, Dill in tow.

"There they are." She pointed a skeletal finger at the huddled group. Everything felt like a dizzy blur of distant action as Aerika thundered on, "You finally have the time to show up for your training session. You think that arranging all this for your entertainment is easy for us? That you can come and go as you please? That you are here on a pleasure trip? Or maybe you think being the top team in the last round gives you an excuse to be disrespectful?"

Kusha shook his head vehemently. "N-no . . . no we don't," he

- 132 -

stammered. "We . . . we had to—"

"Keep lying, maybe that's the only thing you're good at," Aerika said coldly. Kusha turned a bright crimson and looked away in haste. "I don't know how you managed to get top honors in the first phase with such low regard for rules."

"We're never ever late for sessions," Dani chimed in. "Trainer Dill knows we're always on time. But today, we . . . got waylaid."

"Waylaid?" Aerika frowned and then broke into a jeering laugh. "You got waylaid? Well, I think a mistake of that proportion deserves some special treatment. What is your opinion, Trainer Dill?"

Dill seemed utterly helpless in front of Aerika's towering presence. He rubbed his hands together, smiled a little, and mumbled something rather incomprehensible.

"Yes, I think so too." Aerika turned around and faced the group. "Count this as a first strike against you."

"What? You can't do that," Ren exclaimed.

"I just did, young man. Do you want to try getting another strike?" Aerika was in no mood to be argued with.

As Maia stood quietly with her teammates, her head and spirits drooping, Aerika walked over to the center of the room and addressed the crowd.

"I got distracted by the disappearance of your fellow mates, but I was here for another reason," Aerika said as everyone stood in hushed silence. "There have been several reports of unusual activity in this city. Strangest things have occurred in the past few days, incidents that are unheard of in the history of Zagran. I will advise you to practice extreme caution while walking about on your own; we do not want any of you getting into trouble. Please do not venture off into unknown areas, stay in groups, and if you notice any suspicious activity, please alert the authorities immediately."

"What strange incidents, Supervisor Aerika?" Loriine inquired.

"Fires," Aerika replied.

Dani gasped along with all of the other Jjord in the room.

"And that's a big thing? Why?" Nafi asked.

Aerika fixed an annoyed stare on Nafi.

"I did not come here to be quizzed by you but to warn you of what might befall you if you are not careful. If you choose to get waylaid as you did, no one can stop you from getting into trouble anyway," she snapped before clip-clopping her way out of the room.

"Come on, kids, let's get settled," Dill said to Maia and her teammates. He seemed to have found his voice as soon as Aerika left. "We have a lot to learn today."

Loriine and Baecca seemed to be enjoying the whole situation immensely. Not only did they make fun of Aerika's warning, but they also snickered and laughed gleefully as Maia and her friends walked to their seats. Karhann seemed oddly disinterested in everything. He looked bleary-eyed and tired.

"One down and four more to go," Loriine mocked as the five passed by.

Nafi made a face and was about to reply when Maia pulled her away. Ren leaned toward Dani as soon as they reached the privacy of their corner.

"What's it about fires?" he asked anxiously.

"Fires don't happen in Zagran," Dani whispered. "Or in any of our settlements. It's considered a terrible calamity, a misfortune, a bad omen."

"Why is that? I mean, I know fires can be dangerous, but why is it a bad omen?" Maia asked as dread filled her heart. She had suddenly remembered her nightmare from a few nights ago, with the fire blazing across the room.

"Because we've had a history of terrible tragedies that occurred from a fire," Dani explained. "So now, every corner of every Jjordic city is monitored by the most sophisticated temperature-regulating systems. It's almost impossible that a fire alert could be missed or ignored."

"Then how is it happening now?" Maia asked again.

Dani shrugged listlessly. "I have no idea."

"Did you see Karhann?" Kusha said in a very low voice, and Ren nodded. "Looks like he hasn't slept in ages."

"Why do you care?" Nafi asked sharply. "Is he your new best friend or something?"

"Maybe," Ren replied curtly, not even throwing a glance at the peeved Nafi.

"No, it's not that," Kusha clarified. "We've seen him slip out of the dorm every other night, leaving around midnight and not returning until the morning."

"Every other night? Where does he go?" Maia asked. "Do you think he might have something to do with these fires?"

Kusha shrugged. "We can't ask him, given that we aren't exactly friends. So we're doing what we can do, keeping a close watch."

The sound of clapping brought their attention back to the trainer again. Dill stood at the center of the room waiting for everyone to listen to him.

"Now, we are about to begin with a demonstration of a watercraft. As you have already heard from my counterpart, Trainer Palak, you will need to master this vehicle for your first challenge. So without further ado, let's bring up the Aqumob."

A gray water vehicle bobbed up at the center of the pool as if by magic. Eager groups gathered around quickly. Dill took turns speaking to every team and soon he came over to Maia and her friends.

"You may want to read the operating manuals before you try your hand at this, all right?"

"We'll be quite comfortable handling one even without the reading, thank you. My brother owns a Biterrmob and I can recite the manuals in my sleep," Dani replied, in a surprisingly dismissive tone.

"A Biter-what?" Ren blurted.

"It's a bi-terrain version of the Aqumob," Dani explained to her gawking teammates.

Dill's eyes grew wide. "Ah, a Biterrmob. Fancy that! Excellent! Please wait for your turn then."

"I dislike that man," Dani scowled the moment Dill left to assist other teams. "I can't believe he wouldn't say a word in our defense to Aerika."

"Let it go, Dani," Ren said. "Tell us more about Hans's Biter —"

"The Hansmobile," Maia interrupted eagerly.

"Say what?" Nafi's eyebrow shot up.

As the team awaited their turn on the Aqumob, Dani told everyone about the Hansmobile. Dani turned out to be a great instructor as well — by the time the gang had completed their tour of the demonstration vehicle, everyone had a good idea of the basic controls.

That afternoon, Maia and her friends ran into Joolsae outside Dill's classroom. Maia's heart sank immediately. She vividly recalled their encounter with Miir after the team had been taken to task by Master Kehorkjin on Xif. Miir had been furious, to say the least. She was sure Joolsae had heard about their strike and she was here to shout at them.

"Oh, hello." Joolsae showed no sign of anger or disappointment. It did not seem like she knew of the strike at all. It almost felt like she was not even expecting to meet them.

"Haven't seen you in a while, Joolsae," Kusha remarked. "Is everything all right?"

"Sorry," said Joolsae. "I've been so busy with my coursework that —"

"That's no big deal," Ren replied. "Will you set up some meetings to prepare for the challenge? We used to have one every other week during the first phase."

Joolsae seemed startled. "Y-yes. Of course. Will . . . soon." She took off right after, waving a hasty goodbye.

"That girl is weird," Nafi declared. "I still can't figure out if she is a fake or plain stupid."

As Maia stood watching the mentor leave, she realized something — Joolsae was nice without a doubt, but no matter how friendly she seemed, Joolsae simply did not care enough.

CHAPTER TWENTY-SIX

THE WILD RIDE

It was late in the evening when Dani's Urso buzzed for the millionth time that day. Maia had become quite used to it now, the buzzing and the beeping, the notes from Hans and Dani's zillion other friends. Nafi barely lifted her head from the thick history book she had been reading, and across from her, Anja continued to nap. Loriine and Baecca, however, rolled their eyes, sighed loudly, and made their annoyance known. Maia shot a glance in Dani's direction, noting her bright smile as she read the latest message. Clearly, something other than the usual had happened. She was right. Dani rushed over as Maia propped herself up on her elbow.

"Hans wants to take us for a ride," Dani said breathlessly.

"Ride?" Nafi shut her book noisily and shuffled onto the floor.

"The Hansmobile?" Maia asked; feeling the excitement rush to her head as Dani nodded.

Nafi frowned as the two girls squealed with joy. "We can't just prance out of here, can we? Bones will kill us if she knows."

"Don't worry, he has gotten her permission already," Dani

assured. "Let's go now. Hans is waiting for us outside."

The trio scooted out of the room, ignoring icy stares from Loriine and Baecca who had been listening intently to the conversation.

Hans stood at the atrium, grinning. "There you are," he said. "See there, Maia, I haven't forgotten my promise."

"Thank you," Maia replied, grateful for his thoughtfulness. However, other matters kept popping into her mind. She desperately wanted to ask Hans about the Council and the fires, but no one brought them up, and Maia hesitated to be the one to disrupt the happy atmosphere.

"Shall we start from the Upper Docks?" Dani inquired.

"Yes, let's head upstairs," Hans started in the direction of the elevators and beckoned the group to follow.

"You sure you got permission from Bones?" Nafi asked Hans, her face puckered with worry.

"I did, Nafi, don't worry," Hans replied, chuckling loudly at Nafi's nickname for Aerika.

"And what about the boys?" Nafi asked again as they scampered along, clearly still a little in doubt.

"We can't fit everyone in at the same time—my vehicle isn't that big," Hans explained as they zoomed upward. "Since I promised Maia that I would take her out for a spin, I thought of getting you girls first. I'll come back for the boys sometime soon."

They came to a stop at the 550th floor, the topmost level of the city. As the group filed out, Maia felt a sharp nudge on her elbow. She looked inquiringly at Nafi, who had now resorted to an insistent poking.

"Just wanted to check if you were really blushing," Nafi smirked, and then skipped ahead to join Dani and Hans. Maia was stumped for a moment at that comment; then she shook her head and picked up her pace.

"These are the Upper Docks," Hans said. "It's a private launch area for Aqumobs, much smaller than the bigger public ones you'll get to see later."

"The Hansmobile stays at the safest corner of the Upper Docks," Dani filled in the details. "It's almost impossible to get a docking slot in here, but Hans found one after a year of persuading the officials. Wish you could've seen him celebrate after they gave him a pass. I doubt if he'll ever be so happy again."

"Keep in mind that she exaggerates," Hans remarked, smiling.

The Upper Docks consisted of numerous launch bays, and Hans led them to Bay15. This was a large circular room, with a wide ledge running around the circumference of the sparkling water at the center. The roof was domed, the center rising in a high arch and dipping down at the edges. Aqumobs were anchored all around the ledge. There were large ones and small ones, some looked new and some older, but all of them were clean, a shiny craft that were well taken care of. A strapping young man walked out to receive the party and led them to one side of the harbor. Maia spotted the silver body with blue stripes peeking out from in between two larger Aqumobs.

"There," Maia said to Nafi, "that's the one."

It was just about then that Maia felt a sudden heaviness weigh her heart. This was a rare and wonderful opportunity, Maia knew that, but oddly her excitement ebbed. Once inside the vehicle, Dani and Hans insisted that Maia take the seat next to Hans, and Maia had to oblige. But the strange feeling persisted. Something bad was about to happen, Maia was sure.

The craft dipped into the water gracefully and entered a tunnel that led out of the city and into the open waters. It shot out of the spout like an arrow and seemed to stay motionless for a while in the vastness that engulfed it from all sides. Then it inched upward again.

"That is the Ridge of Artemis, it connects Mount Setna to the rest of the Ourean Range," Hans said, pointing at the huge wall of rock that rose behind them. "The city is on the other side of this wall, hooked into Mount Setna much like a cluster of clams. Let's head over to the front and take a look at the city."

Instead of going around the massive wall that seemed to stretch endlessly in front of them, Hans took the Aqumob over its peak.

Rising above the top of the city, the craft briefly hovered overhead before it rose even higher and a little away from the sparkling Zagran.

The city was a sight to behold from there, a view that they had missed when the Aquiccela had crept into the middle of the behemoth. Now, as the structure shone in front and below them, the lights within it almost bringing to life a page from a fairytale, Maia sat wordlessly gazing at its ethereal magnificence.

"Don't the lights look a little dim to you?" Nafi's voice broke her trance. "It's still bright but—"

"You're right, they are," Hans replied. "The bubble meshes screen out certain frequencies to minimize the impact the city lights can have on marine life. It'll get even dimmer as night falls."

"Aah," Nafi whispered.

Maia kept staring at the magnificent city, her heart filling with admiration for the Jjord and their perseverance. They had built a wonderland out of nothing, all the while caring so much about the habitat and respecting it. Maia hardly remembered how long they hovered, coming to her senses only when the craft fell abruptly downward.

A scream of fear and surprise rose through her, but Nafi beat her to it.

"What are you doing?" Nafi shouted.

"Welcome to the Hansmobile," Dani said calmly. "If you want to live to see another day, hang tight."

Down they went, picking up speed as they sunk lower. Maia's heart beat wild and loud in her chest as she grabbed the edges of her seat. The Hansmobile headed straight toward the bottom of the ocean. The floors of the city whizzed in front of them, a thrilling sight by itself, but Maia was not in a state to sit back and enjoy it. They were heading, at a breakneck speed nonetheless, toward where the vast network of transporter lines converged into one and entered Zagran. A few transporter craft could be seen zooming through the tunnels as the Hansmobile drew closer to them.

"You do know what you're doing, right?" Nafi squeaked.

"I'm about to show you line-hopping," Hans replied, smirking.

Maia gulped; this sounded neither safe nor innocent. But as scared as she was, she could hardly ignore the thrill of what she was about to see. Fighting the instinct to keep her eyes shut, she held her breath instead as the Hansmobile shot through the tight knot of transporter lines and weaved through them in a smooth, practiced motion. They coiled around the tunnels, grazed past their length, and ran along parallel to the craft inside. Before long, Maia found herself cheering as Hans hopped and bobbed around the maze of tunnels, skipping over one and under another, spinning across them in reckless abandon.

A brilliant flash of gold from somewhere in Zagran broke the intoxication of the adventure. The vivid light blinded Maia for a brief moment, its suddenness shocking and overwhelming.

"Hans!" Dani screamed.

"What was that?" Hans said as he slowed abruptly and turned the Aqumob to face the direction of the flash.

It came from one of the lowermost levels of Zagran, an orange-yellow glow that leaped across the floor, the colors incredibly brilliant amidst the darkness. Giant flickers of red swung upward like the flames of a burning torch. Then, the whole level was swept by the flickering gold light, a startling contrast from the floors above and below it.

A dread held Maia's heart in a painful grasp. She knew what it was. "Fire," she barely managed a whisper.

Everyone stared at her. Hans and Dani looked horrified. Then Hans turned away and swung the Aqumob upward.

"Dani, notify Emergency Services. Use my code," he instructed, and Dani immediately took out her Urso and started fiddling with it. Not another word was uttered until they had left the confines of the Upper Docks.

"I've to go down there right away. I can't imagine how terrible it can be if indeed it is a fire," Hans said on the way down to the 500th. "This is crazy, it can't be true."

CHAPTER TWENTY-SIX

"I'm sorry," Maia mumbled, hoping that she was wrong in her assumptions.

A loud beep sounded from Dani's Urso as they were walking out of the elevators. Dani's face had paled when she passed the device to Hans who shook his head glumly.

"You were right, Maia. It is a fire. It was impossible to believe the first few small ones we had before. This one was—" Hans stopped abruptly.

"Did people live there?" Nafi asked.

Hans nodded, grief etched on his face, his eyes dark with worry.

"I'm sorry we couldn't have as much fun as I had planned, Maia." He led them to the stairs. "I hope we have some time to get together again while you're here."

As Hans strode away, Dani ran up behind him to say something. A sharp nudge on her elbow made Maia wince and turn around. Nafi stood with her arms crossed, squinting at Maia with all her might.

"What?" Maia asked, rubbing her elbow gingerly.

"Boy, you are sweet on him," Nafi declared.

"That's nonsense, Nafi," Maia protested vehemently.

"Come on, Maia, you blush just like Joolsae does. And I've to say, it's most disgusting." Nafi twisted her face to make her annoyance more obvious.

Maia wanted to make Nafi disappear. This conversation was inappropriate as is, given the situation with the fire. Even otherwise, it was ridiculous. And it would be mortifying if Dani caught a whiff of it. Of course, Maia liked Hans. Maybe she liked him quite a lot, but that was just because he was friendly and kind and . . . just fun to be around. Nafi, like always, was making too much of very little.

"You'll stop this right now, Nafi," Maia whispered as threateningly as she could before Dani walked back to them.

Heading up the stairs with her friends a bit later, Maia felt exhausted. "I wonder what's causing these fires," she pondered aloud.

"Maybe the question is not what but who?" Nafi added.

"I just hope no one is hurt," Dani said with a small sigh.

Maia went to bed in a sullen mood. All the fun and excitement of the outing had been dimmed by the tragic incident.

BREAKING OUT AND BREAKING IN

The next morning, the girls told Kusha and Ren all about the previous night's adventures. Ren was particularly crestfallen at having missed out on riding the Hansmobile.

About halfway through breakfast, Jiri rushed up to their table. "Have you guys heard about the fire on the tenth floor?" His voice was taut with anxiety. "They say about a hundred people were hurt, some of them pretty badly."

Dani shook her head morosely. She had been scanning for reports on the incident but had found none on the news broadcasts. Earlier that morning Dani had asked Hans about it but apart from a plain "Don't worry," she had not heard a word. Maia guessed this was probably Hans's way of hiding the enormity of the tragedy from his sister. But information had found its way to her and now Dani's worst fears had been confirmed.

"How do you know?" Kusha asked Jiri.

"Just heard from a few seniors there," Jiri explained. "They say it wasn't an accident either. Someone set the fire deliberately."

"Who would do that?" Ren asked. "And why?"

Jiri shrugged. "No one knows for sure." Then he leaned closer and whispered, "Some people said they saw masked, hooded men wearing dark capes carrying these long whip swords. The guys back there think it's just a tale."

Jiri left soon after, but the faces around the table had paled considerably at the news.

"Masked men in capes and carrying whip swords," Nafi repeated slowly. "Sounds very familiar, doesn't it?"

It did sound eerily similar to the men Maia and her friends had fought at the Grotto on Xif, the men who had tried to sabotage the Stabilator. Those men, Chairman Phocluus of the Defense Services had explained, belonged to the Order of the Fyrstell. The Order was a covert militant wing of a political faction on Xif that backed the withdrawal of Xifarian energy support to Tansi.

But it still doesn't make sense. Why would they set fires in Zagran?

"It could be a tale, like Jiri said," Ren speculated.

"The similarity is too unusual to just be someone's imagination," Maia said slowly. "If it's the same people, then they must be planning something terrible."

"I think you're jumping to conclusions too quickly," Ren shot back. He seemed tetchy and difficult this morning.

"And I think you're turning a blind eye." Nafi was not one to give in so easily.

"Now why would I do that?" Ren retorted.

"You tell me."

"All right, guys, no point in fighting over things we don't know yet," Maia interrupted.

Dani pitched in quickly. "We're getting late for our session, let's not upset Aerika again."

The atmosphere in the classroom was glum. Rumors abounded concerning the source of the fire, but there was no official news regarding the matter.

Maia had to privately laugh at the absurdity of the situation—she had hoped to feel lighter after revealing her secrets to her friends. The burden of carrying her own story bottled up inside her had not been easy, and having shared it with everyone else was liberating.

And yet . . . I barely feel happy. The worries just keep on coming.

Ren had been slipping into sullen moods now and then, and Maia did not like it one bit. The rift between Kusha and Dani did not show any signs of waning either. Kusha did make some small attempts to start conversations with Dani, but she ignored him steadfastly. The whole situation was, in one word, dismal.

***

The sessions with Palak and Dill went well over the next few weeks. Both trainers were impressed with the progress made by the team. Much of their expertise in the sessions was due to Dani's extensive knowledge of the Aqumob, as well as the effort each one of them put into the reading exercises. It had become an unspoken challenge to prove to Aerika that they were indeed the best.

All that studying left them busy and exhausted most of the time, and that was not necessarily a bad thing. They hardly had time to worry about the Council, and with Hans having disappeared on them completely, they did not have any news of the fires to fret over either.

On a particularly tiring day that included a long study of the buoyancy modules of the Aqumob, Maia fell into the deepest sleep she had had in months. It did not last very long; she found herself being shaken vigorously by the shoulders. She sat up, trying to recognize the face in front of her. It was Anja. She stood over Maia with her arms on her hips, a deep frown etched on her face.

"What do you want?" Maia said in a sleepy stupor.

"Your boys"—Anja pointed an accusing finger at the door—"were making an awful ruckus out there. You're lucky that those two princesses didn't wake up with all the knocking and the calling."

"Boys?" Maia pulled herself out of bed and nudged Dani and

Nafi. Dani woke up without too much effort, but getting Nafi up and ready was quite a task. Soon they had all managed to slip on their coats and the trio gingerly stepped out into the passageway.

Ren and Kusha stood at the top of the staircase, hunched over a piece of paper.

"What is it, Ren?" Maia asked.

"Found something," Ren announced, pointing at the piece of paper Kusha held up reverentially. "A map – "

"Hold on," Dani interrupted. "What map? What would we want to do with a map?"

"And where exactly did you find this?" Maia was growing increasingly suspicious about the whole situation. Something fishy was going on, and she knew this would lead to some trouble.

"I saw Karhann putting this in his satchel a few nights ago after he came back from one of his nightly prowls," Kusha explained. "Today we found a piece of paper peeking out from under his pillow and we decided to grab it. It turned out to be a map."

"You stole?" Nafi, barely awake, stood frowning.

"No," Ren replied emphatically. "We borrowed it for a while and copied it for our reference."

Nafi shook her head and turned away, still too sleepy to argue the morality of this.

"So?" Maia asked. "You've stolen a map. Now what?"

"It's not stealing! Anyway, look at this . . ." Kusha impatiently spread the piece of paper in front of them. He pointed at a red star that marked one of the rooms. "Obviously, this is where he's been going every night. We want to get to this place and find out what he's up to."

"We don't even know what this place is or where," Maia said. "What are you hoping to find there?"

"That seems like a secure government floor. Can you imagine what will happen if we get caught?" Dani asked solemnly.

"Aerika would make mincemeat out of us." Maia had to side with Dani on this.

"That Bones is a terrible woman," was all Nafi would say.

"Yes, we know all that." Ren snapped. "But the question is, don't you want to find out what the sneaking around is all about?"

They looked at each other for a while, and Maia silently pondered over the not-so-attractive outcome if they did get caught.

"Are we going or not?" Kusha demanded.

"Well, you woke me up," Nafi offered a sound reason. "Now we have to go."

And so they started on their mission. Not only did the map have precise directions, but it also had the requisite security codes for any closed doors they came across. All along Maia wondered how Karhann could have found such a map. They had to go up twenty floors with the help of an elevator code, pass three doors from the atrium using three more codes, and finally go down a long flight of stairs to a large arch-top door that stood closed. A panel with an illuminated keyboard on the wall next to the door quietly announced the name of the room.

"CR-470-2R," Nafi read the small letters.

"Stop," Dani whispered even before Nafi had finished reading it aloud. "This is the Council Room. This is where the Trinational meetings are set to happen. We're *not* allowed in there."

"But we *are* here," Nafi stated. "And we have the code to enter. Are you telling us that we should walk back to our dorms now?"

"Nope, we go inside." Ren had made up his mind.

Kusha nodded in agreement. "And watch the proceedings."

"Let's not," Maia said emphatically. She knew the majority of her teammates wanted to get inside, but the idea of breaking into the Council Room troubled her. And she needed to make her opinion clear. "I don't like this map. I don't understand how Karhann could have gotten hold of all these codes. It's all *very* odd. We should go back."

"I agree with Maia, it will be bad if we are spotted inside. Let's leave," Dani pleaded.

"It won't be any worse than if we're spotted out here," Ren

argued. "We're going in."

"Karhann has been going to the meetings almost every night," Kusha exclaimed as Ren quickly punched in the last set of numbers. "Can you believe it?"

As the large door slid open noiselessly, the dimly lit room inside came rapidly into focus.

CHAPTER TWENTY-EIGHT

THE COUNCIL

The rectangular room had a sunken oval center filled with about a hundred chairs lined up in rows. These were arranged into three clearly-demarcated sections—one was empty, which Maia presumed to be reserved for the Xifarians and the other two were occupied by representatives from the Solianese and the Jjord. It was in this central area that the talks were in progress.

Rows of benches ringed the central oval; these were for the audience. This space was half-filled with people who listened to the proceedings with rapt attention. Hardly anyone looked up when Maia and her teammates entered the room. Kusha spotted a row of seats in the far left corner and the gang marched quickly toward it.

A violent war of words erupted among the representatives before the group had time to settle down. A man wearing long robes typical of the Solianese First Continent paced the floor, waving a piece of paper, and shouting loudly at the Jjordic section.

"Have you forgotten this? Your people signed this accord of support. How can you simply ignore it now?"

A portly man in a predominantly white uniform, who sat in the front row of the Jjordic section, raised his hand to placate him. "Calm down, Sahiiraan Tsininio. Let us go over the situation at hand one more time."

Tsininio neither showed any signs of calming down nor did he attempt to take a seat. "We have been trying to go over this for a whole month now. This is a time for action, not deliberation. You fail to understand that time is slipping away for my people."

"Is that so? Then where are all your leaders? I do not see the urgency you speak of in the actions of your House leaders, Sahiiraan Tsininio." A gray-haired woman who sat hunched next to the portly Jjordic man spoke in a clear voice that rang across the room. "Now, take a seat, please."

Tsininio seemed startled for a moment and then his shoulders sagged.

The gray-haired woman spoke again. "Believe me, we do understand your situation. But tell me, Sahiiraan Tsininio, what would you do if you were in our place?"

Tsininio fidgeted restlessly, and his gaze drooped.

"We, the Jjord, have been let down over and over again by you, the Solianese," the gray-haired woman continued. "Our faith in your abilities and your intentions has been tested more than once in the past. And you would know it better than I do, Sahiiraan, that it has been a series of disappointments, to phrase it nicely. Just your promise to try to unite all the Houses in this one cause is not enough to make us rely on you. Look at your attendance—not even half of the Houses have sent their representatives. How do you expect us to trust people who do not even care to show up at the time of such a crisis? After all we have been through, we cannot accept this."

"You keep referring to incidents of the past." Tsininio slowly eased back into his chair. "We need to forget them and move on to the future."

"Yes, and then get burned again by your callousness?" the portly Jjordic man retorted.

"That is offensive . . . you will take that back." A bald, dark man, who sat behind Tsininio, stood up angrily. The Jjordic man wriggled in his chair trying to get to his feet, but his girth held him back.

The gray-haired woman raised her hand, and both men backed down immediately.

"Who is the woman?" Maia asked Dani. "She seems to be the one in charge."

Dani chuckled. "Yes, she is absolutely in charge around here. She is our leader, the honorable premier, 'The Intimidator' Oliena."

"The Intimidator?" Nafi asked.

"Can't you sense that already?" Ren commented wryly.

"This is nothing," Dani added with a knowing smile. "You don't want to see her in action."

As Premier Oliena started to speak again, everyone turned their attention to the floor.

"Sahiiraan Goren, as offensive as it might sound to you, our concerns have valid grounds. You cannot deny that our present is an outcome of a past that we had chosen willfully. And our future will also be a reflection of our actions today. More than a hundred years ago, had you, the Solianese, listened to our concerns, our warnings, and our predictions about the worsening ecology on Tansi, we would not be a divided nation like we are now. You chose to ignore us and practically drove us away; sending us into an exile that was hardly a luxurious living under the waters back then. We, the Jjord, were always expendable to you—we were then and we are now."

Premier Oliena paused and Maia noted the absolute silence that had fallen in the room.

Ren nudged Maia's arm lightly. "Is everyone here named Sahiiraan?" he whispered.

"Sahiiraan is a title for leaders of the Solianese Houses," Maia whispered back. "Each House governs a principality or a region."

Her explanation was cut short when Premier Oliena started to speak again.

"You did not stop to find out whether we lived or perished,

because you were so busy in your extravagant and careless ways. You destroyed the planet that you forgot you shared with others, driving it to the point of extinction. And all through it we suffered and struggled in silence, protecting our refuge from the poison that you unleashed. There were times when we thought it was hopeless, but we labored on."

Premier Oliena paused again and took a tiny sip from the glass in front of her. It was interesting, Maia thought, to hear the other side of things. She had always considered the Jjord unfair and highhanded. While they still seemed to be that way to her, she had to admit that the Solianese had not treated the Jjord fairly either. The Jjord refugees who seceded from the Solianese parliament centuries ago were probably as helpless and scared as the land dwellers of today.

"It was by the grace of the stars that your civilization—the supposed great civilization of the Solianese—perished before Tansi did, or we would have not lived to see this day. When it all fell in a pile of ruin, we could have chosen to ignore your plight, but we did not. Our envoys came to your aid, restoring the lives, the remnants, or whatever survived. We had to put restrictions in place; we could not take the chance of letting you try to destroy Tansi again. It might seem unfair to you, but we had to learn from your terrible and unbridled greed."

Maia stifled a sigh. Premier Oliena was voicing unpleasant facts, but the truth in them remained true no matter how horrid they sounded. The Solianese had destroyed their civilization and nearly destroyed Tansi. The Jjord had a right to be wary.

Oliena went on, her voice calm, unruffled, yet her words firm and hurtful.

"Our uneasy peace lasted only until the Xifarians arrived. Yet again, you did not show the tiniest bit of restraint in befriending them. We had warned you and asked you to be careful, but we were told to stay away. The Xifarians were your chance to escape the chains we had put on you, we were told. Once again you, the Solianese, forgot that we sustain you, that we give you food and water and heat and light.

"That was not the end. Your carelessness let the Damoclian Connector be destroyed. That betrayal cost us precious lives, almost destroyed Zagran, and destroyed our energy independence. We had no choice but to submit to our neighbors on Xif."

Dani sighed softly, and sadness wafted through the stillness and touched them all. Maia had heard stories about the famed Damoclian Connector, but she did not know that it was more than just a myth. Built to share the energy sources between the two nations of the Solianese and the Jjord, it was supposed to be a giant feat of technology, a super conduit of energy that rose from the ocean beds to the planet's surface.

"After all that, what do you expect us to do?" Oliena asked earnestly. "Trust you again with our lives and risk all chances of our own survival for you? Even when you cannot promise to bring forward the leaders of the Resistance? Even when you fail to get all your House leaders to attend this Council?"

"Yes. I am asking you to give us another chance and some more time to convince all the Houses to come to an agreement about the Resistance," Tsininio said simply.

The portly Jjordic man waved his hand in dismissal. "Another chance to a bunch of dishonest and greedy murderers? Why can't you ferret out those rebel rats, those thieves that pose as heroes, and hand them over to the Xifarians? Had you not pampered them and indulged them, we would not be in this situation today."

"Calm down, Aloysus," Premier Oliena said to the stocky Jjord.

Aloysus continued regardless. He seemed to be keen on igniting the situation with his brash statements. "At this rate, forget about us assisting you, Tsininio. Even if you start begging for refuge, I would not provide shelter for your young. Premier Oliena, I think we should give these Solianese an ultimatum—follow our rules unconditionally, meet all our demands, and only then shall we consider letting you live."

A huge commotion erupted in the chamber. While the aggressive

Jjord man definitely seemed to enjoy the effect his words had produced, Premier Oliena shook her head in disappointment and sank back in her chair. She looked drained and exhausted, and nothing but hopelessness showed on her pallid face.

"This is outrageous," Kusha said loudly. "I can't believe they would let someone say such things in the Council Room. Obeying rules . . . I'm sick and tired of it."

In a sudden impulsive movement, Kusha reached into his pocket and took out his red headband. He stared at it wistfully, his fingers lightly caressing the golden emblem of the sun at the center of the band. Then he slipped it onto his head. His face grew hard, and his eyes shone with determination.

"Guess you guys have to live with another strike," he said. "Or if you want, I'll gladly quit the team and the competition."

They had all started to protest Kusha's last statement when a voice made them turn around.

"What are *you* doing here?" It was Hans. He looked inquiringly from face to face, his gaze coming to a rest on Kusha and lingering on his headband. "I do not want to know how you got here, but you will be in serious trouble if someone sees you."

Maia bristled inside at his admonishing tone.

"Let's go," Hans said. "I'll walk you out."

They quietly followed Hans to the door. Dani looked particularly crushed; her head was bowed and her eyes drooping. In the inner chamber of the Council, a furious debate raged. Hans stopped when they were all outside. He glanced briefly at the downcast face of his sister before looking pointedly at Kusha's headband once again; something about it seemed to draw his repeated attention. As Kusha fidgeted uneasily under his stare, Hans chuckled.

"I haven't seen you wear that headband before. Is that the latest fashion statement?"

"No." Kusha shook his head. "It's an inheritance."

"Oh, I see," Hans said. Maia thought she saw the hint of a shadow pass over his face. He broke into a smile almost immediately and gestured at the empty corridor ahead. "Well, you should get going."

They walked back to the dorm in silence. The debate Maia had witnessed in the Council Room played over and over again in her tired mind. The future seemed worrisome, including their inevitable encounter with Aerika over Kusha's headband.

CHAPTER TWENTY-NINE

THE KARNILIAN CHALLENGE

The dreaded confrontation with Aerika came a week later. The days that led up to that meeting were far more aggravating than the meeting itself. The anxiety, the gloating faces of Loriine and her teammates, and the tension that grew by leaps and bounds between Kusha and Dani did not make for pleasant living conditions. Since the trip to the Council Room, Dani had grown quieter, scarcely talking to anyone, and barely glancing in Kusha's direction. Maia asked the girl about what was bothering her only to be replied with a vague, "Nothing, I'm fine." Nafi, on the other hand, was sure that it had something to do with disappointing Hans.

"He expects too much of his sister," she commented with her nose up in the air. "He should let her have some fun."

Maia did not bother pointing out that breaking into the Council Room in the middle of the night might not exactly appeal to anyone's sense of fun.

The unfortunate meeting with Aerika passed as painlessly as it could have, mostly because it was also the day when the first challenge was announced. Everyone was busy thinking about the task at hand, more than about the misfortunes of a certain team. That morning, they found Aerika in Palak's classroom conversing with both trainers busily. Strangely, Aerika did nothing more than raise a quizzical eyebrow at Kusha, clearly noticing the reappearance of his headband, and take out what Maia presumed was a small recorder to note the violation. Not a single word was exchanged, but Maia knew they had been awarded the expected strike.

"We are here today to announce your first challenge," Aerika said when the room had filled up. "You have two more weeks until the challenge, which means you still have a chance to catch up. Those who have been paying close attention will probably cruise through. As for those who have not, we can say goodbye to them right now."

"Goodbye, Nafi," Loriine crooned from behind them, and Baecca joined in with a snicker. Maia saw Nafi's fist clench; she hoped that the girl would be able to hold her temper. They did not need yet another penalty against the team.

"The challenge is simple: you will have to reach the Karnilian Caves in an Aqumob. The first team to reach the caves will be the winner, and the rest will be ranked based on the time you take to arrive at your destination. Obviously, how fast you are will depend considerably on understanding the geology of the area, charting out the best path to the cave, as well as your ability to control and steer your Aqumob. Now, your trainers will explain in more detail."

As Aerika stepped aside, Palak took the stage.

"Up on the screen, you will see the map of the caves. And you also see our starting point, Zagran." Palak pointed at the huge three-dimensional maps that showed the area that lay between Zagran and the Karnilian Caves highlighted in a bright yellow. "You will need to traverse the course from here to the caves in the shortest possible time. It will all depend on the path you select. So, choose wisely."

A hand went up on the other side of the room. It was Jiri; he never seemed to run out of questions.

"Do we have to submit the details of our route in advance?"

"No, absolutely not," Palak replied. "Your vehicle will be tracked and monitored at all times, so we will always know your precise location. You will be free to make changes to your route as and when you see fit, even while you are racing toward the destination."

Jiri's hand went up again, even before Palak had finished speaking. "But we haven't even driven an Aqumob," he said.

"You will. Soon," Dill replied, as he stepped forward to join Palak. "However, since there is not enough time for you to master that vehicle, they will be on semi-auto pilot mode. That means, even if you fail to maneuver it, it will take you to your destination using the safest and possibly the longest route it will be programmed with. So, while you might lose the challenge, you will not be lost."

This time, Kusha's hand floated tentatively in the air. "Will it be just us?" he asked. "Or will our mentor be with us as well?"

He was asking from their experience on Xif, Maia realized. For the final challenge, while the team had been responsible for the navigational tasks and had also helped in flying the craft, their mentor Miir had actually flown his Onclioraptor to the Seliban Temple.

"It will be just *you*." Aerika stepped in at this point. "Although the mentors have been asked to guide you, it is not required of them to assist you beyond simple tasks. But if you have established a good rapport with your mentor, which I hope you all have, I expect them to be more than eager to help you with the planning. Also, you will be allowed to carry your personal weapon with you," she said, looking at the eager but anxious faces. "Good luck."

Aerika left the classroom soon but not before a brief stop near Kusha's desk.

"Just so you know, your decision to wear that headband counts as a strike against your group," she informed coldly.

No sooner than she had left, Loriine sang, "Two down, three more to go."

More snickers and laughs erupted around the room.

Chapter Thirty

Chicanes and Corkscrews

The choices were numerous, to say the least. Armed with stacks of maps, Maia and her teammates studied the maze of currents flowing through the section of the ocean separating Zagran from the Karnilian Caves. The more they probed, the more difficult it became to pick just one path. It was not simply the matter of the length of the paths, but also the properties of water that flowed through them. Kusha and Nafi volunteered to learn more about the heat, the flow, the speed, and every other mundane detail of the waters that could affect their timing.

Maia decided to research the caves, while Ren and Dani focused on the operations of the Aqumob. The Aqumob was definitely not as complicated as the Onclioraptor, but still, it was no mean feat remembering every control, even with Dani's experience with the vehicle.

"The Karnilian Caves is a horizontal chasm halfway down the Zsitanian Abyss. This abyss, which could hold ten cities the length of Zagran stacked one on top of the other, stretches to the deepest deep, the lowest point of the Tansian ocean floor," Maia summarized a passage to her teammates as they assembled in their usual corner of the atrium. "It was found by accident. One stray Aqumob had drifted into the blackness of the chasm when its power systems failed. It was by a stroke of luck that the hapless engineer found his vehicle miraculously recharged while inside the pit, enough for him to rise all the way up to the surface and safety."

The team sat engrossed as Maia described the Zsitanian chasm—how investigating teams explored the chasm soon after, and what was uncovered changed the understanding of underwater energy systems. The Karnilian Caves sat on a long fault line, which hastened the leakage of energy from Tansi's superheated core. To tap this limitless source of power, a series of force spikes were soon driven into the fault line forming a mesh of conductors. The energy that flowed out through these spikes was fed into a grid that led up to Zagran's power concentrators.

Then there were the Zsitanian currents—giant vortexes of water so strong that each could equal the forces of the entire surface waves taken together. No time was wasted in building the massive grid of water turbines that ran across the length of the chasm.

"Thus"—Maia concluded her reading—"the mightiest of the Roqowist farms came to life. In its entirety, this whole chasm is capable of producing enough energy to sustain all the underwater settlements, if not more."

"What's a Roqowist farm?" Nafi asked.

"Any energy farm that feeds into the energy grid is a Roqowist. There are other kinds of farms also, like the Challowist, which are standalone," Dani explained.

"What's the use of an energy farm that is not connected to the energy grid?" Ren inquired.

Maia remembered Dani mentioning the Challowist farms a long time ago in Appian. "They are used to charge up smaller appliances. Right, Dani?"

"Yes," Dani replied.

"I wonder why we're being sent to an energy farm," Nafi muttered, frowning.

"Because of the complexity of the path, I guess," Ren replied. "And maybe to show us the farms. It sounds quite impressive to me."

"Any ideas on the routes yet?" Maia asked Kusha and Nafi, who looked at each other quickly before turning to face the team.

"Well, as usual, there are the safer routes and a few not-so-easy ones," Kusha informed; his face grim. "The fastest one will give us a good lead over anyone else, but it would also mean that we have to depend on excellent driving skills."

"Anything short of perfection might make us crash." Nafi stole a furtive glance at Dani's pensive face. "This time Miir won't be around to help—it's no one else but us."

"We'll be fine," Ren replied. "Dani and I have it all under control."

"We need some more training on the thruster module," Dani said. "We've requested Joolsae to help us with it, and she has promised to spend some time with us."

"That girl is of no help at all," Nafi fumed. "I had asked her for some special maps of the Northern Zsitanian Ridge, and I'm still waiting. I wouldn't depend on her if I were you."

"But she promised," Ren protested.

"Well, of course." Nafi shrugged. "Anyone can make promises, but it's another matter altogether to keep them, or even try."

"She is supposed to be a mentor," Ren grumbled. "Miir was so much better."

"Yes." Nafi let out a long sigh. "Don't get me started on how good Miir was. I admit, he could be rude at times, but he always did what he was expected to do and he *always* helped us. And this stupid Joolsae—"

"She must be busy with her coursework," Maia remarked.

"Maybe. But that doesn't excuse her from helping us," Dani argued. "It's not like she is doing this just out of kindness. Anyone who volunteers for mentoring earns extra credit."

"And yet, she fails to show up," Ren said.

"All right, enough about Joolsae. If she's not here, then we have to figure it out without her," Maia interrupted as Ren was about to grumble some more. She leaned over the large map of the Zsitanian region that Kusha had laid out. "This is what I think we should do. We take the fourth Trans-Zsitanian current from Zagran and head southward on it until we find the Antiotic 270, the cold stream that runs perpendicular to the Trans-Zsitanian. We can follow this until we reach the North Ridge of the abyss."

"We will be with the other teams all along this stretch," Nafi added. "All we need here is speed to pass the others and – "

"Or maybe not," Maia interrupted. "We can simply choose to fall behind and stay out of sight, just like we did during the Seliban challenge. Then we dip into the North Zsitanian Fissure and come out far ahead of the rest, halfway into the abyss itself. From there we simply take a downward vortex that carries us to the bottom of the abyss and into the Karnilian Caves."

"Yes, that *is* the fastest path. But . . ." Kusha stopped, and Nafi sighed loudly.

"What?" Maia squinted hard at Kusha and Nafi. "Something wrong with it?"

Kusha and Nafi exchanged that curious look again.

"It's about the part through the fissure," Kusha replied. "It's a very tight space, laid out like a maze almost. Also, it's not a flat, straight road through the ground—it's far from that. It's a trap of chicanes, finally ending in a corkscrew that stretches halfway through the length of the abyss."

"And then, we're not exactly sure about the mouth of the fissure." Nafi tapped on the map, pointing at the end where the thin line of the fissure met with the chasm of the Zsitanian Abyss. "This is where I needed help from Joolsae, but—"

"I can help," Maia said eagerly. "I'll try to dig up some information. And I can monitor our paths and our surroundings as you navigate."

"At least we're sure there's a way out into the abyss," Kusha added, "we just don't know how it looks."

"So, Dani, maybe we need to start researching the thrusters on our own." Ren lay on his stomach, resting his head on his hands.

"How about asking Dill?" Maia inquired.

"We do *not* like Dill," Ren said, smiling at Dani who looked away rather unapologetically.

"That's all right," Nafi commented as she gathered her books and stood up to leave. "We aren't exactly asking Palak much either."

It was funny to see how reckless they had all grown, Maia thought and chuckled inside. All they counted on was each other and nothing else.

CHAPTER THIRTY-ONE

THE DEEP DIVE

The days leading up to the challenge went by at a dizzying pace. There were a few trial runs of the Aqumob up and down the chute to Dill's classroom, all of which Dani and Ren handled exquisitely. Maia had sufficiently mastered the sounding probes to accurately analyze the environment even before sighting it. Kusha and Nafi had their maps ready without the sought-after help from Joolsae. Their mentor was nowhere to be found; it was as if she had vanished into thin air.

The morning of the challenge did not start well. In the girls' dorm, Anja was sick. Loriine and Baecca did not cast a second look at the poor girl who lay exhausted in her bed. Maia, Dani, and Nafi, however, waited with her until she was taken to the infirmary. When the trio finally met up with the boys at the RC, they were running late. Rushing into the classroom, they found all the teams assembled and ready, but Aerika was yet to arrive.

"I'll navigate; Nafi will help with the backup charts," Kusha informed Dani and Ren as they huddled together. "Dani, will you be steering?"

Dani flinched. "Ren, you steer, I'll be in the co-pilot's seat," she said decisively. As Ren nodded, clearly surprised at what seemed to be a sudden change of plans, Dani stepped away from the group. "I have to ask the trainer some questions. Be back soon."

Ren stood staring for a few moments before following Dani toward where Palak and Dill stood. Nafi busied herself arranging the charts and maps while Kusha continued to gape. He looked sad and hurt, Maia noted, as she waited for him to speak. His gaze skimmed the floor before they came up again to meet Maia's.

"Did you see that? Did you see how she snubbed me? Why is she doing this to me?" Kusha shook his head in confusion.

"She hasn't been real chatty with anyone lately, Kusha." Maia tried to reassure the boy.

"Yes, but I don't see her ignoring anyone else so deliberately either," Kusha argued.

"You're the one who screamed at her, remember?" Nafi piped up. "Without a reason too."

Kusha grimaced and hung his head. "I know I wasn't very polite when I reacted to Hans's message, but I was annoyed and frustrated."

"Maybe you should apologize," Maia suggested.

"I already have and she didn't even say a word," Kusha said with vehemence.

"Well" — Nafi crossed her arms and looked squarely at Kusha — "if you care about her as much as I think you do, you should keep apologizing until she relents. You can't give up on love so easily."

While Maia did not have a clue on how to react to that statement, Kusha seemed like he was ready to strangle the girl. Nafi shrugged and turned away casually, and then she looked back over her shoulder again.

"Just an honest suggestion," she said before turning away.

Maia was about to ask Kusha some questions of her own when the sound of clicking heels reverberated through the corridor. Aerika had finally arrived.

"We are all here, except for one girl. There is nothing to worry about, she will be fine," Aerika said to the assembled groups. "Everyone follow me to the Dive Bay. There we will assign you Aqumobs and provide you with water gear. You will also pick up your personal weapons there, but remember, any use of them during the challenge will have to be well justified."

The Dive Bay was down on the 200th floor and a long walk from the atrium to the public section. It was a sprawling facility, much larger than the Upper Docks Maia had visited with Hans. The waterfront stretched long and wide through the middle of it, and at least a hundred Aqumobs and other water vehicles were moored along piers in the bay. Aerika led the way to the side of the bay reserved for the university, where a series of Aqumobs that bore the logo, the name of the UAAS, and sported the university colors, were anchored.

Aerika came to a halt. "You will find your water gear stacked inside those rooms." She pointed to the series of changing rooms on one side. "After you have changed, you will board the Aqumobs that have been assigned numbers as per your core. Please wait for my instructions once you are aboard the Aqumobs. You will be taken by autopilot to the starting point outside Zagran, and only then will you be given driving control, so please do not try any smart moves before that. Good luck, play fair, and do not forget that all your activities will be monitored."

It did not take Maia long to dress in the diving gear with university stripes. After they were all given mouthpieces for breathing in water in case they needed to dive in, Maia and her friends climbed into their Aqumob. The vehicle was not very spacious—the large instrument deck faced the front window and the pilot and copilot's seats were right next to it. There were desk benches along the side windows, in one of which Kusha and Nafi settled down next to Ren. Since Maia's task was mostly to study than actively navigate, she took the bench on the other side near Dani, secured her sounding equipment, and buckled her safety belt.

As soon as the system checks were completed for all the Aqumobs, the vehicles dove under the surface of the water one by one. They were sucked into one of the long chutes that led in and out of the city and spewed out at the southern base of Zagran. All twenty Aqumobs lined up side by side at the spout, ready to start the sprint toward the Karnilian Caves.

"Pilots ready?" Aerika's voice came over the speaker.

"Yes," Ren replied in a small but resolute voice.

An anxious silence fell for a moment before Aerika said, "Go."

The Aqumobs shot forward like a bunch of arrows streaking through the dark waters. At the head of the line was Aqumob 7, the vehicle with Karhann and his team. Following them closely were three other Aqumobs. The craft that carried Maia and her friends was sixth, and Ren steadily controlled the speed to hold their position. Everyone was heading for the Fourth Trans-Zsitanian current, from which they jumped off into the Antiotic 270 one by one.

"Slow down," Dani said as they hit the Antiotic 270.

"The entrance to the fissure is coming up on the right before the next left turn," Kusha informed. "We've to make a straight descent into a vertical opening."

Ren slowed down considerably. Almost all of the craft had zoomed past them.

"Right ahead," Kusha shouted.

The intimidating blackness of the North Zsitanian Fissure loomed like a nightmare in front of them as Ren turned the Aqumob sharply to face it. Maia held her breath as they careened into the darkness. Then her vision narrowed . . . chunks of gray rained down on her, blocking her mind, making it difficult to think . . . or breathe.

"Maia." Someone shook her vigorously by the shoulders. "You need to focus. Keep scanning the surroundings."

Nafi stood gazing at her.

"What happened? Did I pass out?" Maia said in sudden embarrassment. All she could remember was the overwhelming darkness.

"You made weird noises and looked all funny." Dani shot a quick look backward. "Are you all right?

The Aqumob was speeding along a narrow path that was studded with rocks and reefs jutting out from all directions. A small beam of light from the craft dimly lit the grotesque shapes and forms that fell behind as the Aqumob sped past. Ren was hunched over the controls, jumping from one knob to another at a frantic pace as Kusha barked the directions.

"You all right, Maia?" Ren shouted in between the crazy routine.

"I'm fine." Mortified for creating a distraction at such a critical time, Maia rushed back to her controls at the sounding instrument panels.

"Chicane Three coming up," Kusha announced.

No sooner than he said that, the Aqumob went into a zigzag course through the rocks, coming ever so close to the walls, yet managing to avoid it by a thread. Maia avoided looking at the window and tried her best to ignore that knot at the pit of her stomach. The craft streaked through the dark, grainy waters, in a reckless and frenzied rush that went on and on. Three crazy chicanes later, the Aqumob fell into a relatively long wide stretch of the fissure.

"How's our time, Nafi?" Ren asked.

"Doing well, very well," Nafi replied.

"Last chicane, Ren," Kusha yelled.

"On it."

A wild pitch of the nose and a seemingly uncontrolled roll to the left later, the vehicle followed a straight path again.

"The corkscrew is up next," Kusha hollered.

"Dani, can you take the corkscrew please?" Ren sounded exhausted after the long ride through the chicanes. Dani did not need to be asked again; they quickly exchanged positions. Immediately, Kusha and Nafi swapped places as if on cue. Maia could not help shaking her head at the silliness of it all but decided to hold her tongue.

"We are at the cavern," Nafi said.

They had entered a giant underwater cavern. From its other end, the path took a nosedive downward, and Maia hoped it would emerge into the abyss. The uneasiness she had felt earlier threatened to make a comeback as the Aqumob turned, hovered for a moment, and then fell in a dizzying spiral into the corkscrew. Maia fought it steadily, pushing away the thoughts of the dark unknown as the craft made its way at an ever-increasing speed down the vortex. She diligently worked with the buttons on the panel in front of her. The readings looked fine so far. They were in regular water; the density and the warmth were normal for the depth. Maia continued to look out for the mouth of the fissure.

"The corkscrew ends right here," Nafi shouted. "Turn left for the exit."

The Aqumob swerved, almost tilted out of balance, and rushed headlong into an inclined gap in the wall. The jolt that came immediately afterward threw Maia backward into her seat and then sideways onto the floor as the safety belt gave way.

"Sorry," Dani yelled as she fought to straighten the vehicle. "I must've grazed the walls."

"It's all right, I'm fine." Maia got to her feet and tied herself back in. It did not feel like she was hurt anywhere. She focused on the panels once more. "The path looks clear so far—seems like it will widen up shortly."

"There's no sign of damage to the mob, except for maybe a dent on the right engine module," Ren said as he scanned the body sensors of the Aqumob. "I don't see anything serious yet."

"Not too far to go now," Nafi said softly, anxiety throbbing in her voice.

Right then Maia saw the rise in the thickness of the medium around them, and it rose sharply with every movement forward.

"Guys, there's something ahead of us," she shouted. "It's thicker than regular water."

"Yes, we have to speed up," Dani said, noting the rapidly falling counters on the speed monitor. "Ren, engage the supplementary thrusters."

"Are you sure, Dani?" Ren asked. "We don't know the boost capabilities fully. What if we overshoot?"

"We have to take our chances. We can't delay anymore or we will be stuck in this mire," Dani replied. "Engage them, *now!*"

It didn't seem like they would make it. The fluid around them was thick and dark like black oil. It swirled and slowed the tiny mob down to almost a standstill. And then the thrusters suddenly kicked in and a jolt threw them backward and sideways. The vehicle careened through the murkiness.

Soon the density counters started falling again and Maia breathed in relief. They *were* going to make it after all. "We're getting back to regular waters again," she announced.

Ren disengaged the supplementary thrusters, and the craft slowly returned to its regular speed.

"The opening is coming up now, slow down," Nafi shouted as the Aqumob shot through a crevasse and into a huge ravine that stretched endlessly above and below them.

"Yes!" Nafi shrieked. "We did it. We made it to the Zsitanian Abyss."

CHAPTER THIRTY-TWO

TIMITI

It was a relief to be out in the open again. Everyone laughed, including Dani, who had not smiled in weeks. Their craft descended steadily toward the distant lights of the Karnilian Caves.

The strange agitation Maia had felt within the fissure persisted, however. As a sudden chill sped down her spine, Maia grabbed the desk tightly, wondering what could have gone wrong again. The darkness outside was not in the least unpleasant compared to the suffocating passage she had managed to survive, yet there was something that made her ill at ease. A flash of memories sped through her mind. She remembered her first flight lesson in Miorie with Herc and Dada watching anxiously from the ground. A brief stillness followed, and then the rush of memories started coursing through her again as if someone was flicking through the pages of her mind.

She groaned, clutched her head, and closed her eyes. A small murmur rose behind her. A shuffle and a cry were all she heard before she opened her eyes again. Then she screamed in terror. Rising like a living wall next to the Aqumob was a huge black-and-white presence—a whale, a Timiti, peered through the glass and looked straight at Maia. Its eyes were dark, thick, and fluid. The inky eyes bore into Maia's as she sat transfixed, spellbound by some magic.

"Someone make her turn away," Dani yelled.

Maia felt a scream make its way out from the pit of her stomach and grayness spilled over her eyes. A pair of arms grabbed her, pulling her down from her seat and to the floor.

"Look at me, Maia." Kusha held her by the shoulders. "Keep looking at me."

Darkness overwhelmed Maia's senses. Arms wrapped around her, pulling her close. Sweat streamed down her forehead.

"Faster, Ren," Dani shouted. "Get us past the turbine farm as fast as you can. Engage the thrusters if you have to."

A kick of speed. A faint conversation. A loud whir.

Then, as the whirring grew fainter again, Maia's mind cleared a little. She was sitting on the floor of the Aqumob, and Dani was holding her in a tight embrace. Kusha was kneeling on her other side, fear etched on his face. Ren and Nafi sat at the controls; they kept looking back anxiously every other moment.

"What happened?" Maia asked.

"It was a Timiti whale," Dani said, her face darkening. "Probably the one you conjured in your Saska."

"I thought they didn't exist anymore," Maia said.

"Clearly, they do," Dani replied.

"Why was I so upset on seeing it?"

Dani paused for a moment before replying. Maia noticed the hesitation ripple through her face.

"Timiti whales are the mutated remnants of regular whale breeds we had in the oceans a century ago. Of all the species that perished during the warming of the Northern Waters, the Timiti is the only one that is said to have survived. They are creatures of darkness. It is said they live deep in the burrows of the oceans, but they invariably appear when there is a disaster waiting to happen, as if they like to thrive on the misery and the pain," she said. "I didn't want to scare you when it showed up in your Saska that day. I hoped that it was a manifestation of something you might've read or heard. But seeing that it turned up here when no one else has seen a Timiti in ages makes me think that there is something wrong . . . somewhere."

"So, it's like a bad omen?" Maia asked.

"Something like that," Dani replied.

That explains why Dani had avoided discussing the whale that day.

"They have strong sensory powers also. There are stories of Timiti whales being used to spy on the enemy; they've been used to read people's minds. I don't know if any of that is true, but . . ."

Maia sat in silence as Dani's words trailed off. It had felt as if someone was flipping through her memories. She wondered if the Timiti was indeed trying to read her mind.

But that doesn't make any sense. Why would it?

Maia shook her head in confusion. "How did I conjure it? This is the first time I ever saw one."

Dani shrugged. "I have no idea, but there has to be a link, and it can't be a good one since its presence didn't exactly have a pleasant effect on you."

Maia nodded, yet she failed to understand what that connection could be. The whale reminded her vaguely of something she had experienced before, something she could not remember clearly.

"We've arrived," Ren announced, breaking her train of thought. "But I don't know how or where to get in."

His questions were answered momentarily when the speakers crackled to life and Aerika's voice sounded.

"Congratulations, Core 21, you are the first team to successfully reach the Karnilian Caves. You will be on autopilot mode from here."

The wild cheer that broke out in the Aqumob drowned everything else she said afterward.

CHAPTER THIRTY-THREE

THE SAGE OF THE DEEP

A gray-haired man welcomed the team as they got off the Aqumob. The craft had been towed in by autopilot and securely moored at the landing platform of the Karnilian Caves.

"I'm Gustin, one of the overseers of these caves. You can call me Gus," the man quickly introduced himself before congratulating and praising the team as lavishly as he could. "I would've loved to show you around, but I need to be here to receive the other teams and Training Supervisor Aerika. You can walk around as you please—just stay away from the 'danger' signs."

"Awesome." Ren grinned. "Thanks, Gus, we'll walk around."

There was not much to see if one was looking for beautiful sights. The place was like a huge factory full of complicated structures. Beams, trusses, columns, and spires rose from the floor and crisscrossed the walls. The quiet was a little unnerving, as was the lack of people. The sounds of their footsteps, echoing across the cavernous hallways, were their only company. Large signs hung all over the place, most of them with arrows pointing in the direction of the "Converter Galley."

"What's the Converter Galley?" Maia asked Dani.

"It's where the hydrothermal converters are installed, basically a big room full of them," Dani explained. "Let's go check it out."

"It's strange that there are so few people around here," Nafi observed thoughtfully as the group walked toward the Converter Galley. "Hardly any guards either."

"What's the point of having guards?" Dani countered. "To be allowed access to the dive bay in here, you must clear multiple biometric scans. The gates won't budge if it detects unauthorized access. And remember, it's not easy to even reach these gates."

"True, but still . . ." Nafi did not seem remotely satisfied. "Since this is such a big source of energy, I'd think it would be more protected."

"Don't worry, Nafi. There are complex alarm systems in place. Look at those red buttons," Dani said, pointing at a noticeably bright red button on the wall. There were hundreds of them scattered randomly across the walls. "They are connected to the central security system of Zagran. You simply have to press one of them and there will be guards swarming all over the place in no time."

"I don't know, Dani," Nafi sighed. "I still think they ought to have more people down here."

"Hey, look," Kusha exclaimed.

They had arrived at the Converter Galley. The converters were behemoths, standing like an army of giants in never-ending lines as far as Maia could see—row after row of gigantic upside-down funnels—their wide base resting on the floor and the chimneys touching the roof. Cables as thick as the chimneys led out from their bottoms and into a long line of square silvery boxes that stood in the middle of the hallway. Iron staircases looped around the funnels and rose to the ceiling. Wireframes spread over the tops in an intricate mesh of hanging walkways. Maia felt minuscule, like an ant standing at the edge of a forest.

"Wow," she exclaimed. "Each of these is a converter?"

"Yes," Dani replied.

"And how many of them do you have here?" Nafi asked.

"I don't know. Thousands, maybe," Dani said with a shrug.

"Wow," Maia said again. She could have stared at the gigantic installation forever—it had more than awed her—but she suddenly remembered Aerika. "I think we should get back now. Aerika might've arrived."

"Hey, guys, come here. Look at this." Ren sounded so excited that everyone forgot about Aerika and rushed over to him instead. He was hunched over a porthole that overlooked a small courtyard across from the entrance of the Converter Galley. The yard was bare except for a few plants stacked on one side. On the other end was a door, and light flickered through it. A flight of stairs led up from the courtyard to the nook where the group stood watching.

"What's that thing?" Ren exclaimed.

A bright shiny disc circled the yard continuously, alternately spiraling inward and then outward.

Ren seemed spellbound by the motion. A moment later he traipsed toward the stairs. "I'll go check it out."

"I don't think we should go in there," Dani cautioned, and Maia agreed right away, but the boy was already halfway down the stairs.

Ren leaped forward, jumping into the courtyard with the careless abandon of a child, his eyes fixed on the spiraling disc. His curiosity was quickly overcome by fear when the disc stopped abruptly in the middle of its repetitive course and headed in his direction with surprising agility and speed.

"Ren, get back," Maia screamed as the disc plunged toward the boy, aiming for his head.

It would have been an unthinkable mishap if Kusha had not dived forward and knocked Ren down on the ground. But that only helped for a brief moment. The disc hovered as the boys scrambled. Then it plunged toward Kusha.

As Kusha rolled over toward the inner end of the yard, the disc missed striking him, but only by a whisker. Once more, it paused and then charged. The girls had pulled Ren out of the yard and they huddled near the stairs watching, still shaken. The disc ignored their presence completely.

"Kusha, don't," Maia shouted as Kusha pulled out his sword and stood defiantly, ready to take on the menace. "Just get out of the yard."

Kusha took aim at the disc as it dove for him. His first swipe touched the rim, deflecting it. But then the disc changed direction and came back. Kusha swiped again and missed. The disc whirred toward his face as Kusha fell back against the wall. Someone screamed, someone sobbed, and Maia closed her eyes.

"Bravery wasted on nothing," said a sweet, tranquil voice.

Maia opened her eyes and looked around. Kusha stood pinned to the wall, the disc buzzing incessantly in front of his face, and barely the width of a hair separated them. The man who had spoken stood at the lighted doorway. His slight frame was covered in a flowing multi-hued robe. His wispy, long beard hung over his robe, and his long white hair cascaded past his shoulders. He smiled at Kusha, who stood perfectly still. The old man raised his hand in the direction of the disc; it abruptly turned and swooped on the man's chest. A gasp of terror rose from the watching group, but the disc simply melted into the man and disappeared behind his robes.

"There." The man smiled again. "Nothing more to fear now."

For a while, they stood frozen, and then Dani took a few tentative steps toward the old man.

"You must be the Sage of the Deep," she said. "It *is* true what they say then."

"And what *do* they say?" the old man asked, sitting down near the doorway.

"That deep in the abyss lives the one who wields a chakra, one who can foretell the future, the one who has lived through it all, through the centuries of rise and fall of Tansi," Dani said breathlessly as she kneeled in front of the man.

The man's laughter echoed across the yard.

"They do call me the Sage of the Deep," he said pleasantly. "But I do not know if I can foretell the future. Although I do see greatness in you all, as long as you have faith in each other."

The sage beckoned Kusha. "You, brave one."

Kusha walked over with slow, deliberate steps.

"You confronted my chakra, which is no mean feat." The sage's eyes studied Kusha's face. "You have the power in you to fulfill your desires. Do not question the gift you have been given, embrace it."

"What gift?" Kusha asked.

"You will know in time," the sage replied.

Kusha sat transfixed for a moment before speaking. "Where is the chakra now?"

"Here." The sage held out a bright blue crystal pendant that hung from his neck. It looked as harmless and as innocent as could be, far from the terrifying weapon that had been intent on harming the two intruders.

"But that's not what chased us," Ren said.

"What chased you was the morphed form of this water crystal," the sage explained. "This crystal is made from the Tourmaline waters of the spring of life and it is sworn to protect me. As soon as it detected your presence, it morphed into the chakra. I have long debated giving it the power to morph on its own, but seeing the terrible situation I put you young children in, I know I was mistaken after all. Your days of freedom are over, my friend," the sage affectionately brushed a finger over the crystal. "I shall be the judge of friend and foe from now on."

His tender gaze flitted over each face before it came to rest on Maia. A small frown played on his forehead before it disappeared and he smiled again. He reached out and touched Maia's hand briefly. "Having too many nightmares, hmm?"

Maia's simply stared, stunned by his words. She hesitated a while before nodding slowly. It had been relentless lately; the dreams, and mostly the nightmares, that made her toss and turn through the night.

"Is something wrong with me?" she asked.

"Nothing is wrong with you, my child," the sage said softly, reassuring her. "If you can see things, consider it a blessing."

"You mean . . ." Maia hesitated to ask. "You mean these things I see are . . . real? They could really happen?"

"Sometimes fragments of the past and the future have a way of making their way into the present," he replied in a vague sort of way.

"Won't they ever stop?" Maia asked.

The sage sighed and shook his head solemnly. "I am sorry, child. I wish I could help you, but I do not know how," he said. "Although I do see you with the one who could help . . . the one who treads the snow. Maybe he will set you free. But until then you shall need strength, all the strength in the world."

As Maia struggled to understand the meaning of his words, none of which made any sense to her, the sage rose to his feet.

"And now, I believe it is time for all of you to leave. Your training supervisor is rather anxious for your return."

There was not a moment to spare, not an instant to lose. After the sage bade them goodbye, they ran up the stairs and rushed toward the entrance of the Karnilian Caves.

CHAPTER THIRTY-FOUR

THE NOTE

They were halfway to the entrance when the sound of heavy footfalls came from the other end of the path. Gus and another man came striding toward them, their brows knit and fists clenched.

"There they are, Bikele," Gus exclaimed when he saw the group. "I told you there was nothing to worry about."

The man named Bikele looked livid. He glared at the group long and hard before making a loud grunt to show his dissatisfaction. He was very tall. Dark circles ringed his sunken eyes, and his dusky complexion had an unhealthy pallor. His greasy hair was unkempt—strands fell across his face in a stringy, jumbled mess.

"Let's go, kids," Gus said cheerily as he led the way. Bikele had fallen a few steps behind and Maia felt his lingering gaze at the back of her head.

Maia sighed as she walked quickly alongside Dani. "We're done for. Aerika will be all over us now."

"We shouldn't have gone down there," Dani whispered.

Aerika stood at the bay; she did not look pleased. She strode up to the approaching group, tapped her feet a few times, and shook her head.

"What is it with you?" she snarled. "Waylaid again?"

As everyone else fell silent, in an unexpected and unnecessary urge, Maia blurted out a lame defense.

"We lost track of time, Trainer Aerika," she said earnestly. "We really did."

"That's unfortunate, Miss Maia," Aerika snapped, "I wonder why such calamities keep befalling your team in particular." Aerika was not one to buy into justifications or excuses, certainly not from a group of kids who had done nothing but repeatedly annoy her.

"Into the transporter, all of you." She whipped a bony hand toward a much larger Aqumob that was anchored at the dock. The vehicle they had arrived in was nowhere to be seen, and neither were the craft assigned to any of the other teams—Maia assumed they had already been towed back to Zagran.

"And by the way," Aerika turned back from the sheaf of papers that Gus had handed her to sign. "This counts as your third strike."

"But please . . ." Nafi wailed, but Aerika did not even spare her a glance.

Disappointment of being punished with yet another strike wiped out all the joy of their victory. Maia headed toward the waiting vehicle, dragging her feet as she walked. It seemed impossible now that they could survive the next three months with only two strikes remaining.

"Maia?" A gruff voice made Maia jump and turn around.

Bikele stood with a small piece of folded paper in his hand. "You dropped this." He held the paper out in her direction.

Maia was sure she had not brought any paper with her, let alone dropped it. She shook her head and started to explain that the paper did not belong to her when he spoke again.

"You want to take this, Maia." There was no friendliness in his voice; it was almost an order. Maia was about to turn away when a hand snatched the piece of paper from Bikele.

"I'll take it for her," Nafi said before she dragged Maia away toward the Aqumob.

"Nafi!" Maia protested.

"We don't have time for this," Nafi replied, frowning. "Do you want Bones to shout at us again?"

"But you didn't have to take that paper from that strange man," Maia chided.

"Don't read it if you don't want to," Nafi said and turned her nose up in the air. "I will in any case."

"No, you shall not." Maia voiced her objection loudly as she followed Nafi into the hulking Aqumob. Inside, all the other groups were scattered—some looked sad, some happy. Except Loriine and Baecca, who threw a nasty look at the duo when they entered, no one bothered to glance in their direction. Maia followed Nafi to the back of the Aqumob where the rest of their team was already seated.

This Aqumob was laid out like a transporter vehicle with alternate rows of seats facing each other on both sides. Kusha and Ren sat on one row facing Dani who stared out at the dock. Nafi sat down beside Dani, rested her leg on the seat in front of her, took out the piece of paper, and grinned naughtily at Maia. Maia simply shrugged; there was no point fighting when they were going to hear all about it from Nafi anyway. She slumped down next to Kusha and laid her head back. The doors of the Aqumob closed, and as it gradually immersed itself into the waters, Nafi spread out the paper on her knees and frowned.

"Maia," she said right away. "You should read this."

While Nafi hastily explained their encounter with Bikele to the others, Maia looked at what was written on the small piece of paper. It only had a few words, scribbled in a hurry.

If, and only if, Sophie means anything to you, meet me in 15 days — midnight, 10th-floor waterlock, room 24.

Maia read it out loud as her friends listened with rapt attention.

Even after she had finished, no one spoke. Maia sat still, unable to think, almost unable to feel anything. After a while, the questions came in an overwhelming flood. Who was this man? Had he been a friend of her mother's? Or was he trying to lure her into some trap? How did he recognize who she was? What if he was R'armimon? Or a Xifarian spy?

"Who was he?" Kusha voiced the biggest question of all.

"I don't know." Maia did not know what to say. Not only did she not know who he was, but she also did not know if he meant to do her harm.

"You'll meet with him, right?" Ren asked.

"You can't go alone, we'll come with you," Kusha declared.

"We shall see about going," Maia said. It was too soon to decide whether it was a chance worth taking. She had not liked the man at all, and if going to meet with him meant risking another strike from Aerika, it probably did not make sense. "We have fifteen days to think about it."

Very little was spoken after that. Thoughts weighed heavily on Maia's mind all the way back to Zagran.

CHAPTER THIRTY-FIVE

THE UPKEEP EXERCISE

Palak and Dill organized a little party to honor the performances during the first challenge. There was no end to the praises they showered on Core 21, but they also mentioned the fabulous effort of Core 13, who coped with the last-moment loss of their fifth member, Anja, and still made the second-best time, making their feat even more impressive. Core 7 came in third, but the members of that team did not look happy at all. Loriine and the gang not only refused to congratulate the other teams but also openly scowled at every word of praise the trainers had for anyone else. Amidst all the celebrations, it was sad to see that five of the lowest-ranked groups had already left and only fifteen teams remained. It was a reminder that this was not all fun; they were being evaluated and judged every moment of their stay.

The training sessions changed rather drastically. As soon as the teams met after the first challenge, Palak brought up the new topic of building energy converters, machines that ranged from minuscule to gigantic, that could change energy from one form to another.

"All your assignments going forward will be in preparation for your second and final challenge," the trainer announced. "You will be given three tasks. I shall explain the first two now, and the third one will be explained by Trainer Dill."

Palak paused to take a breath and a wave of murmurs swept through the room. Maia savored the tingle of excitement in her brain. She sat up straight, ready to devour every word.

"First task! Each team will construct a mini hydrosol converter—one that will be capable of capturing energy from the waves and the sun.

"For your second task, all fifteen teams will work together. You might have noticed the hydrothermal converters at the Karnilian Caves," Palak said. "You will build one such converter to be installed at the Karnilian Caves. Remember, for this task, all of the teams have to collaborate."

Maia sat dumbfounded. She liked the sound of the mini hydrosol; it was *mini* after all. But building one of those giant converters she had seen at the Converter Galley, even if all fifteen teams banded together, sounded daunting. Around the room, whispers swelled to the level of a distracting drone.

Palak clapped his hands in an attempt to get their attention back. "I understand, I understand," he started. "Building a hydrothermal converter can sound overwhelming. And it won't be easy working together with your opponent teams, but we shall try our best to be nice to each other. Supervisor Aerika wants you to learn the value of cooperation during this task."

The mention of Aerika did the trick. All humdrum died down, as heads pored over books and diagrams and anything else that could help them build these machines. An exhausting morning session later, Maia trudged toward Dill's classroom expecting an even worse fare.

***

A startling cacophony hit Maia's ears as she set foot in the classroom and the sight that met her eyes made her stop and gawk. A variety of water creatures frolicked in the usually tranquil pool of water at the center of the room. They swam, jumped, bumped into each other, and screeched loudly. There were many snub-nosed dolphins, a lot of large colorful fish, and some larger and strange-looking creatures.

Maia's eyes were glued on a particular dolphin that rested its chin on the rim of the pool and stared amusedly in her direction. Its eyes were a shiny black, its body the darkest ink blue. There was something warm and pleasing about the expression on its face. As Maia slipped into her chair behind her Saska and peeped at the animal, it seemed to peek back at her as well. They played for a while, a silly game of hide-and-seek until Dill walked in triumphantly.

"What do we have here?" he said in mock surprise, pointing at the melee in the pool. "Anyone want to take a guess?"

True to expectations, Jiri's hand went up first. "Maybe we learn to understand the animals better?" he said.

"Yes. And how would we do that?"

"Am I allowed to answer?" Dani asked and Dill nodded.

"Maybe we swim with them," she suggested brightly. "You know . . . like we did as little kids."

A wide smile flooded Dill's face. "You got it right, Dani," he said. "We will indeed swim with our aquatic partners."

"No way," Ren said so loudly that the whole congregation turned to look at him. He flushed a little and shook his head vehemently. "I'm not going anywhere near the water."

"We will see about that, but now let's first get the gear on." Dill pointed at a corner of the room where water gear hung neatly in rows. "The changing rooms are back there."

As Maia lined up in front of the pool awaiting the trainer's instructions, she felt nervous. Waters on Tansi were considered too risky for human use, so she had only ever been in water two times in her life. Once as a child, Maia had waded in up to her ankles in the stream near Miorie. She was about six years old at the time, but the memory of the coolest touch around her feet, and the subsequent commotion it caused among the elders who were watching her, stood out clearly in her mind. She still remembered how Emmy had inspected her feet for any irregularity over the following month. Maia had learned to be wary of Tansi's rivers and streams, and even of the small pond on the farm.

Next to Maia, Nafi squirmed restlessly, her face a mix of fear and eagerness to step into the blue.

"Attention please," Dill said loudly from a small podium he had dragged to one side of the pool. "I'm sure you have heard about two of the three tasks you are expected to complete before your final challenge. Here is your third — the upkeep exercises.

"After you have been introduced to your aquatic partner, you will swim together to a reef outside Zagran. There you shall perform checks and maintenance on the various marine creatures. This will help you bond with the environment outside, it will teach you to communicate with your aquatic partner, and it will improve your balance and endurance — all of which you will need to complete the final challenge."

Maia's mind drifted. She wondered how she was going to hang on to these creatures. *Are we supposed to climb on their backs, like riding a horse?* But the backs of the marine creatures would be too slippery to stay put and there were no harnesses on them that she could see.

Dill droned on. "Your partners have been assigned based on the affinity you have shown to various life forms, some evident from the manifestations in your Saska. The experiment with the Saska has partly been a preparation for this day. Now I will introduce you to your aquatic partners, and you will put on your air mask and step into the pool with them."

Maia stole a quick look at her Saska. Its waters had grown murky lately and much of the vegetation had wilted, but the Timiti still lingered.

What if the Timiti comes for me?

The trainer's voice sounded distant. "Trust your partners, depend on them. Consider them to be extensions of yourself. Only then you shall be truly successful. For starters, just try to mingle in. Now, let's begin."

Dill beckoned Dani and led her to a large table. A plethora of small instruments was scattered all over it.

"Pick a tool," he said. Maia watched as Dani grabbed a curved tube with glass ends.

Dill nodded in approval. "A scope is a good choice. Ready to meet your partner?"

He pointed at a large blue-green dolphin that reared playfully at the edge of the pool.

"Mikoo," Dani shouted and broke into laughter. From the way Mikoo bobbed up and down in the water with excitement as Dani reached out to pat him, Maia concluded that Dani and Mikoo the dolphin had known each other before.

Dani put on her air mask and stepped into the water. Slipping an arm around Mikoo, she straddled his back. In the blink of an eye, the dolphin dropped below the surface of the water and disappeared with her.

One by one, the contestants went forward to be assigned to their partners. Kusha was paired with Carine, a beautiful fish with mottled red-yellow spots. Nafi was assigned a funny-looking monkey-faced fish with an impatient demeanor named Aia.

All hell broke loose when Ren was called to the edge. A wave rushed up to meet the already agitated boy, and when the waters parted to show a mass of tentacles, he simply turned around, deposited himself in his seat, and refused to budge. A giant milk squid peeked over the rim, watching Ren as it waved its tentacles. But neither its attempts to draw attention nor the trainer's cajoling, had any effect on Ren who sat with a stony face, his eyes glued to the floor.

Maia's turn came soon after and she walked to the rim with trepidation. A joyful face greeted her at the edge of the water — the dolphin who had been playing peek-a-boo was the one assigned to her. Maia breathed in relief.

CHAPTER THIRTY-FIVE

It's not the Timiti after all.

"Maia, meet Keiki." Dill bent down and patted the young animal. "Ideally, we should have found you a Timiti whale, but unfortunately that is not something that can be easily procured. So, you have to make do with this one. She is one of our smartest, and I believe you will enjoy your time with Keiki a lot."

After Maia had picked a tool that Dill said was invaluable in assessing water conditions, she stepped into the water. The thought of perching stably on her aquatic partner was still worrying Maia as she reached for Keiki's back. But her fears vanished as soon as she touched the dolphin. It was the water gear—it had a strange sticky quality that almost glued her palms to the animal's body, very nearly like a spider's would. The soft surface swallowed Maia, and as Keiki dipped under, the world changed. Coolness washed over and soothed her. The freshness seeped into her spirit as Keiki sped through the chute leading out of Zagran.

The passageway ran out to the backside of the city and into a sheltered reef much like the one in the front of the atrium. Keiki burst into the area like a blazing comet, spinning in a dizzying corkscrew and almost throwing Maia off her back. Maia giggled at the energy of her little friend who slowed down considerably before heading to the nook where Kusha, Dani, and Nafi seemed to be having the time of their lives. On seeing Maia, they gathered close and looked eagerly around for the missing fifth member of the party. It was not possible to talk with the air mask on, so Maia tried gesturing to tell them about Ren.

Nafi's voice came clearly to her ears, surprising Maia. *Ren got a milk squid?*

Maia looked at the firestone bracelet around her wrist, realizing it had started working again and transmitting thoughts telepathically.

Yes, Maia replied. *And he wasn't happy about it. I don't think he'll join us, at least not today.*

Time to collect another strike from Bones, Nafi said with a sigh.

He'll come around, Kusha murmured.

I will not! An angry shout streamed through their minds. Ren was clearly very upset. *I'm never getting in the water, and certainly not with that basketful of tentacles.*

The fun of the experience was half-dimmed after that exchange. Maia worried about a possible strike from Aerika. She kept thinking of ways to cheer Ren up and convince him to try the exercise. It was not until hours later that their swimming partners carried them back up to Dill's classroom. Ren was still there, sitting with his back to the pool where the milk squid was lounging lazily and observing him. Ren did not speak a word or ask a single question on their long walk back to the dorms.

Chapter Thirty-Six

Chylomyhrra

R en's refusal to do anything with the water lessons continued through that week and also into the next. Palak distributed task lists to everyone for the hydrothermal project. The research and studies in that area came along pretty well, but in the matter of the milk squid versus Ren, everything remained at a stalemate. Dill tried his best to persuade him every day, but it seemed only like a matter of time before Aerika would be summoned. It was an anxious countdown to that encounter as Ren refused to yield. The rest of the contestants were slowly learning to communicate with and control their aquatic partners, and Maia was proud of how well she had adapted to her Keiki.

One glaring exception, an expected exception according to Nafi, was Loriine. She had been paired with a large sword-tailed fish with gray and yellow stripes. Not only did they not bond, but also something she did aggravated the poor creature so much that it threw a fit and took off. Left helpless in the water, Loriine would have sunk like a stone had it not been for the efforts of all who rallied around her immediately and carried her back to the class. She had since been assigned a new partner, Saem, a black leathery fish with a spotted tail, but this partnership did not show signs of a promising future either. Regardless, it did not stop Loriine from sneering and poking fun at Ren now and then, much to the annoyance of everyone in Core 21.

On the tenth day, the team came up from the reef to find Aerika sitting next to Ren. Maia's heart sank, and she rushed forward with her teammates to find out more about the situation. Aerika left the moment she saw the group approaching.

"Don't tell me we got another strike," Nafi said breathlessly.

Ren shook his head.

"So?" Kusha punched him lightly on the shoulder.

"So, nothing," Ren replied, flicking off the droplets of water Kusha's punch had showered on him.

"What do you mean nothing?" Nafi demanded. "What exactly was Bones saying to you?"

"You're dripping all over me," Ren said irritably, pulling his feet away from the shadow of the group. In their hurry to find out what was going on, no one had remembered to change out of their water gear.

"All right." Dani took a quick step backward and pulled Nafi and Maia back by their arms. "There's your space. Tell us now, please."

Ren stared at her for a moment then threw up his arms in the air. "All she said is I ought to give it a try, and maybe it won't be as bad as I think it is." He looked at the pool, sighing deeply as he gazed at the head of the waiting milk squid. "She said that I owe at least one ride to Chylomyhrra. That I should give her at least one chance of taking me out . . . her devotion deserves that much."

"Chylomyhrra?" Kusha chuckled loudly. "That sure is a pretty name."

"And . . . ?" Maia pressed.

"And I've decided to give it a try," Ren said.

"Yay! Take that, Loriine," Nafi yelled, waving a fist in the air. "We're not getting another strike." Before anyone could blink, Nafi threw herself on Ren in such a ferocious tackle that both toppled over the bench. Ren was not pleased at all, while Nafi was so happy that Ren's remarks and glares had absolutely no effect on the girl. She hopped and skipped all the way to the changing rooms, sharing the wonderful news with everyone on the way.

***

That turned out to be a day of surprises. After weeks of absence, Joolsae showed up at the RC.

"I'm so sorry I couldn't be of any help during the first challenge. My little brother got sick and my mom needed a helping hand. But I'll make up for it the next time, I promise." The unhappiness seeping from Joolsae's voice washed away all resentment Maia had toward her. Judging by the looks on the faces of her teammates, Maia knew they shared her own embarrassment for complaining about Joolsae.

"Never mind, Joolsae, taking care of your kid brother is way more important than running around with us." Even Nafi was all soft and gentle. "And we did well at the challenge anyway."

That night, while walking back to their dorms, Maia raised the subject of her meeting with Bikele.

"What do you think?" she asked. She had thought a lot about the situation, and with every passing day, she felt even more intrigued than before. She kept wondering about Bikele and how he knew Sophie. But then, there was the matter of Aerika's strikes. The group could not suffer because of her.

"I think we should go," Nafi said in a heartbeat.

"Go? We?" Maia stopped and turned to look at her.

"Of course. We'll come with you," Kusha waved at her dismissively. "You don't expect us to let you prance around in the dark, do you?"

"But—" Maia started to protest.

"I thought we had talked about that already," Ren interrupted. "We can't let you go alone. What if he kidnaps you or something?"

As Maia rolled her eyes and made a face at Ren's comment, Dani chimed in solemnly.

"The issue is—how do we get to the tenth floor?"

"I thought you'd know," Nafi replied.

"Can't we take the elevators down there?" Ren asked. "The only restrictions were going up to the government floors. No restrictions on going down, right?"

"You're right," Dani said. "There are no restrictions in taking the elevators down. But they only go so far, to the fiftieth floor to be exact. The rest is only accessible through the chutes by watercraft."

"And we don't have any watercraft," Ren groaned.

"That makes it easy then . . . we won't go because we can't go," Maia concluded. A pain she had not expected inched up from her heart and formed a lump in her throat; maybe it was disappointment, or maybe it was just fatigue. As Maia turned to leave, she realized how much she had anticipated the meeting with Bikele, even while she had not consciously entertained the thought.

Dani tugged at Maia's sleeve. "Don't give up so soon, we shall find a way."

Maia managed a brave smile. "Let's instead think about Ren's first swimming lesson tomorrow."

***

Time flew fast and furious the next day, and before long the team found themselves in Dill's classroom. Even Aerika had decided to be present on the momentous occasion. Chylomyhrra seemed to have understood as well, and she was the most excited of all. Her tentacles flew wildly all over the pool, hitting the other occupants of the waters and creating much of an uproar in the process.

Ren took hesitant steps toward the edge of the dive bay when Aerika beckoned him.

"Hurry up, slacker," Loriine said in her usual unkind drawl. "If you take any longer, your stupid, ugly blob of fat will kill the rest of the rides with her silly excitement."

"Shut up, Loriine," Ren shouted.

"All right, Ren, keep coming now." Aerika ushered Ren closer to the pool where Chylomyhrra waited eagerly with an arm over the ledge.

"That was unkind and mean and . . . that calls for a strike," Ren looked beseechingly at Aerika as he walked closer to the milk squid. "Loriine has no business calling Chylomyhrra names."

With that declaration, he put on his air mask and fell feet-first into the water. Chylomyhrra bobbed up in surprise and then vanished, tentacles and all. Up on the ledge, Aerika flashed a small smile, the first smile Maia had seen on her face.

Aerika turned to Loriine when the surface of the water had stilled a little. "I agree with Ren. I also think that calls for a strike," she said.

As a shocked Loriine opened her mouth to say something in her defense, Aerika raised a decisive hand. "I would not argue if I were you. The way you behaved goes against everything we are trying to teach you here. If it were just up to me, I would throw you out of this contest right now."

Loriine did not say another word but quietly followed everyone else into the water for the daily upkeep exercises. Aerika left the room as the trainees took to the water. Maia and her friends caught up with Ren, but the boy was so busy spinning in circles around the reef that he did not even glance at the approaching bunch.

Look at him, Nafi said reproachfully over the wristband communicator as Ren tried a somersault over Chylomyhrra who seemed to enjoy his antics every bit as much.

Yes, just look at him. I better go and work on my balance, Kusha said before turning Carine away to practice some balancing maneuvers under the arched entryway to the reef.

Since that afternoon, Ren was transformed into the happiest person around. Maia's spirits lifted on seeing her friend's happy face, even the disappointment of not being able to meet Bikele had faded away.

CHAPTER THIRTY-SEVEN

UNDER THE ICE PACK

Nafi had a habit of walking around her teammates' workbenches, observing them work. One morning, as the teams built their converter units during Palak's session, she peered at Ren's desk.

"What's that you're building? Doesn't look like a regulation unit."

Ren sat with a small silver-blue cylinder in his hand that looked a lot like the micro-converter hydrosol units. But when Maia looked closely, she realized that Nafi was correct. As alike as the cylinder seemed from a distance, it was definitely not the regulation units they were required to build.

"Nothing important," Ren said quickly before slipping the questionable piece of equipment into his pocket. Then he casually picked up a set of tools and bent over some pieces of metal, ignoring Nafi who stood there for a bit before turning away sullenly. She grumbled for a while, but no one else was eager to press matters any further. A new announcement came soon after, one that brought enough excitement to make Nafi forget all about the silver cylinder.

The trainers announced it was time to visit the energy farm where the teams were expected to install their micro-converters. They led the fifteen teams to the Dive Bay on the 200th floor, and into a giant gray Aqumob similar to the one they had made the journey up from the Karnilian Caves.

Their path lay in a direction away from the Karnilian Caves, Maia noted. First, they went sharply upward and then north from Zagran, skimming along below the waves. They could see the sun shining above the surface, its golden rays seeping through the light blue waters and making it sparkle like a liquid gem. Maia sat spellbound, fascinated by the tiny ripples that caught the light and glistened. Numerous fish swam alongside the Aqumob, their bodies glittering, transporting Maia into a magical world.

A little way through the journey, Palak handed out maps. Maia realized she was right; they were indeed headed north toward the Third Continent of Tansi. The Aqumob was following the Intercontinental Cold, a strong northward stream of currents between the First and the Third Continents.

"As you might have already deduced from the maps, we are heading northward," Dill said. "Our destination is the Roqowist farm on the continental shelf of the Third, where we have one of the biggest near-surface installations of hydrosol converters. These micro-converters use both the power of the sun and the force of the water to generate energy. Since these are small units, we have to install millions of them to generate enough usable power. As you should know by now, these units are mounted along the reef walls and the stream of currents. The Intercontinental Cold, being one of the strongest currents up north, was an obvious pick for a Roqowist farm. Unfortunately, however—"

"There . . . I can see them," an excited shout filled the air. A girl was pointing eagerly to the left of the Aqumob.

Maia peeked outside, as did everyone else around her. The Aqumob had drifted close to the gray rocky walls of presumably the Third Continent. Perched on the wall were tiny units similar to the ones they were building themselves, in never-ending rows that stretched in all directions.

"Well, not exactly," Palak said. "These are the Challowist farms. A Challowist farm is like a giant recharging station. The units used here are micro-converters also, even smaller than the units you are building. These, however, are used to power smaller devices that we carry around."

"Like the LumTorch," Maia exclaimed, remembering what Dani had mentioned about the Challowist farms.

"You are right." Palak smiled. "A LumTorch is powered by three micro-converters that have been charged in a farm like this. Once a micro-converter runs out of its stored energy, it can be brought back here to be recharged and reused. Any questions?"

"Are the Roqowist farms built differently from these Challowist farms?" Karhann asked.

"Yes," Palak replied. "Roqowist farms, like the one in the Karnilian Caves or the one we are about to visit today, are much bigger sources of energy than these. The power from a Roqowist farm is fed into a power grid that runs through our cities, supplying energy. Now, let's allow Trainer Dill to continue."

"Thank you," Dill said. "As I was saying, unfortunately—"

"That doesn't look like a rock," Kusha exclaimed, squinting at the Challowist farm. "It seems like a metal enclosure of some kind."

Again, Dill was forgotten as every head peered to look at what Kusha was talking about. It was barely noticeable, and Maia had to gaze for a while before she spotted it. It was true—something metallic formed the walls of these farms, gleaming and shining in parts as it caught the light.

"Hmm . . . good observation. You are correct. These units are hung on a metal backing, not on the natural rock surface. However, I am not sure if I could explain it all to you," Palak commented. He looked inquiringly at Dill, who nodded gravely. As if reassured by the gesture, Palak started.

"That is the Seal of Separation," he said, grimacing. "It was built after the Collapse, around the time when the land was scorched and the Solianese civilization fell. The Third Continent was the seat of Solianese power; the biggest megalopolis, the capital of Korobieltes, sat right on this shelf. As the city fell to ruins, gases and corrosive acids flowed out of the cities and into the land, poisoning the terrain and everything on it."

He paused for a moment and shot a quick glance at Dill, who looked on pensively. Maia wondered what was making the trainers so anxious and if it was because of Aerika's directive of not discussing politics. But this was hardly that; it was more of a history lesson. She could not fathom what harm could be caused by knowing more of their pasts.

"Since all the poison that was already destroying the lands could flow into the ocean and kill the living waters that we called our home, we, the Jjord, decided to seal the walls from the top to a certain depth. We started slowly, cordoning off one area at a time, eventually building a whole wall around the seas. There was a time when the shorelines used to be patrolled routinely to prevent any accidental contamination. Then we built these walls to rise high up along the coasts, to keep anyone from entering the waters."

Maia remembered a visit to the shores of Miorie long, long ago. There were four of them—Cousin Sana and Uncle Alasdair, Herc, and Maia. It had taken a day to get their passes to see the seas, and they had only been permitted past the walls after each person was carefully sanitized.

"What if something falls from the sky?" Ren asked. "How will you protect the waters from that?"

"Well, we have ways—more effective and efficient ways to shield ourselves now," Palak replied. "But at the time though, this was the only way we could think of, so we did what we had to do."

He paused briefly. Maybe it was the way the light fell on Palak's face, Maia thought it brightened suddenly.

"Maybe someday, when we have nothing else to worry about, we shall bring down those ugly walls." Palak smiled and turned to Dill.

"Now, no more interruptions until we have finished with the details of the Roqowist farms."

"Yes, I hope I get to finish this time," Dill said with a loud chuckle. "As I said, it is unfortunate that the Intercontinental Cold stream is strongest along one of the most difficult terrains on Tansi. It is along the Ice Shelf of the Polar North, the frozen expanse named the GeiFonz Icecap. The GeiFonz Roqowist farms line the sides and the bottom of these ice packs, and that is where we are heading."

Dill stopped, looked around at the worried faces, and grinned.

"You may now ask questions," he said.

There were no questions to be asked; what they had heard so far was thought-provoking enough. Maia was anxious now for a glimpse of the ice packs of the Polar North. Soon the Aqumob sunk lower, maintained depth for a while, and then rose upward again. Maia gasped aloud when they came close to what seemed like an infinitely long roof above them. It was a roof of solid ice, and its bottom was jagged. In every fold of the serrated bottom sat the metallic body of a converter. This went on in all directions, as far as their eyes could see.

"That, my dear children, is the GeiFonz Roqowist farm," Palak declared. "And that is where you will install your hydrosol converters."

Maia held her breath.

This is a long way from Zagran and the waters will be cold. How would we —

Dill pointed at one corner of the farm that looked lighter. It was only the green-blue shadow of the ice, there was no dark metal installed into it yet. Engraved in nooks and corners were plaques that bore the names of each team. Ren spotted their name; Core 21 had been assigned a particularly narrow ledge that curved upward into the ice, a space that looked challenging to reach.

"Nice," Dani sighed. "We've been allotted the toughest corner."

"Of course," Nafi said with a loud grunt. "Bones likes to take special care of us."

Maia was scared herself, but she still had to reassure her

teammates. "We just have to train harder, that's all."

No one replied. A nerve-wracking silence had just about engulfed the insides of the Aqumob when a voice rang out.

"Excuse me, sir?" Jiri was waving frantically at the trainers. "Do we have to use Aqumobs to get here during the challenge?"

Palak and Dill shook their heads in unison. Then Palak replied, chuckling loudly, "Oh no, you will ride with your aquatic partners."

"A-all the way from Zagran to . . . here?" Jiri clearly was having trouble even comprehending the idea, and Maia could not blame him — what Palak just said was unbelievable.

"Yes, of course," Dill chimed in. "That is why it is important to take good advantage of your upkeep lessons. Improve your endurance, you shall need it."

No one spoke much after that revelation. Soon after the viewing, the Aqumob turned around and headed back to Zagran. After worrying for a while, Maia decided to enjoy the ride instead of fretting over what tasks lay ahead. There was enough to agonize about at the moment; the not-so-immediate future could wait.

CHAPTER THIRTY-EIGHT

THE LADDERS

Aerika stopped by every now and then. She usually walked around the room supervising the activities, talking to the instructors, collecting feedback, and observing everyone. The days she came by — her eagle eyes scanning every person — passed slowly. There was no opportunity for conversation, no chance of giving in to a moment of slack, and no fun. It was on one such day in Palak's classroom that the unthinkable happened.

It started with an earsplitting scream. Maia dropped everything and sat up straight, alarmed beyond belief. Then the scream came again. It came from right behind them. Before Maia could turn around, Nafi burst into a fit of loud giggles. She pounded the desk with her fists, her mad chuckles growing louder with every passing moment. Maia tore her eyes off the girl and gulped hard to stop a chuckle from escaping her lips as she stared speechlessly at Loriine.

Loriine sat frozen. Her eyes were wide with terror, her face pale and mouth agape. It was her head. It had turned into a pincushion of sorts, as each hair stood on its end. Her hair crackled strangely, and it seemed like the strands were electrified. Next to her, Karhann sat blinking rapidly. All eyes were on Loriine, who seemed fine in every way other than the shock of getting an unexpected hairdo. Soon, bouts of giggles spilled from every corner of the room.

"Are you all right?" Aerika had marched over quickly. She spoke in a very serious tone and cast an annoyed glance at the still wildly cackling Nafi. "What happened?"

"I . . . I don't know, I just picked this up." Loriine howled. Tears streamed incessantly from her eyes. In her hand was a small silver-blue cylinder, something Maia remembered seeing with Ren not too long ago. She looked at Nafi, who must have recognized it as well, for she stopped laughing immediately and her eyebrows knit into a frown.

"Let me see it." Aerika reached out for the offending object. Maia held her breath when the instructor touched the device, and she heard Ren inhale sharply behind her. But except for a sharp crackle at the instant Aerika picked up the cylinder, nothing untoward happened.

"Seems like a static electricity generator," Palak said. He had walked up to Loriine's desk and was now peering closely at the small device. "Where did you get this?"

"It was . . . sitting here . . . on my desk," Loriine wailed. She kept running her hands through her hair, trying desperately to tame her mane, but the effort only made it stand up even more.

"All right, no harm done, you will be fine soon," Aerika tried to comfort the girl. She turned and shot an angry look around the room. "And I have had enough of this senseless laughing. I do not know how this thing got here, but if I find any of you responsible for this silly prank, you can definitely count on some punishment."

The session returned to normalcy soon after that, normal in all respects that is except for Loriine's endless sniffles, the stray giggles that arose from all over the room, and the glares from Aerika that followed. It was not until they were walking back to the RC that anyone got a chance to talk to Ren.

"Are you crazy?" Nafi went first. "Pulling a prank like that . . . as if we're not in enough trouble already."

"I don't know what you're talking about." Ren shook his head and walked on, looking unruffled.

"Weren't you building that thing the other day?" Maia asked, stopping to face Ren. She was concerned. While the trick was undoubtedly funny, they could not afford to get another strike. Ren looked away. Then he looked back at Maia again.

"Yes, I was. I built it just to get back at Loriine. It was harmless, just a shot of static, that's all," he replied. "It'll keep her quiet for a while, don't you think?"

Kusha laughed and patted Ren on the back. Dani did not say a word, but Nafi was more than eager to express her candid disapproval when a still-sniffling Loriine walked by, her hair still winning its fight against gravity. She looked accusingly at Core 21 as she passed, with Baecca throwing a dirty glare in their direction as well.

"I know it's them," Loriine sobbed.

"Ignore those worthless tramps," Baecca replied. "We'll get them in the next challenge."

"Serves her right," Nafi said when the troupe had disappeared from sight.

"Told you so," Ren commented wisely.

No one in Core 21 spoke on the topic after that. Loriine remained relatively quiet from then on; the days followed an easy, regular pattern right up to the evening of the meeting with Bikele. So far, no one had come up with a single sensible solution to the problem of getting to the tenth floor. Maia had given up on the plan. It was disappointing, but she bore the dejection stoically.

***

Late that evening after dinner, Maia and Nafi sat poring over some problems related to their hydrosol convertor. Dani, who had been suspiciously missing since the afternoon, burst into the room and balanced herself at the edge of Nafi's bed. She held a piece of paper in her hand. Nafi sat up immediately.

"We have to talk." Dani waved the roll of paper. "Outside, now, the boys are waiting."

Nafi was out the door in an instant, as if she had known all along what exactly to expect. Maia was confused; she shuffled slowly out of the room, ignoring the stares from the three other occupants, particularly the hostile looks from Loriine and Baecca.

Kusha and Ren were at the atrium, waiting for the girls to arrive. Dani kneeled in front of the bench facing the glass and spread out a hand-drawn cross-section of Zagran.

"This is the fiftieth floor." She tapped on the top floor of the drawing. "This is where the elevator ends. Now, getting from here to the remaining floors below is possible, as we all know, only through the—"

"The waterways," Nafi piped up.

"Yes, you're correct," Dani said.

"But?" Ren blurted. "There's a 'but,' right?"

"Yes." Dani laughed. It was a burst of carefree laughter, a Dani-like laughter Maia had missed hearing for the longest time. "There is indeed a 'but,' as I found out tonight."

Maia leaned closer; the map looked complicated. A maze of what appeared to be staircases ran through the sides of the building, ending in the lowest level of the city.

"There are ladders." Dani took a deep breath before pointing at the complex series of markings on the map. "These haven't been used in a while, practically abandoned except for maintenance work or some such thing. So, we don't know if they're safe at all. And—"

"We'll try," Kusha interrupted. Dani looked up at him, and her face dimmed like a light had been put out. A stifling silence fell.

"Other than the ladders not being safe, what else should we worry about?" Ren wondered aloud.

"Bones, of course," Nafi chimed in. "But then, she has become quite a buddy of yours."

"Shut up, Nafi." Ren glared at the girl before turning back to Dani. "Dani?"

Dani drew a deep, long breath. "We're talking about climbing down forty floors." She looked squarely at Ren, Nafi, Maia, and then back to the diagram, specifically avoiding looking at Kusha. "The question is, can we endure the climb down and back up?"

"No!" Maia said emphatically. There was no way she was going to take her friends down a set of broken-down ladders into a situation likely filled with danger. She could live without knowing a little less about her mother, but she would die a thousand times if anything happened to any of her friends on this crazy adventure. "I will *not* agree to this. We are *not* going anywhere."

"Well, too late now." Nafi made a face. "Poor Dani has been into so much trouble finding out all this for us."

"Yes, I agree. We can't back off now." Ren shrugged and looked away quickly when Maia frowned.

"I vote for going," Kusha said simply.

Dani nodded and smiled. "I'm going too, Maia," she declared. "Are you coming with us or not?"

Maia stared at her friends for the longest while, not knowing what to say. No power in this world would dissuade this bunch, and she definitely did not stand a chance.

Ren held his fist forward at the center of the small circle.

"Together," he said.

"Together." Kusha's fist flew in.

"Together," Nafi and Dani followed in unison.

Maia was the last to go, the hesitation in her still unrelenting when she put her fist on top of the little pile in front of her.

"Together," she whispered.

CHAPTER THIRTY-NINE

AT THE WATER LOCK

They sneaked out of the dorm a little before midnight, while all the others were sound asleep. The trip down the elevator to the fiftieth floor was eventless. There were not too many people around, and of the few who busily walked past, no one seemed curious about a bunch of kids.

The fiftieth floor was a public floor, a lowly floor. Maia felt the difference immediately—everything seemed dismal and colorless down here compared to the floors they lived on, and a world seemed to separate the two. Down here, a lot of dreary work seemed to be done. Traces of that toil lingered in the dull floorboards and grimy half-scrubbed walls. Bare corridors spoke of a hard life. Dani led them quickly past the first set of corridors that stretched across the width of Zagran to the smaller set of passageways that ran along the edge of the city. She paused, counted, picked the third corridor, and walked briskly into it.

"There it is." She pointed at a door on her right. "The ladders should be in there."

"Let's find out." Kusha tugged at the handle.

The door opened with a loud screech making everyone jump in surprise. A strong musty smell of a long-closed damp room hit Maia right away. It was powerful and unpleasant. Kusha paused at the open door briefly before walking straight to the ledge of the row of ladders. Slowly the rest of the group followed him inside. It was a small stairwell, and the ladders went around the square cage of the well in a prolonged spiral down to the bottom of Zagran. They were made of open metal gratings, not shiny anymore, but not rusted either. Small lights shone dimly in their half-broken holders, casting long, strange shadows on the damp, unpainted walls. It was a depressing path that lay ahead, a laborious one as well.

"We better get going," Kusha said, starting to climb down. "It doesn't feel half as bad as it looks."

"That's good to hear." Nafi was on the rungs in the next instant.

They clambered down slowly, clawing at the metal bars, reaching out for the dark walls for every bit of extra support they could get. Every floor opened onto a platform that extended into the stairwell; between each floor were three ladders. Dani kept count of the number of floors they passed, an important task since it was bad enough climbing down the stairs, and no one wanted to do it more than what was necessary.

Halfway down, on the twenty-first floor, Kusha came to an abrupt halt.

"Stop, everyone," he shouted. "The steps are a little soft on this one."

"Which one?" Ren shouted back.

"The one that I'm stan – " His voice faded into a muted shout as the ladder he was standing on bent abruptly and swung freely downward. Kusha slid down the broken rails, hit the stairs a level below, and collapsed in a jumbled heap.

"Kusha," Maia screamed in panic.

Not a sound came from Kusha. Above him, Nafi crawled to the brink of the unbroken section. "I'll jump," she declared after a while.

"What do you mean?" Ren asked. "Don't do anything stupid."

"Nafi, stop talking nonsense," Maia shouted from the top of the queue.

"She's right. That's the only way to get to Kusha," Dani said in a tone that made Maia look at her in surprise. A cold conviction had overpowered her usually soft voice, making it sound almost like Aerika's. "Do what you have to do, Nafi. Just be careful."

Nafi nodded, scrambled down to the edge, and dropped herself to the lower level. Her feet narrowly missed the rungs, Maia could hear her knees scrape against the metal, but as Nafi slid downward, her hand grabbed the rails and she held. Kusha groaned and stirred as Nafi found space to kneel beside him.

"Are you all right?" Nafi asked as Kusha slowly came to. He tenderly rubbed the side of his head, and he clutched at his right elbow.

"Yes," he moaned. He sat up groggily, looked at Nafi, and then looked up in concern at the other three still dangling above.

"Come on, Kusha," Nafi said, linking her arms through the boy's. "We need to give them room to land."

As Nafi and Kusha moved away from under the broken ladder, Ren slowly dropped down. Dani and Maia soon followed without incident. Kusha kept on massaging his arm so Maia assumed it still hurt, but other than being worried about it, there was not much anyone could do.

"Do you realize that we're stuck below this level now?" Maia blurted, as a sudden clarity swept through her brain.

The ladder was broken above them and the only path was downward. Without access to a watercraft, there was simply no way to get back to the UAAS.

"No point thinking about that now," Dani replied, striding to the next set of ladders. "We better get to our destination in time at least."

They continued laboring down the staircase without speaking; even the injured Kusha did not make the tiniest sound. After what seemed like forever, they reached the tenth floor.

Maia held her breath as she stepped out of the stairwell. They were on the ill-fated tenth floor where the most recent fire had broken out, claiming nineteen lives. Dark walls around them were a grim reminder of the terrible incident from weeks earlier. The entire floor was charred and blackened from floor to ceiling. Remains of burned items lay scattered around the place, and broken pieces of wires and trims hung free from the ceiling and the walls. It was a depressing sight, and Maia picked up the pace, eager to avoid looking around. A few turns around the corridor brought them to a series of dilapidated-looking rooms, each marked with worn-out numbers. Dani stopped at the one marked twenty-four. She looked back at the rest of the group, turned the handle, and stepped inside.

The shabbiest room in Zagran greeted them quite hospitably. It was dimly lit for sure, but what it lacked in luster it more than made up for in character. Dampness spread its wide arms across the walls, creating a pattern of moisture that was eerie yet fascinating. The floors were no better; they were uneven and rough, and patches of the surface had been plucked out unkindly. The only opening other than the door was a large porthole covered with an orange lid that stared angrily from the middle of the dark floor.

"That must be the water lock." Dani pointed at the orange-lidded porthole.

"Does that lead to the outside?" Ren asked, kneeling beside the lid to study it closely.

"Yes, these are the pathways from the early days when Zagran was being built," Dani explained with a lingering look around the room. "None of the fancy waterways or the transporter lines existed back then. It was a few floors of hastily made housing, not even insulated with care. Funny that I've never been to these rooms before, hardly ever heard of them."

"Why are they all kept open without guards or protection?" Nafi asked. "What if someone decides to break in from the bottom?"

"Oh no, that's not possible." Dani waved away her worries. "The bottom of Zagran is protected by a series of moats and locks. No one, except those with the highest government clearance, can pass through the moats into the city."

"Which means" — Maia thought aloud — "Bikele has such a clearance."

"Most likely so," Dani nodded.

"I wonder what time it is," Kusha said as he kneeled next to the water lock.

The loud pop that resounded through the small room, followed by the sudden opening of the lid just as Kusha's hand touched it, made them all jump back toward the walls. A shiny water-gear-covered head emerged slowly from the hole, gleaming eyes scanning the room from inside the air mask. Within moments, the dark figure hoisted itself into the room, closed the lid of the porthole, and took a few deliberate steps toward Maia.

CHAPTER FORTY

A STORY OF LOST FRIENDSHIPS

Ren rushed between Maia and the man. As Kusha planted himself next to Ren, Maia felt Nafi and Dani move closer to her on both sides.

"What do you want from Maia?" Ren demanded. They were all unarmed, and Maia knew that neither Ren nor anyone else would stand a chance against this man who was more than twice as large as the biggest of them. But she also knew there was no stopping Ren, or the rest, from trying to protect each other from whatever came their way.

"What are you? Her security detail?" the man asked as he took the air mask off. Strands of unkempt hair fell free and hung loose on his unfriendly face.

"Yes, you mind?" Nafi snapped.

Bikele chuckled and looked around at the faces. "Plucky bunch," he observed. He bent a little, leveled his eyes with Ren's, and bowed his head a bit. "I mean no harm to your friend . . . only need to talk to her in private."

"Well, this is all the privacy you'll get," Kusha declared. "I suggest you get talking fast."

Bikele seemed angry as he looked at Kusha, muscles tightened around his jaw, and his lips thinned showing a few his clenched teeth.

"Please, let them stay," Maia pleaded, taking a step forward. "We have no secrets between us."

Bikele stared at her for what seemed like an eternity before his eyes twinkled. Then he kneeled before Maia and gazed into her eyes without blinking as if she were a precious long-lost object that had been found again.

"How . . . you have grown. The last time I saw you, you were the tiniest little baby. Sophie's little baby girl. Oh . . . how we had celebrated the night you were born," he said, halting over every word as Maia stood in stunned surprise.

His hard features had melted into a softness that Maia had seen all too often on Dada's face. Love and tenderness streamed down on her and enveloped her in its warmth.

"What? How?" That was all Maia could manage to say.

"You were born under the seas, Maia," Bikele smiled radiantly as he waved his hand around him. "Right here in Zagran, this is your birthplace."

"You . . . you took Sophie back to Miorie?" Maia recalled Dada's account of the night he had first seen Maia at an inn in Miorie—a dying Sophie barely had time to place Maia's hand in Dada's. Maia had often wondered how such a seriously ailing woman had managed to come to the inn by herself.

"Yes, Zaara and I did," Bikele replied. He looked down at the floor, and when he looked up again, his face had hardened. "We asked the innkeeper to call on Sophie's father, and we watched from the shadows as he rushed in. We could not show ourselves—it would mean risking you. We left with you a note containing Sophie's wishes, along with instructions to destroy it. I had never hoped to see you again. But fate brought you back to me. I caught a glimpse of Bellator the other day, and I remembered a girl I had known who had wielded it. Then I wondered if it were you. And when Aerika called your name, I had no doubt in my mind — you had to be Sophie's daughter. In that instant, I knew we were all wrong. Sophie had planned to protect you by shielding you from your past, but there's no stopping destiny. What you really need is the knowledge of your past, of your mother's past. And I have decided I will help you, as much as I can, to rebuild it for you."

"Zaara . . . who's that?" Maia asked.

Bikele smiled and looked around the room again. The five youngsters stood around him, stiff and vigilant.

"It's a long story, kids, so you better sit yourselves down."

Nafi plopped down right in front of the man, and Maia and Ren kneeled next to her. Kusha and Dani remained standing behind the seated trio, watching the proceedings.

"I met Sophie and Zaara for the first time in Zagran, at the Super Convention of Energy Morphers hosted by the UAAS. The two brilliant girls from the XDA were the talk of the university, and everyone wanted to know them and be their friend. I did not care much, but as fate would have it, a botched talk and a misunderstanding later, I found myself chatting endlessly with the two. Zaara talked for the most part. Sophie was quieter. She was reserved and cautious while her friend was fiery-tempered and impulsive.

"When they left after the convention, I did not hope to see them again, but I was wrong. They came back and took up internships with our government, surprising a lot of people, including me."

"Dada said that Sophie lived here for a few years," Maia recalled.

"Yes, they both did," Bikele said. "We worked on the Damoclian Project together. It was a happy time. And our friendship grew stronger; we found deeper bonds in our shared concerns for the world and ideas that tied us together. But I knew there were secrets they kept from me; the shadow of darkness grew every day in their eyes. They would not tell me — I was not in their circle, they said."

"Their circle?" Nafi stared wide-eyed at Bikele.

Bikele nodded. "Yes, the Crae—"

"Craedonnen?" Maia blurted. Mahswa Tabrin had used that word, a Xifarian word that meant a "circle of trust."

"Yes," Bikele nodded. "It was the four of them: Sophie, Zaara, Asiyaah, and Raidyn. No one else could know their secrets. After a while, I gave up asking. I was happy with my friendship; I could do without the secrets."

He paused again, his eyes glazed. He seemed to search for happy memories in those days that had faded and time and again, his eyes sparkled.

"Then one day, Sophie disappeared. She did not say goodbye, not to me, not even to Zaara. I knew Zaara was heartbroken, but she bore it with strength. All she said was, 'I'm glad that Sophie could break the circle. Maybe one day I can tell you, Bikele, and then you would understand.'

"Another year passed, the Exchange happened and turned our lives upside down, and we still had no news of Sophie. I always suspected that Zaara knew, but she would not tell. One morning, I woke up to a loud knocking on my door—it was Zaara, and she was distraught. She had found out that Sophie was being held prisoner in the Gnelexian sector on Xif. They would kill her, she said. I did not understand much but I realized Sophie was in trouble, big trouble."

Something snapped inside Maia. Vivid memories of a conversation flashed through her mind. The Gnelexian sector—the fearsome prison run by the mind-reading Gnelexians. *No one survives their mind probes.* So Miir had said.

"About a week later, Zaara came to visit me again, this time in the darkness of night. She was dressed for travel and she needed me to come with her. I was about to ask her about our destination when she sat me down and said it was time I knew. She told me all about the Verto-balancer Capsule and what Sophie had done with it."

"You know about the Capsule too?" Kusha said incredulously. He was sitting on the floor with his knees pulled to his chest.

"Yes," Bikele replied, his tone guarded. "That's the reason I'm here tonight. How much do you know about that, Maia?"

"A . . . little." Maia hesitated. She had just met this man, and it was a bit too early to share everything about Sophie's message with him. But then . . . he seemed to know a lot already. "I know she broke it. She did it to save Tansi. And she wanted me to be careful."

"She worried about you," Bikele said solemnly. "Had it not been for recent events, I would have respected Sophie's wish of keeping you far away from your past. I would have kept the promise Zaara and I made to Sophie."

"But wait, where did Zaara take you? Did you break into the Gnelexian prison?" Nafi asked.

"Are you crazy? No one has *ever* broken into the Gnelexian prison, absolutely no one," Ren remarked.

"He's right. That's what Zaara said." Bikele nodded at Ren. "We were not about to plan a prison break. We were going to Xif because Zaara received an anonymous note asking her to come and get Sophie."

"And you trusted an anonymous note?" Dani's mouth fell open. She stood with her arms crossed, towering over the small group on the floor. "It could've been a trap."

"Could've been, but we didn't have a choice. Imagine if you were in my place. You were told that this was the only chance your best friend had to get out of that monstrous place alive. What would you have done?" Bikele asked. "You would have done the same. You came here because of an anonymous note from a stranger, didn't you?"

Dani sighed and looked away.

"Did you find Sophie?" Maia asked impatiently.

"We did find Sophie. We had been asked to be at the underpass of Ixiil, behind the fountain of Toomlas. And she was there. Someone had left her there, wrapped in a blanket, slumped on a bench. Why they let her out of the prison, who had contacted us, we did not know. All we knew was that this was our one chance to get Sophie back home. So Zaara and I took Sophie and got out of Xif as fast as we could. And we didn't stop until we reached Zagran."

"Sophie was sick already, wasn't she?" Maia whispered, recalling more of what Miir had said. *Gnelexian scans, along with the information they seek, suck out consciousness from the mind. A subject won't necessarily die but will exist like a mindless corpse.*

"Yes." Bikele nodded. "The bright and beautiful girl I had met the year before was nothing but a broken shadow of what had been. The light of the Sedara had consumed her soul, and the Gnelexian mind probes had weakened her consciousness. But . . . she was still alive. And when we brought her back to Zagran, we found a greater miracle. We found out about you, Maia, her unborn child."

Everyone turned to look at Maia. It was hard enough to hear about Sophie without the attention, and now with all eyes on her, it was near impossible to keep from tearing up. But Maia held strong; not even a sigh escaped her lips.

"And the miracle that you were, Maia." Bikele gently touched her cheek. "It was a wonder that you had survived the light that consumed your mother. We had not hoped for much, but you were born perfect in every sense. In one of her brief moments of clarity, Sophie had named you and asked us to take you to Miorie. 'Call her Maia. Take her to my father. Keep her safe. Don't let my life cast a shadow on hers.' And so we did. We took both of you to Miorie to your grandfather."

Bikele reached out, holding his upturned palms in front of Maia. Maia hesitated a moment before she put her hands in his. He cradled her hands; it was strange how safe Maia felt at the moment, holding the hands of a man she had not even known existed until a few weeks ago.

Someone sighed deeply, the sound breaking the stillness.

"And Zaara? What happened to her?" Dani asked in a subdued voice.

Pain swept through Bikele's face, twisting it momentarily.

"I haven't seen Zaara since that night in Miorie. We had to part ways. There was always a risk that we would be hunted down, so we decided to hide in separate places. If the Xifarians found us, they would find their way to Sophie's child, and we could not let that happen."

"You've been hiding at the bottom of the seas for me . . . so I could be safe—" Maia could not bear it anymore. The hurt overwhelmed her heart and spilled from her eyes.

"No, Maia, not just for you." Bikele wiped a tear from her cheek. "It was all done to protect our future. Sophie did her part, and we chose to do ours."

"What happened to the rest of the circle?" Kusha asked. "Did you hear from Raidyn and Asiyaah?"

"I never heard of Raidyn again." Bikele shook his head. "But Asiyaah never left us; she was always a part of Sophie's unending nightmares. Every night Sophie would start screaming in her sleep. All she said was 'Asiyaah, no. Asiyaah don't. Asiyaah, I'm sorry.' And it went on until the very end."

"What does that mean?" Nafi asked. "She was begging? But for what?"

"I don't know," Bikele replied solemnly. "Zaara didn't say much about Asiyaah, but she seemed to think that Asiyaah could have helped Sophie more. 'She could have given Sophie a better cover' was all Zaara would say. And I have this . . ."

Bikele reached inside his water gear and held out a small notebook for Maia. "Sophie kept scribbling in it. You won't find anything meaningful, but it is something I had of hers. It's yours now. Asiyaah's name is all over it as well."

Maia slowly opened the notebook. It parted right at the center. Broken handwriting filled the pages from top to bottom. It was the same words over and over again.

ASIYAAH NO . . . ASIYAAH NO . . . NO . . . ASIYAAH NO . . . ASIYAAH NO . . . NO . . . NO ASIYAAH NO . . . ASIYAAH NO . . . NO . . . ASIYAAH NO . . . NO . . .

Maia shut the book with vehemence. The Xifarians had turned her mother into a madwoman, a raving lunatic. And no one paid for their crimes. It was not fair that so many people had to die or live broken lives because of the Xifarians.

"Was Asiyaah a student of the XDA as well?" Ren asked.

"No, she was not," Bikele replied. "She was a master. Zaara, Raidyn, and Sophie were her students at the XDA."

"Asiyaah," Ren pondered again. "Did Zaara tell you anything about her family?"

"No." Bikele shook his head vigorously. "She would not tell me anything about the other two. She said it was better if I did not know. I never argued—the less I knew, the less the possibility that the Xifarians would come after me. And I was fine with that."

Ren fidgeted uneasily for a while and blurted, "Asiyaah was the name of Miizuken's only daughter. She was a master at the XDA before her husband became the Xifarian chancellor. After her husband took office, she surrendered her position at the XDA and completely retired from public life."

"Miizuken's daughter? And the Xifarian chancellor's wife? That means she's Miir's mother, right?" Nafi deduced.

Ren nodded.

Maia recalled that Ren had told them once about Miir's grandfather Miizuken, the genius Xifarian inventor.

"Wait. How can you be sure this is the same Asiyaah?" Dani questioned.

"How many Asiyaahs do I know of who has been a master at the XDA about fourteen years ago and have retired since then?" Ren retorted. "Only one. It has to be her, and that explains why Zaara didn't want to tell Bikele more about her."

"Because of her powerful connections, she could harm him more if her involvement with Sophie became known," Kusha concluded.

"But hold on a moment. We're assuming this alleged involvement," Dani interrupted. "All we know for sure is Sophie and Asiyaah were friends."

"Zaara did not talk about it, but she always seemed to suggest that Asiyaah and Sophie were in it together. This plot to damage the heart of the Sedara was more Asiyaah's," Bikele said.

"And it's quite obvious from Sophie's nightmares that Asiyaah betrayed her and let her be captured by the Gnelexians." Kusha inferred, thumping his fists together.

"Well, it all fits together in an interesting way," Bikele said. "Sophie was captured right around the time when the new chancellor, Asiyaah's husband, came to power. This was probably a few months after the heart of the Sedara had been broken."

"You mean Asiyaah could've betrayed Sophie to buy the office for her family?" Kusha asked.

"I do *not* know that," Bikele replied. "But, it's intriguing that so many things happened right around that time."

"How could Asiyaah have betrayed my mother?" Maia felt drained. She could not even think clearly anymore. "They were a circle of trust."

"Don't fret over what you don't know for sure, Maia." Bikele placed a reassuring hand on her shoulder. "But then again, always be prepared to see people change, because they often do."

They sat in silence for a while before Bikele spoke again.

"I have to go now, Maia." He stood up slowly. "I hope to see you again soon. You all be careful now."

As soon as he opened the lid of the water lock, the stubby nose and smiling face of a snub-nosed dolphin popped up through the hole, its dark eyes glittering with mischief. Bikele broke into indulgent laughter as the audience shrieked in surprise.

"Meet Gibbon, my trusted partner over the years. He's blind, but he refuses to stop following me. And I cannot force him into retirement because he thinks he's still smart and strong," Bikele chuckled loudly. "Maia, your mother and Zaara liked to pamper him. Actually, those artificial eyes that he likes to show off so proudly were gifts from Sophie. I was just a struggling apprentice then, and had a hard time getting him fitted with a prosthetic fin after he had an accident about fourteen years ago. But then Sophie gave away two of the black pearls from her necklace, and Zaara, being the gifted healer that she was, fashioned a pair of eyes out of them. It all worked for

Gibbon—he came out as good as new and as conceited as ever."

After they had all said their hellos to a very excited Gibbon, Bikele prepared to leave.

"Now, we need to figure out how to get past that broken ladder," Kusha said, scratching his head as if to rouse his wits.

"What ladder?" Bikele asked. "You took the maintenance elevators down the side of the air shaft, didn't you?"

Maia looked at Dani and caught her blushing profusely.

"Tell me you didn't take the ladders down forty floors," Bikele said incredulously. "Well, at least I'm glad we talked about this. Take the elevators and stay safe, kids."

With another wave of his hand, he was gone. Ren shut the lid slowly, and Maia felt her friends shuffle around her. She had lost the urge to move. She stood gazing at the closed lock, yearning to run away with Bikele to his hideaway under the seas, to keep hearing as much about Sophie as she could.

Chapter Forty-One

Remii and the Apprentices

The world around Maia receded into a haze. It was as if . . . as if she was a thousand miles away from there, somewhere alone in a dark cocoon with nothing but the pain and the misery of her thoughts.

"Come on, Maia, we need to get back to our rooms." Kusha's voice was distant as he patted her gently on the back.

They tortured my mother . . . turned her into a living corpse. My mother gave it all – her life, her sanity – to save her Tansi.

"Maia, let's go," Kusha said again. And she took the first step and the second and kept on going. Following the sounds and the sights, the murmurs and the whispers, all the way to the huge black walls around the airshaft that ran like a spine through the city.

Now they're trying to restore the Capsule. And if they do . . . all the sacrifices Sophie made will be for nothing.

"Down those stairs," Dani said as the group turned a corner, pointing at a flight of metal stairs that wound down to a narrow corridor.

Tansi, Sophie's Tansi, is in danger. Again. No, wait; it's my Tansi now —

"There's the elevator," Dani exclaimed.

At the end of the passageway was another flight of stairs and a pair of huge elevator doors stood beyond them. The group had started walking briskly forward when a loud clanging sound made them stop. The elevator doors started to open with a prolonged screech. The last trace of daze cleared from Maia's mind at the terrible ruckus.

"Stand back," Kusha whispered. They quickly fell back a few steps and hid around the corner. Maia heard heavy footfalls—most likely a group of people had emerged from the elevator.

"Search Keif and Zeiss again," a man said. His hushed voice was cold and bitter. "There has to be something in there."

Maia peeped around the bend of the wall. Three figures clad in familiar black uniforms had stepped out of the elevator. A man she had never seen before walked out first. Following him was a young woman with bright red hair and a young man.

"Miir and Amanii? Who's that other guy?" Nafi whispered.

"That's Remii, Miir's elder brother," Ren whispered back.

Boredom and frustration were etched deep on Miir's pale face, but Amanii looked content.

"We are wasting our time," Miir's voice came up the stairs.

"Do you have a problem with following my command? Or maybe you have a better idea?" Remii snapped. "There is something down here for sure, the pointers can't be all wrong. You heard the chatter about Keif and Zeiss . . . it has to be there or somewhere nearby. The sooner we find it, the sooner we can get out of this mess. So I suggest you stop trying to prove me wrong like you always do and search again."

"Remii, maybe Miir is right. We have looked in there a thousand times over and found nothing." Amanii spoke up hesitantly. "We should look elsewhere as well."

"My dear Amanii, try once more. Use the weapon if you need to. Do what you have to do, tear the place down, but just *find* the thing,"

Remii said irritably.

"Use *the* weapon?" Maia recognized Miir's voice, but it sounded a bit strange. Never before had Maia noted that tremor in his voice. "Do you remember what happened the last time we used it? People live around here and we will be risking—"

"You think I care about these people?" Remii hissed. "I don't. And if you had any sense left in you, you wouldn't either."

Nafi nudged Kusha. "What are they talking about?" she whispered. "What weapon? And what are they searching for? Does he mean the heart of the Sedara?"

"I don't know, Nafi," Kusha responded. "Just be quiet."

"I hope they don't decide to come up the stairs." Dani peeked from behind Kusha.

No sooner than she had uttered those words, Remii started up the staircase and headed toward the corner where Maia stood huddled with her friends, unsure of what to do. Behind them stretched a long, straight corridor, and there was nothing to hide behind, not even the smallest bump. The two groups would have to face each other; there was no other option.

"Act normal," Nafi said as the Xifarians neared the corner. "Let's walk into them before they walk into us."

Before anyone could come up with a better idea, Nafi traipsed out into the corridor. Kusha put on the face of a martyr and followed bravely. Maia, Dani, and Ren brought up the rear. Remii and the apprentices stopped on seeing the gang, their faces frozen in stunned surprise.

"Miir," Nafi squealed. Maia could have sworn that expression of happiness on her face was as good as genuine. "What a surprise!"

Miir frowned in reply. Amanii stared half-smiling, half-confused at the group. It was Remii who startled Maia the most. His brown hair was parted neatly on the right side, and he had a strange, cold, unblinking gaze of a reptile. His dark eyes darted from one face to another until they came to rest on Maia.

"We get to see the whole group today," Amanii laughed. "That is so wonderful. But what are you doing down here?"

"Came downstairs to meet a friend," Kusha blurted the truth.

Remii continued to stare fixedly at Maia amidst all the conversation. It was unnerving, annoying as well.

"We should leave now," Maia whispered to Ren who stood fidgeting next to her. He nodded eagerly.

"You should leave now," Miir said as if sensing their thoughts. "It is past midnight. You should not be strolling around here. It is *not* safe. I have told you that before, but you do not seem to get a hang of good sense."

The last part of his lecture was clearly directed at Maia, and she bristled at his tone. She swallowed the jab with difficulty, thinking only of their eventual escape out of this floor to keep herself from retorting.

"Come on, Miir," Amanii tried to make light of matters. "Don't be so harsh. They're just kids . . . let them have a little fun."

"Fun? This is no place for fun. They do not have the slightest sense of responsibility." Miir did not take Amanii's comments lightly at all. He seemed really agitated. He did not look at Maia, but she felt every word he spoke was a rebuke to her. "They were reckless on Xif, and they are no better down here."

Nafi shrugged and flashed the silliest grin possible. While the others exchanged rather amused glances with each other, Maia felt outraged. Maybe it was the suffocation from Remii's reptilian stare or her pent-up frustration from the conversation with Bikele, but she could barely tolerate Miir's cutting remarks.

"All this fame has gone to their heads," Miir grumbled. "Now they think they are superheroes of some kind."

Maia was not going to take it quietly anymore. She drew a sharp breath, filling her lungs to the brim with air that smelled of fire.

"How does what we do here matter to you?" she lashed out at Miir. "You forget that you're not our mentor anymore. Stop bossing us around."

"Maia . . ." Dani tugged at her arm, trying to placate her.

"You are quite a thankless girl," Amanii said, frowning. "All he did was show his concern for you all."

"I'm not dying for his attention or concern. I don't think my friends are either." An angry blaze was sweeping through Maia's mind. There was no stopping it. Someone screamed, *Asiyaah, no . . .* Asiyaah would pay for her betrayal, for the pain she had caused Sophie. Asiyaah's sons would have to pay as well. "And if he still feels like showing that he cares, he better learn how to do it nicely."

"That's no way of talking to your friends," Amanii countered again.

"Friend?" Maia spat out the word, the vehemence in her voice surprising even to her own ears. But more words kept rolling out, along with the rage. "I know better, Amanii. He was never a friend, and he never will be."

"We have to go. Now." Kusha grabbed Maia by her shoulders and pushed her past the trio before anyone had a chance to respond. They rushed down the stairs and huddled into the elevator as quickly as they could. Maia took one last look at the top of the staircase. Remii and Amanii had turned away, but Miir still stood staring. His eyes were vacant, much like Yoome's dead, lifeless eyes.

"Stay away from me," Maia shouted, as a wave of revulsion at his face swept through her whole being. An instant later, the elevator door screeched shut.

CHAPTER FORTY-TWO

DANI AND KUSHA

A concerned Dani peered at Maia's face. "Maia? Are you all right?"

"I'm fine," Maia replied, still fuming.

The elevator had not even climbed ten floors when she started feeling calm again. And as suddenly as it had come, the fury was gone, replaced by a terrible feeling of guilt and embarrassment.

"I don't know what came over me, Dani. I think I should go back and apologize to Miir."

"No one is going back," Kusha said firmly. "And you don't need to apologize to anyone. The way Miir talks to people, he deserves some criticism once in a while."

"I don't think we should go back either," Ren added. "Maybe we'll see Miir again soon, and then you could explain yourself."

"Yes, he's right, Maia," Nafi chimed in. "If there's anything we know about Miir, he gets mad at people easily, but he usually comes around. Don't worry too much about it."

"I . . ." Maia found it difficult to justify her actions or express her thoughts clearly. She rested her back on the cold wall of the elevator, trying to think what had brought this on.

"I was thinking of Asiyaah when we bumped into them," she confessed. "All I could think of was how she could've broken Sophie's trust. I hated her with all my soul, and Miir's words made me snap. I thought shouting at him was a way to get back at his mother, and that was wrong."

"Maia, it's all right." Dani slipped a comforting arm over her drooping shoulders as they walked out of the freight elevators and headed toward the atrium section of the fiftieth floor. "We will see him again, hopefully soon."

"No, Dani. It's not all right. I said some nasty things . . . unfair things. He saved my life. How could I have forgotten that? I . . . I said he was never my friend. How could I?"

"Cheer up." Kusha decided to try to bring some optimism back. "I don't think you should feel guilty at all. You had a right to feel angry after all you had heard about Miir's mother's hand in all this."

"We don't know much about that, Kusha," Nafi protested. "Not enough to be sure."

"We know a lot," Kusha shot back as they walked through the doors of the main elevator. "We know how his father accused Maia of things that he dreamed up, and we know his mother was somehow involved in getting Sophie imprisoned, and now we've also seen that creepy brother of his. And Miir himself is not beyond the shadow of a doubt. Does Maia need to feel guilty about ending what he started in the first place?"

Maia felt Dani's hand tighten on her shoulder.

"He did save us from Yoome," Ren said.

"Who knows what might have triggered that show of kindness. Maybe there's a plot behind it that we don't know about." Kusha was in a very unforgiving mood. "Knowing what I know about that family, I have my doubts. You know what they say, 'The apple doesn't fall far from the tree.'"

"How can you say such a thing?" Dani's voice was like the flash of a whip. Her lips trembled and her hand shook as it rested on Maia's shoulder. Not only was this the first time she had spoken to Kusha in weeks, but the intensity of her voice was surprising. She glared at Kusha with a ferocity that Maia had never seen in her before.

The elevator came to a stop on the 500th as a silent Kusha continued to stare incredulously at Dani. Dani walked out with Maia, never once letting her gaze off Kusha's face.

"Because . . . Miir and his family *are* vile . . . that's a logical conclusion," Kusha said when they had shuffled out into the atrium.

"Logical conclusion? And *you* would know about that, right?" Dani made no attempt to hide the ridicule in her voice. Maia looked from Dani's flushed face to Kusha's shocked one and back to Dani's again. This was far more than a fight over what Kusha had said about Miir; this looked complicated and deeper than just another difference of opinion.

"What do you mean?" Kusha managed to squeak after a very long silence.

"Is it that complicated, Kusha?" Dani sounded more sad than angry. "Tell us what conclusions we should draw about *you* from what we might know about *your* family. Go ahead, tell us about the tree you're from, we're here to listen."

Kusha stayed silent. No one else uttered a sound either.

"No, didn't think you would say a word," Dani said in response to Kusha's silence. "At least show some concern for people, give them the benefit of the doubt."

She shook her head again and turned to leave when Kusha sputtered back to life.

"W-what do you want to know?" he asked. "I'll tell you."

Dani stopped and turned around.

"You don't need to tell me anything, I already know." She looked heartbroken now. Her eyes sparkled like gems under the pool of unshed tears brimming at the corners of her eyes. "Growing up, I've avoided discussing the Damoclian Connector because it took my parents away from me. But now, thanks to you, I know every little thing about it. I know how it was broken. I know about your family. I know all about you."

Dani paused, but just for a moment.

"Hans always says I put too much faith in people too quickly, even in those who do not deserve it at all. And you've helped prove him right."

Dani stormed away toward the dorms.

There was not a thing in the world that could cheer Maia up at that moment. She stood staring at Kusha, confused, trying to make the tiniest bit of sense out of what had just happened.

CHAPTER FORTY-THREE

THE HOUSE OF THE SUN

Moments of painful silence trickled past. Nafi fidgeted endlessly. Maia could not decide what would be a better idea—to leave Kusha alone for a while or urge him to share his troubling secrets.

"We should get back inside," Ren blurted after a while.

"I agree," Nafi said, nodding vigorously.

Kusha spoke before anyone had a chance to move. "You must want to know what that was all about."

"Of course, Kusha. If you're ready to talk then I'm here to listen," Maia replied.

"I'm as ready as I'll ever be," Kusha declared, gazing at the rippling waters outside the atrium, his voice calm and remarkably composed. "You can probably guess that it's all about the Damoclian Connector."

"What's this thing you keep talking about?" Ren sat down on a bench and looked inquiringly at Kusha.

"Until I heard about it at the Council, I didn't think the Damoclian Connector existed," Maia said. "Most people on Tansi consider it a myth of some sort. But Bikele mentioned it too and now Dani—"

"Oh no, it's no myth. The Damoclian Connector was as real as could be, the path to our future, our hope of achieving greatness again. It was the last link that could tie the Solianese and the Jjord together, the only hope to resurrect Tansi."

Kusha paused for a moment before he continued.

"You know, the Jjord and the Solianese were one nation for a long time until the Jjord had been driven to take shelter in the seas. Since then, our paths have diverged. While the Jjord diligently developed new technology to harness the powers of the waters and nurture the habitats under the seas, the people on the surface continued with their old ways, stripping the planet of its resources for all it was worth.

"It would've continued that way for another century, had it not been for the virus. It killed millions, it killed industries, and in the process of trying to fight it, the Solianese used up all the resources they could lay their hands on. The Solianese civilization was nearing its end."

When Kusha stopped to catch his breath, Maia recollected the stories she had heard since childhood. "Those were the days of the Collapse, a hundred years ago. After that came the Scarcity—pillaging hordes ransacked towns and cities and villages. Fires burned sky-high, and millions of people perished as they fought to salvage whatever was left. Finally, one day, the Jjord came out to help us."

Kusha chuckled. "You'd be surprised if you knew what really happened, Maia. The Jjord didn't choose to help us willingly, we forced them to. After all the pain they had been subjected to by the Solianese, the Jjord had no intention of coming to our aid."

"Forced them?" Maia had never heard this before. "But how? We were on the brink of extinction. We hardly had enough to survive those days."

"We had the foulest of weapons . . . we had poison," Kusha replied. His eyes grew dim. "We threatened to release all our toxic waste into the waters they lived in. Of course, they had the capability of filtering the waters around their settlements, but the ocean ecosystem would've been wrecked. That would've been devastating for the Jjord."

"That's why they built the Seal of Separation," Ren exclaimed, recalling the wall around the coastlines that they had seen a few days ago.

Kusha nodded. "So the Jjord gave in and negotiations were soon underway. They came to the surface with aid for the survivors and they rebuilt the power grids enough to help us subsist. Most important of all, they agreed to build the Damoclian Connector with us. In return, we had to go back to a way of life we led hundreds of years ago and live that way until the planet was completely healed."

"And we did," Nafi whispered.

"We promised to try," Kusha said. "A few years later they started building the Connector—a massive power link between ThulaSu and Zagran, balanced between two enormous converter stations. The two ends needed to be in perfect and steady equilibrium, as anything short of absolute harmony would create a disturbance in the flow of power and result in a disaster of catastrophic proportions. If one end was disturbed, it would not only cause havoc on the opposite end, but that loss of balance would also impair the entire channel.

"The Solianese end of the Connector was placed under the protection of the Order of the Sun—an ancient group also called the Survansam, which had upheld peace and harmony over the ages. Their chief was the Sahiiraan of the House of the Sun. The path to the Connector was at the center of the Coronation Room in the Sun temple of ThulaSu, protected by an elite team of warriors among the Survansam called the Kausakas, who were handpicked by the Sahiiraan himself."

"The Kausakas are legends," Maia exclaimed, remembering the tales she had heard so often from Herc. "The masters of time and space, they can see people from across oceans, they can fly through the air, and their swords can spit fire. Those are the legends of

ThulaSu."

"Some of those legends are real," Kusha said. "I've seen a few masters myself, although not the real Kausakas themselves."

"I knew it. I always told Dada that they weren't just some tale, that they still exist."

"Maia, please," Nafi chided, and Maia fell silent.

"The Survansam took an oath to protect the Connector. They were the proud keepers, the only ones who knew the way into the inner chambers that held the Connector. Then came the night when the Xifarians broke into the inner chambers and damaged the Solianese end of the Damoclian Connector. The massive energy imbalance between the two converters blew up an entire sector of Zagran. The same night the Sahiiraan of the House of the Sun disappeared, as did the Survansam. This also happened to be the night of the Xifarian standoff at Miorie."

Kusha paused for a moment, then continued.

"The Damoclian Connector was destroyed, and our biggest source of energy was lost. We, the people of Tansi had to beg the Xifarians to save us by supplying us with the energy we needed to keep our cities and towns alive. The Xifarians were more than eager to give us a share of their energy in exchange for our submission. And we didn't have an option but to accept their terms. So, we allowed them to draft Solianese children for their mines on Ti every year. All because we couldn't protect the Damoclian Connector."

"What happened to the Jjord?" Ren asked. "Did they lose all capacity to sustain their end as well?"

"The balance was broken, and the converter station lost most of its generative powers. Their main power grid had also been damaged extensively from the massive imbalance. The explosion at Zagran that destroyed a large chunk of the city killed thousands. Dani's parents were probably among the ones lost. At the time, the Jjord had no choice but to depend on the Xifarian offer. Since then, they've rebuilt the grid and invented new sources of energy. Now, the Jjord can sustain themselves, but they'll never forget how they had put their faith in us and how we failed to defend it. The Jjord still believe we betrayed them, and rightly so. They too had to accept the terms of the Exchange, and every year they have to give away technological knowledge to the Xifarians."

"But I don't understand," Nafi interrupted. "How are *you* connected to all this? Why is Dani mad at you?"

"It's simple really." Kusha suppressed a sigh. "I belong to the House of the Sun. The Sahiiraan who took the oath to protect the Connector, the leader of the Survansam, was my granduncle. My family was held responsible for this betrayal, for Tansi's collective downfall at the Exchange. The House of the Sun, my family, was accused of sordid crimes, of selling their conscience lured by Xifarian favors."

"And Dani is mad because you didn't tell us this before?" Ren scratched his head. "So, who told her then?"

Nafi gave him a knowing look. "Must've been Hans. But how did he find out? And why didn't you tell us, Kusha?"

"He could've guessed from my headband." Kusha lightly touched the band circling his forehead. "But I didn't tell you because I couldn't. This is not something I'm allowed to tell anyone."

For a long while Kusha sat silently, his head hung low.

"I was barely a few months old when all this happened, and I've only heard these stories from my mother. My father couldn't bear the accusations hurled at our family and the shame of not being able to protect the Connector. He was the heir to the House of the Sun, but right after this terrible incident, he renounced the position of the Sahiiraan and left ThulaSu with his family. Some of the closest friends of the family accompanied him on this exile and his journey across the world. My father does not speak of his life before the incident or of ThulaSu. He wants to wipe off every link connecting us to the Order of the Sun. We're all sworn to secrecy, and as I tell you this, I'm breaking my promise to my father and my family. But I'd rather break my promise than lose another one of my friends."

Kusha touched the red headband again. "My father doesn't even like my wearing this headband, but I refuse to take off the mark of the sun. This is my inheritance, my right as a firstborn. Someday, I will restore what was taken from us and get my family's honor back. Someday, I will prove to the world that my granduncle was an honorable man who tried to protect the Damoclian Connector. Someday, the people of the world will show him the respect he truly deserves."

"You should tell Dani about your oath of secrecy," Maia suggested. "She would understand that."

"I don't think she will, and I won't try," Kusha declared stubbornly.

A brief poignant pause later, he forced a smile to his face.

"So, Maia, when I said that ThulaSu and the Order are all but extinct, I wasn't lying. Now you know why it's a good thing that you joined the Initiative instead of going to ThulaSu."

CHAPTER FORTY-FOUR

CONVOLHYDRAE

D ani had already left the dorm when Maia woke up the next morning. They found her in Palak's classroom, bent over the model of the hydrosol. Parts and tools lay strewn around her as she worked with undivided attention. Dani sat up at the sound of their footsteps, flashed an obligatory smile at the approaching quartet, and dived back into her work.

Maia cast a quick glance at Dani's pallid face as she settled down in her seat. She made a mental note to talk to the girl as soon as they were alone and tell her Kusha's story. If Kusha was not planning on explaining the situation to Dani, someone else had to. And Maia could not bear to see two of her friends fighting; she had to resolve it somehow.

The assignments were moving ahead well, and the micro-converters were getting built steadily, as were parts of the giant converter to be installed in the Karnilian Caves. For the second task, Core 21 was required to work closely with Core 34 which included a bushy-haired boy named Kenan and his teammates, and Maia was thankful for that pairing. The two teams hit it off instantly, making the whole exercise enjoyable.

One thing that everyone had started disliking was the upkeep exercise. Maia knew that no matter how much she hated the task, there was no escape from it. She also knew this exercise was important, that it would prepare her for the second challenge of installing the micro hydrosol converter in the GeiFonz Icecap. For that challenge, they had to cover the distance from Zagran to the Polar North, only with the help of their assigned aquatic partners. These upkeep exercises were nothing but practice sessions for the second challenge—they helped improve coordination, balance, and endurance.

While the benefits were understandable, the exercises had turned boring. The practice sessions were not free-form anymore; the contestants had to perform specific tasks of checking, cleaning, and sprucing up the reef. There was hardly any free time to romp around in the water with their aquatic partners. Dill had drawn up a schedule, and each team was assigned a place in the rotations. After that, Dill started the teams on endurance training. That mostly involved breath-control exercises. This was necessary, the trainer said, to ensure safety in case there was trouble with the breathing apparatus during the trip to the GeiFonz Icecap. The endurance training was messy, and Maia often ended up swallowing a lot of water, which led to a lot of coughing, wheezing, and near-death experiences.

And then there was the Convolhydrae. And the thing Maia hated the most—clocking her lap times inside it. The Convolhydrae was a gigantic glass tunnel built into an equally massive pool. It twisted and turned, and spiraled and curled. Sets of activator panels with switches were scattered along its length. The training involved getting into this tunnel with the aquatic partners and triggering specific switches on each panel. What made the Convolhydrae a pain was that it had to be traversed one person at a time. While the person inside the tunnel struggled with passing through the curves and enduring the humiliating falls and bumps, the rest of the contestants watched the show from the viewing chamber.

To make matters worse, Loriine was an expert at steering through the Convolhydrae and her teammates were not too bad either. They did not waste a single moment mocking and poking fun at the rest of the participants. Arguments and scuffles had become a common occurrence ever since the Convolhydrae exercise had started. The bruises that almost everyone sported on their bodies were not always from accidental causes.

"I hate all these assignments," Maia grumbled as she went over the day's task list. "This upkeep thing is terrible. The Convolhydrae is awful. Nothing is fun anymore."

"You've had enough fun already." Ren made a killer imitation of Aerika. "Be thankful for this fantastic learning experience."

"Yes, learning," Nafi scoffed. "Hanging upside down from a hotheaded monkey-fish, trying to measure the temperature of a coral the size of my fingernail . . . I would gladly give up on that learning."

Neither Kusha nor Dani showed any interest in joining the conversation.

"At least we didn't have to go the icecap first," Maia said, trying to look at the brighter side of things. "Can you imagine what Core 10 is going through now?"

Core 10, an all-Jjord team, had been selected to go first for the trial run from Zagran to the GeiFonz Icecap. From what Maia had seen and heard Core 10 was far from ecstatic about it.

"That too with all their experience in the water," Ren commented, hinting at the team's Jjordic heritage. "I'm nervous just talking about it."

"I still need a *lot* of practice with the monkey-fish." Nafi rolled her eyes. "Hopefully teach the girl some manners."

"Can't really blame her though," Ren snickered at the thought of Nafi's somewhat cantankerous riding partner. "She takes after you."

Maia broke into a mad fit of giggles as Nafi took a swipe at Ren, missed, and satisfied herself with a barrage of angry mutterings. Kusha did not bat an eyelid, but Dani gave a look of such utter disapproval at the joking trio that they sunk back into work without another smile. Things did not get any better after that; an uncomfortable lunch awaited them at the RC. To make up for the silence caused by two warring teammates, the vocal ones made more of an effort to make conversation.

"You'll be fine, Ren," Nafi said as they compared notes on how difficult it was to balance on their rides. "Chylomyhrra has arms. She holds on to you as if you were her baby."

Maia laughed and so did Ren. It was true, the milk squid had developed a fierce affection for the boy, coddling and fussing over him all the time.

"She *is* sweet." Ren sighed. "I wish I hadn't been so rude to her in the beginning. I'll miss her when I leave this place."

"You'll miss your girlfriend, huh?" The hysterical cackle came from the table next to them where Loriine sat with her team. She guffawed at her crude joke as her friends joined in with her. "I have to tell you, Ren, she's a real beauty."

"Shut it, Loriine," Ren retorted.

"The boyfriend is real touchy," Loriine replied, smirking.

"Don't be so mean, Loriine. It's his first love after all," Baecca teased.

Ren flushed a bright crimson as Loriine and gang erupted into laughter. Nafi squirmed to turn around and yell at Loriine, but Maia's firm grip on her arm kept her from doing so. This was not a time to get into a fight. Maia and her teammates rushed through their meal and left the RC as quickly and as quietly as they could.

Chapter Forty-Five

One Deal and Another

Some squabbles are destined to happen. As eager as Maia and her friends were to avoid getting provoked by Loriine, Loriine seemed equally eager to bring matters to a violent end. She traipsed into Dill's classroom one morning while most of the contestants were already gathered around the pool interacting with their partners. Ren was crouched where the entryway ended, holding one of Chylomyhrra's arms as she playfully sprinkled water over him.

"Are you asking her out for dinner tonight?" Loriine cackled loudly, making Maia want to sock her in the face. "Oh look, she has such pretty blistered hands."

Maia noticed Ren's fists tighten as Loriine's teammates burst out laughing. Chylomyhrra sensed the taunts; she pulled her tentacle out of Ren's hands and sank underneath the surface noiselessly. Ren quietly watched her vanish from sight. Then he rose to his feet and turned to face Loriine.

"You think you're beautiful?" Ren said in a threatening whisper. "Maybe you are. But does that make you better than us?"

A small crowd gathered around them eagerly.

"What?" Loriine asked, seemingly amused by Ren's question.

"I challenge you to a race." Ren crossed his arms and looked steadily into her eyes. "Dare to accept it?"

"W-what challenge?" Loriine suddenly looked a bit scared.

"Chylomyhrra and I will race you and handsome Saem through the Convolhydrae. The one who wins will take over all the upkeep tasks of the other." Ren paused. "Deal good enough for you?"

"You . . . must be out of your mind." Loriine rolled her eyes, shook her head, and waved dismissively at Ren. "I always time the best in the Convolhydrae. There's no way you and your lump of tentacles can beat us."

"Then you've nothing to lose anyway," Ren replied coldly.

"Is this some kind of a joke?" Loriine smiled rather uncomfortably. The unexpected challenge had rattled her somehow.

"I don't think Ren would joke with you, Loriine," Nafi remarked in the most unfriendly tone she could muster. "He only jokes with friends."

A titter of laughter rose from the crowd that had now grown quite large. Loriine flushed deeply and turned to her team. Baecca shook her head and whispered something in her ear.

"I'm not going to fall for that trick. You're trying to get a strike against us," Loriine said.

The crowd booed and jeered.

"What if he races for the whole team?" Kusha said so abruptly that Loriine almost stumbled. "Your team's upkeep tasks are on us if he loses."

Ren stared at Kusha for a moment before a radiant smile flooded his face. The crowd egged on as Loriine hesitated.

"That would mean we do yours if he wins," Loriine finally said. "That's too—"

"Well, Loriine," Karhann interjected, "you started it, so you can't back out now. Take the challenge and be done with it." He sounded a bit annoyed and disinterested.

"But how will we find the time?" Loriine persisted in her attempts to walk out of the challenge. "It's not like we can reserve the Convolhydrae for a race."

"That's no problem at all," Jiri intervened eagerly. "Dill always has meetings with Aerika at the beginning of the session. He usually leaves us alone for a while. We can easily get the race done during that time. Only if you're up to the challenge, of course."

Jiri's jibe was not lost on Loriine. She frowned and flushed before nodding her head.

"All right, I'm in," she said, and the crowd broke into a cheer.

"Yay, it's on," a tall Jjord boy shouted. He punched Ren playfully in the shoulder. "You go, Ren. Teach her some manners."

The chatter and the ruckus ended pretty soon as Dill walked in with a giant chart in his arms. After the groups took their seats, he hoisted the gigantic roll from a hook and unfurled it. It was a roster, a mammoth list of upkeep tasks assigned to the various teams over the upcoming months. He went on to explain how the tasks would be carried out, handed out maps and directions, but made no reference to the day's Convolhydrae exercises.

"Won't there be any practice at the Convolhydrae today?" Jiri voiced the question that stirred restlessly in Maia's mind.

Dill stared for a while at the boy, taken aback by the sudden eagerness. Then he slowly shook his head.

"No Convolhydrae sessions until next week. Some circuits needed repairs," he said, frowning as people all around him sighed in disappointment. He added after a moment of confused silence, "It seems you have come to like the exercises. Good!"

Maia could tell that no one cared for anything other than the Convolhydrae at this moment. If it were up to Maia, she would rush out to the Convolhydrae right then. But concern over Aerika's reaction to such an action triumphed over the urge to see Loriine beaten. She decided to focus instead on Dill's instructions. But as soon as Dill stepped out of the room, everyone huddled together.

"Can't believe we couldn't race today," the tall Jjord boy said.

"It's a good thing that we didn't. We need time to chalk out some rules," Jiri said wisely. "We can't rush into a challenge that has so much at stake. We need to make sure the race is fair."

Maia looked at the usually quiet and sweet-tempered boy with surprise. He surely was keen on the race.

"And what next? You'll want to be the referee?" Loriine mocked.

"Why not?" Jiri shot back, astonishing Maia again. "Do you know someone who can do the job better?"

"No, you'll do just fine," Karhann said before Loriine had a chance to speak. "We need to go over the rules first. When can you get them ready?"

"Soon," Jiri replied airily before weaving out of the crowd, pursued by an unusually large bunch of followers.

"What's with Jiri?" Nafi said as they walked out into the corridor. "Did you see how he snubbed Loriine?"

"Hope he draws up some good rules." Maia could only think of the race now. If Jiri's new personality made the whole thing a little fairer, Ren would stand a chance against Loriine's skills.

"We need to find a place to practice. This week's break is quite a stroke of luck," Dani said determinedly, speaking for the first time since the night before. "Loriine is quite good in the Convolhydrae, and catching up in a week won't be very easy."

"You find us a place and we'll work as hard as we can." Ren looked Dani in the eye, his face steely with resolve. "Trust me, I won't let you down."

"I know you won't." Dani flashed a small smile before she stepped forward and gave Ren a quick, unexpected hug. "I'll find something for you."

They were about to walk in the direction of the elevator when a cheerful voice assailed them from behind.

"Hey, you kids!" A smiling Joolsae swooped on the group. "Haven't seen you in ages." She glanced over each face before throwing herself on Nafi, catching her by the shoulders, pinching her cheeks, ruffling her hair, and driving Nafi into a state of open-mouthed shock.

"How have you been, cute little one?" Joolsae crooned, as Nafi still stood paralyzed. It was a good thing that Nafi was stunned into silence, Maia thought. In any other situation, Joolsae would have had a rough time after calling Nafi a "cute little one."

"How's your brother, Joolsae?" Dani asked before Nafi could get her bearings back.

"Huh?" Joolsae shot a bewildered look at Dani. Then she smiled. "Oh, he's fine. Ummm . . . I have another message from Hans."

She held out a bottle very similar to the one Hans had sent the last time only this one showed a series of cracks along the rim. Dani ran a finger around the bruised cap and looked inquiringly at Joolsae, who shrugged and sighed.

"I dropped it once. These things are so small and I have such clumsy fingers," she said defensively. "I hope the letter is intact. Do you want me to ask Hans to write another one?"

"No, this seems like surface damage. I think the contents are fine," Dani replied.

Joolsae stood in apologetic silence before she said uncomfortably, "Well, I have to go now. Is there anything else you guys need help with?"

There was nothing that Joolsae could help them with now, Maia was sure. She could not even help them when they had asked for it. No one else seemed to think differently either.

Ren shook his head. "Nope. We're all fine." He flashed a charming smile.

"All right then." Joolsae reached out to pat Nafi. By some questionable quirk of fate, Nafi's satchel decided to fall to the floor at that very moment. The head full of auburn curls dived toward the floor, missing Joolsae's shooting arm by a splinter. She got up from crouching on the floor only after Joolsae had left.

"Why does she have to make a pet out of me?" Nafi whined as the group settled in one corner of the atrium and Dani carefully broke the seal on the bottle. "I mean, it's not just me here. She has four more heads to pat."

"You're a cute little one, that's why," Ren said from his safe hideout behind Dani. Nafi growled and muttered and growled some more, stopping only when Dani started reading Hans's letter aloud.

As I have said before, please keep this message our secret. You are well aware of the talks that have been going on. You have been privy to one session yourself. I'm happy to tell you that we have finally come close to a deal that might somewhat avert the disaster ahead of us.

While many Solianese Houses have not been keen on participating in these talks, there are quite a few exceptions. Some Houses have been trying to bring about a peaceful end to this crisis. They have agreed to flush out every suspected member of the Resistance that they can find in their territories. But not just that, we now have reached a quorum to grant long-term UTAP for the land cities to the Xifarians. The Xifarians will be able to seek their lost treasure freely or round up the Resistance on their own.

To thank these Houses, notably the House of the Broken Seas, we have agreed to share our surplus energy with only those who have come forward to find a solution. To the rest who do not care, we have nothing to offer but our sympathies.

Battle lines have been drawn — it is all those who have pledged action to help the Xifarians find their artifact against the ones who refuse to even show up for discussions.

This pact to grant long-term UTAP and share energy is being drafted as I write to you. It will be signed and ratified within ten days by the Xifarians, our Solianese allies, and the Jjordic Council.

As Dani stopped, Maia tried frantically to grasp the meaning of those words.

"What does that mean?" Maia asked. "The Solianese Houses are not united in this? There should've been a committee representing all of the Solianese Houses, right?"

Nafi scoffed. "Never was and never will be. The Solianese have been divided ever since the Collapse. Each House to its own, so the saying goes."

Maia listened on, a bit startled at Nafi's words. Herc always talked about how the Solianese had been ill-treated by the Xifarians and the Jjord, but he rarely mentioned the divisions among the Solianese.

"So . . ." she started tentatively. "What will happen to the people whose House leaders are not present here? They'll not get help from the Jjord, and when the Xifarians stop the energy supply, the people in their territories will perish, won't they?"

"Obviously." Nafi shrugged. "If they don't migrate to an area that has some native source of power, they definitely will."

A prickly silence made its way in.

"What's worse"—Nafi broke the quiet—"is the long-term UTAP. It was bad enough when they had UTAP for a week during the annual drafts, but now they can practically show up anytime to round up an entire village and take them away."

"How can they make a deal with only a handful of houses? Shouldn't there be some voting or some such stuff?" Maia asked.

"They must have a quorum," Nafi said gravely. "That's the minimum number of representative Houses needed to propose a deal. As Hans said, quite a few Houses must've showed up in favor of this pact."

She fell silent for a moment while the rest of the team waited patiently. Nafi was a history buff—everyone knew that and respected her knowledge.

"The House of the Broken Seas has considerable hold, I know. They have a group of others who follow their every bidding. Together, they must've been able to make a good case for themselves."

"These Seas . . . people . . . who are they exactly?" Ren leaned forward, his brows knitted.

"A bunch of slimeballs. Their territories are about a thousand islands between the Second and the Third Continents," Nafi explained. "They're never up to any good. All they care about is getting favors at any cost from whomever they can."

"It's unfortunate that the Jjord found no one else but these people to side with," Kusha said in a vicious, scornful tone. "They should've had better sense than to depend on the slimeballs. Can't believe they chose to ignore the millions of lives that will be sacrificed by this biased pact. Who needs sympathies?"

Dani stood up abruptly. Her lips trembled and her face flushed in a fit of anger.

"There you go again! Why do you always have to be so quick to blame others?" Her eyes flashed. "Have you ever thought that the people who are to blame for the millions of lives that are about to be lost are none other than their House leaders themselves? At least the *slimeballs* chose to come here for their people and so they were rewarded for making an effort to resolve this mess. What are *you* doing? Where is *your* House? Aren't you supposed to be taking care of the people whom you chose to lead? Don't you think *you* are failing them?"

She stopped, shook her head, then turned and walked away. No one made an effort to stop her; it was of no use.

"What's wrong with her?" Kusha said after a while.

"Well, she *is* right, you know," Nafi admitted, she sounded spent and hopeless. "I know the Sahiiraan of our territory is not here because he won't have anything to do with the slimeballs. But in the end, *he* is the one failing my people, not anyone else."

"All right, but she could've said that nicely, couldn't she?" Kusha almost shouted. "And she could've done without the stomping away, don't you think? Why does she always have to scream at me like I'm at the root of all problems? Why can't she understand that my family and I are in a difficult position as well?"

"Because . . . you haven't actually told her that," Maia stated very cautiously.

But true as Maia's statement was, and as nicely as she had put it, Kusha flared up. He got to his feet and glared at the trio.

"So, it's my fault now? You want to side with her as well, do as you please." He stomped away in the direction of the elevators.

Ren, Nafi, and Maia sat in silence for a while before Nafi slowly got to her feet.

"I just remembered . . . I have to go see Palak about some *stuff*," she stated with an air of vagueness.

"What stuff?" Maia asked guardedly, hoping that she would not get yelled at again.

"Some stuff. Nothing important. See you later," Nafi replied, as evasive as before. She took off toward Palak's room before Maia could ask another question.

"I think I'll go and have a chat with Chylomyhrra," Ren said after Nafi had left. "I need to talk to her about the race. Explain matters to her."

"Do you want me to come with you?"

"No, I think I need some time alone with her."

"All right," Maia sighed.

"Sorry."

As Ren walked away, Maia trudged toward the elevators. This was going to be an evening to remember. It was interesting how things had changed over the last few weeks. She remembered their days on Xif, when they were always together and always ready to support and lift each other's spirits. Everything seemed to be broken now, and with the way things were going, the future seemed bleak as never before.

"Can't let this happen," Maia whispered as she leaned against the cool wall of the elevator. Her fists curled as she vowed to take action—she had to talk to Kusha and Dani and try to make them patch up.

CHAPTER FORTY-SIX

SEPARATE WAYS

Maia had a fitful sleep that night. Yet another nightmare had barged in, leaving behind bits and pieces of it in her memories the next morning. She remembered seeing Kusha dressed like a king, and he led an army of people into a dark forest. And then there was a war—a huge, big, and bloody war, with spears and bows and arrows. There was something dreadful about Kusha in the end. He lay on the ground in pain, and deep gashes on his body were oozing blood.

When Maia sat up in her bed, still reeling from the numbing heaviness of her dream, she had no idea of how badly things were broken in the real world. She found both Dani and Nafi missing from the dorm. Anja, who was the first to wake up any given day, informed her that Dani had left while she was still sleeping, and Nafi left a little later. Then, as Maia waited at the atrium for the boys to show up for their usual walk together to the RC, Jiri stopped by.

"They both left pretty early, Maia," he informed. "Would you like to walk with us instead?"

And so it was. No notes, no messages from anyone. They were just gone. Maia wanted to be angry, but she felt only sadness at the situation. Her team was like her family away from home, and the last thing she wanted was for it to fall apart.

"I have to talk to Dani," she whispered to herself as she walked to the RC with Jiri, Anja, and the rest of Core 13.

Breakfast that morning turned out to be a very enjoyable experience. Maia realized that since her team had such strong bonds of friendship, she had not had the time or the need to talk to people outside the group. Even after spending almost a year with Jiri, Anja, and many more, they were all strangers. Had she met them outside the classrooms, she would not know their names and probably would barely recognize their faces. And she felt ashamed of herself at the thought.

"We should've spoken before," she confessed to Nair, a boy who sat next to her, who was as pleasant and friendly as could be. "I mean, it's crazy that I didn't spend much time with any of you before today."

"Don't worry about it, Maia." Luem, a Jjord boy on Jiri's team, shook his dreadlocked head vehemently. "We've all been so busy with whatever they throw at us — we've hardly had a chance of having fun together."

"I just can't wait to see Ren race that snooty girl," Corinilus said as he passed around bowls of steaming hot morning grub. He was another friendly Jjord on Jiri's team. Maia noted how his green eyes always twinkled. "I sure hope he wins."

"Keep hoping, Corin," Anja said from across the table. "And keep praying. It'll take a lot of good thoughts to get Loriine beaten. You have to admit, she's good in the Convolhydrae."

"Ren is not bad either," Jiri countered. "All he needs is a little practice. I bet he's working on a good plan, which is why he's missing."

Maia nodded. She had no doubts that Ren would at least give Loriine a spirited fight to the end. She also hoped that Loriine would remain smug and overconfident, and not take the possibility of losing the race very seriously. That could swing things a lot in Ren's favor, and he needed every little help to win.

Maia walked into Palak's classroom with these thoughts swimming in her head. Kusha sat alone at his desk working intently with parts and pieces of his micro-converter. He looked up and smiled when he saw Maia approaching. If what the sage had said about her dreams being real was true, Kusha was going to get hurt in some way, and Maia decided to warn him.

"Be careful, Kusha," Maia said after narrating what she had seen.

Kusha laughed when he heard the details of her nightmare.

"Maia, it's something your mind conjured up after hearing my story. I mean, think about it, you heard about my lineage and you saw me as king. Then you were upset and worried because I fell and hurt myself while climbing down those ladders to meet Bikele, so that must've triggered the part about my injury."

"I hope it's just a stupid dream and nothing more," Maia said ruefully. She was a little upset at being laughed at, but Kusha's logic sounded reasonable. It must have been just her mind playing tricks.

"You left early this morning," she said and Kusha apologized immediately.

"Sorry, Maia. I should've left a note or something. I just wanted to get away quickly."

"Kusha . . ." Maia decided to make good use of this opportunity to bring up Dani. "I know you're upset, but I think you need to speak to Dani. You really need to tell her what you told us. She *will* understand, I'm sure."

Kusha shrugged. "I'm not upset," he declared emphatically. "If she doesn't like me, that's her problem, not mine."

"But, Kusha – "

"Just look at this, Maia," he said, changing the subject. "Look at the circuits I modeled. You know, these ideas came to me right after I woke up this morning, and I had to run out and start working on them as soon as I could."

The component of the hydrosol converter Kusha had built looked beautiful indeed. It was intricately sewn together like something Palak would have done himself. All of the contestants had been struggling to put together the tiny components with as much care and dedication as they could, but working on the miniature units with magnifying glasses and scopes and microscopic instruments was nowhere near easy. First, the parts had to be built to the right size, and then they had to be fit inside the shell of the hydrosol converter. Every day Maia and her teammates ended up producing clunky replicas of the ones that Palak had shown them. This went on for days, an endless and frustrating endeavor of building, disassembling, and rebuilding. But now, finally, Kusha seemed to have mastered a good technique. He eagerly described his new methods to Maia as she studied his little piece of art closely. She hardly noticed when Ren walked in.

"Wow, that is so cool," he exclaimed when Kusha had finished. "Hope it works for me too."

"What were you up to all morning, Ren?" Maia asked.

"I was reading about milk squids and their behavioral keys." Ren flung his satchel on his desk and sat down noisily next to it. "I thought I should know as much as I could about Chylomyhrra if I wanted to get the best out of her."

Ren eagerly related all he had found about milk squids – their high intelligence, their ability to bond with humankind, and their astounding group behavior. He was about done when Dani rushed in. She looked excited and very happy as she sat down next to Ren.

"I found a practice ground," she whispered. "We can use it every night this week. Now, all we need is to transport Chylomyhrra and your gear to this place and we can start."

"Wish we could've just asked Dill to send her there," Ren said with a chuckle. "We could also have borrowed the gear from him."

"Would've been nice if we could ask Dill" – Dani laughed – "but he won't give us permission for unregulated and unsupervised underwater exercises. Although, he might let us borrow the gear if we tell him we want to study it closely."

"I'll try to make Chylomyhrra meet me at this place you've found. I better read up some more on visual transmissions," Ren said thoughtfully, pulling out a couple of books from his satchel. "One book said milk squids use telepathic signals for communicating among themselves — maybe we could use that somehow."

"You figure that out while I get some more things arranged for this evening." Dani turned toward Maia next. "I need your help after we've finished with Dill's class."

"All right," Maia said before heading back to her desk as Palak marched in for the session.

Soon the screens lit up with charts, diagrams, and models. It was a long session and a tedious one to sit through, especially since Maia's mind was mostly buzzing with thoughts about the upcoming race. She could hardly focus through the day, and by the looks of it, none of her friends seemed to fare any better. Nafi did not show up for either session; her desk remained conspicuously empty, drawing curious stares from everyone. Curiously enough, neither instructor showed the slightest interest in the case of the missing Nafi.

***

Maia found Nafi sitting on her bed surrounded by a pile of thick books when they returned to the dorm that evening. She looked up as Dani and Maia entered, and a content smile lit up her face. Maia stole a glance at the book the girl held in her arms. It was titled, *A Psycho-Historical Study of the Solianese Social Structure.*

"What's all this you're reading?" Maia asked, looking curiously at the other books strewn around Nafi. All of them had equally impressive and intimidating names.

"Stuff," Nafi replied vaguely.

"And where were you all day?"

"Had to collect these books, so I took a leave of absence from Palak and Dill."

"That explains why they didn't ask us about you." Dani flipped the pages of the thickest book, *A Brief History of Post-Modern Times.* Given its ample girth, Maia doubted if there was anything remotely brief in it. Dani went on to explain their plans for the night. "Maia, Ren, and I are going to the practice grounds tonight. Ren will try to get Chylomyhrra there, and we'll likely be practicing late into the night."

"All right, good." Nafi almost sounded relieved. She did not ask another question like Maia expected her to. "I need to get some reading completed. Good luck with the training."

They did not stay in the dorm much longer. Leaving Nafi buried up to her neck in books, the girls took off even before Anja, Loriine, and Baecca had returned from the RC.

"Where's Ren now?" Maia asked, rushing to keep up with Dani, who strode quickly across the atrium toward the elevator doors.

"He'll meet us at the fiftieth. We're going to the tenth floor again. We'll take the service elevators down from the fiftieth this time though," Dani disclosed her plans as they zoomed downward in the elevator. "As you know, the entryways below Zagran are highly protected. Not only by security personnel who monitor the rim of these channels but also by the layout of these channels themselves. They're arranged like a maze, and only the most-gifted navigator with the most-detailed map will be able to get through these narrow, dark water alleys. These are mostly abandoned now, but there was a time when they were watched around the clock. With the help of a friend, I've located an old monitoring post. A few monitors there still work, and we'll use them to observe Ren and clock his timings as he swims the channels with Chylomyhrra."

"What about the security?" Maia asked. "Won't they stop us?"

"They won't see us. Remember, they only actively monitor the rim now," Dani explained.

"And how would Chylomyhrra get there?" Maia asked as they got off at the fiftieth floor. This whole plan sounded quite complicated and seemed like a recipe for certain disaster.

"There are paths from their pens upstairs to the water locks down at the tenth. She'll know how to find us if only Ren can make her understand where she needs to be. There he is now." Dani waved as Ren ran up to join them.

"I think she got it," Ren said breathlessly "At least I hope she did."

"We'll find out soon," Dani remarked.

The trio took off toward the service elevators at the back of the fiftieth. As they walked briskly past people who went busily about their work, Maia could not help but remember the last time she had been in these parts. She had met Bikele and had learned so much about Sophie. The thought of her mother being tortured in a Gnelexian prison was so painful that she had not dared to open the journal Bikele had given her. It was tucked away safely within the folds of her coat, waiting to be read. Maia hoped to muster enough courage someday to leaf through its pages, to be strong enough to see how the mind probes had wrecked Sophie's brilliant mind into senseless mush. She wanted to see Bikele again, desperately hoping her wish could come true. But the chances of it seemed remote, yet another dream that could never be realized.

The service elevator had come to stop on the tenth floor. It was as quiet and lonely as it had been the other night when they had bumped into Miir and Amanii, and as Maia climbed the metal stairs up to the long corridor that led to the water locks, a sense of guilt and shame filled her. The way she had screamed at Miir was wrong. It was no fault of his that Sophie had been betrayed. Yet she had said the vilest things, used the foulest words.

"If only I could see him again," Maia muttered under her breath as she followed Dani and Ren along the dimly lit path. At every turn of the corridor, Maia wished they would bump into the Xifarian apprentices again so she could apologize to Miir. It would not matter if he shouted back in anger; she would endure. But none of her wishes came true in the time they reached their destination at a door marked "10." Dani hesitated a moment, then opened the door and stepped inside.

CHAPTER FORTY-SEVEN

THE MONITORING POST

A room, dark and forbidding, greeted their eyes.

"You sure took your time to stroll down here, didn't you?" a raspy voice said.

The owner of the voice was a woman as shabby as the room itself and every bit as inhospitable. Her matted gray hair was tied in a loose bun that hung at the nape of her neck. She wore a long, dark tunic that fell well below her knees; it was badly in need of some washing.

"What are you staring at?" she said as Maia and Ren gawked at her. "Have you no manners?"

The duo started to mumble a quick apology, but the woman turned away.

"This is Siobah," Dani chimed in quickly. "She used to be a nanny at the Collective where I grew up after my parents passed away. I knew her family worked in the lower levels, so I asked her for help. And, as you can see—"

"All right, no need to waste time on meaningless chitchat," Siobah interrupted. "I have the gear for you, boy. Go change in there."

She pointed at a door in one corner of the room and shoved a water gear at Ren. As he shuffled away, the woman flicked a few switches at a broken-down panel on the side of the room. A large screen flickered fitfully to life on the wall above the panel. It slowly came into focus; grainy pictures of an intricate maze of waterways became visible.

"There it is—Zagran's forgotten entrance. A work of art, a treasure," the woman said as if in a trance. She leaned closer to the screen and pointed at a moving blob of darkness. "And that must be the squid. Hmmm . . . smart animal."

"Chylomyhrra made it." Ren's sudden squeal made them jump. "She understood my directions."

"Now, boy, you'll not screech like that again, do you understand?" The old woman stood with both hands on her chest, her eyes wide. "Siobah is rather old and not used to screaming and shouting ten-year-olds. Not anymore."

"I'm sorry, it won't happen again," Ren gushed. "I'm not ten though, I'm almost . . . practically thirteen."

"Ah ten . . . thirteen . . . it's all the same to me. You'll understand when you get to be as old as I am." Siobah waved in dismissal, grabbed Ren by his shoulders, and led him to the round opening of the water lock. "Now off you go."

It started pretty badly. As Dani shouted directions through the communicator, Ren and Chylomyhrra bumped against the wall, the floor, against each other. They fell, they yelled, and they hurt. But after an endless series of hopeless maneuvers, Ren seemed to have found a rhythm, and Chylomyhrra found comprehension. They were still slow, but the awkward lumbering manner had vanished. Siobah had placed herself on a rickety chair, far away from the screens. She observed the goings-on with an annoyed expression on her face. When Ren emerged from the water hole after an exhausting trial, Siobah got off her perch and walked to where Dani was in the middle of briefing the tired boy.

"You were doing well near the end," Dani said as Ren listened eagerly. "I guess we need to make an estimate of how fast Loriine goes and compare your times with hers."

"How will we do that? We won't even have a session in the Convolhydrae until it's time for the race," Maia said.

"You kids have so much to learn." Siobah grabbed Ren's arm and pushed him into her chair. "Take some rest, boy. You'll need your breath when you get back in there."

As Ren gulped in surprise, Siobah turned toward the two girls.

"You do *not* race against your opponent—that gets you nowhere." The old woman wagged a wise finger at them. "You race against yourself. Once you're the best that you can be, you have the best chance of being better than anyone else."

Siobah turned to Dani. "Let's get that boy in the water again. I'll give directions this time, and you'll relay it for me through whatever thing you've been using." Siobah nodded at Dani's firestone wristband.

Soon Ren was sent down the water lock again, and Siobah barked orders to Dani, who then relayed them to Ren. Siobah's regimen was three times as punishing as Dani's had been, and she continued relentlessly for what seemed likan e eternity. When Ren was finally allowed to come up again, his face had a bluish tinge.

"You'll be fine," Siobah declared after looking closely at a rather large purple welt on Ren's cheek. "When you come back tomorrow, I'll have a map ready to mirror that Convolhydrae you have. And then we'll see how good a rider we can make out of you."

Dani hugged the old woman. "Thank you Siobah-dima. I'm so grateful—"

"Nonsense," Siobah said. "Don't go all fancy words on me. You think you've grown up, but to me, you'll always be that wee little thing."

Siobah paused. For a brief moment, Maia thought she saw Siobah's wizened eyes well up with tears.

"What a catastrophe it was. All those orphans," Siobah muttered almost inaudibly. Maia realized the woman was speaking about when the Damoclian Connector had blown up. "There were so many of you—all helpless little things. Your brother was one of the older ones, and he was holding up strongly. But we could tell that the little tot was as scared as a mouse in a snare. And how he clung to you . . . as if you were his only hope."

"We made it so far," Dani whispered.

"Of course you did. You'll go farther. Both of you. Just like your ma and pa." Siobah paused a moment. "What a waste. Two of our best scientists . . ."

A gloom descended as Siobah's words trailed off. The room was quiet until Ren lumbered out of the changing room, barely managing to stand up straight. The trio left right after. It was way past midnight when Dani and Maia half dragged, half carried Ren to his dormitory.

CHAPTER FORTY-EIGHT

BLOOD, SWEAT, AND TEARS

It was morning again even before Maia could catch a wink of sleep. Their nighttime adventure was like a sleeping potion; Ren was barely awake at his desk the following day. Everyone took turns to keep an eye on him so he would not doze off and fall from his seat. Maia and Dani struggled to keep awake as well. Nafi continued to be distracted. She had carried one of her fat books into the RC and read through breakfast, lunch, and dinner. Kusha was the only one whose senses were properly functional, and he volunteered to put extra effort into building everyone's micro-converters. Ren, Nafi, and Maia heartily agreed to the proposal, but as was expected, Dani politely declined.

It was the same drill every day—a sleepy Maia and Dani, a barely alive Ren, a distracted Nafi, and a particularly wary Kusha herding the bunch around the place. Jiri, along with a couple of worthy assistants he had procured to help the cause of making the race fair, came by with a set of rules one fine morning. Everyone, including Loriine, Ren, and their teams gathered around him. Jiri read out the rules in a brassy voice worthy of a leader.

1. *The race will comprise of three rounds in the Convolhydrae.*
2. *The race will end as soon as the first rider emerges from the gate.*
3. *The final score will be based on how quickly a rider is able to complete the rounds, as well as the number of activators a rider manages to touch.*
4. *A rider who falls off his/her ride will be immediately disqualified.*
5. *Any attempts to cause harm to each other or each other's rides will result in immediate disqualification.*

"Questions?" Jiri asked, looking from Loriine to Ren and back again. Ren, for the most part, was too sleepy to comprehend the goings-on. He simply nodded, and Loriine did not seem to mind any of the rules.

"All right then and good luck," Jiri said, and the crowd dispersed. It was back to the sleepy grind again after that.

On the training front, Ren made progress every day. But it was not until the fifth day that Maia spotted a tremendous change in his style. They had been practicing a routine set of twists and turns that Siobah had drawn up, mimicking the layout of the Convolhydrae. Not only had Ren remembered all the turns quite well, but he seemed to glide and soar with Chylomyhrra. Even before Dani could shout out the directions or warnings to him, Ren cruised through, stopping briefly at the spots that were marked as the activator simulation points. It took Dani by surprise, and Siobah looked a little amazed as well. The customary three rounds looked half as difficult as they usually did, and when Ren emerged out of the water hole, prepared to face the usual ranting and raving Siobah, he was greeted with a warm smile instead.

"You've done well, boy," Siobah laughed and thumped Ren appreciatively on the shoulders. "I'm quite happy. You should go and rest now, get a good night's sleep before we do the final trials tomorrow."

The trio had a spring to their steps as they rushed back to their dorms. Siobah was definitely very difficult to please, and her show of approval was a thing to cherish. Suddenly, winning the race seemed like a possibility.

A strange sight met their eyes as they got off the elevator on the 500th. It was Nafi, pacing the floor like a mad scientist, deep in thought, muttering to herself. She did not even glance in the direction of the trio as they approached her.

"Hey," Ren whispered, careful not to startle the preoccupied girl.

As hard as he had tried, she was still taken by surprise. She jumped and stared with her mouth agape before heaving a sigh of relief.

"You're back," she said, grinning. "How was it today?"

"Good, it was fantastic actually." Ren went on to recount all that had happened at practice, Siobah's approval, and his own joy.

"What are *you* doing here?" Dani asked.

"Oh, I'm trying to get some fresh air, that's all," Nafi explained. "I was tired of sitting alone in the dorm with nothing to do."

"Whatever happened to reading those books?" Maia asked. "And why were you alone? What about Anja and the two loons?"

"I'm done reading," Nafi declared before hastily changing the topic. "And the girls and the boys have gone shopping. Bones took them out on a sight-seeing tour."

"A tour?" Ren exclaimed. "And what about us?"

"Just be happy that Bones didn't ask why you three were missing in the first place," Nafi offered a sensible reminder. "And don't worry about it; I don't think it was much. Kusha jumped at the idea though, took off with Jiri and his team like a rabbit."

"That boy seems to be getting very friendly with Anja," Nafi added after a meditative pause. "Oh well, they should be back anytime now. You want to wait for them?"

They huddled together at their usual corner in the atrium and chatted about the upcoming race, the impending final challenge, and the various tasks that remained to be completed.

The tourists returned after a while. A wave of laughter and chatter floated across the floor as the groups disembarked from the elevator. Kusha, along with Jiri and his teammates, was the first to come around the corner. They must have been discussing something silly, as Kusha, Luem, and Anja were laughing their heads off. Maia noted how happy Anja looked, wondering if there was indeed reason to believe Nafi's comment had some weight. As soon as Kusha saw his teammates, he waved a quick goodbye to Anja and Luem.

"Hey, you guys." He sat down next to Nafi. "Is everything fine?"

"Yes, all is good with us," Maia replied. "Did you have a lot of fun?"

"Yes, as a matter of fact, I did." Kusha turned around to cast a quick look in the direction of the stairs where Jiri and his friends were still laughing on their way up to the dorms. "I'm glad I decided to go out with them."

Maia was about to ask more about the trip, but Ren beat her to it.

"And what exactly did you do?"

Kusha shrugged. "We walked around the shops. Aerika took us to this fancy place for iced cones and that's it."

"That's it? You seemed to have more going on than just that." Ren did not look the least bit convinced at Kusha's description of the outing.

Kusha stared curiously at Ren for a while before he flushed and turned on a serious face.

"You're right. The real reason for going on this trip was something else," he confessed. "I wanted to take a look at Keif and Zeiss."

The name sounded vaguely familiar, but Maia could not quite remember where she had heard it.

"Remember the place Miir, Amanii, and that creepy Remii were talking about?" Kusha reminded. "Where they were hoping to find something? Something that we assumed could be the heart of the Sedara?"

Maia remembered now. She nodded eagerly, as did Ren and Nafi.

"Turns out it was the biggest and oldest antique shop in Zagran," Kusha said in a low voice. "And listen to this, yet another strange and unusual fire destroyed it last week. All that remains now is the metal frame of the shop . . . all the rest is gone. Gutted."

"Fire again?" Dani exclaimed, her voice faint. "Why would anyone do such a thing?"

Ren sighed; it seemed like he wanted to say something, but Nafi burst out.

"Now, don't start again." She shook her head at Ren. "This has been going on forever now. Hooded masked figures with whip swords and strange fires in places . . . it has to be somehow connected to those Xifarian thugs that attacked the Stabilator."

"Why do you always have to fight?" Ren retorted angrily. "I was going to say that I'm now sure people from Xif are behind it. I might be sad to admit it, but I can hardly deny it anymore."

"Sorry," Nafi said, busily studying her fingernails.

"But why would they set fires?" Dani asked.

"I thought a lot about it. It must be the Trial by Fire," Ren said simply. He looked away from them, a distant gloominess clouding his eyes. "This is the only obvious way to locate the Capsule. The heart of the Sedara is indestructible. It can be broken into pieces, but it'll never die unless it decides to die. If anything were to survive a fire, it would only be something that contains either the core or the chalice or both."

A brief silence settled in before Nafi spoke, very gently this time.

"So they're setting fires to anything that they suspect might house the Capsule?"

Ren nodded, still avoiding looking at anyone. "And this can't be some ordinary fire either," he added. "This has to be Tenhihula's Fire."

"Ten . . . what now?" Nafi blurted.

"It's a special fire used to mold and shape L'miere crystals. If anything can survive its intense, super-heated flames, it would be something as miraculous and powerful as the heart of the Sedara."

"Can anyone start such a fire?" Maia asked.

"The process of igniting a Tenhihula's fire is a top military secret, shouldn't be known outside a select few—"

"Like people at the XDA? The chancellor? Top brass at the SDS, maybe?" Maia's mind was racing.

"Something like that," Ren replied. "It can be a dangerous weapon."

"Weren't Remii and the gang talking about a weapon the other night?" Maia pondered aloud. Everything was starting to make sense suddenly. "Maybe this was it."

"That's possible. Tenhihula's fire can get very hard to contain, spreads too swiftly."

"Maybe that's why these fires are not being detected by our systems in time," Dani inferred.

Ren simply shrugged.

"You think they found the shard at Keif and Zeiss? We never even got a chance to look for it." Maia recalled what Ren had said a long time ago—there was little likelihood that a few kids like them could beat a nation in this search. But she did not want to lose hope, not just yet. "But there should be more shards out there. We need to find—"

"How, Maia?" Kusha interrupted. "Let's face it. There's no way we'll ever know how many pieces the Capsule or its contents were broken into, or where they were hidden. The only one who could've known for sure was your mother."

This time the quiet stretched longer. Maia gasped for some air—it was getting difficult to breathe. It was hard to accept that her hands were tied; there was nothing she could do to stop the Xifarians. Here they were, spending time in these mindless games, while the Xifarians were plotting to end their world. For a moment Maia wished that she had not known, at least she would have spent her last days in blissful ignorance.

But now . . .

They would have sat there in silence forever had it not been for Dani. She rose to her feet and nudged Ren.

"You *have* to get some rest," she asserted. "We have only one more day before the race, and you need some sleep."

The whole gang walked quietly back to the dorms. A gloom was weighing heavily on Maia's mind. Something that she could not quite place her finger on kept bothering her. It was something in the conversation they had just had, something strange, out of place. Lying in her bed, Maia wanted to go over their chat in her mind, but sleep overtook her senses far too soon.

***

The day that followed, however, was once again too busy to keep Maia and her teammates from worrying about anything but their present situation.

On their final practice with Siobah, the whole group slinked in much to the irritation of the old woman. And Ren had a terrible run. Not a single thing went right. Even the simplest of maneuvers ended in crashes, bumps, and bruises. Siobah stopped it quickly and called Ren in.

"I think we're being a little nervous here," she told the shivering and shaking boy. "It would be a better idea if you just relaxed a little. Try not to think too much about it."

With those words and a couple of reassuring pats, she sent the team back to the 500th.

CHAPTER FORTY-NINE

THE WRATH OF BONES

Relaxing was easier said than done. As hard as everyone tried to put on a happy face to keep Ren cheerful, he remained morose and sullen. The misery carried over into the following day—the day the race was set to happen. He was droopy-mouthed in the morning, and he grew restless by the moment as Dill's session drew nearer.

An excited and chattering crowd was already gathered inside the observation room near the Convolhydrae when Core 21 walked in. People were talking among themselves; some were arguing about who had the better chance of winning, while others were busy analyzing the racetrack. Jiri stood at the center of the room with his two assistants; next to him stood Loriine and her teammates. On seeing Ren, Jiri scooted over.

"It's all set. Dill went off for his usual meeting with Aerika." Jiri's eyes shone with anticipation. "He won't be back in a while. He asked us to follow the routine. Let's get started."

Soon they were ready to go. Ren plodded forward, his gaze

skimming the floor as he followed Loriine to the gate of the Convolhydrae.

"Ren, wait," Dani shouted, and rushed to the boy as the door was about to close. She hugged him tight before declaring firmly, "It doesn't matter if she wins. It's not like our lives are at stake here, you know. You're doing this for Chylomyhrra, and you should be very proud that you stood up for her."

Ren forced a smile as Maia and the rest of the team gathered around.

"Yes, we'll be proud of you whether you win or lose." Maia jabbed at his arm playfully.

"We sure will," Nafi said smirking. "This scheme is way more decent than the betting rings you used to run at the XDA."

"Just go and have some fun." Kusha landed a good-humored punch on Ren's shoulder.

Ren seemed happier as he walked away, his steps were more confident, and his shoulders a bit uplifted. As Loriine and Ren swam out into the Convolhydrae, conversation died down and all eyes inside the observation room focused on the gigantic viewing screen on the wall, beyond which stretched the serpentine waterway.

Loriine and Saem arrived inside the waterway first, followed by Ren and Chylomyhrra. They waited patiently for the starting signal from Jiri and then zoomed out. It started without much of a tumult, Loriine speeding ahead of Ren as the light flashed a go. Ren and Chylomyhrra got out a little slow, but they were steady. Saem, the black leathery fish with a spotted tail, glided effortlessly through the waters. Loriine surged forward smoothly, touching one activator after another, not missing a single one. Ren trailed behind but did not miss any activators either. The swim so far was easy and predictable.

"Two more to go . . ." Nafi let out a long breath as Loriine completed the first lap around the waterway, followed closely by Ren. "He's doing well."

"As long as he doesn't hurt himself," Dani said pensively.

Inside the Convolhydrae, the pace picked up once the second lap started. Chylomyhrra now tailed Loriine and her ride closely; her snout almost touched the serrated tail of the black fish. She pitched forward and staggered back in a strange rhythm as if struggling to stop herself from overtaking Loriine. Balanced on her long arms, Ren swung and swerved as they passed the turns, reaching out for the activators as they sped past.

Loriine glanced back at him a few times in this round, looking increasingly uncomfortable as Chylomyhrra inched closer. And then, right before they were about to complete the second lap, Chylomyhrra shot forward. As they approached the last activator in the Convolhydrae, the milk squid rolled upward, arching above Loriine and her ride, allowing Ren enough space to reach the activator that was perched high on the ceiling.

"Yes!" Dani raised her fists in the air as Ren touched the activator before Loriine did. "Go for it, Chylomyhrra. You can do it, girl."

"Hold off the celebrations, it's not over yet," Karhann, who stood with his fists clenched, snapped.

"Make him shut up, Maia, or I will break his nose," Nafi whispered.

"Be quiet, Nafi," Maia whispered back. The race was tense enough, a fight in the viewing chamber was not necessary at all.

Meanwhile, in the waterway, Chylomyhrra glided forward with Ren. She swam faster and faster, head to head with Loriine who clearly struggled to hold on to her pace. With every passing moment, Loriine fell behind. The more she lost, the more erratic her gait became.

"I hope she doesn't try anything crazy," Kusha remarked, observing intently. "I jus —"

Right then the unthinkable happened.

As Chylomyhrra surged forward some more, Loriine's ride reared nervously. For an instant, it seemed Loriine would fall off the back of the black fish, but as a collective gasp of horror rose in the observation room, Loriine balanced herself. In the next moment, she raised her fist and struck one of Chylomyhrra's tentacles.

"No way," shouted the tall Jjord boy from Core 10. A loud murmur rose and filled the room at the unexpected turn of events.

But nothing had prepared anyone for what happened next. In a swooshing movement of her tentacles, Chylomyhrra flicked the water behind her, sending a strange swirling wave toward Loriine. As the wave hit and swamped the girl, she staggered, lost her balance, and fell. Chylomyhrra continued, as gracefully as before, with Ren touching every activator on his way to the final point of the race. Shouts of joy filled the observation room as Chylomyhrra emerged through the gates of the Convolhydrae, Ren waving wildly at the viewing chambers.

"This is what happens when you leave them unattended," The voice was so chilling that the din in the room subsided in a heartbeat. Aerika stood behind them, arms crossed, and Dill stood next to her with his head bowed. Aerika's eyes were flashing; she stared fixedly at the Convolhydrae where Loriine tried hard to reassure her ride while she wobbled outside. Not a word was spoken in the room until a jubilant Ren and a limping Loriine walked in through the door.

"Follow me, please," Aerika said to the duo before turning to instruct Dill briefly. "Dismiss the rest for the day."

"You will all go back to your dormitories." Dill nodded curtly at the crowd and then shook his head in disappointment. "This behavior is inexcusable."

Maia suddenly felt sad for Dill. By the looks of things and the expression on his face, he was sure to have a miserable time with Aerika. The room cleared slowly, heads were hung low, and shoulders drooped. But no one went back to the dorms—the excitement bubbling inside every young head was too much to be contained. Instead, they congregated on the 500th, near the glass windows. There was no end to the discussions, of how Ren had touched that last activator, or how Chylomyhrra had taken that particular turn. The most discussed issue was how callously Loriine had behaved and how she deserved to be taken to task.

Time trickled past and the excitement ebbed, but there was no sign of either Ren or Loriine. Slowly the atrium emptied as people retired to the dorms. After a while, the only ones left waiting were Core 21 and Core 7—the two teams whose members had been summoned, sitting at the two ends of the desolate atrium in an endless wait. It stretched so long that Nafi started pacing again, mostly in the area near the elevators, and dangerously close to where Karhann and his teammates were camped.

Maia was about to walk over to Nafi to ensure that there were no new fights when the doors to the elevator opened. A bawling Loriine and a wearied Ren stepped out. Loriine's team rushed and formed a protective cocoon around her. Nafi was not too far behind; she sprinted, grabbed Ren by the arm, and almost dragged him to their corner of the atrium like a lioness protecting its cub. Ren sat down on the floor noisily and cradled his head in his arms.

"So?" Nafi asked impatiently.

"So, you've no idea how mad Aerika can be," he replied, waving his hands in the air like a lunatic, possibly mimicking Aerika's fury. "And her lectures are torture. I hope I never ever have to hear her yelling at me again."

"Do we have another strike against us?" Dani inquired.

"Nope," Ren replied amidst sighs of relief.

"You mean there was no punishment?" Maia asked, unable to believe her ears.

"Not for me," Ren replied. "Loriine had a terrible time though."

"And?" Nafi urged.

"She has been barred from Dill's sessions for the rest of our stay. She also can't take part in the final challenge."

"What?" Kusha's question was almost drowned by Dani's loud gasp.

Ren nodded feebly. "Aerika went ballistic when she heard of how Loriine had spoken about Chylomyhrra. And when she heard about the incident during the race, she practically threatened to send Loriine packing. It took a lot of begging and sobbing to make her relent."

Nafi grinned happily. "She gets taken out and nothing happens to us? This is awesome."

Ren sighed. "Umm . . . Aerika did declare the race illegal. That means our tasks are on us even though Loriine lost."

"That's fine," Dani said. "We can do it ourselves."

"You must be joking." Nafi fumed, muttering loudly as she rose to leave. "After all the trouble we went through, we still have to do the nasty maintenance work ourselves? That's so unfair. Those guys should be made to pick up everybody's work."

"Have a heart, Nafi. It's bad enough that they're down to three members now." Maia felt for Loriine's team even though she knew that Loriine's punishment was justified. She wondered if there was any way for that team to survive this phase of the contest with three remaining members. It must have been difficult enough when they were down to four after losing Yoome during the Xifarian phase. And now they had lost Loriine as well. Nafi, however, rolled her eyes, shook her head, and made a face that clearly said how little pity she had for Core 7.

CHAPTER FIFTY

RATIFICATION DAY

Things changed from difficult to unbearable in the days that followed. The contestants were watched over by the trainers; Dill even got a couple of assistants to keep an eye on everyone. Every request was scrutinized, every action evaluated. To top it all off, Aerika made surprise visits to the classrooms about five times each day, not any of them to shower affection on the youngsters.

The practice sessions in the Convolhydrae continued, but only under the strictest vigilance. No one was allowed to spend a moment more than they were allotted, and any deviation from the regulated movements during the exercise was awarded a sit-out penalty for two subsequent sessions. It was particularly bad on the first day when almost everyone was penalized, which meant the following day the whole troupe was found moping on the penalty benches.

Loriine attended Palak's sessions only; she hardly ever spoke or even looked at anyone. Her team remained quiet as well, not that the other contestants cared about it. Maia felt quite sorry for them though. Ren was also upset for a few days, considering his actions were partly responsible for their misfortunes. Nafi, however, was more than elated. Every time she passed Core 7, she either smirked or snickered or openly laughed at them. It had reached a point that the remaining four had to keep an ever-watchful eye on the girl so they could drag her away before she went on her mischievous rampage.

Then, one evening, the team fell out with Joolsae. The mentor was playfully teasing Nafi about the various exercises they had been assigned and their life in general. As they fidgeted impatiently, eager to get away from the girl, Nafi decided to ask Joolsae about her kid brother again. Joolsae tried her best to recover from whatever it was that puzzled her.

"Do you even *have* a brother?" Nafi asked, fixing a suspicious stare on Joolsae.

"Y-yes . . . yes . . . why?" Joolsae stammered.

"I don't think you do." Nafi frowned and continued looking fixedly at the older girl. "You always look confused when we ask you about him."

As Joolsae shook her head and opened her mouth to reply, Ren stepped closer.

"I think you made him up, so you could use him as an excuse. You want to get away from your mentoring duties," he said, raising an accusing finger. "And I think you also tried to unseal the second message from Hans."

As Joolsae stood quietly in the face of accusations, hardly trying to defend herself, Dani pulled the final straw.

"You know, we can do well enough without your help," she said coldly.

Joolsae shrugged and seemed to come to a decision finally.

"Whatever. Babysitting you was a boring assignment anyway," she said with a grimace. "And if you're the best in this world, as they say you are, you shouldn't need my help. They pamper you spoiled for nothing. I'm much smarter than all of you put together. And about those messages . . . I think you've been getting restricted information. Had it not been for Hans, I would've reported them already."

"Report away, Joolsae," Dani hissed. "See if you can prove anything."

Joolsae stared at her for a while before she turned and stomped away.

As she left, Maia and her friends stood watching, a little stunned on realizing that Joolsae had indeed lied to them and had tried to spy on them. All the smiles and the friendliness had been nothing but a farce.

"Did that girl just threaten Hans?" Nafi said incredulously after Joolsae had disappeared. "What happened? Why did she lose interest in him so suddenly?"

Dani looked thoughtful for a moment. "Hans started seeing someone a few weeks ago," she blurted.

"Aha!" Nafi exclaimed, casting a knowing look around. "I don't know about you guys, but I'd rather have Miir over her any day."

Nafi turned her nose up and stomped away in the opposite direction. No one was in the mood to counter that statement, at least not at that moment.

***

Joolsae's betrayal left the team in a stupor for the next few days. It was during one of these days after the Convolhydrae incident that Nafi went missing right after Palak's session. She appeared at the RC, breathless and excited, as the rest of the team was finishing lunch.

"It's tonight," she announced mysteriously, leaning over the table. "They're going to sign and ratify the deal tonight," she said, pronouncing each word deliberately on seeing the confused faces.

Still, there was nothing but blank stares around the table. Nafi grimaced, frowned, and threw her hands up in the air.

"The deal with the House of the Broken Seas and its minions, of course." Nafi rolled her eyes and shook her head. "Please don't tell me you've all forgotten about the UTAP and the energy-sharing pact."

Maia had not forgotten and from what she could guess from the others' expressions, no one else had forgotten either. The Xifarian deadline to shut off energy supplies was drawing near, and most of the population on the land cities of Tansi had no chance of survival if the Jjord did not help. Yet, most Solianese Houses refused to round up the Resistance as the Xifarians demanded. Most did not even appear at the Jjordic Council. Only a few of them, led by the House of the Broken Seas, were eager to align themselves with the Jjord. These Houses had promised to grant the Xifarians a long-term UTAP for the land cities. The Jjord, in return, agreed to share their energy surplus with only those few accommodating Houses. Tonight, these Solianese Houses were going to sign a pact to aid the Xifarians and ally with the Jjord.

"What's the point?" Kusha absentmindedly fiddled with his food.

"The point is that we need to be there tonight," Nafi declared.

"For what?" Kusha asked without looking up. "It's all over. I don't want to go there to see how the fate of our people is sealed."

"It's not over until it's over," Nafi said with ferocity.

"I know I have no business commenting on these matters," Ren started apologetically, "but I kind of agree with Nafi. Even if there's no way to change things, you should be there to see what happens."

Maia nodded. She knew what was about to happen—the outcome was predictable—yet there was no doubt in her mind that this was one Council meeting they could not miss. She wanted to see it all go down, watch history being made, as failed a history as it might be.

"All right," Kusha muttered. It was obvious that his heart was not in it.

Dani remained silent. She ate her food with quiet concentration, not agreeing or dissenting to the proposal. No one asked her, probably thinking she would not reply in favor anyway. Maia decided to talk to her as they walked back to Dill's classroom.

"You'll come with us tonight, won't you?" she asked as they fell a little behind the other three.

"I . . . I honestly don't know, Maia," Dani replied hesitantly. Not only did she look upset, but also a little nervous.

"Are you worried about getting caught by Aerika?" Maia asked even though she knew that was not the likely cause.

"Not really, no," Dani replied. She seemed to want to tell more, but a hesitation stopped her every time she tried to say something.

"You're concerned about what Hans will think?" The way Dani's face fell and her eyes dimmed, Maia knew she had found the right reason. She decided to press a little further. "Why do you worry so much about pleasing him, Dani?"

"Because, he's all I have, Maia," Dani almost wailed. Her eyes were glazed with tears. "I don't want to let him down. I've disappointed him far too many times lately."

"Dani, I think you should give Kusha a chance to explain." Maia did not waste another moment before jumping to the point. "He really didn't have a choice but to keep his past a secret."

Dani looked away at the mention of Kusha's name. But Maia had no plans of relenting; she could not see them sad anymore, and she would do her best to bring an end to the standoff.

"He was under oath, Dani, and yet he told us everything after you left that night." Maia went on to recount all that Kusha had told them. Dani listened in silence.

"I hid *my* past from you guys," Maia added, sighing. The thought still tormented her and the guilt was still unbearable sometimes. "I'm more at fault than Kusha ever was. If you could brush aside all of that, why can't you ignore something that was hardly a mistake of Kusha's?"

Dani stared at her, not blinking. For the briefest moment, her eyes softened, but that passed too quickly.

"It's different, Maia," she whispered. "You're different."

"I'm different? How? Dani – "

They had reached Dill's class. Maia had run out of time. Maia only hoped that she had done enough to convince Dani of Kusha's innocence.

Their time in the Convolhydrae passed rather smoothly that day, and everyone was alert enough to not break any rules and not be penalized in the process.

**

Day turned into night, and soon it was time for the lights to go out. Maia did not remember dozing off that night, but she woke up to someone shaking her shoulders violently. It was Nafi. Maia sat up with a start and jumped out of the bed as noiselessly as she could.

"Sorry," Maia whispered as they walked out into the corridor. "Are we late?"

"No, but Dani thinks we should be there before the Council starts tonight." Nafi rushed down the staircase, a huge satchel hanging over her shoulders. "She says it'll be crowded, to say the least."

Before Maia could realize the implication of Nafi's statement, she saw Ren, Kusha, and Dani standing under the staircase. A wave of joy swept through her heart at the sight – Dani had decided to join them after all. She grinned widely at Dani as they walked into the elevator and got a half-smile in return, but that was enough to make Maia happy.

They went the same way as they had the other night, but this time around, there was no dearth of people. All roads seemed to converge at one place this night—the Council Room. By the number of people who thronged the gates of the Council Room, Maia had not hoped to find a single available seat. But they spotted a small clearing and the five friends slowly made their way to it.

At the center of the room, people walked around busily. Maia recognized some faces: there was the Jjord Premier "the Intimidator" Oliena; Tsininio and Goren, the Solianese Sahiiraans who had pleaded for unconditional support the other night; and Aloysus, the portly Jjordic man who had opposed them. The two Sahiiraans looked very unhappy, Maia noted, which obviously meant that they were still not in support of this pact. Aloysus, however, looked elated. He was laughing and chatting with a man who stood with his back to where Maia was sitting. This man seemed very familiar to Maia, even from behind. Premier Oliena stood next to these two men, her face a mask of calmness.

"Look who we have here, friends," a recognizable voice rang out. Maia turned, not wanting to see the face she knew she would see.

"Lex . . ." Kusha said the name very slowly as if he did not want to believe who it was. Lex looked as charming as he had the first day Maia had met him at the Xifarian spaceport of Arpasgula. Behind him stood the solid wall of his cronies, looking menacing and formidable as ever. Lex was a bully who had tormented Maia and her teammates during the Xifarian phase until his team was eliminated.

"Yes, the same old Lex," he said with a smirk and bowed. Maia could not help but steal a quick look at his perky ponytail; there was still no denying the fact that it was utterly cute.

"What are you doing here?" Kusha said sharply, not charmed by Lex or by his ponytail.

"I'm here to attend the Council, as all of my House members have," Lex said boastfully. "We're honored to make this piece of history possible. You can't imagine how proud I am to belong to the House that finally brought peace to our world."

"You're a Broken Seas!" Nafi exclaimed so loudly that Maia jumped. "I should've guessed."

"Yes, I am, dear friend." Lex bowed again, lower, and with added grace this time.

"I don't think I'm your friend, Lex," Nafi retorted. She continued without the slightest pause as Lex stared. "And I don't think much of your House either. None of us does for that matter. I think what you're doing is disgraceful. You're doing this to buy favors for yourself, ignoring the fate of thousands of innocent people. But don't think you'll get away with it, because you won't."

Lex froze, then his face flushed and his nostrils flared.

"Who cares what you think?" he snapped. "And so what if we're doing it for ourselves? I don't see you trying to stop us. If you can't stop us, shut up and get out."

"I won't shut up and I won't get out," Nafi shouted back. "And you just wait and see what happens next."

Lex was about to retort when a voice boomed. It was Aloysus, the stocky Jjord. He stood at the center of the Council floor, his face brimming with joy and happiness.

"I would like to request everyone to please be seated as we intend to begin shortly. This will most definitely be a historical session where we take the first step toward a future of understanding, and it is my honor to invite Chairman Phocluus to speak a few words." He bowed graciously at the man who had looked familiar to Maia.

And now Maia knew why—it was the same Chairman Phocluus who had come to visit her at the conservatory on Xif. He had been Sophie's teacher, and he had been kind and nice to Maia. He took the podium, his fingers sparkling with the jeweled rings, his eyes shining with compassion.

"Thank you, Aloysus. I will not take up too much of the Council's time, as we have important matters to discuss. But I am glad we have decided to choose the right path, that we did not lose our way in that maze of impracticalities that could hinder any hopes of our future together. I thank you, Premier Oliena, and Sahiiraan Leeam, for making this groundbreaking pact possible."

The chairman is in favor of the pact.

Maia's heart sank a little, but then she realized that putting the heart of the Sedara back together meant more than anything else to the Xifarians. Although it also meant they would not think twice about leaving the Tansian system, even if it destroyed all life on Tansi forever. She found it hard to believe that the man she had liked so much could stand against everything Sophie had fought for.

Sahiiraan Tsininio, the Solianese man who had spoken the other night, took the stand next. "I know my thoughts and concerns are not welcome at the moment, but I still would like to speak a few words. I would like to make a plea again to my counterparts from the other Houses to consider the meaning of this pact. Signing this means that we will be denying the energy needed to survive to more than half of the people on Tansi. Once you agree to the UTAP, you will also leave the entire population in the land cities vulnerable. Do not punish the innocent for no fault of theirs. Please reconsider your choice. Please give us some more time so all the Houses can reach a consensus and *then* let us take a real step toward understanding."

A series of boos rose from both the Solianese and the Jjord sides even before the Sahiiraan had stopped speaking. From what Maia could see, Sahiiraan Tsininio and his ideas did not have too many supporters. Maia's insides squirmed at the discord. It was not unexpected; Nafi had said the Solianese were divided, but it still hurt to see how the Houses were falling out so openly instead of standing up together for their cause.

A tall man rose from the side of the Solianese and strode vigorously to the podium. He smiled at Sahiiraan Tsininio as they passed each other; there was no friendliness in that smile, only ridicule and mockery. This man's resemblance to Lex was uncanny except for the ponytail; the swagger, the smirk, and the sharp features reminded Maia of what Lex would look like when he grew older. A wave of claps spread across the room as the man took the podium. This man, Maia realized, was popular among the Solianese representatives and the Jjord.

"Must be related to Lex, don't you think?" Maia whispered to Nafi who shrugged in response.

"They look alike and walk alike, so I guess he could be Lex's father or uncle," Nafi said a moment later. "These Broken Seas are a horrible bunch."

"Thank you for the enthusiasm, my friends. Your applause tells me that I am not alone and I know I am doing the right thing. Please believe me when I say that the consensus Sahiiraan Tsininio speaks about is impossible to achieve. How is it possible when half of our House leaders are not even present here at this critical juncture? And how can we depend on the ones who have chosen to turn their backs on their people? How can I wait for them endlessly and risk the lives of my own people? I will sign this pact for my people, and I will urge each of you to sign it for the sake of your people. Let us save the ones we can, rather than losing them all."

Thunderous applause greeted him as he stepped down. Shouts of "Sahiiraan Leeam" filled the room. Premier Oliena rose to speak when the room quieted a little.

"We will now pass the signing papers, so please let your opinions be known. At the end of the signing and after the moments of silence, we will declare the pact sealed and closed."

A man walked in with a small scroll and handed it to Sahiiraan Leeam, who looked at the paper, smiled, and scrawled assertively through it. The paper passed on from one person to another, finally coming to a stop at the last row. The man, who had brought the paper in, collected it and handed it to Premier Oliena.

"We have twelve in favor and three against. We have approval," she declared after glancing through it. Cheers broke out again. Oliena waved at the crowd to calm them down a little. "We will now have the moments of silence. If anyone wishes to voice their objections before this deal is sealed, now would be the time. We will reconvene soon after."

The man, who had brought the paper, now carried in a large gold sand clock and set it at the center of the podium. He turned it around, and as the flecks of sand trickled down the narrow neck to the empty bottom, the countdown began.

CHAPTER FIFTY-ONE

OF HONOR AND GLORY

Around the room, people rose to their feet as the sand clock started counting. Those on the Council floor got up and started walking around as well.

"There it is, Nafi." Kusha let out a loud and deep sigh. "That is how it all goes down. Now, we've all witnessed the beginning of our glorious end."

"You know, it doesn't have to be this way," Nafi said as she turned around to face Kusha. "You can change it."

Kusha's brows shot up and his eyes widened.

"This is not a matter to joke about, Nafi," he said in an admonishing tone after a moment of stunned silence. No one spoke a word. All eyes turned toward Nafi, waiting to hear her response.

"This is no joke, Kusha. You belong to the House of the Sun; you can do anything," Nafi replied.

Kusha raised his hand. "Nafi . . . you don't make any sense."

"All right, I'll try speaking stupid." Nafi rolled her eyes as Kusha glared back. "You, or should I say, the leader of your House, has the authority to overturn all those signatures they collected. That's how power was divided among the Solianese, and it still is."

"All right, I understand that," Kusha said. "What I don't understand is how *I* can do anything at all. In case you haven't noticed, I'm no leader of any House. And I think I've told you already that my father stepped down from his role many years ago. I'm not in any way as powerful as you like to believe."

"Wrong," Nafi smirked. "It's *you* who has no idea. And I'll tell you why."

She yanked her satchel and pulled out a thick book titled, *A Brief History of Post-Modern Times*. Nafi expertly leafed through its pages and came to stop at one of the later chapters.

"Listen to this. The leadership of a House is bestowed on a person at birth; no power can take it away other than the will and the choice of the person himself. A child who is born into a House lineage will inherit it until he or she chooses to abdicate out of his or her own volition."

Nafi stopped and looked Kusha squarely in the eye. Kusha did not bat an eyelid; he sat like a statue staring wordlessly at Nafi.

"You get it now?" Nafi's eyes sparkled. "When you were born into the House of the Sun, your father had not yet renounced his lineage, so you inherited the right of leadership. After that, even when he chose to give up his rights, his act did not take away yours. So you *are* technically the leader of the House of the Sun."

"This is way cool." Ren was on his feet; he could hardly keep his excitement from showing.

"But then . . ." Kusha looked confused as he continued, "I severed ties with my House when I was a child – "

Nafi shook her head vigorously. "Volition means the choice of an adult, one who has come of age at eighteen. Like you just said, you were a *child* when you severed the ties. That did not mean a thing. You, Kusha, have more power than you can think of."

"And . . . I can simply walk over and change everything they've decided to do?" Kusha asked, his voice trembling.

Nafi nodded and smiled.

"No, that'll be crazy." Kusha shook his head vehemently. "Can you imagine what will happen if I do that? That Chairman Phocluus will lose all hopes of getting his hands on the Resistance, so he will come to kill us. Premier Oliena will probably not be very happy either, and that fat Jjord guy will most definitely not be pleased. We won't make friends with Lex, Leeam, and all their cronies."

"But you will have saved a lot of innocent lives," Dani said. Her unexpected words were gentle, yet they had a reassuring firmness.

Kusha looked at Dani, holding her gaze for a few moments. Then he sighed and continued. "Then there's Aerika. She'll surely have us thrown out of the contest, or have you forgotten that she specifically instructed us to not even discuss politics?"

"I don't care if I'm thrown out." Maia felt no hesitation when she said it. "What's the point of trying to win this contest when everything I know and love will cease to exist?"

"And who cares about this stupid contest when there are better things to fight for?" Ren kneeled next to Nafi and Kusha. "I mean, think about it, Kusha . . . who would you rather be? The boy who got top honors at the Alliance Initiative? Or the legendary hero who saved his people from certain doom? I would pick the second without a doubt."

"Time is running out." Nafi cast a quick, anxious glance at the sand clock on the floor and then looked at Kusha. "You know what we all want, so make a choice. Now!"

The moments of silence that followed drowned the din that surrounded them. Kusha sat with his head bowed for a while, then looked around the room, and finally scanned the hopeful faces that stared keenly at him. He got to his feet with a suddenness that surprised Maia.

"What do I do now, Miss Know-It-All?" He stood with his hands on his hips, looking inquiringly at Nafi. "You want me to just walk in there?"

"Yes, that's exactly what you need to do, but I'll walk with you."

Nafi put her book inside the satchel and flung it over her shoulder.

"Can we come too?" Maia asked as the duo started walking away.

"Will you?" Kusha asked. "I'm a little nervous. To be honest, I'm so scared that I can barely breathe."

The team made a beeline for the Council floor, jostling the crowds. Hostile and irritated glares came their way, as well as comments about how children should be banned from such serious proceedings. But finally, they reached the table where Premier Oliena sat alone. She looked surprised and then amused when they lined up in front of her. Dani was in front, and she did a strange handclasp and bowed; the others followed suit. After Dani introduced herself and everyone else to the premier, Kusha and Nafi stepped forward to explain the situation. By the time Nafi had finished speaking, the premier was far from smiling. Her face had turned somber as she looked intently at Kusha, studying him closely, looking into his eyes.

"Tell me your word of honor," she asked him, and Kusha whispered a reply.

Maia could not hear the words he had said, but whatever they were, the premier seemed to be satisfied as she nodded slowly.

"You should know that this will be far more complicated than simply talking to me," she said. "Are you sure you want to choose this path?"

Kusha nodded once and took a deep breath.

"I do." There was no hesitation in that statement.

"All right then." Oliena rose and beckoned the man who had carried the sand clock inside. She whispered something to him and when he bowed and left, she turned to Kusha again. "Please follow me, all of you."

They followed her outside the Council Room, a few paces down the corridor, and into a small but impeccably furnished office. Oliena seated them on one of the long couches that lined the right wall. They had just about settled down when the door was flung open. The portly Jjordic man, Aloysus, walked in, his eyes cross and his face red. He was followed by an anxious Tsininio. Behind them came Sahiiraan

Leeam and Chairman Phocluus, both looking calm and indifferent, but Leeam's clenched fists were a sign of something else. Everyone's eyes fell on the bunch of youngsters huddled on one side. A kind smile played on Phocluus's lips when he saw Maia, and he raised his left hand and waved. Maia waved back gleefully, joy filling her heart at the thought that he still remembered her and did not think of her as an enemy. Not for long though, she figured, this meeting would surely change everything.

"What is this about, Premier Oliena?" the chubby-cheeked Aloysus demanded loudly. "Why were we summoned here?"

"You are here because the pact we just signed has been disputed and stands to be nullified," Oliena replied. As cries of surprise and fury rose around her, she explained the situation until every little detail had been covered.

"Do you have any idea what you are up against, dear boy?" Leeam turned to face Kusha, smiling to cover the snarl that threatened to tear apart his handsome façade. "This is no child's play."

"I think he's faking it." Aloysus pointed an accusing finger at Kusha.

"I am *not* faking it. I'm the rightful heir of the House. And rest assured, Sahiiraan Leeam, I'm fully aware of my choice." Kusha stood, locking stares with the two men. "And it's final, this deal is off. We shall have a deal but before that, we shall have consensus among the Solianese, and you shall wait until that day."

Both Leeam and Aloysus seemed taken aback by what Kusha had said and how boldly he had said it. Even Maia and her friends were stunned by the confidence and strength that exuded from their friend.

"He is but a minor," Chairman Phocluus spoke, breaking the silence. "Can he invoke these rights you speak of?"

Oliena nodded. "In matters concerning public well-being, which this clearly is, he has unrestricted rights and the authority to wield them," she said.

"Well, I still think he's a fake," Aloysus said again. "Has he proved his lineage?"

"I do not have any doubts whatsoever regarding that," Oliena replied. "But then I thought you might have concerns. That is precisely why I brought him to this room, so he can prove his true heritage to you. I have already invoked the GRAVE procedure; it should be ready for the test momentarily. I hope all of us here trust the sanctity of that system."

While Tsininio nodded eagerly at Oliena's words, the other men exchanged quick, fretful glances. One by one, they agreed, albeit grudgingly. Away from where the adults were talking, the group of equally worried and anxious children looked at each other in confusion. Maia did not have an inkling of what this GRAVE procedure could be; she doubted that any of her teammates did either. Oliena walked over to where they waited, and as if understanding their unspoken questions, she started explaining.

"The GRAVE procedure stands for Geneographical Rights and Ancestry Verification and Evaluation. It is a supremely complex automaton that can crosscheck any person's ancestry and verify lineages. Only two things are necessary for it to work correctly: the availability of genealogical information of the lineage in question and the voluntary submission from the person to undergo a complete neurogenetic scan to crosscheck his heritage. The first part is easy in this particular case because we have ample genetic information on every Solianese House in our automaton, and the House of the Sun is obviously no exception."

Oliena looked earnestly at Kusha and continued. "Kusha, while I understand that asking you to submit to this is rather discourteous, I only hope that for the sake of peace and understanding, you will agree to the procedure."

Kusha nodded vigorously. "Of course, I will. What exactly do I have to do?"

"Oh, not much at all, you will step under that frame once it has been prepared and place your palms on the scanners." Oliena pointed at a white doorframe that was set against the wall at one corner of the room, wide enough for a person to stand underneath. Its center

tapered outward a bit and housed two flat plates that Maia assumed
to be the palm scanners, and a set of lights and buttons glittered and
shone on the side. While the gang ogled at the machine, a light on the
roof of the frame turned a bright green and a faint beep sounded.

"There, it is ready for you." Oliena led Kusha to the automaton.
When he stepped inside, Oliena turned toward the men again. "To
make this absolutely fair, I would like to invite Sahiiraan Leeam and
Sahiiraan Tsininio to kindly do the honors of selecting the lineage and
initiating the procedure."

The two men looked at each other and then walked up to the
GRAVE automaton. They took turns punching the buttons on the side
until the green light on the top started to blink in a rainbow of colors.
Maia assumed this was an indication that the machine had started
analyzing the genetics. Everyone in the room fell silent. A long while
later, the dance of colors stopped, and the light turned a steady green
once more. Tsininio laughed and clapped his hands while Aloysus
brought his fist down on the table in a resounding crash. It all meant
one thing: Kusha had won. Nafi exhaled loudly and fell back on the
couch, and the rest of the team had a difficult time suppressing their
wide grins.

"Please step out, Kusha," Oliena said, and then flashed an
apologetic smile. "I am sorry; I should address you as Sahiiraan
Kusha."

"N-no, please don't. I'm just Kusha," Kusha replied, blushing
profusely.

As Kusha walked away from the machine, Oliena picked up the
piece of ornate paper that lay on the large desk behind her. It was the
same paper that the Sahiiraans had signed, the one that sealed the
pact. She looked at it briefly, then ripped it right down the center.
Aloysus stifled a gasp with the utmost difficulty, while Leeam and
Chairman Phocluus stared. Tsininio, on the other hand, chuckled
heartily and walked over to Kusha.

"You, my dear boy, have performed a miracle tonight." He
clasped Kusha's right hand.

Kusha reddened slightly. "It was my friend, Nafi, who figured it out really," he said, pointing at a beaming Nafi.

"Yes, yes, of course," Tsininio gushed, flashing a quick, obligatory smile at the youngsters huddled on the couch, before swiftly turning his attention back to Kusha.

"Sahiiraan Kusha, of the House of the Sun. My respects."

He bowed and touched Kusha's hand to his forehead. Maia noted how Kusha flushed while struggling to keep his poise.

"That is all fine, Sahiiraan Tsininio," Oliena interjected solemnly. "The most important thing now is getting some security for Kusha."

"Security?" Kusha's mouth fell open. "Why would I need security? My friends are with me all the time anyway."

"I have to say that your bravado tonight won't make you popular with everyone around the world," Oliena explained. "And since your role is quite critical in these negotiations, it is important that you be safe. I do not underestimate the capabilities of your friends, but I still think you need some backup."

"I will arrange for something as soon as I can," Tsininio assured.

"It is a pity that I cannot provide you any assistance in that matter," Oliena sighed. "I always thought it a pointless bunch of bylaws that call cross-national protection and security systems illegal. And at this sensitive juncture, I do not want to get caught up in some ridiculous legal technicalities."

A small knock sounded on the door, and a man walked in and whispered something in Oliena's ear.

"It is time for you to go back to your rooms," Oliena said, walking over to the couch where the team was seated. She accompanied them to the door and led them outside. The moment she opened the door, all the happiness and joy of having achieved glory beyond imagination vanished in a heartbeat. Aerika stood in the corridor, her face scrunched in anger. Next to her, huddled together, was the entirety of Core 7.

"Thank you, Premier." Aerika did the same handclasp as Dani had done and bowed to Oliena.

Oliena turned to Kusha. "We will take care of this, Kusha. And I am sure we will see each other soon. We have a lot to discuss." She smiled again and took her leave.

As soon as the door closed behind Oliena, Aerika stepped closer to the gang. "Don't you love attracting attention?" she fumed.

No one spoke. A question like this was not meant to be answered. Nafi took a deep breath, and it seemed like she intended to speak. Maia's hand shot out to grab her arm, to stop her from saying anything, but it was already too late — Aerika had noticed.

"Yes, young lady, you wanted to say something?" Aerika looked at Nafi with cold, appraising eyes.

Nafi twitched but did not speak. As Maia watched Nafi avert her gaze, strength rose through her and spilled out.

"It . . . it was . . . critical that we came here tonight," Maia started. "You see, we were trying to save some lives."

"Oh, really?" A mocking smile played on Aerika's face. She looked threatening and by no means appreciative of what had taken place. "Then maybe you do not mind accepting the fourth strike against you. I believe it will be a small price to pay for all those lives you managed to save."

"But, how can you ignore how important this was?" Maia was not going to accept it without a fight.

"I have half a mind to throw you out of this contest," Aerika said. "Please do not tempt me further with your arguments."

Behind her, Loriine and Baecca broke into a cascade of giggles.

"You told on us?" Nafi snarled at the two girls. "How can you when you've been going out too?"

"You thought we would sit back and watch after what you brought on us?" Loriine shouted.

"You brought it on yourself," Ren shot back. "Had you not been so mean to Chylomyhrra all the time, you'd be fine."

"And how can you not be punishing them?" Maia asked Aerika. This was war — there was no room for feeling sorry for anyone anymore. "They've been going out more than us. It's their codes we've been using to come up here."

Aerika pondered a bit before turning toward Core 7. Loriine and her teammates had stopped laughing.

"Is that true?" Aerika demanded.

"It's all lies," Loriine said with a straight face and unwavering eyes. "They always lie and break rules."

A tumult of protests rose from Maia's team. Aerika raised her hands to make the barrage of shouts and cries stop; matters were getting dangerously close to a fistfight.

"It is true."

That one statement made everyone fall silent immediately. It was Karhann. His teammates stared at him in shock and disappointment.

"I've been coming up here to watch."

"A strike against you too then," Aerika said after a thoughtful pause. "Now you will get back to your dorms; I have had enough trouble for the night. Keep in mind, I do not want to hear another word on this matter from any one of you again."

"Maybe you can send us home already," Loriine said rather adamantly. It was astonishing that she still dared to talk back after all the furor she had caused a few days ago.

"Try me, and I just might do that," Aerika replied in a voice steely enough to stop all conversation for that moment and for that night.

CHAPTER FIFTY-TWO

IN THE BELLY OF A MONSTER

erika's vigilance increased exponentially after that incident. Her constant and rather cruel monitoring of activities now included the time before and after the sessions as well. There was no escape from the dormitories, no late-night chats—nothing other than visits to the RC, the sessions, and back. Dani and Kusha still did not speak to each other. Maia felt that Dani had softened a bit and made a few awkward attempts to talk to the boy, but Kusha somehow ended up botching her attempts with equally awkward responses. Dani continued to be miserable mostly because Hans had sent her a message saying how disappointed he was that Dani had overstepped her boundaries. Maia had tried to cheer her up, but it hardly worked.

Then there was the matter of yet another nightmare, one that revisited Maia over and over again. This one was particularly strange. Every morning she woke up with a hazy memory of Bikele disappearing under a pool of dark water, much like the way he had dived out of sight through the water lock. It was obvious that her mind had cooked up this specific vision just like Kusha had said. It was probably a remnant of her last meeting with Bikele and nothing more. But hard as she tried to drive away the nagging memory of it, with every other occurrence, the unease grew.

The final months of their stay were upon them. Maia found it hard to believe how quickly time had passed since her arrival at Zagran. Palak announced that the model converters needed to be submitted soon, and a long list of tasks to be completed.

"You still have some time to finish your hydrosol units for the GeiFonz Icecap," Palak said. "However, the work on the hydrothermal unit has to be wrapped up sooner. So, from now on, that will be your top priority. All teams have done a great job in joining forces to design the parts. Now all parts have to be assembled before the converter can be transported from the workshop here to the Converter Galley in the Karnilian Caves. Your first trip to the workshop is scheduled for today."

With Aerika, the two instructors, and their assistants on their backs around-the-clock, everyone was eager for a break, and the trip to the workshops provided just that. It promised an escape from the relentless supervision, and Maia looked forward to the outing. She was excited by the prospect of being inside the cavernous machines; spending time tinkering with its gazillion parts and pieces, and conversing without the fear of observant eyes and snooping ears. Maia could hardly wait.

***

The workshop was a gigantic place. It was neither cozy nor warm, only an endless parade of iron and steel apparatus on a shadowy factory floor. Monstrous equipment, mostly hydrothermal converter units, were being built all over the place for the various energy farms under the seas. The units, resembling gigantic upside-down funnels, were sunk halfway into the floor, the upper half protruding above it. Engineers and technicians in overalls milled around them busily, dark masks covering their faces. Palak led all the teams to one side of the floor and stopped in front of a colossal funnel that towered above them in an ominous stance. A large sign on it read "SHTC-9203-KC."

"This is the one you are helping us build, the Singletorrent Hydrothermal Converter 9203 for the Karnilian Caves site." He pointed at the dark structure. "The parts you have built already have to be installed inside, and once all of them have been fitted, we will carry the converter out to the Karnilian Caves where it will come to life."

"Sir?" Jiri's hand shot up. "What does 9203 mean?"

"It's a serial number," Palak replied casually. "This is the nine thousand two hundred and third unit at the Karnilian Caves site."

"You mean there are – "

"Yes, there are nine thousand two hundred and two other converters at the caves now."

As the group stood transfixed, Maia struggled to imagine the enormity of the power grid that the Jjord had built under the oceans. A pang of hurt and sadness sank its sharp teeth into her prone heart.

9203 . . . and this is just one of the many sites. The Jjord have so much . . . too much almost. Yet, they can't find enough to share.

"All right, let's move on," Palak barked, marching forward.

He showed them inside the converter. It was as impressive as it was intimidating. Its interior was filled with huge gears and axles, wheels and spokes, circuits and wires and fuses. The numerous parts and pieces gleamed menacingly amidst the dull darkness. There were ladders built into the sides to access the upper areas and more going downward from the midway line. The subparts that the teams had built were stacked on a table outside and soon everyone was assigned parts and tasks by a group of technicians in charge of the unit.

Maia found it somewhat fun to creep and crawl through the machine's massive innards, trying to put the various elements in place. The groups were put to work together in one particular section at a time, which gave them ample opportunity to chat about things. Palak and Dill, their assistants, and Aerika did stop by routinely, but mostly stayed outside. Inside the giants, there was freedom, and Maia cherished it.

***

About a week into the regimen, Dani took a break from their usual tasks to show Maia how she had installed gears in Appian's wind turbines. The rest of the team gathered around as well, studying and observing, learning various tips and tricks. They were all listening to Dani with rapt attention when the sound of shuffling feet made them sit up and look around.

"There you are, thought I'd never find you," said a familiar voice.

"Bikele?" Maia squealed, scrambled to her feet, and rushed toward the masked man.

"Yes, indeed." Bikele took off the thick black workman's mask. He slipped an arm over Maia's shoulder. "Siobah told me I could find you here, and I've been searching every floor of the converter for you. By the way, I heard of the ruckus at the Council. And I have to say, I'm impressed," Bikele added with a wide and approving smile at Kusha.

"Don't tell that to Kusha, it'll get to his head," Nafi teased. "He already thinks he's some kind of royalty now."

"I do *not*," Kusha protested loudly. "Be quiet, Nafi."

"Did you hear that, Bikele?" Nafi smirked. "That's the Emperor of Tansi speaking."

As Kusha lunged at Nafi, uproar ensued. Maia giggled and Ren joined in the mad scramble.

"We shouldn't be making so much noise." Dani's was the only voice of reason.

"I think she's right. I can't stay here for long anyway," Bikele said. That comment did the trick, and the group calmed down.

"Siobah is a friend of yours?" Dani asked when everyone had settled down in a half circle around Bikele.

"She's a very wise lady who has eyes and ears everywhere. A guy like me needs friends like her to survive, and she has been a good friend and helped me out countless times. She was the one who told me about the Council. I would have never known otherwise since they didn't declare the details to the public. The premier simply called off the proceedings and announced the deal as void. I believe she was concerned about revealing your identity to everyone, Kusha, given that you have not come of age yet. I was so proud of you guys." He stopped and beamed at them. "I hope Aerika didn't have too much to say about it?"

No one wanted to miss the opportunity of expressing their opinions on Aerika and her ways, especially after having all their frustration pent up for so long. They started all at once, loudly voicing their complaints. It took a while before they calmed down a little and finally managed to tell Bikele the whole story of their adventure at the Council.

"We did stop the deal, but it hardly helps us in the long run." Kusha sounded worried. "The Xifarian withdrawal starts in a few months, and since we don't have time to come to a consensus before then, the Jjordic Council still won't give us any support. Maybe it would've been better to get a chance at saving some of the people instead. Now, until there's a new deal to replace the underhanded one we got scrapped, *everyone* on the surface is in danger."

"I have reason to suspect that it will not come to that," Bikele said. "I don't know for sure though, so keep this only to you. We have a lot of energy to spare, we always did. Or I should say that we have slowly built capacity to reach the point that we would be able to sustain the undersea settlements and much more. But, due to our unfortunate history, we have never made that information public. Premier Oliena is a firm believer in peace and coexistence, and I do not think she will turn her back on millions of helpless people."

"Why can't she make it known?" Dani asked as soon as Bikele paused.

"There are many reasons for that, Dani. First of all, there are a lot of people in the Council who still carry a grudge against the Solianese and would not like to help our compatriots from the surface. I believe our Honorable premier is waiting for an opportune moment to make a pitch to save everyone, but in the meantime, she is also making sure that we are ready when we go out to help.

"Then there is the obvious question of whether the Solianese Houses are ready to protect the supplies this time around. Or will history repeat itself? The Houses are divided, and there is little hope that they would come together again. There are new possibilities though—like this boy, Kusha, who showed the courage to claim his right and make a promise. But, it was not an easy promise to make, and it will be far more difficult to keep.

"The biggest issue of all—the Xifarians. They want their lost artifact back, and they will not be happy to find out that we can survive even if they withdraw their support. And who knows what they might want to do then? Attack us? Destroy everything we have built so painstakingly?"

There was absolute silence as Bikele stopped to take a breath.

"We don't have any answers to any of these questions. Now, the premier is a very sensible woman, and I'm sure she is thinking hard about this. I think that Kusha's appearance gave her some answers and she now knows what to do. I have also seen work at the caves pick up rapidly after your adventure at the Council. That can only mean that we are ramping up capacity so we can support and sustain even more."

"Wow, I hope what you say is true, Bikele," Nafi said slowly. "I guess we'll soon find out."

"Yes, we will. I'm hopeful and you should be also."

"I have to tell you something," Maia blurted. She needed to tell Bikele how the Xifarians were hunting for the shards. He had to know that there was a bigger danger lurking, a greater threat that no one knew about. Slowly she related everything she had heard from Sophie about the heart of the Sedara; she told him about the fires and of the suspected involvement of the Order of the Fyrstell. "They're trying to find the pieces, Bikele. Once they have all the shards, they'll try to put the Capsule together again. And then—"

"Maia," Ren interjected, catching her off guard. "Don't you think you're worrying too much about this?" He seemed troubled. A bit irritated as well. "Yes, we . . . they will try to restore the Capsule. But putting it together won't be so easy and it sure won't happen in a day. Remember what Mahswa Tabrin told us? The heart was put together by Ataii, and she was not an ordinary person. Where will they find someone as powerful again? Will they ever find anyone at all?" His tense gaze met and held hers, but only briefly. "I don't know, but I just don't see Xif flying out of this system anytime soon."

Ren's words, simmering with frustration, made Maia's heart twinge. She realized how difficult this situation was for Ren, caught in the middle and helpless. He was most likely correct in his assumptions, she had to admit. But he did not understand what Maia was going through. The fact that she knew this appalling piece of information and did nothing to warn her people about it was eating away at her.

"Maybe you're right, Ren. But, the people of Tansi need to know the truth, our leaders need to know the truth."

"Maia, no!" Bikele had never sounded so vehement. "I understand your fear and your concern. This is indeed an alarming situation. But now is *not* the time for you to come out. Think about it, no one would even believe you. Do you think the Xifarians will admit that they are planning to kill the sun? No. Do you think the Solianese will rally around you? Of course not. They can't even show up at the Council. Do you think we, the Jjord, will protect you? I doubt that. We are scrambling to secure our settlements. Fires have been breaking out across Zagran and we don't yet know who is behind them. So, stay put for now. You will know when the time is right to announce your secrets to the world, all of you will."

Bikele paused a moment to catch his breath. As Maia sat pondering, she felt a tad lighter. Bikele's supportive words had eased her conscience.

"Are we securing the settlements now?" Dani asked.

"Yes, we are." Bikele nodded. "We're also putting up armed guards at all the energy pits and reengineering the alarm systems. We're almost done with the pits in the remoter areas, and the Karnilian Caves are next. That's why I'm here, to approve the systems for the caves. We hope to complete it all within a few weeks."

"It'll be strange for you, won't it?" Maia chuckled at the thought of a zillion security guards running around the Karnilian Caves. "It was so quiet down there, just a few of you."

"It sure will be," Bikele laughed. "Gus is so upset with the idea of more people joining us that he refused to accompany me today. Actually, he has been putting this off for a long time. But a few days ago we had a severe warning—we had to get started, or we would be penalized. Gus still held out and sent me up instead. He says he will have nothing to do with this hysteria."

Bikele stopped and looked quickly over his shoulders. Maia cast a glance around; so far, there had been no intrusions, but it was good to be wary.

"I think I should leave now," Bikele said, smiling at everyone. "I hope to see you all soon."

He patted Kusha and pulled Maia close before he left.

"If I don't see you before you leave, Maia, remember where you can find me. Call on me whenever you need me."

Maia felt heaviness clamp on her heart. It happened every time she had to part with Bikele.

"I will see you again," she said, forcing some cheer and driving out the sadness from her voice. She threw her arms around him in a sudden, quick impulse, holding on to him for a while before letting go. Bikele sighed. His downcast eyes glistened as he flicked a few wayward locks of hair from Maia's forehead.

"How's Gibbon?" Ren inquired about Bikele's snub-nosed dolphin.

"He's fine," Bikele replied with a chuckle. "Threw quite some tantrum when he figured I won't be bringing him along for today's meeting. He's an old guy with strong opinions, and he doesn't like to be told what to do."

Kusha smiled happily after Bikele had left. "We do have hope then," he said. "I didn't even dream of any support after what we pulled the other night."

"I'm glad they have decided to get some security down there," Nafi muttered thoughtfully. "I do *not* trust those Xifarians."

"I'm sorry." Ren turned away. There was a sense of despair in his voice that Maia had never heard before. It was heartbreaking in its loneliness.

"Ren!" Nafi exclaimed as she grabbed his arm and tried to turn him around to face her. "I didn't mean you, I —"

"It's all right, Nafi." Ren looked her squarely in the eye. "I know you didn't, but I'm sorry anyway. I wish I could stop this."

"It is not your fault, Ren," Maia emphasized every word. "And every chance you got, you helped our cause. You've always done the right thing."

"I know," Ren replied morosely. "I only wish that choosing the right didn't mean going against my own people."

"It's not always easy." Dani placed a hand on his arm. "You know what Hans says? That people we know and love often have different ideas and opinions and they might not always want the same things we do. He says what's important is that we know and choose the right things for ourselves. I think he's correct: we have to pick the path that rings true to us, even when people we know and love might consider it wrong."

"She's right, you know," Maia chimed in. "And you will always be our friend. We can never think of you as anything else."

Ren had just smiled a little when Kusha came forward, caught him by the shoulders, and dragged him away.

"Stop being so overly melodramatic, you know better than that," Kusha said as the two took off toward their workspace. "We have plenty of work to finish. Get back to work, everyone."

CHAPTER FIFTY-THREE

THE GEiFONZ CHALLENGE

Bazillion assignments crammed into each day, a pair of relentless trainers, and a still-vigilant Aerika made the last month fly by in the blink of an eye. There were converters to be tested and prepared for installation, extended hours at the upkeep lessons, and lastly, the long practice trips to the GeiFonz Icecap.

It was arduous, exhausting, and simply a torture to make the trip all the way from Zagran to the ice shelf. The first time Maia tried the journey, there was hardly any strength left in her to make the return trip back to Zagran—riding through the cold water drained her body of its energy very quickly. However, with every other trial that followed, her endurance improved. Yet, when Aerika stopped by to announce the details of the second and final challenge, panic held her heart and mind in its icy grip.

"I am here to announce your second and final challenge—the GeiFonz Challenge. Your primary goal is to install the mini hydrosol converter that you have been building, in your assigned space at the

GeiFonz Icecap. After you have completed that task, you will make your way to the Karnilian Caves—that is your secondary goal. You will be expected to arrive at the caves before the installation of Converter 9203 begins. You will make these trips with your aquatic partners, of course. You will be tracked on remote monitors, as well as followed by a supervising craft.

"Remember, you will not be evaluated simply on your speed, but your efficiency as well. We will note how well you manage your rides—how you guide them and use them while being perceptive of their needs. We will also examine the micro converters you have constructed and grade you on how competently you install them."

Aerika paused, her appraising gaze sweeping over the silent assembly.

"You will be allowed to carry your weapons with you, but we expect you to complete this exercise in peace."

Maia and her teammates had scarcely huddled together to discuss the challenge when Palak and Dill marched to the center of the room.

"We need each team to elect an installer," Palak announced. "This person will install the hydrosols from start to finish. This person will have to have an extremely steady hand and an equally steady ride. The embedding process is simple, yet delicate and long. The converter *must* take root. The ice shelf is covered with a thin metal substrate, a film that holds and conducts the energy generated by these converters. The lead circuit from the converter has to be embedded right down to the bottom of this substrate. The slightest instability will destroy the alignment of the circuits. Until the embedding is complete, the installer cannot budge. If the installer moves, the process will be disrupted, the implantation will be terminated, and the converter will remain a lifeless piece of metal."

"So, pick your installer with care," Dill added, "for this person has to complete the intricate task while enduring the cold and the intense water pressure with steadiness."

Maia did not have to think—the choice was easy. Dani was by far the one with the most experience in the waters and she had skills to match. As soon as Maia announced her pick, the rest agreed eagerly. Dani accepted the responsibility with a gracious smile. That did not mean everyone else was free of tasks. Dani had to be supported in the process, which meant many more hours of practice to be completed with their rides and the routes memorized. Maia felt slightly overwhelmed; this was a journey of incredible proportions, every step was critical, and the planning needed to be more than accurate.

***

The day of the final challenge started as ordinarily as ever. Maia wondered why the contest and its outcome suddenly felt distant and small. Maybe because she had become used to the burden of these challenges, or maybe recent events had stressed her too much. She walked in a daze, and after the usual jaunt to the RC, she headed to Dill's classroom with her teammates. Their swimming partners had already assembled in the dive bay. The fifteen remaining teams gathered around the pool and prepared quietly for the journey ahead. Everyone looked solemn; Maia could not find a trace of cheer on any of the faces.

In addition to the tools and hardware needed for the installation, the contestants carried their weapons. They also received special communicator devices that would enable them to speak to each other underwater. The diving gear was different for this challenge as well, equipped to auto-adjust to the vast pressure variations from the near-surface ice packs to the cave in the abyss.

The groups set off one at a time. Maia and her team had practiced the journey a few times, and she was confident they would do well. But still, Maia knew the enormity of the risks ahead; the slightest mistakes could possibly hurt them a lot before any help could arrive. And suddenly, the fear was back and Maia's heart fluttered wildly.

The waters were cold that day. The sun must have been hidden behind clouds since no sparkle or warmth seeped into the endless blue. The chill made its way in through the thick leathery water gear, numbing Maia's bones as she dipped into the sea with Keiki. She clasped Bellator's hilt and braced herself. Chylomyhrra led the way— she skimmed the edge of the Intercontinental Cold, close enough to utilize its power, yet not deep inside to be engulfed by its crushing force. They were followed closely by the rest of the team, with Dani sweeping the tail end of their little procession. It was interesting to note how the group of riding partners had learned to work as a team—all the creatures followed Chylomyhrra in a neat line as if understanding the graveness of this particular journey.

They reached the GeiFonz Icecap as planned and on time. Dani settled into their cove, balancing steadily on Mikoo's back. Nafi hovered next to her, ready with her supplies of instruments and equipment. The remaining three watched from a distance as Dani carefully placed the first converter on the gray metal base. The substrate glowed to life as she started working, placing layers together, joining and fusing intricate pieces with patience. The process was about halfway complete when a gut-wrenching noise made them jump. It was a mix of a wail and a shout, going on loud and strong without showing any intention of dying down. And then it stopped as abruptly as it had started. Dani looked at her teammates, and even through the visor of her breathing apparatus, Maia could tell her eyes had clouded with worry. As she stared at Dani, Maia wondered what to do.

Dani broke the silence—her voice came over the communicator. "It's an alarm. On my Urso. Someone needs to check it for me."

"Alarm?" Maia cried anxiously.

"Pull it out, Maia," Dani instructed, nodding at her pocket in which her messenger device was securely strapped.

Maia pulled the flat silver device as steadily as she could and held it out for Dani.

"Read it," she instructed again. "I can't take my eyes or hands off the installation."

The message that blinked on the tiny screen in bold red letters was from Hans. It was precise and urgent.

TROUBLE. CAVES. GALLEY. HANS.

"Caves?" Ren asked after Maia had read the message aloud. "What's this about? What cave?"

"I . . . don't know," Dani replied, her voice trembling. She was clearly shaken by the message, and quite understandably too. "Must be the Karnilian Caves. Hans was supervising some changes in the supply lines down there. Has to be the Converter Galley he's speaking of. But I can't help him until I've finished this."

"Will it really break everything if you go now?" Maia asked as Dani fidgeted nervously with the complex circuits.

"Yes, it'll ruin everything," Dani replied. "But it doesn't make sense . . . why would he send an alarm? He knows I'm busy with the challenge today. And still—"

The shrill beep sounded again. The Urso was flashing another message.

HELP PLEASE!

Hans was in trouble for sure. Dani stifled a sob with difficulty as Maia read the message aloud, and suddenly it did not matter to Maia whether they completed this challenge or not—someone had to go help Dani's brother.

"I will go and check it out," Maia declared. "I can head over to the caves while you finish this, Dani."

"You can't just leave, we'll be disqualified," Nafi said. "And what will you do there anyway? We don't even know what this is all about. He probably needs Dani there, not you."

"I don't know, Nafi. Maybe he needs someone to give him a hand with something." Maia had already eased Keiki out of the cove. "Maybe there's some way I can help him."

"I'll come with you." Ren followed Maia outside the cove. "We might be disqualified anyway, regardless of how many of us leave. In that case, we might just as well make sure Hans has all the help we can give him."

They had swum out of their niche when a shout made them stop.

"Wait up," Kusha rushed toward them, waving wildly. "I'll come also . . . don't think I'm needed back there anyway."

The trio went flying underneath the jagged bottom of the cold white sheet of ice, following the practiced route back toward Zagran, but keeping enough room between them and the immense girth of the Intercontinental Cold so that they did not get sucked back in the opposite way. The trio reached Zagran quite quickly; Maia felt that it was too quick, almost. But they still had a long way to go — all the way down to the Karnilian Caves.

Ren led the way, continuing past the sparkling city, and jumping onto the previously run path to the Karnilian Caves. Away from the chill of the ice packs, the waters had warmed up a bit. But the relief did not last long. As the trio sped downward toward the bottom of the seas, the waters grew darker and colder again. The lights on the top of their breathing helmets turned on automatically, illuminating a dull path ahead of them.

"We don't need to take our shortcut, do we?" Ren asked as they approached the mouth of the schism they had taken the last time.

"I think it would be too dangerous without the Aqumob," Kusha replied. "I mean, what if we hit the wall or something? We'll be crushed and may be lost in the darkness forever."

"Let's go the regular way," Maia insisted, remembering the experience of her last time inside the crevasse. She was not looking forward to being in *that* darkness, especially without having the protective shelter of the Aqumob around her.

"All right." Ren nodded and shot forward again, Chylomyhrra leading confidently. In the very next instant, the milk squid came to a grinding halt so abruptly that Ren barely managed to hold on. He teetered, scrambled among her tentacles, and somehow straightened himself. Then he let out a scream, a bone-chilling scream that almost stilled Maia's heart. A little distance behind him, Kusha and Maia came to a stop, staring incredulously at the gigantic shadow that loomed ahead and grew bigger and darker with every passing moment.

CHAPTER FIFTY-FOUR

CLOSE ENCOUNTERS

It was the Timiti whale. Its leathery face became slowly visible, moving closer as Chylomyhrra shrunk backward to where Kusha and Maia had frozen with fear. It looked more imposing than Maia remembered. The three of them put together would not measure up to one of its fins, Maia noted as the gigantic creature swam closer. Its movements were graceful like a predator's, yet it did not seem to want to scare them just yet.

"What should we do?" Ren whispered, hovering on one side of Maia.

"Just wait and see what it wants," Kusha replied breathlessly from her other side. "Besides, there's no way we can outrun it."

The whale came nearer until it stopped within arm's length of the trio. Its mouth parted only slightly, as if in a smile, and its dark eyes bore into Maia's. And then the suffocating pull Maia had felt once before snared her mind again in a crushing noose.

She was falling down a dark staircase, along a narrow well that led to nothingness. Her life flashed through, an album of pictures streaming past. A shriek pierced her ears.

"Run, Maia," someone shouted.

Keiki reared below her. A vague rush followed. Her hands slipped, someone screamed, and she fell. She grasped for something, anything that would break her fall, but found nothing. Lower and lower she sank until she hit something soft. It cradled her protectively and pulled her close. There was a rush again. Overwhelming darkness embraced her, and the waters turned unbearably cold.

"Maia . . . Maia . . ." someone called her name repeatedly. As her mind slowly cleared, her eyesight adjusted to the surroundings. She was speeding through a dark tunnel, long and squishy arms holding her around the wrists and waist. It was Chylomyhrra's tentacles, Maia realized. The darkness around was absolute.

We're inside the North Zsitanian Fissure.

"Ren?" Maia murmured as she saw the dim outline of his face next to her. She tried to sit up straight in Chylomyhrra's arms. "What happened?"

"That whale did something to you, again," Ren replied. "And as soon as you tried to get away from it, it attacked. It went straight for you, not Kusha or me. Keiki fell and so did you."

"What happened to Keiki?" A wave of worry rushed through Maia at the thought of her sprightly young companion.

"The Timiti bumped into her. I last saw her spiral downward." Ren sighed. "Sorry, all I could think of was guiding Chylomyhrra to catch you. Once she did, we dropped inside the fissure — that seemed like the only way to avoid that Timiti. Kusha took the other way down to the caves."

"And what if the Timiti attacks him?" Maia's heart sank. "He's all alone out there."

"I don't think it will," Ren assured. "I could hear it making a lot of noise up at the mouth of the fissure. It was stomping around, trying to break in, wanting to get to you, I'm sure."

Chylomyhrra sped past the dark walls of the fissure, never once hesitating or slowing down. They had dodged the whale, but a few things still worried Maia. The hardest part would be escaping the thick medium at the mouth of the fissure. She wondered if the milk squid would be strong enough to fight through it. And what if the Timiti waited for them at the exit? Where would they hide then?

"We will find a way," Ren whispered, sensing her worries. She nodded vaguely, hoping that Kusha was safe, Hans was safe, and they would also be safe soon.

"The corkscrew is coming up, so hold on to Chylomyhrra," Ren cautioned. Maia steadied herself, remembering their tumultuous ride through the corkscrew the last time.

The rush of the fall stilled her heart for a few moments. It had been quite a ride inside the Aqumob, but dangling in the open from Chylomyhrra's tentacles, water streaking past forcefully over her body, her legs and arms almost scraping against the slippery walls of the chasm, was something else altogether. Turn after sharp turn, her heart skipping beat after beat, her mind went numb while the milk squid glided effortlessly through. Maia was frozen with fear, but somehow she also enjoyed the rush. Even under the terrible circumstances, when the path flattened out and Chylomyhrra picked up speed, Maia could not help but miss the thrill of the corkscrew.

"I miss it already." Ren chuckled next to her, making her laugh.

"Me too," Maia replied. "Maybe someday we can come back for another pass-through. Someday when no one is chasing us and we're not rushing to help a friend."

Around them, the waters had started thickening. Chylomyhrra seemed to sense the change; her pace quickened and Maia thought she felt her tentacles stiffen a little. Right after that, the milk squid's whole body lit up a bright orange-red. She flashed red, followed by a dark pause, and then orange. Maia blinked a few times, trying to get used to the blinding flashes.

"What's that all about?" Ren asked. "I've never seen her do that before."

"Some sort of signal? But to whom?" Maia wondered as well. Around them, the waters were as thick as jelly. Chylomyhrra kept going, driving forward with ease, drawing closer to the mouth of the fissure.

An ear-splitting bellow made Maia's heart drop to the pit of her stomach the moment they shot out of the mouth of the crevice and into the Zsitanian Abyss. Just like Maia had feared, the Timiti was lying in wait for them at the side of the exit. It pounced on Chylomyhrra with the joy of the impending plunder. The milk squid reared, fell back a little, and dived, its body still steadily flashing— red, clear, and orange—over and over again. As the whale turned and rushed at the squid once more, Chylomyhrra headed toward the bottom of the abyss, its form as straight as an arrow. But the creature was no match for the gigantic whale, which hurled itself forcefully at the squid.

Maia screamed. Her hold had loosened and she scrambled to get a grip. Next to her, Ren was struggling to hold on to Chylomyhrra's arms as the squid tried to evade the Timiti. Far below them, at a distance that now seemed unreachable, the lighted entrance of the Karnilian Caves beckoned. For a fleeting moment, Maia felt like they would be able to make it past the gigantic creature. Just then, the Timiti swished its enormous tail, creating a vortex of water that spun Chylomyhrra around. Maia barely had any strength left in her arms, but she clung on with all her might. While Ren tried to steady Chylomyhrra, the whale placed itself below them, blocking the path to the caves with its colossal girth. Chylomyhrra froze, well understanding that there was no escaping into the caves.

For a moment, there was quiet. Then the Timiti tore through the dark waters. Maia braced for impact as the Timiti charged. There was no place to hide, the whale was simply too large to avoid. It came with the intent to crush everything in its path. Chylomyhrra shot upward at breakneck speed, Maia and Ren dangling from her tentacles.

It happened right about when Maia had given up hope. The mass of waters above them blinked bright red, paused briefly before flashing orange. And then again. And again. It was as if the whole abyss was responding to Chylomyhrra's call for help. A deep grunt came from below them; the Timiti had seen the colors and it did not sound happy. Maia looked up again—the wall of colors seemed to move. It was heading in their direction like a humongous, lighted wave. The wave surged, sweeping downward as Chylomyhrra rushed to meet it. She reached it before the Timiti could crash into them. Then she shot through the blinking wall and into the soothing darkness beyond it.

"Did you see that?" Ren gasped and turned around to look at what they had passed through. "It was a wall of squids."

Thousands of squids blocked the Timiti with their blinding presence. They were packed so densely together that they looked like one solid barricade. They flashed in unison as they impinged on the whale. From under the flashing mass came a terrified bellow. Chylomyhrra turned around and swam downward again. Below them, the squids continued to flash, sinking deeper into the abyss with the whale, far beyond the mouth of the Karnilian Caves. Chylomyhrra swam slowly, down to the mouth of the cave, and turned when she reached the entrance. Then she twisted herself through the gates and swam into the dive bay of the Karnilian Caves.

CHAPTER FIFTY-FIVE

WINNING AND LOSING

Maia and Ren jumped off Chylomyhrra, and after a few appreciative pats on the squid's bulbous head, they bounded in the direction of the Converter Galley. They stopped the instant they rushed in through the door. The unconscious body of Gus, the cheery gray-haired keeper of the Karnilian Caves, lay sprawled on the floor.

"He's alive, just unconscious," Ren declared, kneeling to check the man's pulse. Together they pulled him aside. "What's going on here?"

"Hans . . . hope he's all right," Maia said, remembering Dani's anxious face.

"Help," someone shouted from the direction of the Converter Galley. It was Kusha's breathless voice.

Maia and Ren rushed forward, taking a brief moment to get out of their diving gear and draw their weapons. They had been at the Converter Galley during the Karnilian Challenge, so they reached it easily. The Converter Galley was always a scene to behold, but on this day, Maia spent little time admiring the installations. Her attention was quickly drawn to the hanging walkways that created an intricate mesh right below the ceiling. It was on one of these suspended walkways that Kusha, Hans, and another boy with flaxen hair were fighting a fierce battle against five masked foes. They were all dressed like the men Maia and her friends had fought at the Stabilator room on Xif. They wore long black cloaks, masks covered their faces, and each flailed long whips ominously. Maia's heart skipped a beat as she recognized the men's garb.

The Order of the Fyrstell! But what are they doing here? Trying to destroy the Jjordic power installations?

As Maia and Ren rushed forward to help, Kusha shouted.

"Check the sage's chambers! They went that way."

"They?" Maia asked.

"Just go," Hans yelled, struggling to avoid a particularly vicious flick of the whip. He jabbed a long pole at the man he was fighting and yelled again. "Go, *now*."

Maia and Ren sprinted toward the sage's chamber.

A loud thud followed by an agonizing scream flooded the area as the duo ran down the stairs leading to the sage's courtyard. It was Kusha's voice, Maia was sure. She stopped in her tracks, frozen with fear at the thought of Kusha in so much pain. Ren came to halt as well.

In the heart-stopping moment that followed, a vision of Kusha lying hurt and wounded flashed before Maia's eyes. There was remarkable clarity in the thoughts that swept through her mind—her nightmare of many nights ago was coming true: Kusha had been called to lead, he had walked into war, and now he was hurt.

"Ren, go back and check on Kusha," Maia commanded.

"But you . . . you can't go in there alone," Ren argued, even as he threw a concerned look over his shoulders in the direction of Kusha's scream.

"You don't understand, Ren," Maia said breathlessly, her voice unflinching. "I had dreamed of Kusha being hurt and wounded, needing help. He *is* hurt, I know. Go help him. I'll be fine."

Ren hesitated one more time, then turned around and headed up the stairs. Maia stood there for a moment, listening to the sound of Ren's footsteps fading into the distance, hoping and praying that nothing terrible had happened to Kusha. Then she grabbed Bellator's hilt as tightly as possible and ran across the courtyard and into the sage's room.

There was no one in sight, but the room was in disarray. Things were scattered on the floor, furniture overturned and ripped apart . . . it felt as if a storm had passed through not too long ago. A door stood open in one corner of the room. In the dim light that seeped past the doorway, Maia could see a flight of stairs winding downward. A groan that came from the other corner of the room startled her. The shock only paralyzed Maia for an instant, and then she strode toward the sound, pulling and pushing through the debris. She gasped in terror when she lifted the corner of a thick rug that lay over what seemed like an unconscious man.

It was the sage—he was buried underneath the heavy matting that Maia struggled to pull away. His eyes were closed and his body limp, his head cradled between his thin arms. Blood was streaming down his face from a gaping wound on his forehead. Slowly he turned his head and opened his eyes.

"Maia . . ." he whispered, recognizing her as she heaved to move away the pile on top of his frail form, his voice breaking. "Maia. Stop. It's no use, child."

He was right, Maia knew that. It was just too heavy—the rug, the stout wooden pedestal that was tipped over the rug and was partly covering the sage's legs—it was almost impossible to move. Maia wondered what could have possibly made anyone hurt an old man, and hurt him in such a vicious way. She inhaled deeply; she was not going to give up, and she would keep trying until help came. The sage groaned again.

"Maia, listen to me." The urgency in his voice made Maia stop and crouch closer to him. "You *have* to leave me here . . . and . . . go down those stairs . . . your fate depends on it . . . our fate depends on it . . . go child . . . go . . . help Gibbon . . . and . . ."

His voice faded and his eyes closed. A thousand questions remained unspoken in Maia's mind. She stood up on shaky legs, her eyes blurry and hands trembling. Beneath the pile of debris, the sage's breathing slowed as Maia stepped away toward the staircase.

Maia hurtled down the worn brick steps, Bellator in hand, barely thinking what might meet her at the end of her descent. She did not allow herself a moment to ponder. She could not risk letting fear in, she did not have time to lose either. Another door stood ajar at the end of the staircase. Maia braced herself, then flung the door open and hurried inside.

It was strange how brightly lit this room was, given how dull everything else was in the caves. A light, white and gleaming, flooded every corner. A large table stood at the center. On the side farthest away from the door where Maia stood was a huge pool of water. Maia assumed it served as the room's private dive bay. A black Aqumob was anchored to one side of that bay, and Amanii, the red-haired Xifarian girl, tugged a large transparent box that floated in the water next to the craft. Inside that container, a fidgety old snub-nosed dolphin bobbed up and down, his unseeing eyes wide with fear, pecking violently at walls that restrained him.

Maia recognized Gibbon. This was Bikele's room, she realized with a start.

"Gibbon!" Maia screamed. "Where's Bikele?" she yelled at Amanii.

"Hurry up, Amanii," someone shouted from inside the anchored Aqumob. The voice sounded familiar, and Maia wondered if Miir was in the craft. Amanii stirred—she let go of the container's handle, pulled out her sword, and faced Maia.

"Where are you taking Gibbon?" Maia shouted as she deflected Amanii's first strike. She did not get a reply, only a sharp swipe of her opponent's sword zipping through the air, not too far away from her face. Maia met strike with strike, parry with parry, never giving in for a moment. She was scratched, bruised, and bleeding by the time she had Amanii in a corner.

"Did you hurt Bikele?" Maia asked, gasping for breath, pressing Bellator against the blade of Amanii's sword.

"This girl asks far too many questions," a voice seethed from behind her. The bitterness that seeped out of every word was like venom and held the room in an icy-cold grip. Maia stepped away from Amanii and turned around.

Remii, the older son of the Xifarian chancellor and Miir's elder brother, was leaning casually at the large table at the center of the room. Miir stood next to him; the black sword Maia remembered so well shone darkly in his hand. The container that held Gibbon prisoner had now disappeared, likely inside the Aqumob.

As Maia debated her next move, Remii raised his hand, and Maia knew he was about to use telekinetics. Space crumbled all around her. Maia did not have time to react, the telekinetic wave was so fast, and she was not used to it anymore. The TEK wave spread like a ripple of currents, breaking into three as it approached. One hit her hand and sent Bellator flying; another hit her in the chest and knocked the air out of her lungs. Maia did not know what else that TEK wave had done, but her knees buckled below her as she reeled from the pain in her lungs and throat. Remii was almost as powerful a TEKist as his brother, Miir, Maia admitted grudgingly as she gasped for breath. For a moment, Maia wished she could do more than simply see the TEK waves, that she could create them and use them to fight.

"Get Amanii inside, Miir," Remii instructed. "I will take care of this worthless piece of filth."

Black boots strode up to where Maia was crouched. With every bit of strength she had left in her, Maia dragged herself backward as Remii walked closer. She rolled away as he sent another wave in the form of spears in her direction, narrowly avoiding the deluge that landed on the floor in front of her.

Maia scampered toward where Bellator had landed, diving as she felt the surging heat of a TEK wave behind her. She found a small table to crouch under barely in time. Above her, the table shook and buckled as the wave hit it. She had to get out from under there fast, Maia realized, or he would pin her under it the way he had done to the sage. Maia flung herself toward Bellator, grabbed its hilt, and rose to her feet. Remii looked amused as Maia took a shaky stance at the corner of the room. A smile as bitter and cold as his voice spread across his lips.

"You are indeed as feisty as I had heard," Remii said, lips twisting into a sneer. "It's your bad luck that our paths crossed today."

He raised his hand again, and a mountain of boulders formed in the space between them. They hovered in the air before shooting out in Maia's direction. There was no space to duck or sidestep the wall that rushed at her, threatening to smash her. Maia did the only thing that she could think of doing at that moment; she took a deep breath and raised Bellator to meet the wave head-on.

What happened next was a blur. All Maia could remember was charging at the center of the formation with Bellator. Piercing each curve in space, twirling and twisting her sword, she slashed through the wall, creating a path for her to pass through. The boulders came apart in fragments, the pieces flying past her and some scraping her painfully in the face, arms, and legs. The parts of the formation that went past untouched by Bellator, hit the wall behind Maia, creating a scorched impression on it. Remii stared at her with glazed eyes, his face twitching with fury as he stood with fists clenched. As some of the fragments flew back violently in his direction, he raised his hand again, possibly to build a shield, but he was not fast enough. He tumbled and fell as they hit him, groaning and clawing at his face where it was gashed and scalded by shrapnel from the wave.

There was a hopeful pause before Miir attacked. His black sword was as vicious as Maia had always found it to be. Once again she was engulfed by the fire of his fearsome swordplay that grew stronger around her with every passing moment. All Maia could think was to fight until her last breath. She could not give in. She had to fight for Bikele, Gibbon, and everything else that was good in this world. Wishing for her friends to arrive soon, Maia lunged at Miir, trying to push him back a little, and hoping to catch him off balance. She had forgotten all about his swordsmanship, about his skills that were far superior to hers than Maia would have liked to admit. He stepped aside with the quickness of a lightning bolt, and as Maia struggled to regain her balance, the hilt of his sword came crashing down at the back of her neck.

Bellator went flying from her hand again and Maia fell in a crumpled heap against a leg of the table. As she slowly brought herself up to a sitting position, she became aware of the sharp tip of Miir's sword resting between her eyes, steady and poised to strike.

"Why are you doing this?" Maia said, struggling to fill her lungs with air.

"Because you are being a hindrance to our operations and . . . you threatened my brother." Miir's voice was cold and unrelenting.

How Maia had hoped to run into Miir over the last few weeks, how badly she had wished for a chance to apologize. Never once had she dreamed of meeting him like this. She had not meant it then, but what she had said to him the last time they had met had indeed come true—they were surely not friends anymore.

"Don't do this. Please," Maia pleaded, the painful lump in her throat choking her voice. "This . . . this is wrong."

"I have—" he started and stopped right away.

The sound of pattering feet came down the stairs.

"Maia must be down there." Ren's voice was loud and clear.

"Get in here, Miir, you do not need to answer her. We have to get our assets to safety," Remii yelled from the door of the Aqumob, his hand still clutching his face.

Miir stood still; the tip of his sword wavered at Maia's throat for a few moments.

"My allegiance is to my nation," he hissed. "Nothing you do or say will change that fact."

Then he strode over to join his brother.

Maia scrambled to her feet and rushed after him, but the door was almost closed when she reached it.

"You'll not be so lucky if we happen to meet again," Remii snarled, and then the door slammed shut. With a loud swish and a gurgle, the Aqumob sunk below the surface of the water.

Maia did not remember how long she stood there staring at the ripples in the dark water. *Our assets,* Remii had said. If one was Gibbon, the other could have been Bikele.

They have taken him.

Hands shook her by the shoulders and tugged her by the arms, and all she could think of was Bikele. The man who had chosen to spend his life in this tiny room so Maia could be safe . . . the man who had seen her come into this world was . . . gone.

CHAPTER FIFTY-SIX

IPSO FACTO

Ren sat down next to Maia. "The sage is dying," he said. "Did you get to speak to him?"

All Maia could do was nod.

"Everyone else is safe. There are about a thousand security guards up there now," Nafi said. "Kusha is badly hurt from his fall, but they managed to stop the Order of the Fyrstell from damaging the Converter Galley."

"Kusha fell?" Maia asked, her mind still wandering through a thick fog.

"Yes," Nafi answered. "Luckily, he fell along the side of a converter and that broke his fall. He has a pretty nasty scrape on his left arm, but it'll heal. One masked man fell as well. He wasn't as lucky as Kusha though. He landed inside a converter . . . must've been killed immediately."

"What about the other men?"

"Escaped. They ran through here," Ren replied. "They must've boarded the Aqumob with Remii and . . . people. Didn't you notice?"

Maia shook her head. She had been too busy fighting for her life.

"I couldn't stop them," the words escaped her lips in an anguished whisper. "I tried, but—"

"Stop it, Maia," Nafi chided. "You should be glad that you escaped unhurt, that they let you go."

"She's right." Ren was quick to support Nafi. "People of the SDS, people like Remii are . . . trained for combat and trained to kill. You got lucky."

"Remii and the Order of the Fyrstell are working together then?" Maia muttered, her words sounded barely coherent to her own ears.

"Seems like it," Nafi promptly agreed. "Who knows how deep the conspiracy goes—if the entire SDS is involved or just a few rogue agents who are also part of this Order."

Maia struggled to fathom the enormity of the implication. The Scientific Defense Services or the SDS was the most powerful government organization in Xif. It made sense that they were running the operation to retrieve the heart of the Sedara, Maia reasoned. But, the Order of the Fyrstell was an immoral militaristic faction that was bent on destroying the Tansians, and quite out of anyone's control. Why would the SDS work alongside the Order?

"The SDS runs a lot of covert ops," Ren stated matter-of-factly. "I'm sure they work together with a lot of nasty people depending on the situation."

A face flashed across Maia's mind. Phocluus, the chairman of the SDS. She clearly remembered his kind eyes and the jeweled rings that adorned all his fingers. He had seemed friendly. He had known Sophie too. And he did not approve of the actions of the Order.

Had he lied? Did he really not know that his organization was working with the Order? No!

He could not be a liar, Maia concluded.

"Is Hans all right?" she asked rather fearfully, hoping that she would stop hearing bad news.

"He's fine, only a few scratches on him," Ren said. "His friend, Jed, is quite all right too."

"They really took Bikele?" Maia still did not want to believe. "And why would they take Gibbon?"

"Maybe they found out about Bikele's connection to . . . Sophie," Nafi said, sighing deeply.

"But how?" Nafi simply shrugged as Maia squinted at her. Maia sat there, confused. Bikele's was a life of exile—not many people knew that he even existed, let alone of his connection to Sophie.

Despite that . . .

"So, they must know about me?"

"Possibly not. Not yet at least." Nafi paused, hesitating. "But Bikele does."

"You mean he could tell?"

"He might not have a choice, Maia," Ren said gravely. "The Gnelexian mind probes don't need anyone to tell willingly."

"But why hurt the sage?" Maia wondered aloud. It was all so convoluted and strange.

"The sage might've gotten in the way and tried to stop them," Nafi replied.

"It's all because of me," Ren whispered gloomily. "If he not taken the chakra off after I almost caused an accident, this place would've been well-protected."

"Don't blame yourself." Nafi tried to comfort the boy. "I think they would've found a way around it anyway."

An officer dressed in a sharp blue uniform came by to record their statements. He left after the youngsters had described the events, and the trio spent some more time in Bikele's room before walking up the stairs. A lot of people were crowded in the sage's room; however, the three friends did not stop there but went out to the Converter Galley. They found Gus limping around, a thick white bandage wound around his head.

"They hit me from the back," he grumbled on seeing the trio. "Sneaky cowards . . . I should have listened to Bikele and got some security in here sooner. Imagine the fun he will have when I tell him this."

No one had the heart to tell him that Bikele was missing. It was too hard for Maia to even think that he might have been captured by the Xifarians and taken to a Gnelexian prison. She wanted to hope, to think that he had somehow escaped and was hiding somewhere.

Hans and Dani stood near one of the large silver boxes where the cables converged, talking to Hans's fair-haired friend Jed. Near them, Kusha sat on the floor, flanked by two men who looked like healers. They were busy tending to a deep gash that stretched down his left arm. Kusha saw the trio walk in and waved at them, as did Hans and Dani.

"Had Kusha not arrived when he did, they would have taken out all the condenser boxes," Hans exclaimed, pointing at the nearest silver box. "That would have been terrible, the end of all the progress we have made so far."

Hans did not know about Bikele's connection to Sophie; he was sure that this was an elaborate plan to damage the Converter Galley.

Hans continued. "I can't thank you enough, Kusha."

Kusha flushed a little at Hans's appreciation. Dani beamed; she looked exceedingly happy and proud.

"It's all so unbelievable," Hans muttered, shaking his head. "This must've been planned over the longest time. Luckily, Jed and I arrived earlier than intended. And we found Gus lying there. Their timing was so perfect—the alarm system here is in the middle of security upgrades, so half of the buzzers didn't work. I'm glad I thought of sending the message to Dani as soon as I saw Gus, otherwise we would've had to stand here and watch while they ripped the place to shreds. Later on, Jed found one alarm that worked, and he called for reinforcements, but it was already too late."

"I don't know how they fooled the biometric scanners," Dani said thoughtfully. "It's next to impossible to trick those."

"Wouldn't Miir and the gang have biometric clearances already? Didn't he say that they were assigned to oversee the Initiative?" Nafi asked.

"You're right. They must have been given clearances to get in here. Once inside, they could have disabled some more systems. I still can't believe Miir was involved in this." Hans shook his head sadly.

"Me neither. Can't believe he chose to go against us." Dani sounded thoroughly disappointed. "I mean . . . arrogant he might be, but he always stood for the right."

"He said he had to defend his brother," Maia informed the group, "and his nation's interests."

"Even knowing what his brother and his nation could've brought upon us had they managed to destroy the condensers," Kusha muttered angrily.

"Maybe he didn't know their whole plan," Nafi whispered. She looked dejected, her eyes lightless. "I don't think he would've done this had he known."

Maia sighed. It did not matter whether or not Miir had known. The fact remained that he was in part responsible for Bikele's abduction. He would have been responsible for the destruction of Zagran had the saboteurs managed to cause harm to the condensers. Maia knew it was hard for her friends to accept that he was against them now, but it was true, he *was* the enemy.

More people walked in as Kusha's bandage slowly took shape. Aerika was among them. Maia suddenly remembered their hydrothermal converter, wondering if the unit had made it to the Karnilian Caves at all. The training supervisor stood surveying the area for a while and then strode over to Kusha. Ignoring the rest of the crowd, she beckoned one of the doctors to the side, possibly enquiring about Kusha's injuries. After a brief conversation with the man, Aerika summoned the team.

"Let's go, everyone," she ordered, "we have had enough excitement for the day."

She walked them to a large Aqumob in the main dive bay and herded them inside. The other teams had already boarded.

"The Jjordic phase of the Alliance Initiative ends right here, right now," she announced as the Aqumob took off. "Given the current circumstances, and the elevated security levels, the installation of your hydrothermal converter has been postponed indefinitely. This task will be assumed completed by all teams."

It was a sad end to the Jjordic phase, Maia thought. She sat with her friends, huddled together in one corner, each telling his or her part of the story.

"Gibbon's eyes," Kusha whispered when Nafi related the sad tale of Bikele and his pet snub-nosed dolphin.

"Yes, poor thing," Nafi breathed deeply and looked away.

"Yes, but no," Kusha muttered again and his eyes sparkled. "Don't you see? Remii had mentioned picking up chatter about Keif and Zeiss, but what if they had misheard the chatter? That's why Miir couldn't find anything when he scanned the store. They still went looking for the shards, they burned down the place, but I'm sure they couldn't find anything. I'm sure the pieces were never at Keif and Zeiss.

"Then where—" Nafi started.

"Gibbon's eyes!" Kusha could barely keep from jumping up. "Gibbon's eyes rhymes with Keif and Zeiss. Remember what Bikele said about Zaara making eyes for Gibbon? That happened fourteen years ago, which puts it at the same time as when—"

"Maia was born and . . . the heart of the Sedara was already broken," Nafi said in a breathless whisper.

"Correct!" Kusha exclaimed. His face was flushed with excitement. "And remember, Sophie had given away those black pearls to make eyes for Gibbon. What if those were not plain old pearls? What if those were the shards—pieces of the heart of the Sedara?"

"That could explain why the Xifarians had to take the dolphin with them," Nafi said.

"Maybe the sage knew . . . that's why he asked me to help Gibbon," Maia pondered aloud.

"So, now the Xifarians have not just one but two pieces," Dani inferred, her voice trembling slightly. "What if . . . what if that's all there is? What if there's no more to find?"

The dread in Dani's eyes held Maia's heart in its fearsome grip. What Dani said was indeed a possibility. And if that were true, if the Xifarians had already retrieved all the shards, nothing else would matter. There would be no Tansi left to matter. A silence crept in, bringing with it the chill of an unimaginable terror.

CHAPTER FIFTY-SEVEN

THE PREMIER VISITS

Aerika called the team aside when they disembarked at the dive bay in Zagran. While the other groups walked away to the dormitories, Aerika led Core 21 to a room off to the side. Maia trudged behind her, too preoccupied with her worries to even care about what Aerika wanted from them. Guessing by her friends' faces, they did not seem any more eager either.

"You need to take care of yourself for the next few days. No more running around," Aerika declared solemnly, frowning at Kusha and pointing at his bandages. "The rest of you are free to do what you want, but try to stay out of trouble."

"You mean Kusha has to stay in the dorm?" Nafi asked.

Aerika nodded, her face turning grim as Kusha groaned.

"And this transgression will be counted as a strike against you, your fifth and final one," she declared. As squeals of protest filled the air, she shook her head. "Do not try to argue, I am not in the mood to listen to your pointless babble."

"But, Supervisor Aerika," Dani protested. "We didn't *want* to break any rules. Is it our fault that these things happened? What were we supposed to do? Sit back while it all went to pieces?"

"You do not follow instructions very well, do you?" Aerika glared at Dani. "I can understand the audacity of the rest of your teammates, but you disappoint me the most with your impudence. You were brought up *our* way . . . you should know better than to defy and dispute your elders."

"She's just asking you a question, not trying to challenge you or anything," Ren tried to explain.

"We didn't have a choice, that's all," Nafi whined.

Aerika looked at Maia and Kusha and raised an inquiring eyebrow. "And you two have nothing to add?" she asked, a mocking smile playing on her lips.

Maia had no interest in arguing, not anymore. The contest meant nothing to her at the moment; all she could think about was Bikele and the likely loss of the heart of the Sedara. Kusha was probably too tired and hurt to fight. Aerika stared at them for a while before speaking.

"This *is* your fifth and final strike," she reiterated. Nafi rolled her eyes and stomped her feet, Ren threw his arms up in the air, and Dani sighed as noisily as she could. Aerika ignored their rather hopeless behavior and continued. "However, that does not hurt your chances since I have already declared this phase of the contest closed. But, you will have the honor of collecting five strikes."

"You mean . . ." Nafi's face stretched into a jubilant smile as she realized what Aerika had just said.

"Yes, consider yourselves lucky that I . . . forgot to award you the last penalty before I announced the end of the Jjordic phase. I do believe you will be one of the top ten teams who will move on to the next phase. Now, whether that part will ever be conducted, given the situation we are in, remains to be seen," Aerika pronounced gravely. "I will admit, quite reluctantly though, that you have behaved in a most outrageous yet extraordinarily brave fashion. Not just once but time after time. For your bravery, I have to commend you."

It was astonishing to hear those words from Aerika, and the team stood dumbfounded. They had even forgotten to feel proud or happy until Aerika smiled a little and turned to leave.

"That does not mean that you are free to run amuck now," she reminded sternly. "You are still expected to follow rules and will be taken to task if you don't. And let that boy get some rest, do not keep him up for too long."

No one meant to keep Kusha up and about, but there was no way to stop discussing all that had taken place. They took the elevator to the 500th and settled down at their usual corner at the atrium, continuing to chat feverishly until the patter of footsteps made them look around.

It was Premier Oliena. As everyone, including a spent Kusha, jumped to their feet as a show of respect to their important visitor, Oliena smiled and took a seat.

"Thank you for defending our resources so valiantly," she said to Kusha. "On behalf of the Jjordic Council, I am here to extend my sincerest thanks to you and your friends."

Kusha flushed and bowed his head quickly. So did everyone else.

"First, I would like to present this to you, Kusha." Oliena held a blue crystalline pendant that hung from a thin black chain. "The Sage of the Deep has passed on. He wanted you to have this. He said the chakra is free again and from now on it will serve only you."

Kusha extended a trembling hand to receive the priceless gift. He cradled the crystal tenderly in his palms while the team silently mourned the passing of the wise man.

"In return for what you have done for us, I would like to share some information with you," Oliena continued. "We have decided to rebuild the Damoclian Connector. This will be the backbone from which all the Solianese territories will receive supplies. There will be no complicated calculations for distributing excess energy — everything we have will be shared equally with people on the land cities. However, we do need to build a protection system to guard this setup. As we have already found out, we are quite vulnerable. With that in mind, we will soon arrange a council at Miorie, where we hope to have consensus among all concerned parties."

"Thank you," Kusha whispered. "I cannot tell you how grateful I am . . . we all are, Premier Oliena."

"You only have to thank yourselves," Oliena replied.

"So, what do the Xifarians have to say about this attack?" Nafi asked eagerly.

"Oh no, we do *not* take names," the premier said. "Not until we have proof."

"But, we saw them," Maia protested. "There was no doubt about their involvement."

"Such is the painful art of diplomacy, dear child," Oliena explained patiently. "Sometimes, it is simply not wise to accuse someone who might be a truly mighty adversary when pulled out in the open. So, we will continue to wait and watch—that is the prudent way.

"We will closely guard our energy farms, which seem to be a prime target. Whoever it might have been, they took excellent advantage of the opening of the Karnilian Caves for the challenges and the lack of security there. One of our caretakers is still missing; we do not know what might have happened to him. We are fortunate that they were not able to damage the condenser boxes, or we would be doomed."

Oliena paused for a moment and let out a sigh. "We should have known better. We should have been more wary. I hear that they even had a Timiti guarding the passage to the abyss. There have been reports of Timiti sightings lately, but I chose to ignore them. I should not have been so negligent. Timitis are forces of the dark—mutated animals living in the unreachable depths of the oceans. They can be manipulated only by the strongest extrasensory powers. The animal's unnatural and heightened abilities make them the best telepathic conduits in this world. I should have guessed that someone was trying to use them to spy on us. All this time, it had been snooping around, trying to read unsuspecting minds, and relaying them to its masters."

"So, you think the Timiti was controlled by the Xifarians?" Nafi asked incredulously.

"No names, please." Oliena raised a cautioning finger, making Nafi blush.

"The Timiti was a spy?" Nafi whispered, recovering in an instant.

"That seems to be the most likely explanation."

"Will we be ready by the time the Xifarians withdraw their support?" Dani asked.

"We have appealed for their understanding," Oliena said. "It is possible that they will extend the deadline by a few more months. You see, that is why we must not accuse anyone of anything."

Nafi leaned forward, frowning thoughtfully. "And . . . are we going to continue this contest?"

"Well, it does not seem likely that the third phase of the Initiative will start soon, given that the governments on Tansi will be involved in matters more critical."

"Will there be a third phase at all?" Maia asked. She wondered about the utility of an effort of alliance when everything was falling apart.

"Oh yes, there will most definitely be one," Oliena drove away any concerns that Maia had. "Our friends are most keen on continuing it even though we are not. I am not even sure they will be interested in delaying it, but we will plead for time."

"And why should they consent to a delay?" Ren asked, twitching as all eyes impinged on him. He flushed deeply but continued. "What will . . . they gain out of giving you more time?"

"Because, to them, a delay would be better than an annulment," Oliena replied. "In all honesty, I do not know why the Xifarians are so keen on this contest. I never understood the need for it in the first place."

"They're using the Initiative as a cover," Nafi blurted. "That's why they keep pushing for it. That's how they can get their spies into our territories, just like they got the team from the SDS into the

Converter Galley."

"Let's keep our suspicions to ourselves," Oliena suggested.

"Yes, but —"

"We have been assessing the situation, Nafi," the premier interrupted. "I like to think that the Xifarians *do* want peace. They also need to locate this artifact they have lost. Our assistance will be valuable to them. We have expressed our sincere intention of supporting them in this endeavor, so helping us would help them."

Maia debated if it would be prudent to tell Premier Oliena about the true nature of the artifact, that if the Xifarians got hold of it, Tansi would be doomed forever. She had scarcely opened her mouth to say something when a warning glance from Kusha and a sharp tug on her sleeve from Dani made her pause. The premier left soon afterward, leaving the gang immersed in thought. Her visit had brought up more questions than answers.

"You can't tell her about Sophie," Kusha said. "Don't you see that there's no open conflict yet? If you expose your connection to Sophie, that makes you vulnerable. Who will protect you when that happens?"

"Besides, we're not sure enough about the shards," Dani added.

"But . . ." Maia started and stopped right away, she barely had the strength to continue. "Do you realize what might happen if the Xifarians have everything they need to put the Capsule together? They'll kill our sun."

Maia paused to take a bracing breath. "Sooner or later, they'll find a way to restore the Capsule. And then, everything comes to an end. We all die."

For quite some time, no one spoke a word. They all knew the terrible prospect, Maia was sure. Everyone was grappling with the truth, but each in their own way.

"No. No, no." Ren shook his head vehemently. "They don't have everything. If they did, they wouldn't have taken Bikele. They took him only because they need more information. So . . . I'm pretty sure they won't be able to destroy the sun, not just yet."

CHAPTER FIFTY-SEVEN

There was a sliver of quiet and then everyone rushed to agree with Ren.

Nafi nodded eagerly. "Makes sense to me," she declared.

"Hmm . . ." Dani muttered. "I think you're right."

"Yes. Why else would they grab Bikele?" Kusha was the last to go.

Maia looked at their faces. Her friends were all smart, and each capable of rational thinking. While Ren's reasoning had merit, there was always a chance that he was wrong. Yet, no one was considering that very obvious likelihood.

Maybe they're afraid to face it.

Maia looked at their faces one more time and decided to contain her panic. She could not blame them—it was natural to seek an easy refuge from the terrifying alternative. It was also true that she could not keep on fearing—she had to find hope, she had to keep on living.

There will be a way to stop the Xifarians and save Tansi. And I have to find that way. I cannot let my mother down.

"And I'm so sorry, Maia." Kusha's regretful voice yanked Maia out of her thoughts. "Seems like what you saw was not a silly dream after all. I feel stupid now, for laughing at you when you warned me."

Kusha related Maia's dream to the rest of the team. When Maia told them about the one she had of Bikele and how she had chosen to ignore it, everyone gaped. Nafi spoke after the longest pause.

"I wonder if those guys really wanted to damage the condenser boxes. Or was it just a front to find Bikele and Gibbon?"

"It might've been a diversion to get Gibbon or maybe they planned to do both," Kusha said. "And now we know what the Timiti was there for—it was a conduit to pick up thoughts. Must've been how they found out about Gibbon's eyes . . . remember the chatter Remii was talking about? But it was weird how Maia reacted to the Timiti every time. That whale was strange too. First, it showed up in Maia's Saska, and then it attacked her and let me pass. Why?"

Nafi tapped her chin thoughtfully. "I think I know why," she declared. "Maia sensed the Timiti when no one else could've even imagined its existence. No spy would like that to happen to them, right? I'm sure the Timiti didn't either. So, whenever it got a chance, it tried to hurt the one person who knew of its presence."

They sat quietly, lost in thought. As always, Nafi's explanation did make sense.

"Seems like we won't see each other in a while," Maia broke the taut silence. "I wonder how long the Initiative will be delayed."

"We'll see each other soon," Kusha asserted. "Remember the council at Miorie Premier Oliena spoke about? We can all travel there and meet up even if there's no contest until then."

"I don't have any excuse to be there," Ren said with a sigh. He flashed a quick smile when he saw faces darken around him. "But maybe I can figure out a way."

"Not a very lawful one I'm sure," Nafi commented wryly.

At this point, the whole group found themselves involved in a loud discussion about the various not-so-legitimate ways of Ren's possible travel to Miorie. The debate did not go on for too long — with Kusha's much-needed rest in mind, the team called it a night.

CHAPTER FIFTY-EIGHT

BACK IN APPIAN

It was time for the final results to be announced. Core 21 made it to the final round but finished a distant ninth. Top honors went to Core 13, second place to Core 34, and Core 7 was in third place. Maia and her teammates had been penalized for their failure to make the trip to the Karnilian Caves together, which explained their rather dismal ranking.

Although, given the circumstances, it was not too disappointing to come in ninth. Maia was thankful that Kusha had recovered well and that none of her other friends were hurt. There was no news of Bikele or Gibbon, and Keiki had not been found either. The installation of the hydrothermal converter in the Karnilian Caves was completed one day, and all the teams were escorted down below in special, ultra-secure Aqumobs. It was strange to find the caves teeming with security guards clad in full armor, strolling every path and corridor.

There were no announcements about their departure schedules or the final phase of the Initiative. While Maia and the gang knew very well that there were too many things going on for the contest to continue without any hiccups, some of the other teams who did not know the details were curious and worried. About a week after the results were announced, a harried Palak called the ten remaining teams into his room.

"The third leg of the Alliance Initiative has been postponed indefinitely," he declared when everyone had gathered around him. "We know it will happen, we are not sure when. So, you are free to leave for your homes and await further instructions."

"However," he resumed as the groups broke into restless murmurs, "we have decided to arrange for some supplementary sessions for you should you choose to stay a while longer with us here. It is entirely up to each of you—we are honored to be your hosts—but we will also understand if you need to leave. Let us know of your decision within the next two days so we can notify your family in time."

Ren hardly took a moment to decide that he was staying.

"I'll stay. I wasn't planning to be home for more than a couple of weeks anyway." He grinned at a rather surprised Palak, who definitely did not expect an answer so quickly.

"Maybe I will too," Nafi said meditatively.

Maia did not know what to do. While the offer was undoubtedly tempting and she wanted to be with her friends, she also wanted to visit her family. She wavered for a day, trying to pick between the quiet and peaceful monotony of her sleepy village and the excitement of the dazzling underwater city.

Ren and Nafi were both wildly excited and that did not help making her decision any easier. To top that, a very attractive set of activities were announced the next day that Maia felt was downright cruel to everyone who had decided to leave. Every time she convinced herself of the benefits of the supplementary activities, a picture of three faces waiting eagerly for her in a little house in Appian flashed before her eyes. And Maia knew she could not be happy if she stayed. The only good thing was that Kusha was leaving as well, not that

Kusha was any happier than she was, especially since he was not expecting a warm welcome from his father after his bold action at the Council. However, Maia was glad she had some company on her ride back home.

***

On the day Maia and Kusha were set to leave, Joolsae stopped by. She was all smiles, as usual. The members of Core 21 hardly cared about her anymore and promptly ignored the girl, but Joolsae decided to hang around anyway. She continued to shower praises on the team's achievements and apologize for her earlier behavior. This went on and on until Nafi could not take it anymore.

"All right, Joolsae." Nafi looked the girl squarely in the eye. "We forgive you. Can you please leave us alone now? Or is there something you need from us?"

Joolsae stared for a moment, gulped, and stuttered to life. "Y-yes. I mean . . . c-could you write me a . . . note of thanks? Please? It would help get those extra credits. I did take care of you . . . every now and then, didn't I?"

"You must be out of your mind," Ren guffawed.

"You're the *most* selfish and rude person I've *ever* come across," Dani snapped. "Just go away, Joolsae, or I'll file a complaint instead."

Joolsae blinked rapidly, as if unsure of her next move. Then she stomped away. The team, disappointed yet again, spent a while discussing Joolsae's shameless behavior. Before long it was time for Maia and Kusha to leave.

***

Aerika came to bid them goodbye at the terminal. She looked very different from the day the teams had arrived at Zagran, more than six months ago. She was smiling, speaking to everyone, and even seemed sad at times. Maia and Kusha stood together on one side waiting for their Aquiccela to arrive. Dani was there with them; she had not started on the supplementary activities that Ren, Nafi, and almost everybody else had, because she planned to spend some time with Hans instead. She seemed cheerful, and Kusha looked quite happy and carefree too. But Maia sensed uneasiness—a remnant of their past disagreements lingered, making them strangely uptight with each other.

"Thanks again, Kusha," Dani said after she had hugged Maia farewell. "Thank you for helping Hans."

"No problem," was all Kusha could say after smiling rather bashfully.

Dani took a hesitant step toward the boy, Maia presumed to give him a goodbye hug. Kusha seemed frozen; he stood awkwardly as Dani embraced him lightly and stepped away in a hurry.

"See you soon," Dani's voice was barely audible.

"Yes, soon," Kusha replied hastily. He almost ran away into the train and slumped on the nearest empty seat.

The Aquiccela left soon after. It took them to the Fringe Port where another journey, one toward different destinations awaited. Maia made a solitary trip back home as Jiri and Anja, who usually accompanied her on the pod trip, had both stayed back in Zagran. It was late in the evening when the pod touched ground at the Troughs. The pale golden rays of the sun illuminated the farms in a dim glow. The cold days of winter were almost upon them, and the bare trees and the rusty grasslands looked morose. But it was liberating to be under the open skies once again, to breathe the free air and feel the warmth of the sun. As soon as the stairs rolled down, Maia rushed out and ran toward the tall figure that stood next to a carriage on one side of the road.

"Herc!" She flung herself at the man who laughed and patted her head affectionately. Soon they were on their way to Appian.

The sun had dipped below the horizon and the pale moon was up in the sky when the carriage pulled through the gates of the farm. The lights were out, except for a small one shimmering in the kitchen where Emmy sat waiting for them to arrive.

"Dada has gone to bed," she informed after Maia had released her from a tight embrace. "He . . . hasn't been feeling very well lately."

Emmy did not seem to know or would not tell what was ailing Dada. "He's getting weaker" was all she said. Maia hardly had any interest in dinner after that news, but she lingered on, trying to do justice to the fare Emmy had painstakingly prepared for her.

***

Later that night, Maia snuggled under her blanket, unable to sleep. After staring listlessly at the ceiling for hours, she decided to do something else. Grabbing her coat, she reached into its pocket and pulled out her mother's journal. Until now, Maia had found it hard to even think about reading it, but this night, with a heart already leaden with worries about Dada, she did not feel the least bit afraid.

The cover of the notebook was a matted gray, its numbered, faded yellow pages were filled with writing, and most of it was the same words or sentences over and over again. Maia thumbed through the pages, immediately noting the opulence of the word "five." Some small sketches snuck into the rows and lines of "five" as well, some of an orb, some of a set of weapons, including a long dark sword, and another that looked much like the famed Seigvard. There were also a few sketches of a house—a flat-roofed structure with two small trees on both side, and a mountain that rose like a spire from right behind it. None of the pictures were of anything Maia had seen before.

And then, there were a million places where the name Asiyaah appeared—it filled every nook and cranny of the notebook. It was quite distressing to see this book after seeing Sophie through her memory six months ago. Maia wondered how her mother had managed to capture that perfect piece of memory if her mind was indeed as hazy as it seemed from her scribbling.

She flipped over the pages one more time, stopping to linger on a word or a scrawl that stood out. Maia was about to close it and try to get some sleep when something caught her eye. It was one word, the tiniest little word carefully hidden along the central seam of the page. At first glance, it had looked like ornamentation around the center, but as Maia held the book closer to the flickering candlelight, the word jumped out at her.

It spelled "out," the lettering different from the sprawling and convoluted scripts that filled the rest of the page. Somehow, there was no incoherence in the penmanship of *this* word. Nothing else on the page resembled the scripting of the "out," and nothing looked as poised and graceful. Maia wondered if the word was written by Sophie, or if someone else had put it in later. She flipped through the pages again, paying careful attention to the seams and the borders, looking twice as closely at every embellishment she came across. After a breathless search of the next few pages, she came across the word "soul," hidden in the body of the elaborate sword that seemed to entice Sophie so much.

"This can't be an accident," Maia whispered to herself, leaning so close to the candle that she singed a hair. She went over page by page, returning soon to the two pages with the words "out" and "soul."

Maia groaned. "Two words. That's all you could write."

She flung herself back into her bed, lightly caressing the page number "35" etched on top of the long sword. Maia flipped back to the page she had discovered the first word. Before her eyes could trace the center again, she noticed the page number — twenty.

A sudden idea swept through her mind, and Maia sat up with a start. Frantically she flipped the pages over to the one marked five. She pored over every little marking on the page until she spied the word "Five" hidden in the sketch of a cloudy sky. With a squeal, Maia skipped over four more pages, and as expected, she found the next word spelled backward near one edge of the tenth page.

This is a book of clues! Clues about what Maia was not sure of, but every fifth page held a word. Taking a piece of paper, Maia jotted down each word she found, until she had come to the end of the book. Four lines, strings of words that were far from senseless, lay complete on the piece of paper.

> *Five gems carved out of the soul*
> *Each part of the luminous whole*
> *All is empty but the light is alive*
> *And free until the dark claims its life*

Her mother must have written this in a perfect frame of mind, Maia thought, or during the brief sessions of clarity that Bikele had mentioned. Maia did not know the meaning of the words, but as she stared vacantly at the verse, she wondered about their significance, or if there was any. Did Sophie mean the shards? Did her mother break the heart of the Sedara into five pieces? If two pearls from her necklace were the morphed pieces, maybe the rest of the pearls were shards as well? But then, where were the rest? Whom did Sophie give them to? And what exactly was empty?

Maia did not remember when sleep made her eyelids heavy. As she slept, the candle kept burning, its golden flames flickering over the journal a young woman had held close to her heart many, many years ago, and the peaceful face of a girl lost in her dreams. The light swayed joyfully, forever darting between the two, binding them in an everlasting bond. Outside the house, as the night grew older, a new day slowly came to life.

— THE END —